I0575221

LOVE AT THE CENTER OF GRIEF

Cindy McIntyre

Copyright © 2020 by Cindy McIntyre

All rights reserved. No part of this book may be used or reproduced by any means or used in any manner without written permission of the copyright owner except for the use of quotations in a book review. For more information, address: missouriauthorcindymcintyre@gmail.com

For journal prompt approvals, write the address above.

Disclaimers:

The information contained in this book is not intended as a substitute for professional, medical, or emergency treatment. Do not use this information to make a diagnosis or to develop a treatment plan for a health problem or disease without consulting a qualified medical professional. If you are in a life-threatening mood or situation, seek assistance immediately.

This book is a work of realistic fiction. Names, characters, businesses, places, events, and incidents are either the product of the author's imagination or used in a fictitious manner. Any other resemblance to actual persons dead or alive is purely coincidental.

Cindy McIntyre books may be ordered through booksellers or by contacting: IngramSpark

The cover image is for illustrative purposes only and is a stock image.

Editor: Shirley Rash

FIRST EDITION

E-book 978-1-7349228-0-6
Softcover 978-1-7349228-1-3

Library of Congress Control Number 2020907545

Dear readers,

Thank you for choosing to read *Love at the Center of Grief*. Everyone processes grief differently. As you explore the pages of the novel, I hope the storyline resonates with your heart. My grief journey involved a lot of journaling. After losing both parents, writing letters to them had a therapeutic effect.

For this reason, I felt "nagged" by Gretchen and Hayden to write this novel in a comparable manner. Seeking ways to honor my parent's lives, celebrate their memory, and help others with grieving, I reached out to the Lost and Found Grief Center. Here, I trained to become a volunteer.

This book represents more to me than just words. While dreaming about a fictional place named the Summerfort Grief Center, I fell deeply in love with the reality of creating a cast of characters so real to me. I am invested in the lives of Gretchen and Hayden and seeing what comes next for them. Already, I am working on a Summerfort series to bring you book number two. Stay tuned for more information about *Beyond the Center of Grief*.

I would love to hear from you. Please feel free to share your thoughts on the book or your experience with loss. missouriauthorcindymcintyre@gmail.com or write to me:

Cindy McIntyre
PO BOX 356
Richland, MO. 65556

Consider seeking help if you're hurting. Many organizations and resources are available online or in a community near you. Find one that fits your needs. Please don't suffer through grief alone. Or think about reaching out to help others in need. Is there a cause you can make a donation to in honor of your loved one?

"Are there other kids here
whose moms have died?
Do they dress up for Halloween?
Do they still have Thanksgiving?
What about Christmas?
How do they have presents?
How are they ever happy again?"
(8-year-old participant of
Lost & Found Grief Center)

Used with permission/online post

For the motherless child

LISA

Prologue

Meeting Marks in Summerfort (2012)

Welcome to Summerfort, Missouri. Offering all the perks of nearby Branson, this quirky bedroom community with a population under five thousand, rests near the Arkansas border. Plus, it remains somewhat hidden among the Ozark Mountains.

Will Summerfort grant me, Lisa Marks, a niche worthy of calling home?

Because I'm back in my hometown with the expectation of sorting out my life during a time I'm labeling the "Summer of Despair 2012," questions keep nagging me: What am I supposed to do with all my grief? What am I doing with my life that makes a bit of difference to anyone? Who can I turn to and not lose hope? Where do I belong? When will I trust and love again?

Traveling down the backroads, I locate the old Methodist church I attended as a child on Cinderella and Golden Streets. I ponder those names, thinking *how misleading.* My first impression when I turn into the parking lot to view the vacant property: unholy.

This old church building and me—kindred spirits, I think, staring at the condition of the building—run-down, abandoned, in need of a smile, longing for love, purpose, a breath of life.

Where to begin? A "for sale" sign pokes through the grass, but due to the elements of time, weather, and nature, the phone number of the selling agent remains a mystery.

I close my eyes, allowing my mind to drift back in time. My hands pull open the glass double doors as I walk through. I see my mother standing upfront, wearing her favorite purple dress with the white lace collar. The lyrics to the hymn "Take My Life, Lead Me, Lord" ring out in my mother's voice. My father sat next to me, dressed in his Sunday best, his hand latching on to mine. As the lyrics continue, Dad smiles at me and glances toward my mother with admiration. Love enveloped me here.

When my eyes open, the reality of life stings: I'm alone. Footprints of my past lie in ruins. Piece by piece, the little church and I are crumbling. But with a name like "Marks," I should have a plan, a place, a goal. Dad always used his joking line, "Lisa, go and leave your 'Marks' on the world with your big heart."

Inside my purse, I fumble, searching for his letter. Unfolding it once again, I reread my father's final words, hoping to find inspiration.

Dear Lisa,

Please use the trust fund your mother and I set aside to help others. We always believed assisting others helps open up the world to love. When we do for others, we become better versions of ourselves. It's time to put that fancy psychology degree I helped you pay for to good use but do it creatively. Leave your 'Marks' in the world!

Take care of yourself too. Complete updates on your fixer-upper by placing a checkmark next to each of the wishes you keep plastered to the side of the refrigerator door. When the repairs are complete, celebrate by replacing that refrigerator.

Do not let the deaths of your mom and me make you bitter. We worried sick about bringing a child into the world at our age but having you was the biggest blessing of our lives. Over the years, when asked, 'What's your greatest accomplishment in life?' I never hesitated to answer: Lisa, my daughter.

I know you didn't bargain for a husband to walk away, but in time, a resolution will come. Life throws out topsy-turvy things. People we believe in don't always turn out the way they should. Our plans don't always fall into place. Then, somehow, life designs some fancy schemes, serving up miracles, by guiding us with faith. It teaches us to believe in something unrealized as our culminating dream.

Don't be afraid to try adventures—travel, photograph the world, find new love. Show people your heart through kindness. It will be easier for them to forgive mistakes. Remember, mistakes can be made, so stop being so hard on yourself. If you're surrounded by the right people, they aren't looking for you to fail. Embrace this kind of love.

Above all, I <u>hope</u> you find a place to <u>heal</u> your heart. Or maybe a place or a person will find you? And then you will know that's precisely where you <u>belong</u>.

I love you,
Dad

Mom, I'm singing your tune, 'make my life useful. . . .' Dad, I think you'd rejoice at my creative idea.

Can I do this? Was I brought back to this location for this reason? Could this really be my true calling? But in a run-down church? Will people accept me and welcome the idea of a grief center? Is this where everything begins and belongs?

Dad, is your letter telling me it's alright to try? To go for it and make my 'Marks' in Summerfort? I should see if this is the place to heal, hope, and belong?

My treasured note finds its way back into my purse for safekeeping. Not sure if service would reach through this wooded area, I dig through my phone looking for the information my realtor mentioned. Punching in the numbers on my cell, I fumble because my fingers won't stop trembling. I'm amazed when my second attempt at dialing works.

"Hello. Is this Gene Tucker Construction?"

"Yes, this is Gene?"

Chapter One

*T*O KNOW SOMEONE FROM the time you're six years old, then one day, as you're looking at them, you realize something changes. When my world shifted like this, I needed to show Hayden Oliver Tucker my desire to orbit inside his universe—to a place outside of grief. Instead, I did nothing. At the Summerfort Grief Center in May, during the end-of-the-school-year party, every time Hayden stood near, my heart rattled in a new way. Our history, our situation, still feels so confusing.

I've always cared about him, maybe even loved him. I used to think the saying "I love him, but I'm not *in* love with him" sounded strange. Now, I believe I understand what people mean when they say these words. My question: what happens when the feelings jumble and cross into the area of *both*— love and in love? All summer, I've gone Hayden-less. Not seeing or speaking to him in person. Stuck with zero answers about love. Left alone, just imagining him tossing around footballs while he's at his sports camp. This is why I'm clueless.

But tonight, my damaged heart hammers, fearful with hope, wondering, Will he be here?

Back-to-School Grief Bash
August 17, 2019
Special Teen Night
6:00–10:00 p.m.
Group Session, Pizza & Movie,

The "Grief Bash" postcard from Mrs. Marks rests in my hand. Sad to realize, death creates these invitations. My first one—the invite—arrived before my seventh birthday party. That's when my mother's death occurred. Without notice, Mom vanished, even before my birthday celebration.

Eight years later, the offers to participate continue. So, I head to the building sitting on the corner of Cinderella and Golden Streets. Oh, the irony of some roads. Pretty names with paths leading to them behaving with turns so twisty. As Dad drives, I gaze out the window at the tree-lined hills, considering fairy tales. I can't bring myself to laugh or even smile at how ironic it all seems. Because how can a heart like mine ever learn to trust, accept, or understand love without a mother?

Within a rectangular frame behind plexiglass, a marquee sign is displayed. Each block letter stands in line, written in black and white. Positioned in front of the single-story redbrick structure, it states:

Welcome to the Summerfort Grief Center:
A Place to Heal
A Place to Hope
A Place to Belong

A repurposed Methodist church on the outskirts of Summerfort, Missouri, exists as a hub of grief. The Summerfort Grief Center, at times, is my home away from home and where I met Hayden.

My dad, Dr. John Gardener, drops me off wearing his white lab coat. It's the one with a pocket protector that has a flap where he stashes ballpoint pens advertising our family's business: Gardener Veterinary Clinic. With his seatbelt secured in place and both hands glued on the steering wheel, he looks stiff, like a plastic model of the do-gooder Clark Kent sitting ramrod straight. Dad waves good-bye, driving off in his Nissan Rogue hybrid. Practical reasons: safety, dependability, gas mileage—Dad's reasoning for purchasing that thing. Before walking in, I let out a slight snort. Dad knows nothing about going rogue.

At the sound of a diesel engine racing away, my ears perk up. As I scan the logo, Gene Tucker Construction, written on the black truck before it disappears in a puff of smoke over the hill, my internal organs take a roller-coaster ride. Every step I take builds excitement, knowing Hayden Oliver Tucker has arrived. Standing at the height of the drop-off, I look down, close my eyes, scream, swallow my heart, brace for the impact: I open the door—knowing Hayden Oliver Tucker's inside.

I try giving myself a little pep talk strolling to the check-in desk—Breathe, Gretchen. Inhale. Exhale—

New people may join, so I stop at the entry, sign in by writing my name on the clipboard. Claiming a sticker, I slap on a "Hello, my name is Gretchen." This covers up the Gardener Vet Clinic stitching in the upper left corner of my navy polo T-shirt. All summer, this acted as my makeshift uniform while I worked, helping Dad.

"How in the flippity-do-da are you tonight, Gretchen?" Kelsey asks, standing in line behind me. Hearing my catchphrase "WTFDD" used and remembered by one of the newer girls makes me laugh. I turn around.

"Hey, Kelsey. How are you?"

"Okay," Kelsey said, but her sad eyes tell a different story.

"I'm glad you're here," I say, looking down at myself. *With khaki shorts on, I resemble that Australian crocodile hunter girl. Oh, crikey! What's her name? Oh, yes. Bindi Irwin. She's likable. She's also sweet. Plus, aww—she suffered the loss of her dad. My mental thoughts torment me.*

4

Chapter One

From the check-in desk, I scoop up my grief journal and folder. Items were waiting for me since I attend regularly. Mrs. Marks creates folders for first-timers, so no one is ever left out, though. All the prompts will be so similar that even a new-comer understands and relates. With curiosity, I glance inside, shuffle through the papers, reading tonight's activity. Since I'm a regular who texts or calls to RSVP, so I had a personalized prompt waiting for me.

Gretchen, please describe ways in which grief might challenge you as you head to Summerfort High School this year.

For a brief moment, tonight's activity makes me think back to grade school when I was asked, "What did you do on your summer vacation?" Let's see, oh, I know—I spent time at grief camps coping with kids, some motherless, like Hayden and me.

Pretending I'm still reading, I plop down on the sofa. Using quick sideways peeks, I'm well aware Hayden's lounging at the other end of the couch. Our school colors accentuate and match the hue of Hayden's cloudy blue-gray eyes. After this evening's visual, I've decided I'll become a Summerfort Eagle's football fan. A new and improved super-fan. I might even go to every game this school year to make up for not going in our junior high years. Seeing Hayden in his practice T-shirt and shorts gets me channeling school spirit. Go, Summerfort Eagles!

Five teens and Mrs. Marks, our group facilitator, make up tonight's attendees. Mrs. Marks goes over the rules: silence cell phones, remember confidentiality, listen with kindness, and don't tell others they're grieving wrong. We begin with introductions by stating who we are, who died, how, and when. It's not easy for any of us to speak up and go through this portion. Still, it's part of the process of grief healing, and according to Mrs. Marks, it's the one thing that's non-negotiable if you come to the group.

It impacts everyone emotionally to hear someone's story for the first time. Sometimes—near anniversaries, birthdays, holidays—it still stings, but Marks says it's important to honor the deceased by name. We must learn to acknowledge and process those feelings. For some, that's the hardest part of grief—saying anything out loud. For others, it's writing down their pain. There's not a one-size-fits-all here.

Tonight, all of us present are familiar with each other. Three girls—Kelsey, Mia, me—and two boys—Hayden and Miles. We all lost at least one parent—some lost both. Their stories touch me.

Kelsey lost her mom in a car accident. They were on their way home from her band practice. Suicide by gunshot caused the death of Miles's dad, who's the newest boy to the group. Kelsey and Miles attend the same school in Branson. Miles usually sits by Kelsey. I often wonder if he wishes he played the drums, so he could chat up Kelsey easier. He's always tapping his fingers or pens on surfaces. I overheard him tell Hayden he enjoys computers and math. I guess he's kinda cute? Miles has *miles* of hair on his head and dark features. The words "charming" and "sexy nerd" once came out of Kelsey's mouth to describe Miles.

A drug overdose (heroin, I believe) took the lives of both parents for Mia, the other girl. She now lives with her grandmother, who brings her quite a distance to come to our center. It's still hard for her to speak without crying. And we all understand that. During introductions, we can discuss how we are doing or share other facts as we want. Kids sometimes come and go quickly. Some leave feeling ready to face grief on their own. They may return for special events. But I'm hoping this little group right now stays connected for a while.

"Gretchen, let's start with you," Mrs. Marks says.

"Hi. I'm Gretchen. My mom died of a stroke when I was six, almost seven. I remember she and I were planning my upcoming birthday. She's been gone almost eight years now. I've been coming here on and off for the different age groups and special events ever since. It helps me a lot. Sometimes I feel okay. Other days I don't think I will ever feel normal again. Going into high school seems big. There are lots of questions I wish I could ask my mom right now." I see everyone nod in agreement.

With Miles and Hayden as the only boys present, I conclude Hayden's the one responsible for stirring the air with a woodsy pine scent. Across the contours of Hayden's summertime skin, he sports a golden glow. Since the last time I saw Hayden at the end of the school year in May, Hayden's taller and broader in the arms, legs, and shoulders. In the face, he looks *older*. I imagine Hayden fresh from the shower, spritzing on this new cologne.

"I'm Hayden. Like Gretchen, my mom also died, but with uterine cancer. Yet we experienced our mothers' deaths around the same age and time frame." He glances my way.

My heart leaps into my throat at the way Hayden says *Gretchen*. That deep masculine, southern drawl, each word seeping out of his mouth with such slow precision as the letters of my name go across those thick kissable lips. *Holy crap, that's me. I'm Gretchen.* Since when did a guy's voice give me these weird tingling shiver bumps?

Wait, did I hear what Hayden said? He did turn *me* into *we*, didn't he? At first, I go all floaty and giddy thinking of Hayden and Dr. Seuss rhymes in my head. My skin experiences some kind of electrical sizzle. Was I hot? Was I cold? Maybe the couch could become as animated as my imagination, and with two big chomps, it might just swallow me whole?

I'm so wishy-washy. Now, what I really wanna do—perch on the edge of the cushion, bounce up and down, saying, "Hey, say my name, Hayden, and do that goose-bump thingy to me again, please." I feel so weird and out of control. Unsure of how to label anything.

Most of the time in the group, I'm used to Hayden staring at the floor, speaking in one-word answers, saying "pass," or choosing to do the written work but rarely adding to the group's conversation. But Hayden listens and cares. He speaks with his eyes and heart.

Because of the impact Death has on a heart, I worry that in the wake of Death, is Grief going to permanently alter my ability to ever truly love? And the question inside the folder tonight toys with me. I'm scared to attend high school. I'm scared to trust. I'm scared to love. Grief is a scary business—period. Speaking of the word "*period*"—That's a newer problem for me too. Oh, now I'm just rambling.

The emptiness between us screams. A tiny box of Kleenex separates us. It's only one cushion, but Hot Boy appears a million crushed dreams away from me. Hot Boy, that's what I sometimes call Hayden Oliver Tucker now because his initials make the situation humorous, and somehow Hayden grew up. The name really fits. I would never tell a single soul about this nickname.

Hot Boy's a snack—appearing like a double-dipped caramel apple and smelling like the coming fall. He's created a layer of craziness inside me. My concentration's all over the place. Crushing on him like mad. Well, that's just one of my big secrets.

Secrets. Tell me anything you want. I'm the best secret keeper. I'll place labels on them, store them, even categorize them. Also, hoard them away, whether by color, number, or day. Nobody has to find out. I'm filled to the brim with secrets. In fact, I brought secrets to this meeting. I'm literally sitting on secrets now. Some stay trapped inside my head because they hurt so bad. Details of unknowns I left back in my bedroom.

I grab the throw pillow from behind me, trying to play it cool, but knowing the real me is an epic dork. Flopping the throw pillow on top of my legs, I pretend to use it as a lap desk. It's to disguise my skin in contrast to Hayden's. My seasonal tone: off-white-death-gray. Did I need to match the topic of the evening?

I lick my lips. I'd plastered on peppermint lip gloss, but I'm wondering, *does this red clash with my hair?* I almost laugh out loud at my own joke: Who wears Christmas peppermint lip gloss in the summer on a nonexistent, secretive grief safari in Missouri while ogling a boy, anyway?

A million more things short-circuit my brain. Like what if I could dissolve, turn to dust, and fly away? Or melt and float away? Or just jump up and leave this room? I would love a superpower like this because I feel like I'm so freaking stupid.

Chapter One

Why can't I sit still, calm my brain, and just be normal?

Panic starts to set in because I hate remembering some things about what happened this summer. Recently, I suffered through an unkind ordeal. Tonight, if only in writing, I need to share *part* of it. Elastic cuts deep grooves into my legs, all the way around my thighs. I fidget, but this only causes my underwear to begin creeping up higher and higher. I'm uncomfortable. Escaping appeals to me, but more of me wants to hang on, stay, get noticed. More than anything in the world, I know what I really want is the one thing that I can never have: my mom.

My mother's dead. My heart slams hard and then plummets. Tears sit on the edge of my eyes, my lashes holding them back like a dam. I pray the mascara doesn't trickle and give me away. It's too early in the night to cry. Nothing said so far warrants tears falling.

All the kids finish speaking in the circle. Mrs. Marks says, "Time to look at the question tonight. Describe ways in which grief might challenge you as you head to school this year. Take some time to write, and then we will discuss."

Hayden and the others reach for pens or pencils on the rectangular coffee table at the center of the room, so I use a single second to swipe a Kleenex out of the box and dab the corners of my eyes.

Although I select last, I come out ahead with my favorite aqua-colored ink pen. Or maybe after all the time we spend together, the people inside this room know me better than I realize. *Had they left the pen for me on purpose?* To believe in the kindness of others would feel good, but I can't allow myself to get sucked into a world of make-believe.

My fingertips roll at the corner edge of my paper, back and forth and back and forth, reliving one of the hardest parts of the back-to-school routine and being motherless.

In all caps, I jot: **BACK-TO-SCHOOL SHOPPING SUCKS** on curled-up paper. The room shifts to about a hundred degrees, the air in the room zaps away, and the humidity renders me breathless. As I write, my face must flash to red, like a stoplight.

Aqua ink flows across the page as I recap my incident: With high hopes, I'd looked forward to shopping with my friend and her mom down at the Branson Landing. Victoria's Secret had announced their seven-pairs-for-$28 sale days. In addition to the money I'd saved working with Dad at the vet clinic, Dad had given me extra for clothes and lunch.

Indulging at Joe's Crab Shack for some peace, love, and crabs was part of our plan. I needed a bit of summer adventure and fun. Not the weird, constant reminder of how awkward I always feel being Motherless. Going places with friends and their moms makes me see myself as a charity case, a burden, a third wheel, or an afterthought. Trying not to get jealous as I watch people my age with their moms creates a lot of emotions in me that I must learn to overcome. I'd love to take for granted the ability to shop for school clothes and go out to eat with my mom.

I only received my mom's help to buy school clothes during kindergarten and first grade. Memories of these events don't exist, as I don't recall either outing with my mom. Realizing this brings a lot of sadness about back-to-school shopping. Buying my first bras and underwear (especially after my first period—not long ago) brings up some traumatic matters.

Hayden taps his pen against his notebook. When I glance at him, he mouths, "Sorry." We exchange a grin. With his journal rested flat on his lap on full display, I can't help but steal a quick glimpse into the heart and mind of Hayden. I long to learn everything about the guy who kids teased in grade school. They used to call him "Hardly Speaks Hayden." He's still a quiet, brooding, shy loner. Well, he also writes in shorthand. All I'm able to gather from my vantage point is a bulleted list:

*Don't fit jock mold
*Q-AF issue/teammates
*Shy/misunderstood loner
*HS class load with sports
*G

I'm ready to slither over, remove the distance between us, throw that freakin' box of Kleenex to the floor, and plant my first real kiss on Hayden. Then I'd ask, "What does the letter 'G' stand for on your list? Grief, goals, grades, God, girls? Or pretty please, dear God in heaven, could it be for *Gretchen*?"

Get a grip! That's more likely—Goofy Grief Girl Gretchen! This boy's too cool for you. He plays sports, while you're at home playing your Dad-created game, One to Twenty-Seven—the United States Constitution Amendment trivia. Amendment Eighteen equals Prohibition; Amendment Nineteen equals women's suffrage; Amendment Twenty equals the president takes office on the twentieth (20/20); Amendment Twenty-One repealed Prohibition (think of legal drinking age). You can list them all. I bet that's really sexy to a jock? Then, using mnemonic devices with the numbers eighteen and twenty-one, if you combine them, you have the year Missouri became a state.

For even more "good times," Dad used to challenge you with presidential flashcards while other girls at school played with dolls. Perhaps my father's grooming me for the gig of First Lady of Missouri or of the United States?

I know little about throwing a ball across the field for a goal, but I'd like to. By the way, I long to know what those other bullet points mean too?

That whole Q-AF? What's upsetting you, Hayden? What's so Q-AF? And who or what is G?

I hang my head, resisting the urge to react to tears forming. At the same time, I scribble the initials L.P. Seeing "L" on my page, knowing it stands for Lilly, the cheerleader with sunshiny hair, the girl who boys adore. Not meaning to, I moan and shudder too loudly. It's my turn to look over as my mouth forms the word "sorry." Hayden and I exchange another grin.

"You okay?" Hayden asks. It's effortless to study and read his lips, but it's so tough to focus my eyes away. I answer in a nod, dragging myself back to my paper to write.

As we start discussing group issues with our back-to-school thoughts, we all realize nothing mixes well with grief. "Gretchen, thank you for sharing your thoughts on listing back-to-school shopping as a chore, but do you want to be more specific or share a recent story?" Mrs. Marks asks.

I inhale a deep breath. On exhale, I hope I huff out enough of the negative energy. "I guess I'll try. My back-to-school summer outing ended when a girl from school [I don't say her name out loud to the group/*Lilly P.*] pranced into the store. As she threw shady eyes at me, she whispered *loudly* to my friend [*Darcy*] because she did it on purpose so everyone could hear, 'Just because Gretchen's mom is dead, it doesn't really give her the right to

15

come in and steal your mom right out from under you."'

My voice cracks, but as I reach for a Kleenex, Hayden beats me to it and hands one to me. He moves closer, placing the Kleenex in his lap, and puts his hand on my arm.

"I guess what hurts me most is knowing that everyone involved heard—my friend, her mom, and the girls with her—but everyone pretended not to. Their eyes darted all around to each other in the store. They all waited for someone else to speak up. I suppose an apology or defending me seemed out of the question? Death talk makes others ache too much, I guess?" I shrug and wipe tears. My voice cracks. "I don't think I did anything wrong?"

Hayden didn't move.

"I'm sorry that happened to you, Gretchen," Mrs. Marks says. She sits up straight and makes another statement. "Gretchen's right. She did nothing wrong, and death talk makes many people uncomfortable. You'll have times in life when people will avoid the topic, avoid you, change the subject. Or you may experience a similar situation. It can be hurtful. Try to remember that most people don't mean to be cruel, like this girl. Often, in times of sympathy, people don't know what to say. I wish we could teach people to say—'I don't know what to say, but I'm sorry. I'm thinking of you. I can't imagine. I care. I wish I knew what to do.'"

Of all people, Hayden says, "Mrs. Marks, I remember a phrase you gave me once that works under challenging situations."

It sounded like Mrs. Marks starts talking with clenched teeth when she looks at Hayden. "Please, remind us, Hayden."

"I'm sorry you feel that way." Hayden follows up with a slight smirk in Mrs. Marks's direction.

Mrs. Marks throws her hand over her heart, "Oh, Hayden. Yes. That line works well under a lot of struggles." She grins at Hayden, but we all smile. Marks uses this line on Hayden a lot in the group.

"What else might we say about grief and school?" Mrs. Marks asks.

Mia mentions shopping at the mall, only to witness kids fighting with parents about something so dumb. All of us join in, talking about how envious it makes us all feel to see kids with parents.

Kelsey cries because she has no idea how difficult it will be to help her dad organize school lunches, bus schedules, and different school events for her three younger siblings. Without her mom's income, her Dad said he's going to depend on her to babysit after school, so he can work extra shifts at his factory. "So, this coming school year," she says, "I will probably have to give up playing in the marching band."

Students from nearby school districts and churches attend Summerfort Grief Center because our center is unique, nondenominational, and hosts frequent youth events. Hayden and I make up the only two long-term *local* high school students.

"After group, come chat with me in private," Mrs. Marks says to Kelsey. "I want to share an idea with you."

I cringe and hate myself for thinking thoughts like this, but I say to myself, please don't share new visuals tonight, Kelsey.

My heart knocks so hard and loud against my chest every time Kelsey starts to speak about her mother's death. Too often, she works through grief by describing the sounds of the car metal twisting and bones piercing. The mixed smells of rubber tires burning on the pavement, along with diesel gas, blood, and tears. Eyes can't see anything but can't stop looking at every flashing light. Ears hear people trying to help. Numbness comes with the knowledge of death. She and her mom were on their way home from her band practice when the car accident occurred. She lives inside this crashed car each day with guilt—that's her grief.

I hate this for Kelsey. I carry her home in my heart. With her brothers and sisters, I often wonder if it adds sorrow to worry about them or if it helps to have them to lean on? As an only child, I often wish I had someone else to talk to, but during groups, people with brothers and sisters often complain about the misunderstandings and unfair treatments. Some see one as grieving harder than another. Grief changes the dynamics of their family roles too. A lot of adult expectations are placed on kids, like Kelsey. Even with my dad and me, life changed drastically.

I've heard Mrs. Marks over the years pull kids aside during events and offer scholarship money, telling them about the Summerfort and Branson programs offering after-school daycares at no charge. Nonprofits for kids, like latchkey kids run by churches or YMCAs. Mrs. Marks ensures kids and teens in her care don't suffer any more than they have to through grief. Young people give up so much of their childhood during grief as it is. Everyone deserves hobbies and outlets. I hope Mrs. Marks finds ways to work things out for Kelsey and her family. A thought comes to me about asking Dad to create an after-school program at our vet clinic for kids—working with me to help feed, water, and walk the animals. Maybe I can do something in the future?

"Let's break to eat," Mrs. Marks says.

As I walked into the commons area, a voice calls out, "Gretchen, do you know what classes you're in this year?" I turn, my insides knotted, knowing it's Hayden asking.

As he rifles in his pocket to pull his wallet out of his shorts to retrieve his schedule, I dig in my purse to do the same. I find my list of classes, and we compare them.

We walk through the pizza buffet line, chatting.

"Honors English together. Didn't know jocks liked reading and writing," I say.

Hayden follows me to the table to continue our discussion. I pick at my cheese pizza, taking tiny nibbles and washing them down with raspberry tea. Three dark Godiva chocolates sit by my plate. I hoarded them to enjoy while watching the movie. While my legs bounced with nerves, I focused on the purple-and-gold wrappers, but I longed to dive into Hayden's eyes without fear of rejection.

"I'm *atypical*. I thought you knew that about me, Gretchen," he says, giving me one of *those* grins. It's wide enough—it's the toothy kind—where I can see Hayden's sliver gap in his two front teeth and the slight dimple in his cheek. *I want to kiss your atypical mouth*, I shout in my head.

"Nice. Good use of a fancy word. By the way, I like the Netflix show *Atypical*. Are you telling me you're autistic, Hayden?" I ask, then give my closed-mouth giggle.

"I'm not familiar with that show. Wanna come over sometime, Gretchen? We can have a marathon binge-watching session?"

"Oh, okay," I say. Knowing Hayden's just playing me, I scoot my chair back, gather my food to toss, pointing in the direction of the bathroom. With a little wave and smile, I leave the table, stomping as fast as possible.

Chapter One

Once in the bathroom, I let the stream of hot tears flow. Why can't I be normal? I want to fit in somewhere? Anywhere? Why does he pretend to like me when I know he's way out of my league? I'm a nerd. He's a jock. Those two groups don't run in the same school circles. He runs with girls like Lilly. But Hayden is atypical—his word, not mine. He doesn't even run in his own circle. What's wrong with me? I adjust my underwear for comfort and reapply my lip gloss, so I can face the group.

When I go back out, Hayden pats at the space beside him on the couch, motioning for me to sit down in the seat he saved for me. So torn about Hayden's true feelings for me, I flop down. Hayden opens his palm, showing me the three Godivas I'd abandoned.

"I hope you plan to share," Hayden whispers.

I smile, leaving one in his hand.

When he leaned over, his naked leg brushed mine for a moment. If I didn't eat these chocolates soon, they'd melt because of the heat stirring inside me, as well as beside me.

"Our feature movie tonight is *The Breakfast Club*. I chose this film for several reasons," Mrs. Marks says. "*First*, it offers us the back-to-school theme. The *second reason*, I hope to challenge you to look beyond labels this school year. None of us are one-dimensional. Simply because somebody has a pretty face or a beautiful home doesn't mean their life is picture-perfect."

Mrs. Marks stood and gestured to the photos she'd taken of us over the years. In a collage, they hang on the wall behind us, over the couch. Some included Hayden and me as children. Recent ones involve kids in the group now. Highlights of hands grasping one another. Or our hands busy helping one another through activities. Other snapshots show us writing our journal prompts.

"I want to share this knowledge with you: Over the years, I've served as an eyewitness. Inside rooms of stories filled with loss, life's daily labels and social statuses melt away. It seems there's equality with death. And with grief. It comes to everyone. When it does, it flatlines each and every heart. *Sameness* comes to people in a grief-filled room, bonded by pain."

Mrs. Marks sits down, holding up a map of the world. "Think big. Like, the-size-of-the- universe type of big. Go in every direction of the globe where people live because grief reaches all of these lives. That's because grief is universal. The pain of loss touches hearts all over the world."

Mrs. Marks pauses, looking at each of our faces. "Grief sucks the life out of *everyone* at some point—sick, healthy, young, old, wealthy, poor, Caucasian, African American, Asian, Hispanic, Christian, Jew, Republican, Democrat, jock, and nerd—to name only a few. I don't mean to leave a soul out, but there are too many to mention. I ache for each of them because I understand the longing for a parent.

This movie is based at a school, but it offers back-to-school grief and parental issues at a deeper core. It contains so many themes we can relate to and discuss. Think about the characters in the film as we watch."

Mrs. Marks starts laughing. "What am I at—the third, fourth, or fifth reason for choosing this film?"

We all laugh with her.

"I'm not sure," Kelsey says but adds, "Mrs. Marks, I like it a lot when you pick movies with an '80s theme because then I feel connected to my mom when we watch. I can imagine her watching these movies as a teenager because I bet she did."

"Oh, I agree," I say. "I could never put it into words why I felt so obsessed with '80s films, and I think you just solved the mystery." My body relaxed, so I leaned farther back into the couch with a smile. This took me even closer to Hayden, allowing me another quick brush against his naked leg. He poked me in the ribs and smiled.

"Oh, I love your sentiment. What a great way to view these movies. I'm stealing that line and thought from you," Mrs. Marks says. "Can I include it in my reasons for picking this movie?" she asks.

Again, we all giggle.

Mrs. Marks picks up a sheet of paper. "One last item before the film rolls. I purposely didn't put this in your folder tonight, but I will hand one out while we watch."

For your journal thoughts later:

1. Explain ways in which you get mislabeled like some of the movie character(s) from The Breakfast Club are.

2. If you were honest with yourself, in what ways are you like each of the characters?

3. What goes on behind the scenes of your life no one knows about, but you wish they did?

4. Does grief add extra layers of concern for you that you wish others knew? If so, how?

5. Who do you like but feel you can't/shouldn't because it goes against social norms?

Chapter Two

September 2019

Dear Mom,

At the grief center, I got asked: What goes on behind the scenes of your life no one knows about, but you wish they did?

No one can fix me. Or reverse the world, allowing me a chance to feel normal again. Is it too late for any hope? Everything goes unclear when your mother vanishes from the earth. I'm off-axis, off-kilter, off-center—all sorts of messed up with thousands of racing thoughts. All the time, reverse reminders surface of you. Sure. A motherless child's human heart thumps out beats and survives a profound loss, but I wonder if portions fail to thrive, function, or even grow? Without my mother's love, am I able to be anything at all? Your final kiss good-bye left too many lingering questions.

I recall how we planned my *Little Mermaid* party early. *"I know your birthday is months away, but let's buy these candles today," you'd said.* My mind reenacted the day. Like a vise, I clenched my fists, listening to your voice—now only vapors.

Light from the candles you selected trembled, casting shadows across the dining room walls. "Happy Birthday" rang out of tune as Dad belted out the words. "Under the Sea," I stood, drowning in unfulfilled wishes. Wax teardrops trickled down, so I assumed the seven mermaid candles cried for me. Under streamers and balloons, with my eyes closed, I pretended to eat cake with you. *"Ariel's a redhead too. Or as Dad says, 'copper beauty.'"* I had to remember one of our many past talks because, by my seventh birthday, you had disappeared.

Rewind. Play. Pause. Flashbacks operate as digital recordings in my memory bank. Three family members gathered Christmas morning near the tree. My mind won't release this visual. Nor will my heart turn it away. So, I hoarded the last Christmas gift from you, although you meant them only as a joke. Plus, thankfully, you bought the wrong size, way too big for me at the time. On the back of every tag, I wrote, "From Mom" using a black Sharpie with a fine tip. Advertised on the marker's label is the word permanent. What a lie, I thought, considering my experience with you and the realization that nothing and no one survives forever, regardless of tireless efforts attempting to make it so.

It may seem unbelievable, but inside my dresser drawer, I *still* have stashed each Christmas pair in a neat pile by the rightful day of the week. The elastic now stretched and frayed around my waist, thighs, and hips.

Daily, I follow my routine:

1. Open the dresser drawer.
2. Stare old memories down.
3. Choose a pair based on my mood or "Mom Memory"—not by the day of the week.
4. Allow hope to enter the day.
5. Enter comments into my personal or Summerfort Center journal as a way to bury grief.
6. Ensure each item's accounted for.
7. Close the dresser drawer.

Faint echoes swarm inside my head, but I listen, believing I might really hear my mother's voice arguing with me. *"Gretchen, pitch the underwear. Move on. Wear your size, and be age-appropriate."*

"Fine! How about I go buy myself some thongs, G-strings, or something just really cheeky to start Summerfort High School, *Mother*? Would those suit me?"

"Gretchen, why do you need, or want, thongs at your age?" Mother, you *might've* yelled or asked?

This privilege of knowing, I'll never experience with you. But, let's just say *if* you asked, shouted, or talked to me, I imagine myself blurting out a bunch of facts about a shy boy at school, a friend of mine, but this title *friend*—well, he's held that far too long.

"Perhaps if I wore something sexy, Hayden Oliver Tucker (Hot Boy) could catch wind of the fact. He might acknowledge me in English, instead of *only* talking to me at the Summerfort Grief Center. The place full of promises: "A Place to Heal; A Place to Hope; A Place to Belong." Why doesn't he like me? Or talk to me beyond the walls of our grief? He's barely EVER spoken to me outside of there. School seems to make floundering idiots out of both of us. So, is the problem awkward shyness?

Mom, *if* you could chat with me, maybe you might ask me how my school year started. Let me share some of that with you.

WELCOME TO FRESHMAN YEAR, SUMMERFORT EAGLES! This oversized banner greeted me in the school hallway. I imagine this year the school budget's doomed. No extra field trips because Mr. Marshall assures we all sparkle on the inside. Principal Marshall orders such garish signs. A glitzy, emcee job in nearby Branson suits him better. Maybe even Vegas. Indeed, he's a game-show host hiding in the hallways of a southern Missouri high school. I think it's a shame to waste his talents.

The gigantic girth of the dangling blue-and-gray plastic poster seems aimed right at me. Reminiscent of a Civil War battle flag waving in a warning. Every day, distress signals shoot out with cannonball messages: **THINK! BIG STUFF AHEAD**:

*Credits matter
*Full-on womanhood
*Real periods
*Bigger boobs
*Fuller hips
*Boyfriend, perhaps?

Am I ready? I wish you could answer. Living with zero knowledge of what you think of me kills me. This denial of the right to listen to the sounds my mother's voice once made—I get none of your wisdom, secrets, laughter, nagging, or the words "I love you." I get nothing. Everything is just gone. Dead!

Sometimes, I pretend to prance around my room, swaying my hips, twisting and turning—stopping to pose. Gazing at your photos, with intense eyes (the smize, as the fabulous Tyra Banks taught us), and sporting a stern, pouty mouth. I model until my over-the-top performances end in silent shudders. Hard as I struggle to recreate our childhood game, I always turn up a loser. I hate playing *America's Next Top Model* alone.

My whole body aches and craves my bossy best friend. To design a world, one in which I understand *normal* in—one you remain a part of—I slip on old, extra-small Christmas underwear on a size-small body curving her way to medium. What's happening to me?

My freakazoid hips, with their loopy-loo cray-cray uncontrollable thickness, expand more each day. Spanx (also in thongs) to smooth out my ruffles are now required, I think. "Tucked all in for Tucker." What a slogan. Do you believe Hot Boy Hayden would approve? As I'm wearing these new undergarments, I could humor myself in secret (if I can still breathe) as I continue to long for Hayden Tucker. Instead of only seven items, I'll go buy thirty-one tiny articles, a whole month's supply.

Besides, won't shopping ease all my anger? You're not here stopping the madness, making sure I don't steal anyone else's mother right out from under them. Plus, NVPL. Do you know what that means? It represents No Visible Panty Lines. Are you disturbed, Mother?

I creep myself out. One minute I'm a trapped child, and then I'm one giant hormonal mess discussing sexy undergarments, such as butt-floss bloomers, with my deceased mother, so I can lure a (teenage) man. *Who am I?*

Part of me understands grief. The little girl you kissed good-bye refuses to grow up. She stalls, marking time, standing by in scraps of left-over underwear. Birthday cakes, pecan pies, and presents, all with hollow longings on her face, she celebrates each holiday's passing. She yearns to CRY and SCREAM and SHOUT and KICK and PUNCH and SPIT and RUN and FLY and perhaps DIE for the chance to hug you, see you, and talk to you.

Not today, though, because today I refuse to listen. Your voice, a constant ghostly reminder, telling me what to do. My days-of-the-week panties shall remain. I love you but eff you for leaving me. I won't spell it out because we understand the intended meaning. Every effing, godforsaken stitch—until the last ones disintegrate in the washer—stays. Circulation may cut off, but I'm planning to let them hang on tight. Quit the preachy moments: *"Pitch the underwear, Gretchen."* Like a swarm of stinging wasps, your imaginary words hurt and haunt my brain. Please. Stop.

Grief Girl Gretchen—Sometimes, that's all I feel I am to this world. Tonight, I fight through pain and puddles, writing more of the story, seeking understanding. You and I *guess*— God—realize the truth. My underwear so tight now each pair looks like an amateur artist painted them on. To keep memories alive, this inventory sheet offers physical evidence I can touch. Should anything happen, like more colors bleeding and fading away—I *need* a full, *detailed summary* of the current stash.

My Days-of-the-Week Inventory Sheet:

Monday: The monkey might be faded, but I remember the smile on his face, as he hung from the letter O and his tail twirled to the Y. He wore a green hat on his head. With the muscles of his long arms, his hands held firm as he dangled. The greeting "NOEL" written out on a field of felt material.

Tuesday: The turtles appear tattered, but I recall momma tortoise's proud blue eyes, along with her long eyelashes—her focus and confidence, as she led her babies—all adorned in identical red scarves and boots. Her eyes matched ours. She deserves to stay alive, so she can care for her kids. I understand how much they need her.

Wednesday: The non-whimsical wolf remains a powerhouse creature, with threadbare spots. The snowfall scenery is now splotchy, so the season undetected, but who cares—he is so unforgettable.

Thursday: The turkey developed a mini hole in the waistline, easy enough to ignore. I visualize a bird donning a Santa hat, with a sled of toys—dolls, trucks, and stuffed animal bears are a tad visible. This alone warrants them as keepers.

Friday: The frogs hint at long-ago lily pads addressed with a secret message: Merry Christmas. The frogs suggest a growth spurt, perhaps too many years playing leapfrog without my permission. Qualities of age show as waterlogged damage streaks across my holiday amphibians.

Saturday: The silly squirrels reign as my favorite underwear. On them, triplets lounge around a campfire, their mouths stuffed. Beneath matching mittens and puffy winter coats, their bushy tails can't be contained. In their hands, they're holding a songbook opened to the page "Chestnuts Roasting on an Open Fire."

Sunday: The coral reef and starfish died. Like you, Mom, gone forever. Destroyed. While wearing a stupid pair of underwear, I started my first "official" period. The period that chose to stick.

Gloominess had hung in the air that morning. My mood caused me to select the coral reef and starfish pair. I should've known something would happen. Even though they're reserved for Sunday— "Under the Sea" moments we'd shared—decorating my bedroom in shades of aqua, watching Ariel in the *Little Mermaid*, planning a birthday party in a theme you didn't even get to attend. Reliving these memories, I'd stood inside my aqua bedroom, staring inside my dresser drawer. Missing you, I chose and then slipped on that very pair, Mother.

False summer surprises of "hello, two days of womanhood," then good-bye for several months? At thirteen years old, my body betrayed me, but my fourteen-year-old self said, "Time for the real program, I guess." Ugh. Changes with age put a lot of pressure on me. Will I successfully navigate through?

School, of course, the worst possible location to detect my body flipping out on me and where I acquired "woman" status. I needed you so badly that day. Every day, though, I want and need you. What freak wears Granny panties with a multitude of themes: Christmas-gift-days-of-week-Sunday-zoo-animals-starfish-dead-mother-undies?

With a single swooping motion, I bunched a fistful of childhood memories. Through blurred eyes, I flung everything across the room. My mission continued until every pair I owned, the past mixed with the present, sprawled before me. Among the piled mess I created, I curled into the fetal position.

Mommy, what am I going to do? The new underwear I bought scream out warning reminders, over and over. Lilly's voice saying, "Just because Gretchen's mom is dead, it doesn't really give her the right to come in and steal your mom right out from under you." I just can't seem to put an end to it. Mommy, I never wanted anyone else's mother because I only ever wanted you. I still do. But I can't have you, and I don't know what to do. I loathe every effing pair of those summer underwear. Wearing them is out of the question. I didn't know what else to do. My heart found a solution. A way to try and fix my brokenness and be close to you.

For a while, I allowed myself time to grieve: what was, what could have been, what might become of me. A million thoughts stung my brain and flattened my heart. I gasped. For far too long, I suppose, I suppressed sobs. My body lurched, rumbled, and howled.

Grief frightens me. The emotions and the powers gripping, crushing, and detaining my life cannot be defined. Am I angry? Am I sad? Again and again, I ask myself: Am I able to be anything? Or become anything at all without my mother's love? Too many questions. Rambling thoughts I just gotta share:

How do I live the rest of my life without you? How do I pick out my prom dress? What if no one asks me to go to any of the school dances? What if they ask, but I don't want to go—how do I say no, subtly? Should I push myself to take the advanced classes in high school? Will I be informed enough to realize what I should major in at college? Should I take driver's ed before the written and driving exams? Will Dad's feelings be hurt if I don't ask him to help me learn to drive? But who else will step in to guide me?

My mother's death leaves a hole for all of life's events: her absence. High school and college graduations?—How will I walk the stage and not crumple with emotion? How might I even arrive at such a place? Which universities should I apply to? When you dreamed about my future, where did you see me attending? My parents worked hard to build the Gardeners Vet Clinic. Do I have to live near home for the sake of helping out? Should I prepare to work at Gardeners Vet Clinic? What do I do if Dad meets someone new? Is it a betrayal of you if I like a person he decides to date? One day, if Dad were to remarry, would it be alright if I called someone else, *Mom*?

How do I honor a wedding? My wedding, with enough love, without a mother guiding me? Is it wrong to feel guilty or cheated because my mother will never meet her future son-in-law? Or meet her grandchildren? My ability to offer someone a history, roots, a full past, is gone. What if I don't want to find love at all because to lose them involves risks too painful to face? What do I do with the deep feelings I harbor for a boy named Hayden, who I like so much? How do I resolve this? I pretend that when Hayden wrote the initial "G" during our grief group, it meant Gretchen, but there's zero proof. Why is love something I don't trust or understand?

Here I go again: Rewind. Play. Pause. All the buttons I wish to add to my Christmas list. Reenactments operate as digital recordings in my memory bank. Three family members gathered for Christmas morning near the tree. Laughter intermingles with sobs I choke down, envisioning myself digging into my stocking. Embarrassed, I pulled out a package of underwear. You and Dad giggled, flirted, and acted so alive that morning. I recall you said, "Oh, we bet *someday* those silly animal bloomers will be your favorite gift." Now, I listen to the echoes, the whispers, "Someday, those silly animal bloomers will become your favorite." Every morning your words greet me; your words comfort me; your words continue to be worn.

By the following Christmas, my mother had had a stroke, and you had deserted me. Holiday underwear, blinking lights, my parents kissing—I hoard those lasting moments. Ironic, one package meant only as a gag gift, created little laughter. Panties bought in a size too large for me at the time, I grew into. Years passed, and the days of the week and I, along with other problems, expanded out of extra-small.

Mother, please help. My experience with full or real periods is now occurring. Confusion alert ahead: PMS? Pads versus tampons. When it comes to tampons, I'm so confused about all the types and sizes. The cotton sticks intrigue me for the convenience, but their appearance intimidates me. Unpleasant situation. I'm not 100% accurate yet because my approach, aim, or something with these things seems a tad off. I'll keep on keeping on and try. What choices do I accept as a "woman"?

Do they really expect people to wear internal "absorbent bullets" or mini crotch pampers? It's downright cruel. I *hate* both options. This "wing" business that's supposed to protect underwear *seemed* like a nice bonus. Available on one of the brands, but all the excessive stickers sure get on my nerves. One night the sticky part that folds over your underwear to help you stay clean did me no favors. In the morning, I peeled off clustered nonsense from my legs. No more wings; I clipped them!

Midol versus Pamprin versus generic? Why must my innards flip-flop, cramp up, and explode? This is devilish. Am I possessed? I almost asked Dad if he thought so. I wanted to climb on top of the school's roof and hide.

Mom, on that day in May toward the end of the school year—the day I started my period—I bawled my eyes out on the toilet at school. Some nosy person (Period Narc Girl) listened to me flushing the stool a thousand times without exiting the stall. So, she wrangled the counselor, Miss Gabrielle "Gabby" Garcia, who I love and all, but sometimes she's too honey-bunch for me with all her sweet talk: "Oh, sweetie, I brought you some supplies. I understand what a difficult time this is, sweetie. Do you want us to call Mrs. Marks from the grief center or your dad, sweetie?"

"No, thanks. I'll be fine with these." Miss Garcia shoved a bag of goodies beneath the bathroom door. I scrounged through, finding a pair of white Granny panties. Held them up, hoping when I put them on, they didn't reach past my belly button. A travel-size package of feminine wipes for use "down there" also floated in the plastic abyss. She provided me choices—cotton sticks, along with pads. For now, I thought, go with ease, so I selected a crotch pamper. After I cleaned up, my emotions confused me—saddened anger. Quiet, giant tears formed as I grasped my freakin' starfish, plotting ways to smuggle them out and keep them protected. Miss Garcia started in again: "Sweetie, everything alright in there?"

"I'm fine. A little nervous. Can I come to your office for a while? I promise to do my work. Will you please explain to Mr. Porter I'm not feeling well? And pick up my assignments for me?"

I imagined snagging a megaphone to shout at Miss Garcia: *Go, sweetie, please, I beg of you. Give me one effing sweet minute alone with my old bloody bloomers. You wouldn't understand, lady. I'm crazy, beyond crazy, with a side of crazy baggage! Sweetie, my dead mom got me these old undies, but now my body's betrayed me. I've ruined them forever. Hey, while you're gone, sweetie, yank **Hayden Oliver Tucker**, out of class, so I can listen to him laugh out loud for me. Hot Boy Hayden might be the one thing to produce a smile out of me today. He may not realize I entirely exist, but he does at least call me by my name. Together, we go way back. Like, we crossed paths with death and such. Now, how does all that sound, sweetie?*

"Oh, what a terrific idea, sweetie. I'm on it now. I'll meet you in my office soon, sweetie."

"Sure," I managed, swallowing and coughing down tears, snot, and more rude thoughts.

Once the noise from her booties stopped clip-clip-clip-pity-clopping across the bathroom tiles, I gulped down a few sobs and swiped at my last few tears. With several deep breaths, I faced the final period (no pun intended) of the school day. Inside my backpack, I crammed the menstrual bag of tricks. My starfish panties were folded with care, as I said a little prayer, "God, please let me be able to save them." A hush-hush compartment never put to use would tote my soiled treasure home.

Inside a cubicle in Miss Garcia's office, I completed my work. Photos of Poco, her Boston Terrier, littered the area. In one snapshot, Poco's dressed in a Summerfort Eagles costume as the unofficial mascot for SHS. Eagle wings on a puppy equal a lot of cuteness. Of course, in the background, Principal Marshall's photobombing for Instagram, I assume. "Gretchen, I'm checking in on you," Miss Garcia said, peeking her head inside the doorway, noticing me admiring her many photos.

As I held up one of my books, I said, "I finished everything." I picked up a 4" x 6" silver frame adorned with the saying, "I heart my dog." I asked, "So, Poco's your only pet?"

"Yes, he is my one and only. I never told you how much Poco and I *love* your dad. He's our hero and our vet." She straightened her silky blouse, positioning her hand on her hip, smiling wide at the photo, and then back at me. I grinned.

"Your dad once explained to me how Boston Terriers are usually known as the 'American Gentleman,' like him. Your dad's a hoot. So fun and charming. I bet he's a wonderful dad." She laughed, every tooth gleaming as she tossed her dark hair off her shoulders.

I returned her laughter with a little giggle. *My dad: A hoot? A charmer? And my dad, Dr. John Gardener, said all that?*

"Yep, my dad's great." She smiled as the final bell rang. We waved good-bye. "Thanks for everything today, Miss Garcia."

"Hey, Gretchen, how was school?" Dad asked as I slipped into the front seat, securing my seatbelt, kicking my backpack, giving my feet extra room.

I shrugged. "Same old stuff, I guess." Staring at the rearview mirror studying the message, 'Objects in mirror are closer than they appear,' and I practiced my speech to Dad. *"Dad, I need female things now."* Without tears, that's how I desired to blurt out this horrific reality of my life. I should've told him right then and there while we were already out and about. Instead, I waited.

At home, in my bedroom mirror, I continued rehearsing, "Dad, I need female things now," until I no longer cried, which helped. When the courage to approach him occurred, I didn't bother looking him in the eye, I stood at a distance. Who wants their father made aware of their monthly? Who wants their dad so familiar with such private information? Who urges to question their dad about period things—it seemed perv-ish or inappropriate on some level. But what else could I do? The saying

41

"it is what it is" fits the situation. Life required me to speak out. Plus, through marriage, he understood all about this nonsensical period stuff, right?

"Dad, I need some female things—"

"Wow. Well, do I say congratulations?" Dad asked, adding an awkward smile. Dad responded somewhat decently about my pharmacy needs. He played it cool, I guess. But Dad required me to go with him to purchase all the crap I wanted to try. Down the aisle, strolling, he said, "Gretchen, I'll let you make decisions. I don't want to push you into buying anything you don't want. Choose a small variety of products to discover what you like." I nodded, scanning the boxes, unsure.

"I think Miss Garcia and Mrs. Marks talked to you about everything? Oh, Miss Garcia followed up in an email to check on you. I got it just before we left the house. How do you like her as a counselor?"

I picked up yet another box of tampons. This situation required too much reading. So many labels or claims: plastic, cardboard, gentle glide, deodorant, sizes ranging from lites to ultras. I didn't comprehend, but I felt too weird asking my father a vagina-related question.

Little white lies rolled out of my mouth, "Yay, I think I got all of this." I gave Dad an odd look because I was trying to read into his questioning. "I guess Miss Garcia's fine, except for her sweetie this-and-that all the time. Poco's cute. Why?"

"Oh, I thought her email seemed very genuine. I like making sure my daughter gets cared for at school. Yeah, I like Poco too." Dad leaned over the handle of the cart, his knuckles turning white from gripping. He was prepared, in case someone tried stealing feminine hygiene products from us, I suppose. His face offered a lopsided grin, though—thinking of Poco's face, I guess. I hoped not imagining tampons.

I despise every single moment of this. I needed my mother's explanation of the finer details. Sure, I got the gist of my schoolhouse and grief center learning: "You're going to have a monthly cycle now, but products are available for you. Let us know if you need anything, Gretchen, a.k.a 'Sweetie.'"

So, as I mentioned, I got myself a variety pack of tampons, which promised me a gentle glide experience (false advertising). Plus, I added super thin pads with wings (never again) for all those extra protections. Perhaps my friends can offer some insight?—*Dingy* Darcy? *Mediocre* Meghan? Or *steal* their mother's advice away? No thanks, I'll pass. I know Mia and Kelsey would help me, but they have so much going on already, so isn't it wrong to text or call and bug them? Wouldn't I just be added to their troubles? But maybe at the center, I'll ask Kelsey because she likes to talk about Miles and Hayden in the bathroom with me. Kelsey got me to confide a couple of secrets. ☺ Google may sell me on the top brands or products? Someday, I'll manage to figure out the whole thing.

Final thought: the name "period"—what man recommended the name? A more precise identifier—Exclamation point! An appearance of a sharp, pointy tip: a poisonous dart!

Chapter Three

September 2019

What goes on behind the scenes of your life no one knows about, but you wish they did?

Yo, Mom,

CAN YOU BELIEVE YOUR son sat down to write? A long time has passed. Call me a grief slacker, I guess. Many questions about you run through my mind every day, but I dislike writing them down. This diary idea—all Mrs. Marks doing. Soon, she'll harp, spy, nag, and do all her nosy crap to invade my life.

A lot to tell you about. Plenty, in fact, but by putting words down, in black and white, like inside a notebook, I risk everything. Like, getting caught, for one. Tooth marks will surround my entire pencil before I finish this page. Fear jumps out as my number-one reason why I hate putting information in my journal. Teammates at school taunt me. I can picture them now.

"Momma's Boy Hayden, Queer AF, listen to some of the stuff he shares with his dead mother!" they'd continue. My notebook, substituting as a football as guys pass it around the locker room. At the "interception" plays, laughter at my expense would come right off the pages of my grief. A winning game—or being good at football, basketball, or baseball—isn't enough to help me.

I grow tired of being different. Somehow, since I'm quiet, attend youth events at a grief center, and because my mother's died, I'm gay?

On the other hand, being a jock equates to being socially accepted *most* days and by *most* people? Back and forth, they go on whether they like me or not. Under the radar, I fly, quiet, hoping they leave me the hell alone. They're always looking for ways to slip in their hazing phrases. "Momma's Boy Hayden, Queer AF" is the new slam on me this year. "Hardly Speaks Hayden" lingers on, but I don't hear it as often. Guess I remain an easy target?

The frame now hangs on the wall at home, but when I won the sportsmanship award, I overheard the comments: "The coach takes up for him. He's a sympathy case. People feel sorry for him. Coach only gave him a pity award." Whispers circulated among the young as well as the old. Coach Ryan handed me the award and said, "Tucker showed up, played hard, and tried encouraging everyone on the team."

To offset the fact that usually there's no one in the stands cheering for me. Still, I show up boosting other players. I use this behavior to make up for the fact that I'm dying inside. No one comes to the games for me except the "Death Crew Kids" from the Summerfort Grief Center. *"Practice what you preach, Hayden"*— Somehow, I now hear you nagging at me. No, I do not call anyone these names, Mother. Listen to my underlying message. "Death Crew Kids" equals kids like Gretchen, Kelsey, Mia, and Miles this year.

Where's Dad, you might ask? Why's he not in the stadium during football? How about during baseball? Are you able to encourage him to stop working construction in the colder winter months for basketball? Those are all excellent questions, Mom.

I ask them too. Dad says he cares about me, and he's proud, but since he's the only provider now, and kids are expensive, he makes "difficult decisions." Let me put the phrase in quotes because when he said those words, his blue eyes opened super wide—they went icy, I mean, glacier cold. Dad made double fists that night, took a deep breath, walked away from me—even plumb out of the room.

After storming out on me, here's how the next convo went down: Dad and I gathered in the kitchen, intending to make dinner. Our typical meals are self-service style: microwave dinners, frozen pizza, cereals, or sandwiches.

"Hayden, you want a sandwich?" Dad asked in a normal tone of voice.

"Sure, thanks." I tossed the mustard into the air. Dad grabbed the bottle out of my hand and slammed it down on the counter. He stared and gritted his teeth at me. Mom, he acted like an eff-ing rabid dog.

"Sorry. Calm down. Chill, Dad."

"Hayden, does the idea ever occur to you not to be so disrespectful in my home?"

"Sorry?" I guess my "sorry" came out like a question. I suppose I shrugged, crinkled my eyebrows, nose, or something, which apparently set Dad off.

Dad yanked me by the wrist! I jerked away, spinning. "Dad? What the heck? I told you I was sorry."

"You're not the least bit sorry," Dad said, as our game of tug of war raged on. He yanked on my arm again. My mind rattled in conflict—*joke or real? Joke or real*? I figured Dad would chill.

"Dad!" But he struggled with me till I fell on the ground. This felt so foreign to me. Dad has never acted this out of control. And the battle endured.

"Dad?" My hands flew up to block him when I realized he intended to hit me. A brand-new plastic bag of Wonder Bread adorned with smiling kids and polka dots twisting in Dad's hand came swinging hard at me. The first blow clunked me on the shoulder because I pivoted my body, trying to catch it.

"Ouch! Dad, stop it! What the—?"

Pinned to the tile floor by dad, he continued using the Wonder Bread like a weapon, slapping my butt repeatedly. Dad's never acted this insane with me—ever!

On the floor, I laid, like a wadded-up sandwich bag. Or an empty bag of bones—*am I supposed to laugh? Or cry? Or apologize*? No. No apologies because "sorry" pulled me into our current predicament. Stunned, I misunderstood our whole situation. I still don't know what the hell happened.

"Well, now what are we gonna do? What's the plan? We can't eat air sandwiches." Dad said, throwing his "I surrender" hands into the air, along with what little remained of the pulverized bread. Remnants of Dad's mess, piled, tumbled, strewn to the ground because my father "spanked" me.

Looking down at the food, he pointed around the tiled floor, opening his mouth about to speak. Better for me—no, for both of us—he remained quiet. *Please keep your mouth shut, Dad.* With his breathing labored, he stood against the kitchen counter, surveying his damages.

This has to be the dumbest effing thing you've ever done, man. Dad didn't want to hear the other words exploding in my head.

After about hit two, the doughy bag had ripped right open. Our kitchen looked overwhelming—downright ridiculous, in fact. Mom, our home—that kitchen—still belongs to you. On its rightful hook, your red-and-white checkerboard apron with the embroidered words "Kiss the Cook" hangs against the wall. Those bold black letters came into focus right after my fight with Dad. They were the first thing I saw.

I considered punching Dad to get his attention. Or to prove a point, I thought of smashing bread in his eye sockets because I don't think he ever really sees me anyway. Or maybe I could cram dough in his ears because I don't think he ever listens or hears me either.

But I love Dad. I just want Dad to love me too. You're not here, Mom, and I need him. I just need him to want me too. I hate being a burden to Dad and sucking up all his air in life.

Or I guess I could grab Dad by the neck, squeeze him, pointing him in the right direction. Maybe I should shove, kick, or push him until we crossed the entire room. At attention, Dad should stand, front and center, right by your message, "Kiss the Cook." I'd make him hold the fabric, touching the words as I sometimes do. Dad should learn the quote by reading it out loud to me. Then I'd say, "Repeat. Repeat. Repeat." Does Dad need to be reminded: Mom's stuff doesn't read "Beat Your Kid?"

Chapter Three

Something about the way Dad's shoulders slouched inside his dark blue work polo kept me from lunging toward him with my fists. Or maybe it's that he wore the shirt with the sewn-on oval patch promoting GENE TUCKER CONSTRUCTION, the fabric so bunched and disheveled.

One man stood, but he served dual roles. I thought: he was once the husband of the late Rose Tucker, whom he called "Rosie" with love, and he's my father. Dad grasped the edges of our granite countertops, the very ones he installed, like he better start pushing down gravity.

Never have I ever wanted to hurt Dad. To my knowledge, he's never been that aggravated at me either. Dad never laid a hand on me like this before. So, what the hell happened? Sometimes I deal with the wrath of Dad's lectures, but most of our problems stem from his lack of interest in me. Yeah, I understand the stressed, overworked, grouchy parts of him sometimes. But this incident equaled a whole bunch of crap.

Bread crumbs, pieces of crust, scattered and flung—I do mean effing everywhere. Our 12" x 24" tiled floors, the travertine ones Dad had said "Rosie would enjoy," the exact ones he laid in a herringbone pattern—oh, yes, the very ones Dad claimed his pride in, but still, he filled the grout with freakin' teeny-tiny pieces. He treated me, the kitchen, and your memory, all like forgotten garbage.

I remember Dad once said, "I wish your mother could've seen the kitchen remodel finished. She would love the overall design." So much for showing respect, Dad.

FML (F my life). I'm sorry, Mom. I doubt the "F-bomb" language is mother-approved. Mrs. Marks isn't such a fan, either. When I'm angry, she allows me to use the word. Then she's all, "Hayden, enough. I get it. One F-bomb's enough. Let's pick new terms, please." Well, today, eff her too. This grief diary offers me a chance for honesty. Mom, I want to tell you the whole story because of the importance.

With my hands cupped over my face, I closed my eyes. I leaned against the counter. Memories of our life with you in the kitchen haunted me. We colored Easter eggs, decorated cookies for school, carved pumpkins, and ate all our meals nearby, all with you, in this location. All areas Dad destroyed.

After the incident, my guts turned hollow. I failed at trying not to snivel, and I ached to hide from Dad. With nothing left in me to fight with and not even anything to fight for, my back slid down the cabinet door until I plopped down to the floor, sobbing. Dad joined me, sitting on top of all our chaos. Stretching his arms out, he pulled me to him.

My body, along with my mind, returned to a six-year-old little boy. Convulsions of heartache shuddered my body, but I didn't care. Life backtracked, and as a resounding announcement all over again, it's like realizing you're dead once again. I leaned until I disintegrated into Dad's chest. Thoughts like *My mommy's really gone* plagued me.

With my head on Dad's shoulder, my arms squeezing his neck, my body heaved. Over and over, I repeated, "I just want my mom back."

"Me too, buddy. I wish it too. I know you miss her. She loved us a lot. I'm so, so sorry about the bread nonsense. And about your mom. Her death feels unfair. You lost her so young. God, you suffered most, I know. I-I remember what you went through." Dad choked out the last sentence. I felt Dad's body rise and fall as he let out a massive sigh before he rubbed his forehead. "I didn't mean to overreact today. I'm so sorry, Hayden. This is never how we've dealt with things."

I shrugged.

Until I calmed down, hauling myself away from Dad, he stayed with me, draping his arm around my shoulder. Our backs rested against the lower kitchen cabinets of the island until we both sat upright, side by side, legs stretched out in front of us. "Look, you're almost as tall as me now," Dad said, wiggling his feet.

Dad stood up, held out his hand, offering to assist me off the ground. We did the bro hug thing—one quick squeeze with two snappy back slaps signaling the end of our struggle. Later, Dad placed a call for a large pepperoni pizza for delivery. He pretended to "order" me by saying, "Hayden, now go take a shower and start on your homework—*or else*." Dad said it all with a slight grin.

Smooth talking, Dad.

"Oh, and "BTW" (Dad actually used air quotes and said B-T-W) you kinda stink, kid. Peel yourself out of those football sweatpants and T-shirt." Dad tossed a piece of crust at me, with a smile. He headed toward the pantry, retrieving cleaning supplies. Dad picked out the broom and dustpan. With sweeping motions, he teasingly swished me out of the room. "Go, go, go! I do love ya, Hayden."

"Love ya, too, Wonder Bread," I called over my shoulder as I left the room.

"Ah—my kid, the jokester."

As Dad had gathered the cleaning supplies, I noticed the markings in the pantry. Mom, your last pencil measurements of all your boys took place in 2011. As your youngest, I stood 3 feet, 10 inches tall. Remember, I tried to stand on my tiptoes, my arms lifted way up high? I filled myself with hopes to grow as big as Drew, Cole, and Dad.

You hugged me and positioned me for a piggyback ride. You said, "Hayden, don't hurry to grow up. Enjoy the fact you're my special boy." Mom, I'm suffering like a freak! Lingering inside of me is a little boy's mind, with all his memories. But on the outside, I'm supposed to be all man.

How ironic, after you died, my eagerness to grow up ended. Early on, Dad found me hidden in the pantry closet, preoccupied with my toy cars. "I located my little buddy," Dad had said. "Where are you going with your cars today?"

"I'm looking for '*Home*.'" I had answered.

Across the ground, I had stacked all your cookbooks, laying them staggered. The books formed roads I traveled, with their various twists and turns. These stacks, the cookbooks I watched you use, were items your hands touched, so I assumed they brought luck. I looked in every possible direction, searched all the paths leading through my mazes. I seemed to always be on the lookout to finally find my way back to you—"my mommy, my '*Home*.'"

"*Home*" happened to be the location of your apron. Some nights, Dad came in, turned out the lights, and brought in his flashlight to join me. Perhaps, he only braved your loss, too, hoping to help his son.

"Smells like '*Home*' in here, buddy. Can you smell the cinnamon, vanilla, gingerbread, or maybe pumpkin, I think?" Fearing punishment, I diverted my eyes downward, only nodding my head. On this occasion, I dragged a chair from the kitchen, improvising its use as a ladder, I climbed up high in search of your red-topped McCormick spices. Once I found them, I clicked open those flip-top lids. Sniffing through perforated holes, I inhaled memories of you.

Among the top shelves, I launched the sweetness of my mother. Cinnamon, once sprinkled on my breakfast toast, now dusted up and down my arms. On this day, I made dirt roads out of your pumpkin spice on my way to locate you. Dad joined me and allowed me to play until I grew so tired. I fell asleep in search of "*Home.*" Together, Dad and I equaled two broken, wayward souls, *homesick*, I now realize.

At night, I cried the most for you. "I want my mommy! I need her to tuck me in! I only liked the way Mommy bathes me! Why won't she come home? Does she not love me? Daddy, I gotta sleep with you. Daddy, I'm so scared!"

Dad allowed me to bunk with him for years. As I got closer to age ten (double digits), I urged myself to try to sleep alone. I worried if Dad got out of my sight at night or got sick, like you, what would happen to me? The images of death which I loathed due to fear, trailed after me for years.

My eyes saw you every night in the photo on Dad's bedside table, smiling. In the morning, you greeted me with the same happy face—wearing your graduation nurse's uniform. How could you just be gone? I never understood how my mommy, a nurse, who saved lives and cared for others, died. Why did my mother disappear out of my life forever?

At first, I remembered how you spent so much time away in the hospital. I learned to understand quite a vocabulary at the age of six years old: cancer, uterine, hospice, good-bye, death, grief, new routines. For a lifetime, I'll live inside these words with the hope of finding their meaning.

I once experienced a mother's love. But with only six years of love, I wish I knew if those few years will be enough for me to fully understand love. My heart still aches, and I believe it always will. I want to be honest and say a couple of things. First, I'm so pissed you're gone. At whom I don't have an answer. God? You? An explanation is too hard for me to pinpoint when I can't find anyone to blame, or it does me no good. Second issue: God cheated me at six years old. I was way too young to lose you. Mother, my need for you never stops. My craving for buttery cinnamon toast nags at me every day. I worry my heart will stay behind as a six-year-old forever lost inside a kitchen pantry.

And not too far from where your beloved apron stays hung remains our pantry door. Today, Dad measured me, and I reached 5 feet, 8 inches. I'm gaining on Dad's 6-foot height. Since you're my mother, you're right—I will always enjoy the fact I'm your *special boy*. Your voice whispers to me every time I see your pencil marks.

People don't seem to understand. Death doesn't end a parent's job. But death completely ends a parent's ability to complete their work. Mom, if you're able to see me from heaven, I hope you're proud of who I am. If you can help me or ever step in and intervene, feel free. Don't be too ashamed of my social media, thoughts, and those very private behaviors. Remember, I'm a guy—flawed and human.

Hmm.. . . . crazy Mrs. Marks, my "grief mom," might be right about a few things too. Perhaps, writing to you isn't such a bad idea. Otherwise, sorrow builds up, bottles up, and erupts! All issues come out of nothing when we wait—effing mustard and bread. Never will I allow Dad to live a *food* "beating" down. Someday, our mustard-bread fight can become a humorous story, but since you died—what a dark day for us.

Oh, and no, your college boys don't come home much on weekends. A theory: I'm guessing they're too scared of Dad? LoL moment. Well, do my brothers harbor secrets or wicked stories about your Mr. Gentle Giant Contractor, Mom? Topic number one next holiday: "Nutty Dad Moments and stories of the Wonder Bread Beater."

Drew texts me a lot. I think he pretends to study. He will take a pic of himself holding books with a caption, "on the way to class soon," but I can see in the background of his photos, he's getting ready to walk into Starbucks, the school's cafeteria, or something. So, he's still "goodhearted-full-of-dreams-harmless-fun-good-intentioned Drew" Mom. Dad still calls him his Dennis the Menace.

Cole checks in with Dad a couple of times a week, either with a call, email, or text. On the big holidays, he comes around. For the last couple of visits, he's brought the same lady. This one might stick. They both graduate with their master's degrees from college in May. She's going to be a professor, but I don't remember her telling us what area. They met in a class, so probably a dull subject. I can't recall. She's hot. I liked her. She asked about my school, sports, and girls. I enjoyed chatting with her. Kind of think of an exotic, slightly curvier Catherine Zeta-Jones or Jennifer Lopez-type. A tanned body with dark features.

Cole's got a job lined up through his internship program with an impressive boring business title. Sorry, Mom, but Cole's a bit arrogant sometimes. Mr. La-Di-Da Cole needs to dial it back and learn how to have some fun. Guess he does with Ariana. I hope she's the one for him. She's kind to Cole—always smiling or holding his hand, qualities you might like for your son. That's my goal for a girlfriend. . . . . More info to come on that topic, I hope.

I bet Mrs. Marks from the grief center will be calling soon to check in with me. "How's the journaling?" At least I won't have to lie to her. I'm opening up, finally. I *wonder* if she's ever been assaulted by bread? Do you like my "punny" joke? A pun is funny = punny. ~~Mom, did Dad ever spank you with dough? Ew.. . . . . perverted—forget it. I don't want to consider the details of my parent's intimate life. I sound like a creeper, pervert, sicko. But~~

~~how funny. I might even erase or scribble through~~
~~this at some point because the mere mention of it~~
~~makes me laugh but cringe with awkwardness.~~

Sex (the word), conjures up one girl at school. I bet you're screaming, "You're too young." I can't help it, Mom. This girl, who I wrote down on my back-to-school list during group as "G," the initial stands for Gretchen. She's responsible for giving me all the "feels."

Chapter Four

September 2019

Dear Mom,

Thank you. Your letters, inside the pages of my aqua baby book, provide me hope. It helps me to know a little more about myself and how my birth made you so happy—you described meeting me as "the most unimaginable joy," when I came into the world. You adorned the cover with extra gems and a monogrammed "G" in a darker shade of ocean blue. "For girly-girl-Gretchen," you inscribed on the front cover flap. I swear I can hear you say these words.

Sometimes my fingers trace the raised jewels, aware of your energy, hoping it's near. Maybe it resides in me? I want to believe in something. Perhaps you've become part of my soul now? God, I miss you. Between my mattresses, I stash the notebook for easy retrieval. Often, I slip open to the page titled, "Gretchen Growing up Gracefully." I reread those pages anytime I can't sleep. As I pour over the sentences, I close my eyes, imagine you holding the pen as you wrote the sentiments. Your face comes back to me in flashes—blue-green eyes, freckles, copper hair. Every page I treat like a tiny treasure—I visualize each like a photo for my photographic memory. Soon, I'll be capable of imagining them anytime my heart wishes. Our time together slipped by too fast.

However, the record of these moments kept will provide a lifetime of inspirational thoughts, warmth of heart, and depth of your love for me.

I'm ready to add a TMI section (Too Much Information)—the Tough Stuff. It's about to get real. Dad cringes when I say the phrase, "Hey Dad, I got a TMI story for you." Life's tough, Mom. So, lately, I've found myself in need of time to chat with you about the BIG issues—the stuff nobody likes to talk about with teenagers. I'm about to write down some blunt thoughts.

This section got labeled "TMI" because sometimes people shy away from difficult subjects. But that fixes nothing. Why isn't this wrong? So what if life offers taboo topics? Why can't we live in peace, among others, even if we don't like their politics, religion, sexual orientation, gender, race, etc.? The list appears endless. Social media, the internet as a whole, and the word "interconnectedness?" Yet, with all these options to keep in touch, I notice people speak face-to-face even less. Plus, their language toward each other falls out of their mouths as rash and crude. They bash one another in the form of pictures called memes if the communication is nonverbal, which seems to be how most people choose to communicate. Life's about little blurbs, Mom. To insult someone with the tackiest photo using the fewest words declares you the "winner." They call the whole process, "gettin' burned or gettin' served." I'm hopeful it's gettin' outta here quick as another fad.

Many gather information from Facebook, Instagram, and memes, treating them as accurate news. Oh, if I could tell you about the concept of the term "fake news," you might not believe the connotation. By the way, in case I didn't tell you this before, Donald Trump got elected the President of the United States of America. He moved from the New York Trump Towers to the White House.

I'm too young to vote. During election years, a swamp of campaign advertisements "reign" down from all angles (all parties/sides—local, state, national), giving me the impression of a lot of empty promise making. The data doesn't add up? Zippy and snappy campaign trail visits, power-hungry people feeding the poor what they want to hear. Do I see this correctly? Or am I too jaded already? Nobody listens to a young kid about politics, though. Maybe they start out hoping to create a better world, make a difference, improve lives. Still, greed intervenes and runs the masses of politicians.

Imagine sitting on your couch as a preteen girl watching the news with your dad, hearing "Grab 'em by the pussy" blaring through the TV. Well, in 2016, when Trump ran for president, his words came back to bite him. Previously recorded, he still said this, Mom. Talk about an embarrassing moment for *me.* However, I'm not the one who said it, yet I felt all sorts of emotions—like this odd guilty weirdness. Like growing up as a woman in this world will always be seen as second best or out of place? *Grabbed?*

Dad's take on the situation—"Yikes. That's such an inappropriate message to get caught saying."

I've thought about this since. What did you mean, Dad? Oops, he got caught? Or those words don't sound presidential? It came out before the election in response to the reporter sharing the information. The reporter got fired from what I understand, but Trump went on to win. People thought Trump meant "grab 'em by the pussy" as a *joke*? Can you fathom a president saying those words? It shocked me.

Locker-room chat, boys will be boys—how the story played out. I guess that's the way the major-ity heard it. As a girl, I pray guys in a locker room, like at my school, never talk about my body like that to other guys. It sounds and feels degrading.

Do men ever defend women against these types of comments? Or do other women stand up for each other and not accept this behavior? There's so much I could write about concerning the state of the Union. It confuses me. My social studies teacher, Mr. Porter, Dad, and the nightly news mess with my mind.

By the time I'm eighteen, old enough to vote, let's hope presidential candidates conduct themselves with diplomacy, so I can cast a ballot with pride. Politics often appears twisted, ugly, and mean. Dad takes me with him to vote, so I can "observe the process," he says, or "come see democracy in action."

I don't like it. Local candidates' signs stolen or destroyed by spray paint—graffiti, with horrible name-calling. Like a bunch of mean girls or school bullies, all grown up. I view commercials as they run day and night, blasting each other, twisting words around, numbers, data, and that idea of "throwing people under the bus" keeps on happening, a lot. I can only imagine what's ahead for the upcoming elections in my lifetime. Maybe halfway listening to too much *Animal Farm* in English corrupts me. Or perhaps it's thoughts of Hayden, who's sitting in front of me during class?

Back on subject: we must research and beware as well as be aware of what our government is up to, I suppose. After all, I thought democracy had to do with some American dream, like a set of freedoms, people helping each other, and stuff? I'm all sorts of confused about humans all the time. I mean, *all the time*. What's this world all about? Where do I fit in?

Your death made me grow up too fast. I'm way too sensitive about everything, but I refuse to let the masses turn me into a robot. I love my country, technology, most people, but my brain power means more to me. You encouraged me to read, write, and spend time outside. As a teenager of today, I'm considered too much of an old soul, labeled outdated or obsolete.

Dad and I hang out in the living room a lot before bed. Guess we established this somewhat "new normal" as part of our routine after you died. Neither of us knew how to unwind and sleep without you. Truth be told, I'm not sure, after seven-plus years, we've got a perfect pattern of hope down. I remember Dad and I on the couch together, night after night, as we pretended to be okay. Some nights we fell asleep, huddled together, watching the news. Other nights, Dad carried me to my bed after I fell asleep on the couch, or he hauled me into your bed.

"Come on in here, Gretchen. I'll read to you," Dad would say, motioning me into your bedroom from the hallway. Dad had enrolled me in the grief center, where we learned about books to read together. "Breathe in, hold it, hold it, hold it, and now let it out." Dad puffed his cheeks out as far as they'd stretch as he played the part of the angry octopus, the character from the book we often read. Sometimes I thought Dad might turn as purple as the little sea creature because he often held his breath too long to entertain me.

"Ahhhh . . . let it out," Dad would gasp. The book guided us, early on, in our grief journey—two goofy lost souls. Not a day goes by that I don't glance up at Dad's face to see a hint of his octopus characteristics. For almost two years, we mastered the craft of deep breathing, reading, and learning to laugh again. We busied our hearts, our minds, and our souls with the words of the deep sea until one of us dozed off to sleep. I woke up many mornings on your side of the bed. Dad and I love you, miss you, and it never ends. At some point, I "aged" out of your bed. But news and madness continued. The search for "normal" rages on. Welcome to Gretchen's World.

Often we scrutinize the news. Dad starts with Headline News, CNN, and then he flips to FOX News because he says, "Gretchen, it's essential to view the world in an unbiased manner, if possible. Let's analyze how they spin the stories, the data, and let's guess which headline they come back with from commercial break."

It overwhelms me. School shootings, hate crimes, immigrant children dying at the United States-Mexican border highlights some of the current events that occurred since your death. The reality of your death and death in general—how possible it is—makes me ponder the state of our world. I worry more than I should—about the safety of others, about what might happen next. Who will care for me if something happens to Dad? What if I die and Dad's left alone?

Ouch. I don't want to hurt Dad's feelings, but our nightly news program stresses me out. Mom, can I say, "Dad, remember the saying, 'ignorance is bliss'?" It makes perfect sense now. Some nights, I wish I could sit beside you, but we could tune out the evils of the world. And maybe turn the channel to something else? I'm not sure what wearing earbuds in protest, tuning a parent out, must be like. Or listening to the world through rap music. Or turning my music up too loud, staying up super late, going out past curfew, or just acting my age. Part of my soul is still a child who cries out longing for her mother, while the other part of me has grown so old."

Mom, is my message too harsh for Dad to hear?

He's a wonderful father. Because of him, I do learn a lot about current events. And I earn decent grades at school. I apply a lot of what I hear on the news and my discussions with Dad in history class. Dad's talks spur me to write poetry too. Still, sometimes, I just want to binge-watch comedy and laugh. I could use some mindless humor and fun. I do watch Netflix now and then.

Instead, Dad and I play this game called One to Twenty-Seven. Can you guess how much fun this might be? Well, here's the guideline on how to win: Write the numbers one through twenty-seven down your page and summarize all twenty-seven United States Constitutional Amendments. No, I'm not kidding. This isn't a joking matter. Your daughter received an A+ on her US Constitution exam. Thank you, Daddy, for game nights. With Dad, I'm always contemplating, though, on how to make our world a better place.

Designing a world pleasing to the majority—an impossibility? Pros and cons: left or right, black or white, Republican or Democrat, pro-gun or Second Amendment, pro-life or pro-choice, prayer in school or separation of church and state, immigration sanctuary or Mexican border walls, legalize or criminalize marijuana? The world's a fury of issues. Somewhere in the mountain of angst, is there an answer?

"You think you're only a kid today, and you can't vote, but someday this country will need you to step up, make choices, speak up, and represent. You represent the future of our government." Written on the whiteboard in big letters, those words strung together to form a statement in my classroom. Sometimes the teacher writes on the board to grab the attention of students who won't listen. Or to inspire kids who like to pretend they're dumb and play ignorant. I loved how my teacher also underlined the word *you*. For a day, my thoughts about our country got restored. And I realized maybe I could make a difference in some way, someday.

My history teacher, Mr. Paul Porter (some of the lame/dumb kids like to refer to him as Mr. Pee Pee), works so hard trying to show us how history isn't dull. For example, Mr. Porter put a graph on the board in the colors of red and blue to explain to us the two political sides and all the differences. I like that he said, "In the middle when red mixes with the color blue, a blending occurs and that color is purple. In politics, if the two parties blended, we could have some balance on issues. If people researched with honesty, most of them would fall somewhere in the middle."

Mr. Porter gave us a list of assignments to choose from. Write a one-page review of the two main political parties, design a poster, create a slideshow, or write a poem or a short play to explain *your* point of view.

As I wrote every stanza, I asked myself, what would Mom say? How might she react? Through the tears, I worked because I realized my wish—to hear your commentary—*only a wish*—that could never be.

So, I tried to work harder and do it for the benefit of me. Self-motivation and sacrifice are worth celebrating. But with who? Even when the world emerges as useless and cold and grief continues

to strangle, choke, and drown me, I promise you,
I will seek a way to live. You see, though, the state
of the world pulls me into dark places sometimes,
Mom. My soul hurts and always wants to talk to
you. I guess the words I feel are pure yearning.

We the People
Written by Gretchen Gardener

We the People design America's face
At a glance, we represent every race
Life, liberty, the pursuit of happiness too—
An old Declaration started something new

Families at a harbor dreaming at the teeming
     shore
Escaping persecution, hunger, wars, and being
     poor
Constitutions were written about We the
     People
Granted rights, such as worship under any
     steeple

Red, blue, elephant, mule—political labels
"United" cannot become a storybook fable
Red and Blue turns a purple hue: A Party of
     Compromising
To form a more perfect Union is known as
     democratizing

Establish justice, insure domestic tranquility
  too
And the general welfare of We the People—
That's me, and you

I got an A+ on the assignment. Mr. Porter awarded me his Top Student Award, and the United States Citizenship Award, on the night of the parent-teacher conference/assembly. Summerfort started this odd tradition of hosting assemblies before parent-teacher meetings. In front of the whole school (including Hayden), plus most of the parents, I trotted out on the floor, crossed the gym, and shook hands with Mr. Porter and Principal Marshall. A local reporter from the *Summerfort Daily Journal* snapped photographs—the kind people wanna frame. So, I stood all prim and proper, grinning all classy-like for the pictures. I held back tears. My mother should be here to see me. I deserve to have a mother. I need to be happy. I need to smile.

Dad took me out to Dairy Queen after to celebrate. I ordered something with peanut butter, of course. About halfway through, I looked around the room, noticing so many people from school there with *both* their parents. My go-to is to hide inside bathroom stalls and flush the toilet over and over, so I can sob. This way, no one hears me. Most of the time, Dad's pretty easy to fool.

When I returned to the table, Dad studied my face with more intensity than I liked. His series of questions began: "You okay, hon? Do you have a headache or something? Gretchen, have you been crying?"

Signaling to Dad with a shrug, I gave a half-hearted "I don't know," glassy glare, followed with an eye roll. My hands curled, forming into fists. If I'd said anything or done much more, I would've created a scene, and cried at the table. What's to complain about in public of a small-town DQ with ice cream treats nearby? Especially when these very people just watched you win awards, saw your Dad hug you, and purchase you a blizzard. Some even overheard the reporter talk about my picture and poem when he said, "It will run as tomorrow's front-page news story." He patted me on the shoulder, then he shook Dad's hand.

The headline should read, "Grief Girl Gretchen look, she smiles; she writes; she's a pro at hiding her emotions. Or so she thought."

"I'm fine, Dad. I wanna go home. Too much sugar, I guess. My stomach hurts. I just wanna go." In haste, he pushed his chair out, scooped up our empty containers, threw them away, and shoved the exit door of DQ open. Outside, Dad marched to the car several paces ahead of me, keys rattling in his hand.

My gut told me: you're busted. The "daddy knows" glares were already going down. In the DQ parking lot, he slammed his side of the car door harder than usual, clicked his seatbelt louder than usual, and somehow, even the blinkers operated at a faster pace. As Dad drove, I felt trapped in a driver's ed film.

Dad's hands sat perfectly on the wheel—like at ten and two o'clock, or something? He sighed, huffed, and seemed to be harboring a breath. I thought of the purple octopus book we used to read together, but I didn't dare mention it. Against the steering wheel, he pretended to perform a strange drumming routine but to no music. "What's all your drumming about?" I wanted to ask. At the stoplight, he looked over at me. Awkward silence. More drumming yet still no music.

Dad didn't take me home. Instead, he pulled into the parking lot of the park nearby, away from prying eyes. Dad slammed the car in park, then turned off the engine. When he undid his seatbelt, it signaled to me Dad's planning to stick around awhile. He stared at me for far too many seconds before he started talking.

I prepared myself because of my experience with Dad and his once-in-a-while "stern" tone of voice. Ugh, I hated long lectures about my not doing something. Or I better start doing this or do that, yadda, yadda. *Now what?*

Before he even opened his mouth, I glanced away from him, out the window. As a family, we walked those trails I see. We slid down that very slide inside the playground in front of me. And flew, seated in those swings—

"Look, Gretchen. Hey, I want—I need you to look at me." Dad put his hand on my wrist as a way to comfort but also to command attention. "I'm not here because I'm mad. But I don't want you to lie to me. Don't tell me you're okay when you're not. You need to start talking. Our life is not perfect, but it's also not that bad either. I am trying really hard to do all I can for you. Please tell me what I can do better. I need to be able to take care of you because it's my job as a father." Droopy eyelids covered up more of Dad's dark blue eyes tonight. I hated hurting his feelings.

I shook my head. "You didn't do anything wrong, Dad. I promise." I could feel my heart beating inside my throat, throbbing inside my eardrums. Tears formed, gathering at the edges of my eyelashes. What little mascara and eyeliner Dad allowed me to experiment with filled my eyes. It pooled into acid, where it burned until it flowed down my cheeks.

"Come here," Dad said, leaning over, helping me undo my seatbelt, encircling me into a bear hug.

"What's wrong?—Come on, what's wrong, GG?"

Inside Dad's arms, I embraced Old Spice, Irish Spring, pieces of childhood. Like mine, his heart communicated in a pattern so fast. Our fear, love, grief—both connected and comforted us. He placed one hand on top of my head and one on my back, capturing me inside a bubble of love and safety.

Words remain beneath the surface for me during pain. My nickname, GG, from long ago, transported me. Dad must've realized saying the nickname GG out loud might trigger excessive tears, offering me a chance to speak with my heart the words I longed to express. Dad gifted me time to grieve.

"Dad, I can't keep saying the same things over and over, like I'm a broken record." With my index finger held out by my temple, I spun loops to show Dad how people must view me. "I just go around and around and around. Nobody wants to hear it anymore—people tell me to get over it; I'm lucky I don't have a mom to get in my business—"

"It's okay. I'm here, GG. I want to hear. Tell me anything—tell me everything you want."

"People don't understand. I miss Mom. Every. Single. Day. I wake up, remember, oh, right, my mom's gone. At least once a day, there's some dumb reminder that mom would find funny. I'd give anything to share the joke with her and laugh, but I can't. I will never get to. When I realize this, I feel the muscles in my face drag and go from smiling to frowning." I gasped, choking on sobs.

Dad held me close, nearly rocking me like a baby, whispering, "I understand."

"At the stores, I deal with seeing Mom's favorite candies, those pecan logs. Or I walk the aisles at Bath and Body, smelling and choking down her favorite type of scents. Girls at the mall who shop with their moms, most of them act rudely. I hate all of them so effing much, but it's because I envy them. I never told you about Lilly P. calling me a mom stealer because I went with Darcy and her mom."

Dad seemed to understand the fists I made, as well as the grip against his arms as I sobbed and yelled because he only listened, squeezing me back so tight to acknowledge he shared the pain. "I'm sorry about these things. I know they hurt, GG." Gasping for a second wind, I used the back of my hand as a Kleenex and forged on.

"Mom will miss everything—good or bad—I do my entire life. Just like my stupid poem. I really wanted Mom to be there to see me win an award. I can't hear her voice anymore. I will never know how she feels about me. I can't just talk to her, text her, email her. Ever! I can't touch her, hug her, see her. Nothing. I hate it. I just hate it. Dad, I eff-ing hate it. Sometimes I need to hear her say, 'I'm proud of you' or 'I love you.' Dad, I just want my effing mom to be alive."

My backpack sat in the floorboard, and I felt inclined to ram my feet into the books with a few kicks as I screamed for the second time that night, "I want my effing mom!"

I love Dad, but it's a different love than the love of a mother, I think. I remember you, Mom, but I'm scared those memories might fade since they come from the mind of a six-year-old girl. Dad tells me stories as we look through scrapbooks and photo albums.

At the grief center, Mrs. Marks assisted me in the creation of "My Mother from A-Z" project, where I wrote stories—I placed pictures of the places we traveled to as a family together. From what I recalled, "A" stood for Arch in St. Louis. Dad provided copies of the photos from our trips. The "Z" represented the St. Louis Zoo. There are photos of us at animal exhibits. Sometimes, I'm stuck inside those pages—it's a dream world, a little fantasy to play among the alphabet, and stay where I still know what it's like to have a mommy. I'm afraid to jump out. Or grow up without you.

"I get it. I miss Mom too. I'm so thankful for you and glad we have each other. I bet she's proud you, proud of both of us. I know I'm not your mom, but you can always talk to me. I love you dearly, GG."

I nodded, attempting a smile. "Okay." Again, I leaned into Dad for another hug. When we pulled apart, Dad wiped at my tears, trailing his thumb down my cheeks, capturing the last of the silent pain falling wayward. To rub my nose, Dad utilized the sleeve of his shirt.

Dad cleared his throat before he nudged me. Then forcing a half-smile, he made me smile by using air quotes and saying, "Hey, GG, I miss my beautiful "effing" wife, but I know she's proud of her daughter. I know I'm proud of *her daughter* too."

"Thanks, Dad." I smiled. But I noticed his knuckle swiping quickly at the corner of his left eye.

By now, we'd entered our weird, giggly, teary-eyed emotional state. Every once in a while, I experience mini-meltdowns, but Dad comes to the rescue. Now, I wondered and worried too. Where's Dad going when he encountered these issues or meltdowns if I happen to not be around?

HAYDEN

Chapter Five

September 2019

Dear Ma,

My relationship with Mrs. Freaking Marks goes from love to hate a lot. I remember the day Mrs. Marks gifted this freakin' journal to me. I stood to leave her office, but she stopped me.

"Wait for a second, Hayden. Just because you're a boy doesn't mean you can't write your feelings out on paper."

With that, she placed my nondescript journal in my right hand. Immediately, I tucked it between my arm and side. With my book of dreaded death thoughts out of my sight, I squeezed the already-flattened paper against my rib cage. Whatever those spiral metal bindings are called, they hurt like hell when they dig into your gut. Mrs. Marks used her stupid notebook against me in our grief counseling sessions too often.

I needed a break from her, grief, notebooks, even life. But then she ended our session with one of her side-hugs. Mrs. Marks's love keeps me going, maybe also keeps me alive. After her simple touch, I realized she's one of the few people in years I received any affection from. Aside from Daddy's loving loaf of bread. Oh, and if I've got to count Spin the Bottle and Truth or Dare.

With a thumbs-up, I gave her a half-smirk, hoping to avoid talking. Sometimes fewer words mean less gloom. Less gloom means less chance for tears to make an appearance. That day, I chose less of everything.

But I said, "I know. I'll use it."

God, I hated myself. What a liar. Easy solution: Flip up the lip, fling this piece of crap inside while I imagine I'm playing a childhood game of Hungry Hungry Hippos and feed Summerfort Grief Center's can some trash. No one cares what I think. I paused. Mrs. Marks works too hard, I realized, and if she happened to catch me dumpster diving with her gift, it would cause hurt feelings.

A couple of pages are scribbled on, which seemed to be items asked of me from previous group meetings. If I threw it all away, I needed to do so in a more private location, so people couldn't read my stuff. Taking it home seemed the right solution.

I suck today. I sucked yesterday. I'm pretty sure I'll suck again tomorrow. What do I know about anything? In fact, I know even less now about life than ever, Mom. Really, what's changed? After seven, almost eight years, I'm still feeling so childish.

My journal/notebook *still* looks crisp and new. I appreciated the help from Mrs. Marks at the grief counseling center, the hope her gift offered me, but I thought, it ain't gonna work; this ain't happenin', lady. Sometimes that woman infuriated me. Every time that woman made me sit, and *talk, talk, talk* about you until I wailed, I effing hated her.

One day while sitting across from her, I even screamed, "Oh, my God, I hate you!"

Mrs. Marks said, "Hayden, you think you hate me now, and you may. But I think it's the grief you hate, not me. See, when we reach the core of pain, love moves in and resides. Let the pain out, Hayden." Then she started side-huggin' on me.

Who can hate a person who says things like this? And one inclined to come around hugging on you? What's that all about? Sometimes she's so mother-like. One second she's too darn harsh, bossy, and freakin' annoying. And the second thing you know she's all loving, kind, real, and just what someone like me needs.

As I try imagining you, what you'd be like as my mother now, I like to picture your behaviors or actions toward me, and I always compare you a lot to Mrs. Marks. She's the closest thing I've got now to a mom. If you could still be here, I bet you'd nag

Who I was before the death:	*Who I am now, dealing with the death:*	*Who I will become; what I am going to be, despite the death:*
Part of a real family. I felt whole and normal. I got to be the baby of the family, the youngest boy of three. My mom and dad adored me. My brothers played with me some.	I don't know this person? I feel lost. A little weird. My family changed. My dad works a lot of hours. My brothers are busy, older, off to college. The house feels empty. I'm a burden. My extended family isn't close by, or they're gone too. I have very few friends. Mostly trust those at the grief center. I'm shy. I like sports. It's hard to fit in. I enjoy most of my classes at my school. People might be surprised to know I enjoy reading, writing, and building things.	I wish I knew. Someday I hope to be a good worker, husband, and father. I'm a loyal person. Sometimes I feel smart. I don't know much about anything?

me more than her. Just kidding (well, maybe not). However, I doubt anyone would love me more than you.

Mrs. Marks's journal lecture continued like this: "Hayden, you'll notice I chose a simple black composition book. No one needs to think of it as anything but a school notebook. Hayden's Grief Diary—hide it away in a dresser drawer, where it will be all yours. Let it be your place of honesty." A prime example of Mrs. Marks for ya: Always hittin' the mark.

With the best of intentions, I placed the note-book inside my sock drawer, burying it deep among the various shades and lengths of my Nikes, Adidas, and Hanes. Below the tubes and rolls of my athletic junk, it's a tad easier to forget about the pain and hope. I can ignore it at home, by keeping all of it hidden away.

So, Ma, starting *again* today, I'm pulling out and using my big 'ole underutilized black "*GD* grief booklet," where I'll vent to you about what's up with your little boy. Oh, come on. That's supposed to sound freakin' funny. Chill, Mom. You're loved and missed. I'm only kidding with the implied cursing. At least for now, anyway. I tend to keep my mouth quiet or the dirtiest words to myself most of the time. Well, I'm human—remember that as I write.

From my grief center prompt: Who do you like, but feel you can't? Today's entry: My Grief

Diary—Hayden's GD Big Black Book of horrors, sins, rages, hopes, fears, and dreams. Hey, I need to talk to someone about a girl. All of the above emotions come to mind when I write her name: Gretchen. I used to consider her my private Golden Girl, but then recalled the funny old lady show, the one I used to watch with you. Well, thanks a lot, Mother, because that ruined that. Dorothy, Sophia, Blanche, and Rose—I act like I don't remember every character. No need for secret keeping on these pages. When I can't sleep, I get out my remote, hoping these ladies' antics will relax me enough to lull me back to sleep—much like you used to do when you tuned in to view episodes with me.

During English class, Gretchen might be what I call a bit of a spaz. She sits right behind me, all fidgety. Sometimes she props her feet on my desk, entangling herself into my wire basket, all jumpy. It sure takes a lot out of me not to reach down and touch her. Every time she invades my space, I contemplate how to make a move. But I like her there, all up in my wire "book grill."

From the Summerfort Grief Center, Gretchen and I bonded as children when we were placed in the same group. Her mom died too. She's always been this cute redheaded angel. Smart, quiet girl who flies off on wild tangents sometimes. Damn her. Now, she's all "grown-up"—if you know what I mean. How do I write about *this* (curves) to my mom without sounding like a total ass-jerk? How about this—hey, Ma, I remember how much you loved babies. Did you hope *one day* I would give you grandchildren? Well, Gretchen makes me think about doing things, so I can create new Haydens for you. There, I said it. Ugh.

The other day, Gretchen won some awards, so I liked her photos online and wrote, "Congrats." Gretchen replied with a heart symbol. I blew up her picture and studied her smile. Hidden behind her grin, I bet she missed her mom. God, she's a beautiful person. Part of me wanted to send her a private message and ask, "How do you feel about your award?" Because I knew to win likely brought on the pains of sorrow. I've been right there, inside Gretchen's shoes. I recall how much I wanted you.

Ask any kid without a mother. They will agree because every kid desires to look out into a crowd, spot their mom being present, watching them be proud when they succeed. Isn't that just the nature of life? Gretchen and I have been denied that. I didn't want to stress her out, but I also thought of how I could've and should've been a better friend. I *hate* my shyness. Reaching out and possibly being further rejected sounded like pure torture. Does this come from a place of fear, failure, and the pain of loss? My fingers tried typing her a message.

Disappointed in myself *again*, because I know I won't finish the message to Gretchen or hit send. Too much fear holds me back. Fear of not knowing.

Fear of success. Because, if Gretchen replied, I'd fear what the hell to do next. This happens over and over. I hide behind the keyboard, dreaming about her. Technology makes it too easy to distance ourselves from speaking face-to-face. So, I never even considered talking to her a real option.

After she won that evening, I struggled with insomnia. Visions of Gretchen standing with her award pretending to be happy, smiling . . . gripped my heart. I caught myself pinching the bridge of my nose, trying like hell to ward off the blues from turning into full-blown waterworks. When I hit this level, I often fall into an emotional snowball effect—by taking a trip down my own memory lane, remembering too many "mommy moments," and creating a longing nothing can fix. Across the hall from me, Dad slept. Like a little boy, I even contemplated climbing into bed with him. Instead, I squeezed my eyes tight, shoved my mug, and fists into my pillows and surrendered to the sobs. Replaying so many of our life events wore my body down until I eventually drifted to sleep.

During a group counseling session, Gretchen rambled on one night with her "WTFDD" What-the-flippity-do-da and her cock-a-doodle-doo and the occasional shittle-sticks stuff—getting super passionate about life, and that's when she comes up with her own language. We all adapt. Well, for me, it's more like devouring her words like a doctrine. Anyway, she was upset about people not "kickin' it old-school" anymore. As Gretchen spoke, I hung on to every word: "Why don't people put any effort into relationships? Today it's too much about one-word texts or a quick like on social media. Chivalry's dead, people. Someday, if someday ever decides to come, I hope to be romanced by handwritten letters, homemade cards, maybe even some snail mail. A date isn't driving in circles around the square of Summerfort, hanging out in the parking lots of the Dollar General or Walmart staring at other girls or texting on your phone the whole time. People make me sad—"

"WTFDD?"—I observed Gretchen's mouth as she talked. Her words carried with them the scent of Christmas. Did Gretchen live at the North Pole munching on candy canes? Maroon-tinted lip gloss sparkled and bounced across her lips as she ranted, the words spewing. Which one's scented, I wondered? Peppermint mouth or lips? My mission and longing were to find out. What in the world do the smartest lips in the town of Summerfort, Missouri, taste like? I wanted to find out. I love candy canes and the flavors of Christmas. Cock-a-doodle-do, Gretchen, I like you. And one day, I want you to be aware, Hayden will provide you those old-school letters.

WOLG (Watch Out Little Girl)—Hayden's versed in the language too. I might be super quiet, but I'm athletic (muscles), and, like you, been through a lot (sensitive), so I might as well rock your world through the lens of a poet. When and if our time ever matches up, I don't plan to disappoint. A little work in progress now, "Oh, Little Angel."

Oh Little Angel
Grief filled my childhood
then an angel sat beside me

Her hair glowed like
a summertime sunset—
layerings of amber,
copper, flecks of gold—

Mom, too much? I worry. I may act and write to Gretchen on a level too cheesy? My poem, so far, does speak the truth, but does it come across as a corndog-ish freak? Or sound like a creeper? Too needy or greedy? Also, over-the-top? Gretchen desires, as well as deserves, all this. I wish I worried less but understood more. Maybe I should question, Dad? Not sure he's up for any birds-and-bees talk? Before I approach him, I'll hide all the Wonder Bread—I'm kidding. Mrs. Marks? Now she's someone who will tell me like it is. Her lectures on safe sex, emotional readiness, grief triggers, etc.—really not what I'm asking about. First, I gotta be able to talk to the girl. The answer is no, as well, for Miss Garcia, the school counselor, who's nothing but kind, but I can't do her "sweetie" this-'n-that chats.

Do you think Miss Garcia or Mrs. Marks may have the answer to solve my problems in the form of a pamphlet or flyer since they're counselors? Something along the lines of titles such as *How to Chat with Chicks*, *How to Score a Girlfriend*, *How to Speak English to Girls in English Class*, *Open Your Grief-Filled Mouth, Boy*.

Sometime, someday, I guess the timing will fall into place? During class, I attempted to write a "normal" note:

Gretchen,

I thought you might want to work on the *Animal Farm* study questions with me sometime? "My mind's good, but your mind's better." Just kidding—a little sheepish humor.

Hayden

God, Mom, I hate myself. I wrote the note but couldn't deliver. I choked. I pulled off her old-school handwritten note, but I flippin' failed. Maybe Dad's on to something? The night of our bread fiasco, I peeled out of my sweaty football jersey before I left the room, and Dad said, "Dang, bud. Where did all that come from?" Dad pointed to my abs—"You've got the faintest outline of a six-pack. Keep lookin' that good, it won't be long, you'll be able to wash clothes on your chest—you'll be a regular washboard." Dad may exaggerate, but sports do keep me in pretty good shape.

Hmmm . . . kickin' it old-school, Dad. Another pondering thought: So, now, do I create a plan of action to take my shirt off in her presence? Show her what the mighty little Hayden has under his sports jerseys? Rip off my Summerfort Eagles shirt, let our blue-and-gray colors fly? *"Fly like an eagle. . . ."* How does that go with the themes in English—"Oh Romeo, deny thy father and give me thy shirt?" During grief counseling, I can give her the clothing off my back to wipe her tears? Good grief, Mother. I'm insane. Why do girls need to act so confusing and tricky?

I wish I could dare myself to step out of my shell. I feel like I could become so much more for her, but I'm stuck in our little grief world. A few strands of Gretchen's long curly hair calls out to me, begging me to tuck them behind her ear. With her ear exposed, I want the courage to whisper, "Gretchen." I long for more time to dive into her eyes—explore the depths of those blue-greens. Her eyes remind me of a rock quarry—danger-ous, edgy, filled with intensity. An infinite beauty worthy of being studied. Those eyes sat beside me, crying for years. Of all the people in my strange little world, Gretchen "gets me." Our relationship, though, offers a strain of pure weirdness, at times, making no sense at all. Do all young people feel this unsure about love? Through our grief, we gel, but that's at the Summerfort Grief Center, I guess, like a bubble, a safe haven, offering a quiet essence, fitting for both of us because of the comfort level.

At school, we might wave, smile, say "Yo/Hi/ Hey" or on a good day, when one of us feels outgoing, we might even exchange the greeting, "Hola." Maybe she's just not that into me? Could she think like me? I've always been more relaxed and comfortable talking to her at the grief center. I guess we've got history and safety there. At school, too many eyes seem to be watching, and too many ears are listening. Plus, there's a lot of ass-jerks at SHS who have no business knowing any of my business.

Besides, what's a girl like Gretchen Grace Gardener (Sexy Little Miss GGG) ever gonna see in a shy, gap-toothed, B-average-student jock? I'm not sure she likes sports much. If Gretchen weren't so shy herself, she'd probably be the ideal candidate to run as President of the United States of America one day. When forced into doing speeches, reports, or papers, Gretchen's freakin' mind-blowing. Even the awkward WTFDD and cock-a-doodle-do stuff I like. I fantasize in awe of her. I'd drape myself in the flag and salute her while singing, "Yankee Doodle," "The Star-Spangled Banner," and Katy Perry's "Baby You're a Firework." You lack knowledge of the last song, Mom. Gretchen's not only freakin' smart, but she's also hot. She tortures me.

Daily, Gretchen walks by me in English, before she begins her wrestling matches with my desk. Perhaps Miss Gretchen has hidden frustrations or desires to "wrestle' me? It sounds like a psychology application to me. I'll keep on telling myself these things. I like to humor myself, now and then. Want to know what's even hotter about her? She doesn't understand, notice, or care about the fact she's so stinkin' hot? I don't get it. But I'd like to get it. If you know what I mean.

If it weren't for my sports, private moments at home, and workouts, I'd request a pass to bail from English every day—my testosterone surges around her. Once in a while, I catch a whiff of her peppermint bark, so I bite my own lip, pretending I will capture a taste. I can't visualize—but, oh, that scent—Christmas candy-cane lips—behind me, all shiny, beckoning me. Peppermint Tic Tacs, gum, and a tube of Chapstick—I gotta buy myself something, or I'm going to go plumb crazy. I'm afraid I'll lick my lips off and eat the whole tub, though. Dang you, Gretchen, with the festive holiday cheer you bring to class. She's like a present underneath the Christmas tree or hidden, hanging in a stocking. I'm not allowed to touch, shake, peek at, unwrap.

One day she dropped something that rolled up to my desk. She prepared to untangle herself from my wires, but I scooped the little bottle of body mist. And magical potential hung in the air.

I read the label aloud. "Love Spell? Does it work?" I followed with a slight laugh, continuing, "Have you put one of your spells on me?" Perspiration lurked on my forehead, hands, pits, feet, everywhere—my whole body went on the verge of a meltdown. Dear God, I spoke.

Gretchen collected the bottle from my hand, grinning. Electrical currents sizzled through me when her fingertips grazed the palm of my hand. My heart jolted. "Well, would you like that, Hayden?" Her answer, given in the form of a question, offered me a flare in her eyes, and her mouth upturned in a new level of confidence I'd never witnessed before. Feet soon slipped back into the motions of entanglement into my desk wires, where she belonged.

She's flirting, right, Mom? Yeah, of course, I'd like that. I froze like a freaked-out kid. I'm an ass-jerk with a dirty-minded soul. My mind began singing, "Pour your 'Love Spell' on me, in the name of love . . . you're hot . . . sticky sweet. . . ." WOLG—I can kick it old-school. By the way, Gretchen, there's this letter in my notebook I meant to give it to you.

"Hey, Hayden, thank you, by the way." Gretchen held up her Love Spell, spritzing herself with one pump, "You're always so kind," she whispered to the back of my head as the bell to signal class rang. Gretchen's wicked legs and feet continued weaving her intricate black widow spider webs beneath me.

She made it freakin' impossible to concentrate. Peppermint danced in the air, wafting around, smacking me in the kisser. Spun like a fluffy bunch of cotton candy, that one tiny mist of Love Spell shimmed up my nostrils—giving me fruity sweet nectar of the god's moment. *Animal Farm*, the audiobook, droned in the background. Animals succumbing to sad fates, like humans. My own destiny wavered, as the hot girl wove baskets behind me. Mottoes echoed from the teacher's computer about legs. Sheep bleated once again, "Four legs good, two legs better."

Gretchen's two legs intrigued me. Scents billowed, placing me in a stupor. In a daydream, I sang an old religious tune, which sure didn't *feel* very Biblical to me. *Oh, her toe bone connected to the foot bone; the foot bone connected to the ankle bone; the ankle bone connected to the knee bone; the knee bone connected to the thigh bone; the thigh bone connected to the hip bone; the hip bone. . . .*" Sweat leaked from my pores. Nothing compared to her. Smells, sounds, and items in this room hoped to compete with her, but Gretchen's the winner, every time.

As she continued squirming, Gretchen stirred a concoction of peppermint, Love Spell, angel feathers, and pixie dust. I yearned to twist around, tangle myself inside her beautiful, wicked web, and say, "Here I am. Take me. I am willing prey." Yeah, right. Sounds like a once upon a time love spell fairy tale, Mom.

Chapter Six

Dear Mom,

Mother, public education offered me some engaging daily lessons over the years. Dad signed a paper allowing me to participate in the sex ed course at school. School officials tried to show us videos and talk to us about puberty, including such stuff as STDs and preventative measures—waiting for the right time.

So, abstinence is the best and only answer? No wonder young people have so many crotch critters, teenage pregnancies, and other confusing issues. They use big words on us. Therefore, no one understands. Traumatized, we stare off into the distance, filled with questions—we have no idea how to ask them, so they go unasked, which means they go unanswered. Until we load up on the school bus. Here, older kids are more than willing to share their beliefs, pretending to be knowledgeable about sex.

Let's also add in the fact adults don't realize abstinence may not always remain feasible, so other options might need to be openly discussed. Too much embarrassment and judgment continue going on. Girls easily get labeled as sluts and whores and "hos" as people like to say, but a guy becomes a stud or a man-whore worthy of a high five? How's this fair? I don't understand the injustice or inequality of my gender. Rumors ruin reputations. Online bullying of this nature goes so far as to cause kids to commit suicide. After reading too many sad articles, I'm convinced society needs to step up and make it stop.

Boys talk. I sit, often quiet, and just listen. How I can maintain silence through the gibberish is beyond me when it's usually pure rubbish. Maybe I should speak out? What does one say to such nonsense, Mom? One recent example: "Mountain Dew in a six-pack or in a two-liter bottle a day lowers sperm count, so no one gets pregnant. Bam, that's a birth control solution." Idiots think drinking excessive amounts of Mountain Dew will lower their sperm count. It will only increase their caffeine. Soda birth control works on some gullible girls, but that's taking advantage of them, right? Guys utilize this line, roping in girlfriends. My body will *not* join the Mountain Dew rodeo challenge. So, no, Mother, I'm not engaging in sexual behaviors *yet*. Since we're on the topic of *intimacy*, though, let me broach the subject of one boy in particular.

Hayden Oliver Tucker sits directly in front of me during my imperfectly perfect English class. His woodsy scent drifts, taunts, delights me, Mother. When he's reading or writing, his head bends in a slight downward angle, so his neck becomes exposed. My transformation begins as I fantasize about the needy vampire inside me launching. Fangs may not be in vogue any longer, but an inner longing stirs. I wish for a sample—one taste—perhaps a single nibble of his flesh.

Hayden Oliver Tucker, Hot Boy, the boy with three first names. I want to touch, kiss, date, and talk to him outside of this English classroom. IRL (that's in real life, Mom), which seems too scary a place.

Today, as we listened to an audio version of George Orwell's *Animal Farm*, the tiniest laugh escape from Hayden. As the reader's rendition of the British sheep's bleating motto played: "Four legs good; two legs bad," I imagined Hayden's imperfect smile. The slight overbite—combined with the tiny sliver gap between his two front teeth. If you looked too fast at him, you would never notice any of these things. Hot Boy's imperfections set my world ablaze. Four legs good, two legs baaad, indeed.

My two human legs jiggled—alive in a mixed-up world of teenage angst: nerves, numbness, impure thoughts. My sweat glands kicked into overload. Sweat beads rolled down my back. The clinical strength deodorant transformed from powder fresh into little wet clumps—tiny balls of stink. In a pool of sweat, I shuddered with a cold chill. Forget my success at vampire life. My armpits and I got sidetracked and went on a tirade.

Dear Secret Deodorant Company,

Here is my secret. While wearing your luscious lilac clinic strength deodorant, the flowers wilted into a stinkball bouquet. Here's a secret—you need to fix this problem!

I so kindly need a refund, so I can buy a different fragrance. Perhaps one day I might get lucky enough to go on a date.

Thank you,

Gretchen Gardener

Pit stain circles, the announcement to the world: Yes, Gretchen is just as weird and awkward as we all thought! Light gray? Why did I wear light gray? It will show all my grossness when class ends. Too young for hot flashes? Pass out? Throw up? Grab the hall pass and run out of here?

I stayed. I decided to keep staring at the back of Hayden, as I held on to *Animal Farm* in my unstable hands. The book bounced up and down as I pretended to hold my place. My mind, eyes, heart, limbs, focused on my future—inside the dream of a boy who sat ahead of me. With my hand placed beneath me, temptation out of view, where it couldn't win with ease.

Because I wished to reach out and stroke his chocolate hair. My fingers could caress his scalp and twirl the wayward dark curl that often lands near his left ear. "Hayden," I longed to whisper. British words continued floating inside the classroom, as fictional animals dealt with horrible situations. *Hayden*, I said inside my mind, using my best accent to sound like the reader, which makes Hayden smile *that* smile.

Yes, time for self-talk and distractions other than Hot Boy Hayden. Gretchen, glance away, pull yourself together. Internal drama, all the chitter and chatter—is this typical, Mom? Most days, I struggle to comprehend my backpack full of mixed emotions.

I'm optimistic about each new day, but I'm not gonna lie, it doesn't always last long. Once in earshot of Meghan and Darcy, anger can overwhelm me because of how they speak about their moms.

Here's an example from earlier this week: "She's so nosy; she's so mean; she's such a witch. Now, I can't use my iPhone after nine o'clock. She's going to 'charge' it overnight in 'her room' for 'safekeeping.' This way, I get plenty of sleep. I posted *one* night on Facebook at one o'clock in the morning. So, like now, the world's gonna end!" Darcy said every word without taking a breather as she used her numerous "air quotes" along with her hand gestures. Her voice almost sounded "chipmunk" annoying. "You're so lucky, Gretchen, you don't have to worry about your mom getting in your way and doing stupid stuff like this." I hope she didn't really want to speak to me this squeaky, piss-poor way.

Oh. My. God. Mommy, my whole body—literally everything ached. I don't know what a heart attack feels like or what you went through before your stroke, but maybe I do just a tad if it's anything like the punishing sting of Darcy's words. Too stunned, I didn't move or speak. My brain replayed her words, my heart pounding in my throat. My hands went too numb to move and slap her face.

My eyes built a wall of wetness, but I prevailed. In my head, I screamed and shouted until the rawness ended. Shut up, you freaking insensitive brat! I'd flush my effing iPhone down the toilet if it meant I could have one more day. No, even just one more flippin' second—one more hug, one more smile. I'd give away everything I have for a single moment to hear her voice again. Swallowing down sobs never allowed to escape while at school made my throat sore.

With my game face on, I survived the pain of Darcy's commentary, without the utterance of words. Meghan and I don't often have an opportunity to share our thoughts with Darcy in our midst.

Meghan's not Miss Innocent either. "Go away. Get out of my room," she said, slamming her bedroom door on her mom and sister last night. Our FaceTime seemed ruined, so I said, "I better go." I shut my iPhone to silent, tossed it. It landed atop a spare pillow on my bed.

To reach my aqua notes, I rolled to my side. Once in my grasp, I latched on, pulled them in close as I embraced your words—valuing them, like pieces of fine gold jewelry. Pillowcases absorbed my tears again last night. Stress exhausted me to sleep.

I'm thankful for some extra time in class right now to share some thoughts with you. It's not unusual for me to have my nose plastered inside a notebook, so no one should disturb me.

Nighttime brings out the hours I contemplate life most. Some evenings, especially with a full moon, enough light shines through my bedroom curtains and lands on the surface of my notebook. And a thousand beams scatter, twirl, waltz, and spin and spin across my walls. The crystal gems play magic tricks with me, but I love and welcome them. I imagine the sparkling pearls as you—your particular way of visiting me—my childlike secret, my beautiful mother, and my favorite rays of light.

Darcy used the word lucky when she mentioned you, Mom. In that one aspect, she was correct. I learned a valuable lesson: God granted me a wonderful mom. He allowed me a winning ticket, just shy of seven years. Then, He robbed me. Yes, Mother, God robbed me. I am sorry if that disturbs people. I must write honestly. My heart hurts. God plucked you up and away from me, away from Dad, and away from earth. You were the greatest gift I was ever given. Sadness hits me hard knowing this. Especially when I remind myself how much you loved me. I wish I could keep my eyes closed long enough to see you in person and not only in my mind. Or in my dreams.

A painful welt formed across my stomach today. My skin's burning red-hot. I can sense the bubbled-up markings coming from Tuesday's turtles. Elastic sliced into me, the rubber strands, I guess, became exposed and snapped against my skin. I'm uncomfortable, but that's nothing new.

Why am I punch-to-the-face angry? And deep-down-damn-damn-double-damn-Darcy-depressed today? Mom, I've got this "I want to go home" feeling. Once home, I'll want to leave because our house really isn't home without you. Such an emptiness lingers. Grief's a homesickness that never goes away. Why does being half-orphan equate to the dread of feeling like a loser? I lost a mother. Why should I be the one to be so out of place still, so nutty, so everything not quite right, so not normal?

My purse buzzed. The vibration sizzled my foot. My iPhone lit up with a text message from Meghan. From a quick glance, I got the gist of her thoughts: Meh, school! Ugh, Darcy! She's clueless, but she loves you. ☺

Thank goodness for emojis and emoticons—the shorthand of youth. Later, I can send a smiley face and a random heart to Meghan, and our friendship remains golden. Superficial living—my friends mean well, but they don't comprehend the sinking depth of grief. And I can't burden them with all my problems. Or I'll have no friends. Not sure I do anyway.

After you died, I believe Darcy and Meghan's moms invited me over or took me places out of a sense of obligation because of *your* friendship. Death got treated as a taboo topic, which they practiced like a devout religion. My mom died, but I was supposed to understand what to say (nothing) and how to act (deny) and ensure everyone else felt better? Freaked-out faces appeared when I mentioned your name. Immediately, the subject switched.

I'd love to dig through their photo albums, searching with the hope of finding unknown pictures of you. Sharing snapshots and stories would bring bits and pieces of you back to life for me. Asking for this isn't possible—timing's way off. Fear, or maybe grief, holds them back from having the ability to listen? What I need, I guess they just don't have inside themselves to give.

These friends could help me laugh. These friends could help me build the history of your life. These friends could help me remember your time on earth. These friends should help remind me of the fun times, but these friends do not do that.

I don't know what to do? I like having people to spend time with, but when friendship becomes too painful, shouldn't I peacefully walk away? Like, drift away but remain kind? Is this normal?

Does this sometimes happen with bonds? Is this how or why childhood pals sometimes change to acquaintances? What a lonely feeling to stand in the presence of others and still feel so alone. ☹ But I ache to surround myself with others who won't disapprove or deny me the right to talk about my mother.

My digressions occur so many times while writing you these journal entries, but my mind spins in circles, like the Spirograph thingy we used to play. I can't fathom you not hearing the happenings of my heart and knowing what's going on in my life. Details—all in the details, right?

Mrs. Tweed's English class ranks as one of my favorites. She's enthusiastic, encouraging, and I enjoy reading, as well as writing. As you now realize, I have diarrhea of the pen in notebooks, where I spend time doodling and writing random poems. Off I go, jump online, and my fingers contract the dreaded poops, as well. Splat! Ha ha! I'm so gross. Sorry, Mom. Sometimes I can't help but have a giant blowout. My emotional release, or catharsis, the fancy word for this. Mrs. Marks at the grief center discussed the topic of tears, journals, and hobbies, all ways to cope, and I learned the word catharsis. Writing to you is mine.

Now, back to the subject of Mrs. Tweed.

What might possess an attractive young teacher to grow arm hair longer than Dad's? Eeekkk— suppose she decides to wear a sleeveless shirt or dress? I'll be subjected to armpit whiskers! Gah—that thought disturbs me on various levels. But I dwell on the absurd issues. I know it's too rude to ask her my inquiry out loud, but every Monday through Friday, I ponder the question, tossing it around in my mind during class. With her sharp mind, whimsical classroom décor, wordsmithing ways, and kindhearted personality, she's almost 100% what I wish I could be, minus her beast-like, hairy quality.

"Gretchen, I admire your creative soul. You're wise beyond your years. You painted the most beautiful picture of your family. I understood your thoughts and pain. I'm sorry for your loss. Your mother would be amazed by you." Mrs. Tweed wrote those words in my last English paper.

Mom, it's only a journal essay, but she liked my response to "Feeling Alone Challenges." I addressed it once in my grief diary. I borrowed it from a prompt about describing the person you miss. Mom, I couldn't give all my "hairy" secrets away, but here's some of the story:

Guess no one ranks as an actual ten, not on any human interest scale. Humans, by nature, appear flawed to some degree. Some flaws enthrall us, touch us, all the way to the core. Mom, I remember how faint freckles peppered your nose and cheeks, and in my mind's eye, I play a game with them of connecting the dots. I form heart patterns until the tears burn on the tips of my eyelids.

My mom used to say, "Oh, I dislike all my freck-les."

Dad said, "That's part of being a copper beauty." He loved her so much. Not because he fancied copper hair, Irish pale skin, and freckled noses but because those qualities represented a whole package.

"You're the luckiest 'penny' I ever found. My wife shines brighter and more prominent than any dime," Dad's saying went. My parents walked hand in hand in the city park, along with me. We stopped along the way, feeding ducks. Or we flew high into the clouds during swing races.

Nowadays, I'm well aware my father called my mother a "dime piece." Dad used a fancier format to share and describe how sexy he thought my mother was. I want to be disturbed or freaked out by this, but I'm glad my dad considered my mom this way. So, my dad's romantic, flirtatious, and poetic? As I think back, I envision all the signs.

One sign I wish would appear for me is a stop sign. Make it a four-way stop because I'd like a break from sorrow in all directions. No chances for the hurt to go to the right. Or go to the left. No chance it can turn and follow me. No option for it to pass me. And no possible road rage events to occur.

"*Signs, signs, everywhere there are signs. . . .*" Oh, as the music played, I recall watching my parents from the hallway. My father attempted to lead their dance, as Mom twirled. They paused with her feet on top of his. Their stolen kisses lingered. Once again, he tried spinning her. Their laughter ended the scene. They caught me peeking but invited me into a family group hug. Christmas tree lights blinked across our living room floor, scattering colorful shadows, like a holiday disco ball.

We all blinked. When I opened my eyes, Mom died. Now, the sorrow doesn't want to end. Every day it continues to sneak up on me. I don't understand how to dance to grief. Or which direction to turn or spin because no music matches its tune. Daily, I watch for signs. But how does anyone learn to dance again without a parent or a partner? And who two-steps all alone?

Mom, it's so true. One minute, I'm having impure thoughts. Within seconds, I'm looking at the physically *unnecessary* imperfections of a lovely English teacher. Stories pour out from us because of our unique flaws. Maybe people see my weaknesses too. Like the neon flashing sign I carry around all the time: Gretchen's Grief.

Well, Mom, I'm fifty percent genetically you, a copper beauty. Is half a cent worth much? Do I stand much of a chance? This half business scares me. When I watch people like Lilly Pullitzer, who go around channeling the "Pulitzer" name—pretending, pretty, peppy, Lilly, the one thing I know she's not is a prize.

Here's a recent list of things I'm not: Pretty enough 2. Preppy/peppy enough 3. Skinny enough 4. Normal enough 5. Simply "enough." Wow, I'm no prize for Hayden either then.

Hayden, Hayden, Hayden. . . . It's no use to take my thoughts elsewhere. *ROMEO & JULIET* appear closer each day, as the posters in English class close in. And the walls might squeeze me to death. Claustrophobia? Maybe I suffer from more than a grief-stricken heart? British words drifted across the *hairy* English classroom as overworked animals donated their entire well-being to humans in *Animal Farm*.

Ugh, Hayden's brown hair offers flecks of sandy highlights along with caramel streams flowing throughout. His ocean eyes reminded me of a cloudy day, a blue-gray, but you grasp, beyond the sadness, the sun will shine again. He's my silver lining during the school day. I lick my lips, contemplating how to steal the grin off Hayden's face; then, transfer it on to me through a first real romantic kiss, perhaps. I hope to smile this way soon. I'm so ready for a boyfriend, a first kiss, a chance to experience romance. All the time, I fear I'm not enough. So, I sit worrying boys don't stare at the back of my head with a longing to run off into the future to romance me. In my imagination, only one boy really matters.

At the end of class, as routine, we passed our books forward, so Hayden turned, where he met my nervous gaze.

"Hey, Gretchen," Hayden said in a whispered voice.

WTFDD, Say something, Gretchen. SPEAK!

Rendered speechless, only one side of my mouth functioned. Well, part of my face managed to perform some kind of half-curled smirk, as the other portion twitched then failed me. 50 percent—see, I'm a half lump-lump. A 50 percent failure freak.

He must think I'm crazy. Hayden scribbled a little note on his desk but scooped it up and hid it away inside his notebook before he left the room. Obviously, it's meant for someone more like Lilly Pullitzer, who pretended to be related to the real Lilly Pulitzer—the prized beauty. Every day she wears the darling bold, sunny-patterned clothing line. Sorry, Lilly, but Nantucket summer resort fabric is quite a long way from the Ozark Mountains. Off down yonder, in fact.

Summerfort isn't quite the Possum Holler hillbilly location with the backwoodsy, banjo-plucking crowds that Netflix, TV, movies, and the pages novels portray. Missouri, or *Misery* as some want to pronounce it, often receives a bad rap, but Summerfort's charming reputation could help change all of that. With Branson nearby, including Paula Dean's (Mom, you had one of her cookbooks) new Family Kitchen restaurant offering ooey-gooey butter cake, hope remains for Summerfort. Even if Lilly P must reside as one of the negative side effects. Perhaps one day, a new town will "steal" her away.

I'm on to you, Lilly. Even if other idiots who roam the school halls and streets of Summerfort choose to live in a state of oblivion, Hayden deserves less fakery. Why does he want to write *her* a letter? Yep, that's *atypical*, alright. What does someone like Hayden have to say to a hateful girl like Lilly? She's pink, orange, and yellow. Bright on the outside and darkness on the inside. During the winter months, she wears floral bouquets. A money-back guarantee says, deep down, every flower Lilly wears stinks of plastic fake rot.

Not my usual **WTF**DD? I only feel like the first three letters today.

Mom, I thought Hayden and I shared a special past connection. Our hearts already broken, healed, and aligned together. Both of us shy and awkward. Now, imagine hormones stirred into a giant cauldron creating warm, magical, happy love spells.

Mentioning "love spells"—I thought Hayden and I truly experienced a moment in English class after I dropped my perfume. "Love Spell," he said, picking it up, reading the label with the slightest smirk of nervous guilt or something, or as if he had committed the name of my scent to memory already. I felt bolder and stared longer into his face. Then he asked me if I had been casting spells with it before he handed it back to me. Hayden's skin barely touched mine, but wow—high voltage! Then no follow-through from either of us. POOF! That's the only love spell I seem capable of conjuring up.

I wish I could cast spells: Poof! Begone, Lilly! But, right now, it sure seems like no spells are working because I'm the one still left empty, unsure, alone. Except I'm stuck with a bottle of Love Spell that doesn't seem to work any dang magic at all.

Will anything I attempt in life ever stand a chance? Does the word normal exist anymore for me? Mom, what do I do? OMG—to most teenage girls, the acronym stands for "Oh my God," but for me, it overlaps with "Oh my Grief!" Plus, I *thought* I understood the world pretty well for my age.

HAYDEN

Chapter Seven

End of September 2019

Dear Ma,

I wanted to write in my journal and tell you a story about Dad. This one's much better than the bread fiasco.

"Hey, your birthday's coming up. What do you want to do?" Dad asked. "Want to invite some friends over? Go somewhere to eat? Or just hang out with me, your cool old man?"

Dad acted so over-the-top and giddy I just went with it. He could be a lot of fun some nights if he didn't work late. Or if someone from his crew didn't call him with issues. Tonight he looked more rested. Seldom do I find Dad kicked back on the couch with the TV on, which is the sign of a good mood.

"Hang with a friend, I guess?" I approached Dad, decided to lean then sit down on the arm of the couch opposite Dad. Our throw pillows, the ones with the floral fabric from the early 2000s, need to be replaced. I never say anything to Dad about them because I figured you bought them. Anyway, they still function. I hugged one up to me for emotional support, I guess. It puts layers between me and my emotions. If I focus on the ugly purple flowers, while tracing their outlines as Dad and I talk, maybe I won't say something too stupid.

"Singular?—you said only a friend?" Dad's eyebrow perked up. "Tell me more."

Dad clicked the TV remote to mute. He even sat straight up, grinning. At that moment, Dad reminded me of a scruffy version of the movie star Paul Rudd. Except for a few more gray hairs around his temples and the signs of recession now showing on the hairline. Plus, middle age granted Dad a bit of stomach pudge. But for just turning fifty, Dad's not so bad. He actually rocks his dad bod pretty well. *Behold, my future,* I thought—*is this me, thirty-five years from now?*

"Well, what's *her* name, son?"

"Gretchen."

"Oh, Dr. John Gardener's daughter, the cute strawberry shortcake girl from the grief place?"

Pleading my case, I said, "Dad, you just can't call Gretchen 'Strawberry Shortcake Girl.' Makes you sound weird—like a creeper." I rolled my eyes.

"Why? She's a cute little redhead. Description works—fits. No biggie." Dad laughed at his own joke. He followed up with some dumb-accented voice. "You can be her very own Huckleberry—oh my, Strawberry Shortcake and Huckleberry Pie." Dad started laughing out loud again at his own stupid jokes. "Go be her Huckleberry," Dad repeated *once more.*

"What does that even mean, Dad?" I muffled my voice with the pillow over my face, so I could block out the sight and sound of Dad's insane cackling. Every time Dad opened his mouth to speak, he stuttered out his explanation about the Strawberry Shortcake and Huckleberry Pie dolls and some kid's TV show through insane fits of giggling.

Dad, who's the parent here? "Gene Tucker, are you drunk or high?" I struggled to get my question out because Dad's giggles were contagious.

"Good God, no, buddy." Dad tossed his throw pillow. "But what's your major malfunction?"

"I ain't got no game with Gretchen, Dad."

"First, you might want to speak English to her. 'Ain't got no game'? Really, Hayden?"

"Okay, I do not have a game plan as to how to effectively speak to this girl. Any better?" I shrugged.

"Well, when you hang out or when you're around her, what do you chat about?"

"To be honest, death, I guess." I stared at Dad, before lowering my gaze to the floor, where I tapped my foot, waiting for a reply. I sighed, worried I had said the wrong thing once again. I peeked back over to Dad. He looked back at me with a straight face.

Time seemed to drag on forever. Finally, Dad said, "Hmmm. I can't imagine you want anything like that for your birthday."

"Not at all, Dad—but—well—I think Gretchen tried flirting with me in English class?"

Dad grinned, shifting around on the couch, fluffing and adjusting his pillows. "Hey, I love a great story. I'm comfortable and ready to listen." He rubbed his palms together. "Give me all the deets."

"Okay. The 'deets' or details, Dad—I'll give, like, the shorthand version." My hands talked for me a bunch, and the workout I put them through made them clammy. I stammered, trying to formulate words right, or trying to piece together the correct way to share my story with Dad. I rubbed my sweaty palms over my knees.

"Alright, anyway, Dad, her perfume is called Love Spell, and well, she knocked it off her desk, so I picked it up for her. After I said something like, 'Does it work; did you put a spell on me?' she said, 'Would you like that, Hayden?' But, then, I froze, like an idiot."

Dad sat there, both his eyes and mouth wide open. He leaned toward me, motioning me to come in for a high five. I slapped at his hand, all confused. "Dad, what are you doing?"

"You're in. Strawberry Shortcake likes you. No question about it, bud." With a lopsided smirk, Dad piped up with: "Seal the deal, Huckleberry. Because, my dear boy, that's what's called a 'done deal.'"

"But we still have *no deal.* Or there's no plan? Do I invite her here? Do I go somewhere? I know she likes old '80s movies. Order pizza—I guess, maybe? Do a little cake? I don't think I want other people here? Let's do something midweek? Low-key?"

I paced the floor, sweat beaded on my forehead. Dad stared at me, rubbing both his cheeks, stroking at his five-o'clock shadow like he's the one stressed out or something. Dad's confirmation of Gretchen's like for me made me sweaty, tingly, and high-strung. And so I rambled on and on, adding to my questionnaire.

"Dad, do you think just dinner and a movie? Less time might make it easier for my anxiety?" I swiped my forehead and rubbed my temples. "Oh, I got a football game on Friday night!"

"Chill, Hayden. How about something simple after your game?"

"No. Gross. I'm all hot and sweaty then, Dad!"

"I would allow my son to take a shower, Hayden."

"Hey, my favorite idea of all, Dad. I'll just invite Gretchen over here to take a shower with me—be serious, Dad!" When I looked over at Dad, I realized I'm the one who misunderstood him.

His non-dirty statement sure sounded like an innuendo under the circumstances. I picked up a pillow in time to block the one I eyed Dad reaching for as he prepared to whack me with it. By anticipating Dad's move, I got in the first couple of swings and won our pillow fight.

"Okay, Dad, so I'm supposed to go say, 'Yo, Gretchen, this is Hayden. Daddy said I could invite you over for a 'Happy Birthday' shower!'" I burst out laughing.

Dad shut his eyes, covered his ears, and scrunched up his entire face. In his extreme southern accented tone, he jokingly shouted, "Please, Lord Jesus, make him stop! I'm shocked. La-la-la-la-la-la. Where did my shy little boy go?"

"My dad ruined me. He flipped me into a freak like him, I guess."

Dad continued speaking in the worst possible southern accent he could muster. He threw his hands into the air in an over-the-top drama king manner. He faked tears, kicked a pillow across the room, picked up the one remaining pillow nearby, and tossed it at me.

"Where did I go wrong, Huckleberry? My kid's a sarc-*ass*-tic brat, now? My poor baby boy's corrupted."

"I'm leaving this room, Dad. You're a total nutcase." I started walking away, but Dad called me back. In an instant, he fell into serious Dad mode.

"Hayden, in all honesty, do you need to talk to me about the bigger issues with Gretchen?"

"Nope," I said. "Let me learn how to talk to her first, you know?"

Later, an idea for a joke came to me. With my hair lathered up high with shampoo, I leaned out of the shower, towel-dried my hands off, grabbed my cell from the bathroom sink, and snapped a couple of goofy headshot selfies. And I saved them as I plotted the best possible text messages—like the funniest I could fathom. But at the same time, ones not too inappropriate to get me killed by Dad, either. Here's what I came up with. I attached my fav photo with the caption:

Me: Hey Dad, Strawberry Shortcake agreed to the whole shower thing. Thanks, Daddy. You're the best.

In my picture, I'm winking with a giant grin on my face. Plus, I'm giving thumbs-up.

Dad: BTW, Huckleberry, Daddy bought new loaves of Wonder Bread. JK, Bud.

In Dad's photo, he's got his face all snarled up as he's biting into the heel of the bread, the piece we both hate and always throw out.

Me: LoL! ☺

Chapter Eight

Dear Mother,

WTFDD does a letter like this from a boy like Hayden Oliver Tucker mean? He plopped this down, right before our English class started. Slid it across the desk to me, with that cocky grin on his face, those come-hither lips parted, as he said in his quiet sexy voice, "Hey, Gretchen."

Gretchen,

I thought you might want to work on the *Animal Farm* study questions with me sometime? "My minds good, but your mind's 'betttterrr.'" JK—a little sheepish humor.

Hayden

PS You busy casting spells behind my back?

***

Okay. Mother, shall we rationalize the situation?

1.) Great, he sees me as just the nerdy girl to study with? So what, he still picked me. I'm not so disgraceful that he doesn't want to be around me. He thinks I'm smart? Why can't that be positive? For today, it equals positivity.

2.) Or he's a flirt and really wants to hang out with me? But, what if he's using this as just a study facade with me? Is this some sort of "guy method," Mother? So what, take advantage of that. Go for it. Right? I like it. Clever words intrigued me. In fact, I'd probably utilize this method myself.

3.) He's been told to do this as a joke by the football players? Nope. Not really able to buy this one as Hayden's style; he's not into the jock practical joking. A Quinton Anthony or a Thomas Sharp move, I buy, but not a Hayden Tucker one. I've witnessed those other jerks in action before. They both flirted with me for notes in the past. Or they tried to copy answers off my papers. Sometimes they private message me on social media to ask for help. Oh, the flattery: "Yo sexy." Or "Little Miss Red Riding Hood, can you take a screenshot of today's assignment?" Blah. Meh. It doesn't work on me. Thomas Sharp might be the typical tall, dark, handsome guy, but something's lacking. Quinton's average cute but more California surfer dude with blond features. To me, he's only a Sharp minion.

4.) Or he remembered how much I liked the concept of the old-school effort of handwritten notes?

5.) If he remembered those things, it means he's listened to everything I've said during grief groups and activities?

6.) So, if he remembered, listened, put in all this effort. . . . Then I declare it: ***Best Letter Ever!***

Hot Boy Hayden offers me a sense of humor. Intelligence is sexy. I love a guy who can string together more than one sentence and use words like *atypical*. And if Hayden's "spell" comment is his flirty, I like the innuendo style. My goodness, perhaps Hayden Oliver Tucker, will resurrect chivalry back from the dead.

Time for the freak fest to begin. I needed to figure out what now? *Gretchen—play it cool—you must not act like your usual whack-a-doodle-kook-a-choo self.* Wadded papers lined up all around me on my bed. First letter draft of my reply to Hayden:

Hey, Hayden:

I enjoyed your note. I can only imagine how excited the author, George Orwell, would be to hear his animal motto used in such an intelligent way. Run your ideas for a time and place we can meet.

Capital N. Capital O. NO! In the first part, I sounded like a schoolteacher, grading a kid's essay. Why does creativity elude me when it mattered most? Throw away!

Perhaps a funny poem? Ideas, take two:

Dear Hayden,
Thanks for providing me some smirks
Indeed my spells must've worked
With delight, I'll study with you
Two magic minds will see us through
When shall we discuss *Animal Farm*?
Let me know, turn on your charm

Nope. Also, way too friggin' ridiculous. Cute, but it opens the door for Hayden to call me a whack-a-doodle. Like Hayden Oliver Tucker wants to hang out with a psycho-chick. So like a whack-a-doodle-psycho-chick, I shed a couple of frustrated tears but decided to add a PS to my poem with a laugh. Mother, I suppose I'm PMS-ing again. I hate my moodiness. Anyway, here's my PS. I enjoyed adding it since no one's ever going to view it. PS. You're like a smokin' hot fire alarm!

Take three—fifteen wasted pieces of paper later, with my eyes closed, I take a few moments to think. *Breathe. Calm thyself.* Only for one second do I consider a FaceTime with Darcy or Meghan for ideas. The fewer people who know, the better. I don't need the whole school involved in my personal life. Small-town life confines me already. Facebook, Instagram, Twitter, and Snapchat design an "instant" chain reaction in life, and boy, then you can't take back what's out there—photos, words, or captions. Hayden and I like our lives private (what I learned from the grief center), and the way I'll keep it for now. Maybe Dad? No. Dad's too direct and honest. Besides, Dad's not ready to hear about how much I like Hayden. Or is he?

I growled into my pillow, scrunching my fingers until two fists punched said pillow to the floor. While I'm at it, I thought, might as well sling the crumpled-up pages of paper high into the air and kick the loser letters I'd written to Hayden across the room. Besides, they'll never see the light of day. *I* should never see the light of day. Freakin' baby—I'm the biggest one I know. Cock-a-doodle-doo. Shittle-sticks. Why do I lack the courage to send a simple, fun reply to Hayden?

Wait. Just do what everybody else my own age does. Use Messenger? Yes. A fast and easy but not too cheesy or nerdy schoolmarm response. Try not to be like my typical self.

Sidetracked by Hayden's social media profile pictures because they required a bit of study. I'm not into football. Once the town of Summerfort dresses Hayden Oliver Tucker in drab blue-and-gray Eagles practice jerseys like he's headed to the Civil War battlefield, I sure become a fan. In fact, toss me some pom-poms. I'm ready to perform a few rah-rahs, high kicks, and spirit fingers.

I love the way he's propped up against the wall holding his helmet, with his trademark smirk. How can a person, such as the shy Hayden, be so dang photogenic, standing in front of a camera? He appears so sharp and clear. "I'm a winner," Hayden's photo states. Did he feel like a victor on the inside too? Hayden wears the number forty-one, and I aim to find out why. My curiosity piqued as to the why of the number forty-one.

Out on the field, what in the heck does the term and position tight end represent or mean? Who understands all this? Maybe someday, I'll make it to the "end zone." Isn't this where touchdowns go down? Perhaps I'll learn all about Hayden, football, and many other exciting things.

Social media allowed me to learn the more delicate art of becoming a stalker-creeper. I'm not alone in this phenomenon. Someone can say a name to someone else, and the first thing people do is Google it or head to social media to track their photos down. I people watch. Trust me, Mother, it's how the world operates now. Look, if I scroll down, I can find pictures of him with his family.

The whole family sports the image of pure deliciousness. Greek god blood must zip through the veins of every one of those Tucker boys: Hayden, Drew, and Cole. Mini statues could be created by adding their muscular arm contours combined with chiseled facial features and a dash of plaster. They're excellent works of freakin' art. Even their dad, Gene, makes growing old look pretty good.

Dear God in heaven, I want you to trust me, but can I trust myself alone with Hayden? Well, yeah, probably. For now, anyway. Because I can barely speak to Hayden on most days. He's pretty quiet around me also. Although I realize what lies beneath the silence. After all, I'm one of those silent types. Why do you think I'm so excited about the potential for the future?

Ew. A freakin' photo of Lilly screechin' out at me from in the background of one of the group pictures he's posted. Here's a cheer for you, Lilly: "Go away, Lilly; go away!" Recall how folks take their index finger and thumb and squint to manufacture a crushing blow to people? With super high shakes of some pom-poms, magic in my make-believe fingers, Lilly's face disappeared. One pom-pom fist covered her rah-rah mug from appearing on my computer screen. I didn't long to be reminded of Lilly. Poof—begone, Lilly. *Go try to steal the scene from someone else's computer.* Then I remember all too well.

Days after Lilly's "mom stealing" remark, it would be Darcy's FaceTime that haunted me even more. Exaggerated expressions came back into focus. Darcy's unblinking brown eyes, flared nose, tiny pixie face, and her Minnie Mouse voice saying, "I heard *Hardly Speaks Hayden* kissed Lilly at some back-to-school sports party. Can you imagine?"

"No way." I skyrocketed up from my bed. I remember the moment well. "Ugh!" I yelled, and I "eeked" straight into Darcy's face. My eyes rolled.

Through gritted teeth, my rant began: "Lilly's so freakin' fake. Why would Hayden go near her? Do you think this might've been some stupid Spin the Bottle game? Or Truth or Dare? Maybe a weird, lame-ass sports game we've never heard of before? Maybe? Right? Or even just some he-said-she-said lie? Darcy, he's way too nice for her."

Lilly, you will not make me crap myself. I hate you enough already. My stomach churned and gurgled, imagining her lips pressed to his mouth. I wanted to puke all over Lilly, with her dang silky straight sunshiny hair. Her pretty-in-pink everything resort wear. Hairs on my arms stood at attention. Every nerve in my body awakened. Fight or flight, fight or flight? Thoughts of Lilly's look-at-me lips outlined in her plumping watermelon berry bliss lip crayon that she toted around disturbed me. I hated the way she applied it in class, her feathery strokes. Lilly loved to admire her reflection as she smeared on the color, smacking her lips together. Lilly posed between each layer. The whole time she applied her hideous, painted on, fake-ass smile.

How far might a phony face faker go while kissing someone? Was this party scene a little peck? A full mouth display of affection? Because when I dream of kissing Hayden, I predict moments with him as a full-contact sport. Sure, I may not understand what to do now, but I'll let my emotions guide me. The mystery of romance unfolds when the moment's supposed to. My soul hurts not understanding the how and why of all this. Why do I care about gossip? Or about a boy who would rather bounce beach balls off Lilly's summer-ready skin? Or about a boy who may only consider me as his "grief sister"?

Darcy rambled, but I failed to focus on her and listen because my heart traveled to the dreadful sports party beach resort, where the alleged kiss happened over a month ago. "By the way, I don't know, but, like, it's kinda cute how defensive you can get about Hayden," Darcy said.

Dingy Darcy loves to dish out dirt, and I did not want myself to be the next platter she served with a heaping side of Hayden Tucker talk. My mouth fought hard not to smile back at her. If I held back, played cool, displayed my poker face, Darcy wouldn't have visuals on how much I cared about Hayden. "He's a good friend to me at the center," I said. Surely Darcy didn't hear the pep in my voice or see my eyes dance?

I don't know what goes down at these sports things, but I'm not gonna worry (much) about an incident I can't change. Hayden's not buddy-buddy with Lilly at school. I had to try setting aside rumors and the memories of Darcy's FaceTime.

With my Facebook Messenger opened, I planned to craft a note to Hayden. Now, what do I say? Hey—did you kiss Fake Face, Lilly? If so, you can study with her big fat lips and layer after layer of her lipstick all over you. If not the case, then come on over and put your lips on mine.

Hey, Hayden,

Your note inspired me to study. My spells will not help me pass the test all alone.

Message back times and ideas for a get-together.

Hey, Gretchen,

Glad you're available. My study questions are done, but I could use your input and help. My house, after Friday's game? Dad can drive you home.

Mr. Tucker,

My father agreed, but only if he drops me off and picks me by midnight. Might be his sneaky way to spy on me. Lol.

Miss Gardener,

I understand spy missions. Glad this works for you. Snack ideas? Any special requests? Small town— you know where I live? 726 Lavender Lane (just outside city limits) not far from the school. Look for Dad's big black Dodge: "Gene Tucker Construction" truck in the driveway.

Dear Tight End #41,

I'm easygoing. I'll sample or try new things. You know my snacks from the center—Doritos (spicy), sugar cookies, dark chocolate, anything peanut butter, water & tea. I know where you live. As I kid, I think I've been to your house, Trick or Treating? I actually live a couple of blocks away (the whole town does). Lol! I'm at 1127 Maple Leaf. I could just walk.

Dear newsworthy girl,

You're not always easygoing.
WTFDD! Don't walk in the dark to my house.
I mean this in the kindest way. ☺
See you tomorrow.

Nite, Hayden!

Chapter Nine

End of September 2019

Dear Mom,

After the game Friday, I itched all over. My mind raced with thoughts of *Animal Farm*—or at least my study buddy. I imagined Hayden as he rushed home hot off the Summerfort Eagles battlefield, all sweaty, his #41 shirt likely piled on his bathroom floor, while I broke out in hives.

"Dad, what's wrong with me?" I showed Dad my red blotches as I scratched.

"Gretchen, rub the Benadryl cream on," he said. He grinned, cocking his head to the side, waiting. He resembled one of his patients—the puppies who come into the veterinarian clinic. "Do you need to cancel this study *date*?"

"No way. I'll be fine. It's not a date." I side-glanced at Dad. My head now cocked, I say, "Well, at least I don't think it's a date?" Shrugging, I stand clueless.

I wished this study night was a date, with my whole entire itching heart, Mom.

For a minute, I walked in circles, checking to ensure I prepared and gathered everything I needed. I wanted to arrive on Hayden's doorstep with the appearance that I gave two flying f's about studying. Checklist: paper, pencil, book, and *Animal Farm* (a.k.a. "Tell me about yourself, Hayden") questions.

"Dad, I wish you could give me a shot to help my nerves and hives, something that wouldn't make me sleepy." I sniffed the tube of cream. "Oh. Ick. This gunk better not funk me up and make me all stinky." I shoved it in my bookbag.

Sitting nearby, Dad went into an extreme fidgety mode. Throwing his hands up, he brought them down, slapping his knees, with a warning, "Your mouth, Gretchen."

"What, Dad?" In a sing-song voice, I said, "F-U-N-K, funk, *funk*, Dad. You know, like, the tune?" I started to sing, "I'm Gonna Take You to 'Funky Town.' I promise that's the word I said." After I sang the title of the song, I wondered if Dad's mind swirled with visions of his wayward daughter hanging out with a boy. And if he worried he'd wronged me in raising me on his old music. "The music is *your* fault, Dad." I smiled, pointing at him.

"Fine," Dad said, indicating for me to sit down in front of him on the gray ottoman. He sat with

132

his arms crossed on the couch, his feet propped up behind me.

"So, have you got a secret weapon shot you can give me?"

"No, GG, I'm not giving my daughter animal drugs, so she's relaxed enough to hang out with a boy." He glared at me until he made sure I got his drift. Then he used one of his feet from behind me, pretending he might kick me for being ridiculous.

I laughed.

"Also, if anything, at any time, isn't what you expected it to be, I want you to call me. Are we clear, *Gretchen Grace*? Plus, no, 'Funky Town' stuff, either; understood?" Dad smirked.

"Yes, I understand." I hugged Dad, giggling, adding, "Please, let's go before I never have a social life."

Dad's lecture about how I needed to behave, be aware of my surroundings, be studious all night, continued for the most extended two blocks of my freakin' life. I should've walked. The crisp end-of-September night air may have conditioned my prickly skin.

"I'll text at midnight when I arrive, okay."

"Thanks, Dad." I smiled and waved him on.

The porch light glowed at the Tuckers' for my arrival. I only got a couple knocks in before Hayden's dad answered the door.

"Hi, Gretchen, come on in. I'm Hayden's dad, Gene." He shook my hand and led me through the foyer.

"Nice to formally meet you, Mr. Tucker. I've seen you at a few events before."

"You can call me, Gene. Feel free to put your things down there if you like." Gene motioned to a bench positioned near the staircase. Outside the foyer, against this wall, the gray, beachy, drift-wood-looking piece sat. Not an ordinary bench, it seemed more like a mini hall closet, with hooks for coats or bags that hung at eye level on the back of the item. One of Hayden's Summerfort football hoodies hung there, as well as one of Gene's white hard hats. Hinges on the seat appeared to lift up, so it included hidden storage. My curiosity piqued, wondering what Tucker men hide in there—shoes, sports gear, out-of-season wear?

"Wow, Gene, your home is beautiful. I love how open the downstairs is. Did you and your crew build it?" I asked, walking to drop my backpack and purse on the bench. My eyes scanned the rooms, guessing their purpose—foyer, staircase, hallway, den, living room, kitchen, dining room, office, and bathroom.

"Thank you. I bought it. Been remodeling it for several years."

As I heard Hayden's footsteps on the staircase, my stomach and heart did a race to leap or explode.

From the bottom rung, Hayden said, "Hey," He paused, standing on the last set of stairs. Gene threw him an odd wink. Hayden offered a wide-eyed glare back that I think meant, "don't embar-rass me."

134

Chapter Nine

Hayden's gaze shifted back to me. He was fresh from the shower. I imagined his chocolate hair feeling damp to the touch. I'm used to admiring him in the context of school. Now, *I'm inside his home*, seeing him wear a big smile for me. In jeans and a form-fitting Nike T-shirt that he left untucked, his posture seemed more relaxed. Even though he's not in any sports uniform or comfy workout gear or sweats, like at school or the center. Also, I've never seen him shoeless. All these visuals, I appreciated.

Oh my God, I'm standing in the home of Hayden Oliver Tucker. WTFDD.

"Want a tour of the house? Or a snack?" Hayden asked.

"Yes, and yes," I answered, sounding goofy with a nervous giggle. Following Hayden, I feel like we walked right into the pages of a fancy design magazine.

I took in the built-in china hutch and shiny appliances. "Wow, your kitchen's gorgeous."

"Thanks. Dad and his crew designed and remodeled it."

"Do you or your Dad cook a lot?" I asked, noticing the island bar, and the countertops that seemed never-ending but inviting.

Hayden smirked. Shaking his head, he said, "No. Not really." He paused. "Mom liked to, though."

At first, I didn't know how to respond, so I smiled. "Did your mom teach you how to cook a lot of things?"

Hayden's grin read like he wanted to protect childhood secrets, but he said, "Um, basic stuff. I'm not a real cook."

"Well, for some reason, your kitchen makes me want to learn to cook, Hayden." I gave him a closed-mouth giggle.

This kitchen provided a lot of space, but at the same time, it's not so big because it seemed filled up with love. And this kitchen offered the most family-friendly areas. To sum up the kitchen in one word: "*Home*?" I felt at home, Mom. I couldn't wait to see the rest of this place.

Right away, though, I spotted at least a dozen unfrosted sugar cookies in the shape of footballs on the counter. From the date on the box, I saw the order had been placed yesterday to Summerfort's Bakery. My mother once used their specialty department. I caught the tell-tale signs. Due to the eye-catching aqua color, I recognized the pastry boxes. Beside them, tubs of frosting for decorating, also special-ordered. Two candles rested nearby, in the shape of the numbers one and five. I performed the math.

Hovering over the evidence, I asked, "Hayden, is your birthday coming up?"

"Yep. Welcome to my birthday party." He conducted a game-show host gesture of the desserts, fanning the wares, offering me a happy birthday smile.

"Why didn't you tell me about your birthday?"

"I didn't want to make a big deal about it. I'm sorry."

"It's okay. I would've brought you a present, though, other than *Animal Farm* questions." I laughed. "Who else is coming?"

Hayden pointed from me to him and back again. "It's just us." Biting his lower lip, he lowered his gaze down to the ground. Slowly he raised his eyes to meet mine, quickly he glanced away again, shuffling his feet, moving closer to cling to the bar. He let out a sigh.

For some people, not knowing the date of someone's birth that you've known for years or at least an approximate day or month might seem weird. Okay, it is weird. Hayden values privacy. And whatever his reasons might be (maybe someday I'll know), he only lets a few people inside the intimate facts of his world.

Oh. My. God. I'm one of those people inside his world. Hayden trusts me. One plus one equals two. Maybe I am on a DATE?

Stealing glances at Hayden, I sensed he harbored undertones of sadness. Standing in my tight underwear, as squirrels gathered around their campsite singing Christmas carols, I related to his sorrow. Wearing a long shirt with my leggings helped camouflage my panty lines.

Hoping to make Hayden feel less awkward, I asked, "Is it okay if I decorate a cookie?"

"Yeah." Hayden's hands stayed glued on the countertop, but he looked me in the eye and smiled. "Duh. Sorry. I should've asked if you wanted one." As I slathered brown frosting on the football cookie, he watched with a grin. Relief seemed to appear on his face at the fact I chose to stay instead of running away.

"Wanna help me? Or we can have a contest—like compete? A football decorator showdown. Hmmm—your dad can pick the best one. But I'm frosting one of these suckers now. Then I'm planning to chow down."

He full on smiled. Laughter caused his top teeth to shine, exposing the tiny sliver between his two front teeth. Tonight, Hayden offered a broad, full mouth, along with thick kissable lips. His eyelashes curled out, dark against the foggy blue-gray of his eyes.

Reaching to grab a "naked" or unfrosted football, Hayden's surprised me by shouting "Go!" in a tone louder than typical Hayden. He dipped his spoon into the frosting. With a spin of his wrist, fancy swirling started. I forgot about the possibility of his inherited abilities in architecture. Naturally, Gene, who's a contractor/architect/designer, might've passed on artistic ways?

I stood back, viewing him cutting the #41 design. With his tongue sticking out, he bit the sides, I guess, as a concentration mechanism. He sliced the edges of each number with precision. With white frosting on his spoon, he whipped and flipped, creating little peaks carefully, throughout his numbers. The whole mission completed with dollops of frosting and a spoon.

"So unfair, Hayden. I'm gonna grab a plate and load it with icing. Then I'm going to sit here in awe, gawking at you"—*I do all the time, anyway*—"I'm breaking my junky cookie into pieces and dunking them in icing, so I can eat them like chips and dip. Birthday Boy, I crown you the winner, Mr. Cookie King."

I offered him a piece of my cookie loaded up with white buttercream. Without a word, he retrieved the cookie piece out of my fingers, with just his mouth and a flash of flirtatious expression in his eyes.

This meant his mouth—lips and tongue— touched me. Hayden didn't lick or suck on my fingers like some *Fifty Shades of Grey* crap, just a very sexy, flirty little act of fun. Mr. "Hardly Speaks Hayden" communicates at a professional level nonverbally.

I fell quiet in the moment of realization. My heart thump-thumped so fast and out of tune, I was confident Hayden might hear. Instead, he stepped closer to me. He frosted a piece of cookie, held it in his fingers for me to sample. Even though I feared I would mess up or make a fool of myself, I chose to dive into Hayden's offering. This was about as close to French-kissing as two people could get. He smelled delicious, like vanilla buttercream icing, sugar cookies, and woodsy cologne.

A part of me wished to flee and hide from my thoughts. Only because I also desired to grab a handful of icing and sample Hayden's neck, ears, chest, arms—I longed to finger paint him. To relax the mood, I put one tiny drop on the tip of his nose before wiping it off. My actions only heightened the moment. He tucked my hair behind my ear, moved in, close. I mean, super close. His breath in my ear stirred goosebumps up and down my arms.

"Mmmm. . . ." He put a little gift of icing on my ear, and whispered, "Thanks for coming to my party, Gretchen." He wiped away the frosting. Noticing the goosebumps, his knuckles skimmed my arm. A quick "aha" smile told me he enjoyed the reaction he'd caused.

Holy crap. This guy does like me. I'm the only person who's at his party with frosting remnants on my face and hands. Um, when he's at home, he's not quite so shy.

Stomping down the hall toward the kitchen, Gene asked, "Did you save a treat for me?" Hayden and I slipped apart. Hayden looked so much like a younger version of his dad, but when Gene entered a room, he arrived to care about things, settle things, and check in. Gene stood straight, making direct eye contact like he meant business.

"I challenged Hayden to a cookie-decorating contest, but he won. You should make one, Gene." I pushed the platter toward Gene to encourage him.

Hayden popped up with, "Duh, I never got out the other food, Dad." He jogged to the fridge and began setting up picnic-type sides—potato salad, coleslaw, a plate of cheese, crackers, and sliced meats. By taking only a couple of significant strides, Gene crossed the room. As a football cookie dangled from his mouth, he reached for the bread.

"What can I do to help?" I asked.

"Nothing," Hayden mumbled, as he carried and balanced the last items—mustard, mayo, and my requested spicy Doritos. Gene patted me on the shoulder as he passed. Along with Gene's bread, he carried a bowl of dark chocolate truffles, the kind I raved about at the grief center—shiny-wrapped purple Godiva.

"Hey, Dad, those Godiva dark chocolates— Gretchen says those are 'simply spectacular.'" Hayden did air quotes, followed by putting his hands on his hips with a smile. He pivoted his feet in my direction, cocked his head, and with a lopsided smirk, he added, "Gretchen labeled them in her WTFDD category."

"WTFDD? Should I even ask? Should I be scared?"

"Hayden!" I buried my face with my hands, laughing, feeling the heat of my cheeks from blushing.

Gene unwrapped one, tossed it into the air, catching it in his mouth. With a grin, he glanced over to me, giving approval with a thumbs-up.

"WTFDD—What the flippity-do-da? Do you agree, Dad?"

Gene closed his eyes, pausing, savoring another piece of chocolate as it melted, waiting to reply with bliss written on his face. He finally said, "Gretchen, I get it. I concur. WTFDD, indeed."

Gene slapped the counter, reached into the bowl, snagging another piece. "Gretchen, Hayden, you guys better take some before I eat the whole flippity-do-da bowl." He slid the candy down the island bar toward me.

Although my heart worked on overtime, sweat beads formed, and my hands reacted a bit unsteady, the night seemed like a success story for Hayden's birthday. Usually, I don't enjoy dining in front of too many people, but I felt pretty comfortable and at home with Hayden and Gene. This kitchen held a lot of fun and warmth. For the most part, I was at ease, especially for the first visit.

The calories I ate that night added up to more than what I ate all week combined. The anticipation of spending time with Hayden kept me from being able to eat, and then stress caused me to be ravenous. My food habits might be summed up like this from the week: sugar, grease, peanut butter.

"It's still pretty nice out. Wanna go outside for a bit?" Hayden asked.

We all stood. Gene jumped in. "I'll clean up in here if you two want to go. I think I'll go upstairs soon or watch TV to unwind. If you need me, though, holler." Gene found his way to the candy bowl again, popping another Godiva in his mouth. Then he snapped his fingers for Hayden's attention. He mumbled, "Put shoes on before you go out."

"Can I take Gretchen upstairs?" He pointed to his feet to indicate the location of his missing shoes.

"Sure, if your room's cleaned up," Gene said, with the bowl of chocolate Godiva poorly stashed behind his back. "WTFDD, Gretchen, this is all your fault. You caught me trying to sneak this out," Gene added as he held up the evidence. We all laughed.

"It's less than horrible upstairs, Dad." Hayden led the way to the staircase. At the upstairs landing, an arranged display of family portraits greeted me. I wished I had more time to ask Hayden questions. I wanted to hear his story from birth to the present, explained to me through pictures. Wondering if I might be a snapshot on his wall someday made my gut summersault.

"Hayden, will you share your family pictures and stories with me sometime?" I asked.

"Of course." But he walked over to the photo wall, covering up a frame with one with his hands saying, "This kid is a mess. Why his family chose to incorporate this picture here is beyond me." He used the thumb of his free hand to point back at the photo.

Revealed to me under his hand—*Oh, the very fingers he held next to my mouth*—displayed the sweetest little boy. Hayden's sitting on Santa's lap, looking up, scrutinizing his face. Hayden's mouth is open in a half-pout, showing a mix of fear with a bit of awe. Hovered over his eyes, his tiny fingers seem to be playing a game of peekaboo with Santa, but Hayden's on the verge of tears. "My dad said I didn't like that Santa watched me." Hayden moved me along.

"My room's to the left, next to what used to be Drew and Cole's rooms. I moved into Drew's bedroom since he had more space. I pounced on it as soon as he left. Drew thinks I don't miss him because I only wanted his room. Since it had a bathroom, I jumped to take that over too. Master bedroom and bathroom to the right." Hayden pointed, smiled, and continued tour-guiding.

Once in Hayden's room, I expected a lot of boyish paraphernalia. A typical dresser with five drawers in a dark wooden tone rested against the wall as you walked through the door. Sports trophies decorated the top. Hayden played on at least one winning team for each sport he participated in: football, baseball, and basketball. Beneath the window, Hayden's laptop, black notebook, and schoolbooks lay piled on his desk.

"Since my dad works in the construction field, he tracked down these old signs for me." Hayden gestured to the green oversized *Hayden Avenue* street sign, which hung above the one reading *Tucker Drive*. Both items served as pieces of art Hayden used above his bed. He had a full-sized bed that matched the dresser and included a platform storage unit. "Some of my dad's handyman work." Hayden slapped at the drawers like he enjoyed showing off his dad's talents.

"I love the effort and detail. I want someone to build hidden storage for me, just like this in my room."

"Thanks. I know. I like it. By watching and helping Dad over the years, I picked up some of his skills." He grinned. "Maybe you can show me something you want. I'll try making you something sometime."

"Deal."

To the left side of the bed, the nightstand contained a display case with a toy car set inside it. I motioned to the items asking, "Does this little set tell a compelling story?"

"Well, yeah, it does. The cars were the last birthday gift my mother ever bought me. I don't want to part with them. I understand they're only toys, but—" Hayden stopped mid-sentence, holding up his hands. A second later, his mouth parted, but still, no words came. His shoulders couldn't form a full shrug.

Hayden, do you want me to kiss away the words too painful to say? I wish I could hug you, love you. His wide eyes welled. Like a wounded deer, he just stood motionless. Looking lost for what to say or what to do, he slumped down on the bed.

"Oh, I get it," I said, sitting down next to him. For a minute, I considered spilling my guts to him, confessing to Hayden about my squirrel underwear and telling him everything about all the days of the week. About my daily routines, plus the need to keep a running inventory. I knew he wouldn't judge me. My mouth failed. No words formed. I just couldn't. Not today. Perhaps another time.

At times that are supposed to be the happiest moments, like a birthday celebration, something might trigger the saddest memories. Stuff like this happens every day for Hayden and me. For a few moments, Hayden and I both remained silent, letting the quiet speak for both of us because our hearts were just too broken for any words.

But since this day should be memorable for Hayden, I reached over, tapped his arm, saying, "Thanks for the invite today." Hayden cracked a hint of a smile, but I detected his glassy-brimmed eyes. Hayden struggled, doing all he could to hold back the flood dams.

"I'm glad you're here, Gretchen." He pushed off the edge of the bed, rubbed at each corner of his eyes before he added, "Duh, still no shoes." He used both index fingers to point down to his socked feet. Hayden walked toward his bedroom closet, grimacing at me while begging me, "Please divert your eyes. My closet's a complete disaster zone."

He rummaged with the closet door slid open but only a tad. He reached in, tossed shoes around until he found a matching pair of black Converse. "Oh, you might like a warmer jacket to wear tonight too." With that, Hayden produced his Summerfort Eagles letterman jacket. He approached me, draping the coat around my shoulders, smoothing the fabric down my back. His touch sent an electric sizzle through me, which formed goosebumps down my arms.

"Wow. Thanks. Now, I'm preppy and warm." For a moment, Hayden stood there, gawking at me with an expression I couldn't identify or one I didn't understand how to read. It certainly wasn't a bad look. It seemed quite the opposite. Maybe I'd call his expression a *muted* grin? Hayden's pupils did some dance by growing bigger. When I raised a brow and almost asked, "What?" his gaze lowered until he bent down to fiddle with his Converse shoestrings on the shoes he just put on? No guy ever eyed me with such a fierceness before. *Was I doing something wrong?*

Hayden placed a finger to his chin, tapping while hunting around his bedroom as if he's taking inventory or something. Next thing I remember, he yanked the two-toned comforter off the bed. He folded the blanket into a bunched-up wad of tangled dark and light blues. "Thought we might want to have a late-night picnic?" Hayden shrugged, followed by that trademark smirk of his as we exited his room for the stairwell.

Hayden flipped the lights to the master bedroom as we passed it. "Dad's set up," Hayden said as he stabilized the comforter in his arms. We only peeked in from the doorway.

"Oh, I love the fluffy white bedding. That giant king bed looks comfy.

"I hang out with Dad sometimes to catch a movie or something on TV," Hayden shared before shutting the light out. I noticed a framed photograph of his mother on the nightstand, but I didn't bring attention to it. A beautiful lady wearing her nurse's uniform. Too far away to view all of her features, but I could see her shoulder-length light brunette waves. Hayden resembles Gene overall, but his mom's hair reminded me of Hayden's—the caramel highlights and that curly piece he gets by his ear sometimes. I wished I could've known her. Realizing I will never experience learning from her what parts of her personality Hayden picked up made me sad.

Each step down the stairs enveloped me. The warmth of Hayden's home offered me floating ease or a puff of clouds ambiance. Peace of mind existed for me on this staircase. The location created *déjà vu*. I experienced something odd but fascinating—a surge, a current through my body, it provided glimpses of hope.

Somehow, someone led me here—the message came to me in a feeling that said, "Welcome." Perhaps the core of me recognized this place. Or my soul loves it here. Or I already resided here long before I arrived—another lifetime if reincarnation is such a thing? Or when I'm with Hayden, my heart senses *Home*? God, Mom, is this too Cinderella? Is it all too cheesy to believe in?

This staircase offers a place for future photoshoots to occur. "Endless Dusk, that's the color I'd name these walls. And I like the way they transform into a tranquil foggy blue-gray mist, among the clouds," I said.

"Wow, you made my house sound like heaven," Hayden said.

You know, Hayden, your eyes kinda match the gray-blue mist. You're heaven.

We paused on the stairs, standing side by side. "I kinda wanna run up and down the steps like a little kid for some reason," I said, chuckling.

Hayden stopped abruptly, looking at me with a lopsided grin. "Funny how you mentioned playing on the steps and running up and down them."

"You did that a lot?"

"Oh yeah." He said every word through a wide grin. "Crazy Drew convinced me one day to get on a blanket and pretend like it was a sled. So, laying on my stomach, he told me to hold on tight. I had fun for the first few times. Until he flew me into the banister headfirst coming down 'Drew's Ski Slope.'" Hayden pointed out the crash site.

"Aww. You poor thing. I can't believe your Dad let Drew play so rough with you."

"Well"—Hayden paused, grinning—"Drew waited until Dad got in the shower. Drew's the *fun*-but-also-*sneaky* brother. Dad often called him Dennis the Menace. Dad still calls him that some-times"—we giggled—"So, you're familiar with that character?"

"Yep. I bet Drew was and still is a handful then."

Hayden nodded his head, with wide eyes and a closed-mouth smile. Sitting down on the stairs, he gestured for me to join him.

"Sometimes, I think Drew and Dad seem the most alike—same weird sense of humor, both kinda outgoing and loud with high energy, good-hearted and fun, but both can be so temperamental at times."

"Oh, so you're quieter and more reserved, like your brother, Cole? Or maybe like your mom, even?

"I wish I knew if I were more like my mom. It's hard to ask those questions, you know?"

I nodded.

Hayden continued, "If you look at Cole as quiet and reserved, then I guess we've got more in com-mon than I thought. He's so much older than me, by almost twelve years. After everything with mom, I don't remember Cole being home much. Felt like he left us and went to college so fast. Cole's a good guy and all. Do you wish you had brothers and sisters?"

"Sometimes, I do. Hearing your stories about playing with Drew makes me wish I could've experienced something fun like that. But I also like knowing I had my mom and dad all to myself. Dad alone can be a bit too overwhelming and demanding of my time. We watch way too much news and play Constitution games." I buried my hands in my face, giggling. "Sorry, embarrassing, TMI." When I removed my fingers from my eyes, his smile greeted me.

Hayden pointed back to the banister, rubbed his head, saying, "Remember, brothers aren't always fun, but I understand your point of view. I wish I related to having Dad all to myself. But after I got older and Drew and Cole left, Dad got busier and busier with work. I just felt more alone."

"I'm sorry, Hayden."

"It's okay, now." Hayden quickly changed the subject, "Soooo . . . these Constitution games, wanna teach me how to play?"

"Nope," I said with my voice on the verge of cracking up. "Too embarrassing, too ridiculous, and it's way too nerdy for you to call fun."

"What? Why? I'm more intrigued if it's this freaking funny." Hayden poked me in the ribs. "Tell me." He scooted closer. My laughter remained contained. The situation still funny, but now I felt his body heat, including his eyes, which bored into me so hard they scorched me. So close, I could count his eyelashes. "Please, share your little game secrets." I watched his mouth move, his lips close enough to touch mine.

The US Constitution's the last thing on my mind, too far away to reach, with everything else so close. Somehow I pull myself together. "I'm going to win, Hayden. Will you be a sore loser?"

"Alright, you're gonna tell me how to play. No, I'm not a sore loser"—wearing a smirk, Hayden added—"except on occasion." He playfully shook my arm.

Just go ahead and put your arm around me if you wanna touch me. "Players take a sheet of paper and number it from one to twenty-seven. As quickly but also as accurately as possible, each player writes an abbreviated version of all twenty-seven amendments to the United States Constitution in order."

The corners of Hayden's mouth start twitching. He can't hide the edges of his lips as they pull higher and higher into full-on grin mode. "Yep. You win, Gretchen. I'm not even the least bit upset about it."

"Hayden, I can see you holding in all that laughter, you know." That does it. One more glimpse at each other, and we lose it.

Hayden grasped my arm, saying, "You've memorized *all* twenty-seven?"

I nod.

"Gretch, that's impressive. I knew you were smart, but dang, girl."

Sitting like this, so close to Hayden, I notice just how comfortable I am talking and joking about anything. Or nothing at all. And after all the time I spent dreaming, hoping, and praying for any kind of moment or chance to be invited inside Hayden's private world—it's happening. I'm in his home. More importantly, he makes me feel at home here, with him. My whole body goes to high-alert happiness. My face literally aches from smiling and laughing. It's tingling and feels a shade of pink from blushing. But I'm able to say, "Thank you."

"I always did think of you as a future president. Or I thought you might take over your dad's vet clinic—*Doctor* Gretchen?" I liked Hayden's flirty tone with me but also his willingness to know me as a person. His visions of the future me as president? Doctor? All those titles appeared in a positive light to him. I loved his confidence in me. Plus, Hayden seemed to be unintimidated by women in power.

I shrugged, saying, "One never knows Hayden. You'll have to share your plans for the future with me." We stood up, heading downstairs, and of course, I got us sidetracked by trinkets.

As we approached the last rung, I asked, "What's this *doodle-dee thing* called?"

"I called you doctor and president, and then you go using words like *doodle-dee thing*, Gretchen?" Hayden shook his head, chuckling at me. "You're clutching what's called a newel post cap." Hayden stared at the peculiar way I admired the cap. I wanted to touch every groove, but I wondered if I might look to be fondling the item. I released my grip. "It holds up the banister."

"In other words, it's part of a fancy post? The squared-off decorative cap provides intricately carved layers, helping to make it all pretty?" I asked.

"Something close to that, for sure, Gretchen," Hayden replied, smiling. "I helped Dad with the remodel."

"Cool. I'm amazed by you, Hayden."

"Thanks."

The *newels* rested on top of each post, in the corners, at the bottom steps, which curved out more extensively than the rest. I left the stairwell with a "come again" sentiment. At arrival, at the top of the landing, I'd received a big "welcome."

From the foyer, we heard the TV running inside the den. Gene was watching with a pillow crammed under his head, stretched out on the whole length of the couch. Hayden and I slipped through the kitchen and out into the backyard. I snagged the platter of cookies and icing, along with two bottles of water from the bar, as we bypassed it. Even as we stepped outside, the deck area embraced me in a hug.

"What? Hayden, you have a pool?"

"Yeah. No advertising, though. If word gets around at school, I might become too popular, and I couldn't handle all that." Hayden gave a slight chuckle, peeking a look at me.

"I understand."

"The pool's small. No diving board, slide, or special effects, but I still enjoy it. Since you know my backyard secret, come over and swim this summer."

"Okay, sounds fun." *Ugh, my hippy pale ass in a bikini with Hayden Tucker? On the flip side is Hayden Tucker wearing only swim trunks? Done!*

"Dad does home improvement projects around our house every couple of years. When I mentioned a pool, I never thought I'd see any follow-through. Ta-dah. My dad really surprised me by doing this. Cole and Drew call me a spoiled brat now. Oh, well."

I laughed.

Hayden tossed me a glance and said, "I wish it were warmer tonight. We could've jumped in. We already started preparing for winter. The pool will get covered soon." We walked around the perimeter of the pool, a basic rectangle in shape. Hayden reached for a stack of lounge chairs nearby but turned away.

"Hey, you want help setting up the chairs?"

"Oh, no, thank you. I think I've got an even better idea. Let's go this way." Hayden nodded toward the trees. Hayden placed his comforter near a small section of trees. It still offered reflections of the water. A full moon, chilly autumn night, millions of stars, and Hayden Tucker all combined.

He lounged back first, gazing at the sky, both his arms tucked behind his head. My heart played a game of hopscotch as I looked over at him. Like a copycat, I followed his move and laid on my back. With Hayden lying there so perfect, I enjoyed ogling him out of the corner of my eye. My stomach spun the waltz as my heart moved on from hopscotch and started pounding out the tango.

I continued to follow suit, staring up toward the same sky. "All of it—so intense," I said, peering into the night. "Do you ever wonder what's out there? What lies beyond those stars?"

Hayden positioned himself so he could face me. He rolled to his left side, propping himself up with his arm. I turned into him to do the same. Under the blanket of the universe, Hayden Oliver Tucker and I shared the same moon and stars. Our bodies so close, I anticipated the warmth of his skin. As we inhaled and exhaled, our breaths circulated the same air. The whole wide world drifted away when Hayden's eyes locked down on mine. Inside this space, just big enough for Hayden and me was our own creation—our little universe.

"Most of the time, I think about the reason for pain and suffering. Then moments like this make me wonder if life connects us to people to help us unfold our destiny, you know?" Hayden said.

"Super powerful words, Hayden. Do you believe in heaven, though?"

"Hmmm?" He let out a puff of air from deep in his lungs. I studied him as he closed his eyes, pausing. He sucked in a new breath. "I'm not sure how to answer that honestly, Gretchen. I guess I do believe in something bigger than us, something watching over us, helping us, guiding us. I think there are good and bad powers in the world. But I still waver on the whole God-and-faith thing. It's more of not liking the religious labeling people get hung up on that I don't like, not the kindness behind it all. You know, I like the fact that at the core, good can—and does—often win over evil. How 'bout you?"

"I like your answer a lot. I believe in something, too, I guess. Not sure at the moment what *that* something is, though." I reached off the blanket, pulling a bunch of grass out of the yard and tossed it. "Hayden, I know I started it, but would it be okay if I completely switched the subject now? I think I may have gotten us too deep in a subject."

"Sure. What else is on your mind?"

"Well, let's go over this number forty-one business." I traced the outline with my fingers on the #41 patch sewn on his letterman jacket I was wearing. "I don't understand much about football. Explain why you're a tight end. Oh, and why you wear this specific number."

Hayden placed a hand over his heart. As he fell backward to the comforter, he said, "I'm crushed that you don't follow football." He pulled himself back into a sitting position, saying, "Just kidding."

Scooting closer, he realigned himself, until his eyes directly lined up to look into mine. As he spoke, I could see the outline of his lips in the darkness, feel each word he spoke as puffs of air against my cheek, and I imagine some letters falling to brush against my lips. "Football players are numbered by the positions they play on the field. As a tight end, I had the chance to choose a number in the forties."

He fumbled around, reaching for the bottled water on the ground near us, took a few swigs, swallowing hard. Hayden cleared his throat before he continued. "I've never shared this part of my story with anyone before. No one but you will hear this information. My mom died when she turned forty-one. Ugh, do I sound nutty saying this?"

"No. I understand it." I reached for him. My arm stretched only inches to him. His wrist I touched immediately. It was just there. With such ease, I could have grabbed his hand and interlocked our fingers together. I longed to weave or lace my fingers with his. The realization of our closeness startled me. Under the stars with Hayden Tucker, Mr.

Forty-One, tonight, I lounged on his blanket, wearing *his* jacket as "Miss Forty-One."

"You know, you should become my cheerleader," Hayden said, out of nowhere.

Hayden, WTFDD, did you just say?

I sprang straight up. My brain processing only one function: a mental image of Lilly's lips all over Hayden. Memories of Lilly crept up, I heard her saying, *"Just because Gretchen's mom is dead, it doesn't give her the right to steal yours. . . ."*

With my arms in the air, hands spiraled into fists, both of them flew into a rigid formation. I performed a cheer: "Ready. Okay. Hee. Hee. Hee. Look at me. I'm Miss Fakery, Lilly P. Rah, rah, ree. Come watch me: Crotch shot! Crotch shot! Wiggle, wiggle, down. Yippee. Now I'll do spirit fingers."

Wearing extra-small Christmas underwear cutting into my thighs and everything *in between*, I ended my heated tirade. I even mimicked extra spirit fingers, along with a mock high kick. I flopped back down to the blanket, finishing the whole scene by swatting toward Hayden's arm once I caught a single glimpse of his approval rating.

Hayden fanned me before exclaiming, "Whoa. Go, Gretchen. You just performed the all-time best Summerfort Eagles cheer. I mean the greatest I've ever heard or seen in my entire life. You should try out for the team. You know, you should stand and demonstrate that again for me. Dang, girl. That will go down as the best birthday gift ever."

I nudged and poked him in the ribs. But he only started laughing harder, to the point he had tears rolling down his face.

"Hayden!" I kicked in his direction.

"So, what I hear you saying"—he can never stop tee-hee-hee-ing before getting a full word out, but he goes on—"I guess you're not a big Lilly fan?"

After he got the final words out, he laid on his back, tapping his feet on the comforter, still cracking up at me. He received a light shove, plus a playful tap to the arm.

"No. I'm not a fan of hers. Oh, but I overheard you are. Actually, you *really* like her!" I scoffed. I crossed my arms in front of me, pulling my legs up, getting into a position, so my head rested in hiding on my knees.

"What?" Hayden sobered up from giggling. He vaulted up, steadied himself by placing a hand on my back, leaving his hand to rest there. Face-to-face, the starin'-and-glarin' match began.

"Well, rumor has it, Hayden, you sucked face with Lilly at some back-to-school-sports party."

"Gretchen. No, I didn't. Did Ding Dong Darcy tell you this crap?"

A shrug is the only reply I could muster. I thought I might blubber if I tried words—or much else. My eyes filled with hot sea salts. The liquid pooled and hung in place, on the verge of a free fall.

"Wanna know what really went down, Gretchen?"

"Yep. I guess." I amazed myself with my ability to utter anything through clenched teeth. Hayden's mouth locked onto my upper lip. Out of nowhere, a simple little kiss. But the power of it awakened me. My whole body desired more. He pulled away from my mouth but stayed close by. I hoped he meant it as an intermission and not the ending.

"See? Do you understand now what Lilly did to me? That's how she did it. I got blindsided. Plus, she did it all on a dare. Only a peck. I didn't give in. I didn't even enjoy it. In fact, it meant zero, nada, nothing." Hayden created double zero symbols using both his hands. After, he raked his fingers through his hair, sighing.

"Hayden, what if I dared you to do that again?" He leaned into me, reached up with the back of his hand, stroking my cheek. Hayden pulled me as close as possible into him, wrapping me into his arms. Cross-legged, we sat, on the ground, encased, adjoined as close as two bodies could get and yet still breathe. We remained, spending several moments spellbound.

"I can feel your heart beating," he whispered, rubbing and patting my back to the tempo. "Thump. Thump. Mine's strumming so fast too," Hayden murmured. He placed my hand over the top of his, so I could feel his heart. We interlocked our hands. Holding Hayden's hands sent a voltage through me. My scalp tickled, my skin formed goosebumps, my mouth ached, my body throbbed, my cheeks burned red-hot, and even my toes curled. Hayden awakened every part of me.

Hayden floated toward me. No dares. He longed to and chose the moment too. First, feather-like kisses touched the back of my hand, then forehead. Next, he arrived at my nose. Hayden grazed the tips of each earlobe. He pulled each of them into his mouth with the tiniest nibble. I anticipated touching his ears the same way. I ran a hand through his hair, finding my favorite wayward curl, and caressed. Soon, I longed to return the exact favor— taste Hayden's ears with my lips and tongue. As he explored, a moan escaped from me. In his hot, breathy voice, he asked, "Is this okay?"

I reached around his waist, squeezed him tighter, nodded my head, waiting for more. My mind entered a euphoric state, lost inside a dream coming true. And, finally, he leaned in to capture my bottom lip. My own lips parted to meet his, so greedy to learn.

Hayden kept his arms wrapped around me, like a halo. While next to him, the solidness of his body, his warmth, every bit of his being, safeguarded me. Among layers of blue—the darkest sky, Hayden's eyes, a picnic blanket upon the ground the world gifted a miracle.

At the moment, I believed in God, heaven, and the universe again. When I glanced beyond the stars, beyond my grief, I wondered if you could see me, Mother. If so, were you overjoyed for your child? Because my heart exploded and shattered into a thousand pieces, Mom.

With each embrace, each kiss, stitches of my soul mended. I thought, maybe, with enough love in my life, one day, I might grow up with the ability to live a fulfilling life without you.

Chapter Ten

September 30, 2019

Hey, Ma,

Well, it's your birthday boy. Leave it to your husband to produce a light show SOS code from the back porch during my "studying" party. Like, Gretchen and I were lost in a full-fledged moment—our eyes-closed—but our lips, tongues, hands, and face were open for business.

"Ugh." I pulled away from Gretchen, the girl I not only dared to openly communicate with tonight but also finally kiss. *Really* kiss. "What's happening, Dad?" I asked.

"It's now 11:30. Remember, Doc Gardener said he'd be here about midnight. I have something for you before Gretchen leaves."

"No problem." I huffed, stalling long enough to draw Gretchen back into me for another hug. She scanned my face. Was she sizing up my expression?

Blinked her eyes and gnawing at her bottom lip, Gretchen smirked. Our eyes locked, washing away the awkwardness from Dad's interruption. The corners of her mouth lifted into a full-on smile.

I dissolved. My eyes closed, my hands cupped both sides of Gretchen's face, and before I knew it, I padlocked on to those happy lips. Did I care if clocks struck 11:30? Suspended animation, if such a thing, another birthday wish. I desired to remain inside this date in time. In fact, I wanted to stay, right there, under the universe of stars, at that juncture.

Mom, I was the happiest I've been in a very long time. With Gretchen, my body, my heart, my head—all free, and I experienced similar feelings to the six-year-old little boy who longed for home, but he found a place to belong, Ma. With her, I sense "home" because I can relax and be myself. I pulled Gretchen from our blanketed planet and back into the real world. My fingers laced with hers. We walked back inside, our arms swinging in time together.

"Surprise!" Dad yelled. With the lights dimmed, Dad lit the number fifteen candles and placed them on top of an ice cream cake. The biggest surprise came from Drew and Cole because Dad arranged to Skype with them over the phone and laptop. At the same time, (or as close as possible) as Dad, Cole, and Drew also shouted, "surprise!" Then everyone got through a horrible rendition of "Happy birthday to you." After the second attempt, the laughter erupted, and the song thankfully ended. I surveyed the room. Everyone important in my life was present, wishing me a happy birthday. Everyone but you, Mom.

"Next, I'll have you blow out the candles and make a wish," Dad said, smiling. He stood right next to me, on my left, and Gretchen to the right. The laptop and phone sat on the bar, angled down, viewing the whole scene.

Across the room, your apron hung. My heart ached and broke, recalling birthday cakes had been your specialty. Six homemade birthday cakes shared with my mother. To your little boy, number six just isn't enough to last an entire lifetime. Now, I lived trapped inside those photos and memories. A frosted-faced little boy who *had had but lost* a mother.

I managed to smile and be grateful for all Dad had done for me. He arranged so many things like purchasing food and cake. Topping off the night by allowing one special guest to attend. Also, he added other surprises, like my brothers singing happy birthday. Plus, Dad's behavior throughout the night earned him a decent score. Maybe I should subtract for the freaking wink when Gretchen arrived and the SOS light show interrupting my lip-locking? ☺

To stand in a place of excitement, happiness, and joy as emptiness persists remained overwhelming. I hoped my face didn't convey the expression of my mixed emotions—how does one show gratitude, anger, depression, grief, happiness, and confusion all at the same time? *My mother's not here. But I'm happy Gretchen's finally here. I'm grateful, Dad, Drew, and Cole care. I feel like bawling or bailing, but I keep on smiling. The smell of vanilla sickens me.*

Part of me wanted to run and hide in the pantry nearby and weep. I wanted to scream, *"The person responsible for this birthday's gone! My mother's dead!"* The boy who forever remains inside me longed for his mother to hold him. The aroma of my mother's cinnamon and vanilla, I craved. Her arms, which once rocked me to sleep or hugged me—I wanted to rest against them at least once more.

At my football, basketball, and baseball games, I wanted to grow up with her ass in the bleachers, listening to her voice cheering me on. Inside the pantry door, I needed her hands marking off my height chart. At the dinner table, I yearned for a typical family—all our chairs full and my mother toasting buttery treats with cinnamon in the mornings. Evenings, I desired to peek into the living room, den, or bedroom, and see my parents together, sitting or lying next to one another in bed or on the couch. Mother—life at five years old included my only years of unified normal—T-ball, toy cars, family celebrations, two brothers, two parents—those days now gone.

So, I stood, about to shed waterworks, like a child, but I didn't give a damn. Vanilla ice cream played tricks on my mind, swirling a gentle Mommy-like scent into the air. Dad said, "Blow out the candles; make a wish." I complied, forcing a smile.

My one wish for Gretchen fulfilled, I reached over and touched her pinky finger. I might have wished for my mother to be alive, but my dream for you needed to end. Since the age of six, I laid in bed on the night of each of my birthdays, hoping against hope my mother would come back. At fifteen, I must abolish this wish as this achievement is an impossibility upon this earth.

Gretchen received a text from her dad. She showed me her phone. "Sorry, kiddo. In ER w/dog. Ask Gene—need to call a taxi? Or, ok, if I run 30-45 min. late? DON'T WALK."

"Dad, Gretchen's dad sent a text. He's got an emergency vet call on a dog. Can she stay later—an extra thirty to forty-five minutes? Or do you want him to call for a taxi?" I asked on Gretchen's behalf.

"Of course she can stay. I hope the dog's okay. Let Doctor Gardener know we're up late tonight. I can take her home if he can't get here in an hour. Update me. Let me know what's happening with the dog."

"Thanks, Dad."

"Gene, I'm sorry. Thanks for understanding." Gretchen said, near whimpering, like me. *Good grief, what a party, I thought. It's my party, and I'll cry if I want to.* That thought made me smile. And the fact I'd earned more Gretchen time.

"Gretchen, no problem at all. You and Hayden eat cake and continue with your fun."

"Oh, Dad just sent a text to say its Miss Garcia's dog, Poco. He swallowed something blocking his airway. A minor surgery's required."

"Well, I'm glad your dad thinks the problem's minor, Gretchen. Don't worry. Go enjoy."

After we nibbled on the cake, Gretchen and I chose the darkness of the front porch rocking chairs. Mom, I remember Dad told me once that you picked out the color red for the door, and Dad found the matching rockers to compliment the décor. It makes me think about how Gretchen gets me, like Dad understood you, Mom. You looked out for each other.

"I'm sad about Miss Garcia's dog, Poco," I said, reaching for Gretchen's hand. Without hesitation, she nested her fingers with mine. "Hope he's going to make it."

"Dad's cautious. He won't perform surgery without hope for the animal's survival."

"I'm glad. Also glad for more Gretchen time." I gave her hand a shake with a little extra squeeze.

"Me too." Gretchen smiled. Not an everyday smile, the beaming extraordinary. She reached places deep inside me, reawakening hope. A full moon, along with a sky full of stars, made

Gretchen's eyes easy to capture with my own. Eyes unafraid of staring directly into mine. Studying my face for clues, Gretchen asked, "What did you wish for tonight, Hayden?"

Without much thought, I chuckled, thinking in my boyish evil ways. But I answered with diplomatic truth, "You, Gretchen."

"Me?"

"Yes."

"Explain what you mean." She draped herself far over the arm of the rocker in my direction.

"Well, if I go by a checklist of wishes, let's mark off wish number one: A girl named Gretchen showed up to study with me, but we decided to party instead, even though she brought her best 'studying' materials, fun occurred."

"Good answer, Hayden." We laughed, pretending to question each other about *Animal Farm*. I gripped her hand, which still clung to mine. "Provide me the sheep's motto while speaking in a British accent," Gretchen said.

"I used this line to rope you in on this date, but I never dreamed you'd make me perform for you," I stalled and stammered before stating the lines— "Four legs good; two legs bad. Four legs good; two legs better."

I spent a lot of time giggling my way through each part of the whole event. Gretchen leaned even further over the arm of the rocker, initiating a hug, but instead, I received an unexpected kiss.

"Whisper the words, Hayden."

"Four legs good; two legs bad," Gretchen *loved* British Hayden. She rewarded me with clapping, hugging, and kissing. My life slipped again into so much perfection. I started growing quiet with worry.

"Happy birthday. You sure everything's fine?" Gretchen *eased* into the zone.

"Of course." I considered Gretchen's truth-seeking eyes, her concerned smile. From her expression, I assumed she longed to say more but refrained. A gleam of fear appeared because she worried saying the wrong words on my birthday?

Checkmate. My appearance so hollow to Gretchen. She peers through each delicate layer of me. With her head tilted, is she anticipating my shortcomings as needs? And summoning the strength to express herself?

"On my birthday, my mood sometimes turns odd. I'm just checking on you, Hayden." Gretchen's eyes dampened, so mine headed in the same direction. I knelt beside her rocker. After what seemed like a long minute, I stood up, reaching for Gretchen's hand, slowly pulling her from the rocker and into an embrace.

I choked down and blinked back pain, even swallowed hard. Gretchen deserved honesty.

Most of my words probably felt and sounded like mumbled groaning in Gretchen's ear. Leaning into her, I tried saying my peace. "Every year, all these signs, the same weirdness. The aches never cease. Those 'Missing Mom' emotions all get fired up and triggered. I admit, celebrating birthdays without her cramps up my happiness. Gretchen, I feel like such a kid sometimes. I grasp, trying to accept the fact she's gone, not able to return, but I can't change or fix anything." Hard as I fought back, my eyes wouldn't obey.

"I understand. I get it, Hayden. I experience those 'Missing Mom' things too."

Arm in arm, her head on my shoulder, we attempted making sense of our grief. I kissed her again because her mouth controlled a magical realm with an ability to evaporate the negative energies surrounding the world. I realized kissing only solved tiny portions of sorrow. A person cannot hold up the entire universe for another. To think like that is unhealthy. For a moment, however, my lips went numb, my body surging alive, tingling all over.

My emotions felt raw but understood. Overwhelmed, my eyes flooded. In the quiet moments, fresh tears slipped. "What can I do to help you, Hayden?"

My voice cracked, chin grew jerky. I stuttered, "I don't know. I miss my mom. I wish I had enough courage to take flowers to her grave and talk. I hate the cemetery. It's crushing." By gulping down breaths, I withheld more sobs. My head rested on Gretchen's patient shoulder.

Chapter Ten

We stood, propped against the front porch banister. Gretchen's head rested against my chest, near my heart. "Our moms take a ton of courage to talk about, Hayden. You're the most courageous person I know. I admire you every day. You're one of my favorite people in the world."

"Thanks, Gretchen." I hugged her. "I think the same of you."

She's never judgmental of me. Gretchen calls me Hayden. In all the years I've known her, she's never participated in the name-calling. Just Hayden—because that's who I am. Not Hardly Speaks Hayden, Momma's Boy Hayden, or Queer AF Hayden. My shyness and loner tendency don't offend her. If anything, she knows where I'm coming from, knows more of my backstory than anyone. When I'm ready, I'll tell her *everything*.

I might only be fifteen, Ma, but I'm thinking, maybe, I really do understand some deep concepts of love? Gretchen likes tough, sporty Hayden and Momma's Boy-Crybaby Hayden. Gretchen's the one person who recognizes, plus accepts, the six-year-old boy hiding behind the muscles of a teenager turning into a grown man. She knows all these people. Gretchen understands he's all one person, and regardless of which person the daggers are aimed at, his heart breaks just the same. Gretchen's kindness outshines everyone.

"Hayden, I'll go to your mom's grave for you."

"Thanks, but—"

Gretchen placed her finger to my lips, silencing me. She continued tracing the outline of my upper lip, before meeting her mouth with mine. Our eyes dried. Things heated up again. White noise from Dad's TV in the den faded. Gretchen and I blurred into our little universe. We stood, swaying on the front porch as a combination of old souls, young fools, and two childlike hearts dancing on the mend. All of us sharing a moment under the same starry sky.

A text from her dad interrupted us. "Be there in about fifteen minutes." Gretchen showed me the phone with a pout before replying.

"I hate leaving. Thanks for '*studying*' with me tonight." Gretchen nudged me. We both giggled, and as she reached for the doorknob, I grabbed her before she pushed the door. Wrapping my arms around her from behind, I pulled her to me. With her hair lifted, I kissed the back of her neck, exploring new territory. She squeaked with approval. She spun around. "Hayden, not fair."

Gretchen planted another kiss, a lingering one with a slight suck and nibble to my bottom lip. "Like that awesome kiss, just a second ago when you ravaged me? You labeled it fai—?"

Lights hit us as we stumbled back inside. Gretchen blushed the moment she registered Dad's voice calling to us from the kitchen. We stopped in our tracks. I didn't even finish my mumbling question to Gretchen. "Hey, you two, I made Gretchen and her dad a plate of birthday goodies, so we don't overindulge all night and weekend, Hayden," Gene said.

"Thanks for having me, Gene. I'm sorry for the extra delay. Dad said, Poco recovered. He texted to say he's on his way now."

"Come back again soon. We enjoyed having you."

I walked Gretchen back outside to wait. We sat on the front porch steps, hand in hand. I desired more of her neck and some more of her lip-nibbling action. *Gretchen, what have you done to me, Love Spell Queen?* Her dad's headlights approached. She stood, removing my jacket. I said, "Nah. Keep my coat tonight. Gives me an excuse to arrange a plan for tomorrow?" I threw her a smile.

At fifteen, who am I? Sometimes an old soul, a little boy, a grown man. A much more brazen Hayden emerged today. Perhaps, I'm more willing, ready, or even capable of being myself and speaking up. Ma, I like who I am with Gretchen. I love the idea of being me. With her, I allowed my vulnerable side to shine, which required a lot of inner strength.

To quote Dad: "I think I wanna be her Huckleberry."

Chapter Eleven

October 2019

Dear Mom,

The "study session" at Hayden's house equaled success. Tonight (today, I guess), I came home with my mind swarming. Hayden is officially fifteen. Mr. Hayden Oliver Tucker (Hot Boy) invited me to an impromptu birthday party. Now, I can't sleep. I'm still too giddy. My lips still tingle when I close my eyes and think of Hayden. I don't think I could ever see enough of that boy. Since the party side of things caught me off guard, I didn't take a gift.

I decided I should design him a homemade birthday card from some of my scrapbook supplies. I used sparkly numbers to create the number forty-one, his football number. Plus, I found a few stars and a moon, which reminded me of the night sky. Instead of writing out "Happy Birthday," I picked colorful puffy stickers to use in my A-Z poem I wrote. Let's hope my sentiment isn't too overwhelming. I don't want to scare him off, but I think he might enjoy my thoughtful gift. For me, taking the chance is worth the risk as long as I can see Hayden smile *that* smile.

Dear Hayden,

I hope your birthday was all you imagined. Thought about what to get you, and I came up with a few crazy A-Z thoughts on the matter. Wishing you many smiles.

Happy Birthday,
Gretchen

Animal Farm notes disguised as a date
Bashful birthday boy (oh, not really)
Cookies, cakes, and endless party treats
Disastrous cheer that ended in fun
Elaborate schemes, backyard of dreams
Football fans, I'm a cheerleader for #41
Gold-trim wrappers, Godiva dark truffles
Happy Birthday Skyped song surprises
Icing shared across our hands and faces
Jackets wrapped 'round me in warmth
Kisses ignited; two mouths set ablaze
Light shows from stars, full moon, and Gene
Moments surrounded in heart-pounding hugs
Nighttime noteworthy study session for sure
Over and over, the kisses and laughter spilled
Picnic blanket transported us to "France" (oh
    la la)

Quince (15) candles lit up to make a wish
Rah rah ree! What a night for me
Swaying together, starry-eyed embraces
Tucker's house, tender moments to pass our
    pain
United States Constitution facts, us hand in
    hand
Vanilla frosting, ice cream, kisses, Vet (ER)
    situations
Wowzer, thanks George Orwell for *Animal
    Farm*
X-tra special moments, too numerous to count
You and me, a night I wish would last forever
Zoom—our time together flew by much too
    fast

When I woke up, I greeted October with a happy jack-o'-lantern grin. Last night flooded back to me. All those memories were fresh in my mind. With my fingertips, I touched my lips. Yes, it happened. I kissed and kissed and kissed Hot Boy last night. Hayden's jacket served as a comforter for me, all night long. I did not stir in bed, toss, nor have nightmares. Nor did I lie there overanalyzing my world in a list of worries. I slept.

Dad pounded on my bedroom door. "Gretchen, what's happened to you?"

"I'm up." I staggered to the door and peeked out with a smile. "Hey, Dad," I said, in a sing-song Saturday voice. There seemed a dreamy, hangover tone quality about me. Although I've never actually been drunk, I could imagine it might be this brain-swarmy-squishy feeling I now experienced. Happy party thoughts from living in the moment of fun, but a loopy wobbly mind also that needed private, quiet time to process everything said, done, and experienced the night before.

Dad looked at me with a quizzical stare, his eyes darted around my room, and his one eyebrow raised. "Gretchen, do you want to contact Gene and Hayden to invite them to a thank you barbeque later this afternoon?" I stood in my doorway, leaning against the doorjamb with a blank expression, absorbing Dad's words before they registered.

"Like, today?" *Dad inviting people over?* I stayed leaning, eyes half-closed, against my door frame, dumbfounded.

"Yes, today. The weather's supposed to cooperate. Is today unacceptable? I thought we liked the Tuckers?" Dad coughed as if to make me open my eyes. "They were so kind to allow you to stay late, and I want to thank them. We can extend Hayden's party into today even." Dad paused, smiled down at me, and gave me one of his "well, what do you say" kinda looks.

"You knew it was Hayden's birthday?" I asked, confused.

"Gene and I talked about it early in the week. Gene called me, explaining Hayden's wishes for a very low-key, private birthday. As your dad, Gene wanted me to be well aware of the situation. I've known Gene for a very long time, Gretchen. Not that long ago, Gene helped me out with a quick repair on the roof of the vet clinic."

"Oh, okay," I said. Dad offered me a high five. That gesture seemed unlike Dad/Doctor Gardener, but I complied. Maybe it suited happy, fun John but not so much the doctor.

"Tell them I'll grill steak, chicken, hamburgers, and/or hotdogs. Come tell me which they prefer. I'm thinking of a late lunch, around 3:00 o'clock, if that's not a problem for them. I bet Gene takes calls on Saturday sometimes."

"I'll let you know, Dad." I glanced at my wall clock: 10:30. "Oh my gosh!" I pointed, my hand slipping to cover my mouth.

"Yeah. You slept in."

"I'm so sorry, Dad. I told you last night I'd help you feed the animals this morning." My eyes got wide when I looked at him.

Dad held up his hand and said, "Ah, its fine." But, then, he did a little finger spin, nitpicking about my various piles of stickers, dirty clothes, unmade bed. "Take care of this, and this, and this, and all of that—if they can make it, please. You're usually Miss OCD Queen." He laughed at me.

"I guess I just got too tired, Dad."

"Looks like a princess party bus wrecked in here." Dad wrinkled his forehead before closing the door. "Remember, I need a decision on the barbeque."

I rummaged through my pieces of scraps, located a section of blank paper, sketching out the script of my phone call: *Hello. Mr. Tucker. This is Gretchen. My father would like to invite you and Hayden over for a barbeque at three o'clock today to thank you for allowing me to stay late at your house. We are sorry for the last-minute invite, but Dad said the weather is going to be nice today. He's offered to grill steak, chicken, hotdogs, or hamburgers. Do you have a preference? We hope you can accept the invite.*

Aside from a stutter of "Um, Mr. Tucker, um, I mean, Gene," I believe my call reigned as a success. It ended with Gene saying, "Thank you, Gretchen. Tell your dad we don't expect this, but we will be honored to come over. We're not picky at all on food. Please tell him to cook any of the foods he enjoys most. See you at three o'clock."

~~~BBQ~~~

"Come on in." I opened the door, welcoming Gene and Hayden into the entryway. They arrived with Hayden carrying an armful of items.

"We brought some leftover birthday treats— some cookies, cake, plus a *new* bag of spicy Doritos and a bag of dark Godiva chocolates," Hayden said.

"Gene, are those Godivas for you?" I asked. We chuckled as I led them through the house toward the backyard.

"Ah, everything smells great out here," Gene said, as soon as I opened the French doors leading into our screened-in porch and patio areas. "Hello, Doctor Gardener." Gene reached for Dad's hand.

"John's fine. I'm informal around here." Dad sat his spatula down to extend his hand. He motioned for Gene and Hayden to sit down and make themselves at home. "Help yourself to a drink over on the picnic table. Thank you for bringing so many extra treats."

Instead of Dad choosing one or two meat options to grill, Dad had selected all four: steak, chicken, hotdogs, *and* hamburgers. As our sides, he roasted zucchini, squash, potatoes, and corn—overkill. However, our patio setup appeared welcoming. Dad bought the rectangular, thick paper plates, with the dividers. He had splurged on aqua Solo cups and napkins with a fall design, and he used matching platters and bowls to display some of the foods. Dad planned to create the main food table, next to the house, in a buffet style. From the vet clinic, Dad borrowed a narrow card table, and to complete the mission, he covered it with a tablecloth, making it look "outside" elegant.

"Dad, can I show Hayden around?" Dad nodded yes, as he took a swig of his drink hidden by the sleeve of his Gardener Vet koozie. Dad always acts weird about drinking in front of me. He'd blended a small batch of some slushy adult beverage for him and Gene. Big deal, Father—*only* drink behind my back. I'm not sure if Dad's trying to set an example for me by not drinking or what? He didn't have to be weird and secretive all the time about alcohol. He's over twenty-one, and I'm not carding him. It's not like he's an alcoholic or anything. Besides, Prohibition was Amendment Eighteen and got repealed by Amendment Twenty-One. You taught me that, Dear Dad.

Once inside, Hayden bit his bottom lip, smiled at me, and went in for a hug. His heart pounded against my chest. My own heart palpated. As he pulled away, he looked me in the eye, his mouth inching closer and closer to mine. I longed for him to kiss me again like he did last night. Thank God, some wishes come true.

"Hey," he said when we pulled apart.

"Hey." I grinned. "I'm ready to give you a quick tour now." I pulled him along. "Here's the dining room. We rarely eat in here. We usually sit on the couch or at the kitchen bar." I'm rambling, both out loud and in my mind:

No need to linger. I HATE this room. It's like a vacuum that sucks all the childhood joy from my memory bank. This place reminds me of how much my mother loved me, but that she's will never again sit in her place at the table. At that chair, right over there. This room screams at me: empty, alone, gone, dead! Happy Birthday. . . .

Grabbing his hand, I led him into the hallway, up the stairs, doing a brief tour with finger-pointing, saying, "Here's one of our spare bedrooms, a bathroom, and Dad's master bedroom." And I pulled him into my room.

Whimsical accessories scattered around my room, which included peacock-feathered floor lamps in shades of aqua. Mirrors bejeweled in various hues of blues around the edges. "Looks like an aqua princess lives here," Hayden said, glancing around at my all-white furniture. First, at my full-sized canopy bed, which lacked in storage. Then, my white matching desk, dresser, and nightstands completing the set.

"Kind of 'Under the Sea.'" I fidgeted with my hands, licked my lips, trying to think of something halfway intelligent to say. "Soon, I guess I'll need to reconsider. Maybe do an upgrade?" I shrugged. "Hey, I wanted to ask you and your dad, can you guys create a storage system, like yours, for my bed?"

"I bet we could do that." Hayden sized up the room, measuring the length and width of my bed with his eyes. I studied him, amazed at how his mind worked. I offered my desk chair for him to sit down in while I lounged across my bed. He continued to take inventory of my room, even snapping mental photographs, I think. Hayden possessed strong capabilities at mixing business with pleasure, I realized.

"This is what I'm going to tell my dad I want for my birthday—a handyman to work on my drawers!" Sitting up, I covered my mouth before saying, "Wait. Double take! I better reword that, or my dad will *never* approve." We both started cracking up so hard.

"Oh, look over there, Hayden. I put something on the desk for you." He picked up the A-Z birthday card, held it up, tried to peek at the contents inside, shook it, and smiled *that* smile at me.

"Can I open it?"

"Yep."

After he read it, he stood up, reached his hand out for mine, and pulled me up, so I stood right next to him. "Wow. Thank you, Gretchen. You're so sweet and creative." He kissed the top of my head, forehead, nose, cheek, and mouth.

Dad called us out to the patio. Hayden nudged me with his elbow, smirking. "Should I be the one to ask your dad if I can work on your drawers?" We laughed about it as we walked to the backyard.

Quickly my laughter tapered. *Ugh, if anyone only knew my real daily "drawer" issue.*

The four of us enjoyed the barbeque and birthday leftovers. After our meal, I walked with Hayden, showing him our property. By taking him to a clump of trees in the backyard, I hoped to recreate the magic like our first night. We found a comfortable spot, beneath a weeping willow tree. When we climbed beneath it, leaned against its bark, it fits us. The willow branches formed an umbrella or a private oasis. After the small talk ended on how much food we ate, I plunged right into an important topic.

"Hayden, do you want to act normal at school? You know, friendly but quiet? Like, keep people out of our *friendship*? You know, like, not post pictures together online and stuff?" I waited, with my heart throbbing and eyes glued to his face. I searched his eyes for signs of an honest answer.

Hayden shrugged. "Well, I *guess* we could do that for now?" He slumped over, lost in a bit of confusion, I guess, going around with his thoughts. For a minute, Hayden swatted at a few willow branches, staring at the grass, as if these actions might lead to some answer. I didn't press or push him.

When he looked back at me, he said, "We have nothing hide, though. I think people already assume a lot about the two of us. Don't you?" He didn't wait for me to answer. Hayden rambled on in an agitated state. Not angry at me, but I could tell Hayden had something he needed to vent. I nodded my head, anyway, and let him continue.

"I mean, your ding-dong acquaintances/friends aren't too terrible, but maybe a bit too much into gossip. To play sports, which I enjoy, I'm stuck putting up with lame teammates who *tolerate* me, but then sometimes some of them call me the "*Momma's Boy who's queer AF.*"

This phrase Hayden mentioned for the first time made me cringe. I wanted to comfort him, but he went on talking, so I stalled. *Queer AF, this name-calling ate away at me.*

Hayden appeared clearheaded and willing to communicate his honest thoughts about the world, so I just took the time to listen. He used some exaggerated facial expressions for Hayden—fuller eyes, excessive hand gestures, mocking tones, but they all fit the emotions he expressed.

"We've been grouped together since we were kids. The people at school labeled us years ago: Those quiet, weird, goofy 'gay' grief kids. We struggled with all the sad scenario crap. And the bullying BS for years, Gretchen. Let's be done with it. To hell with all of them. The ignorance of people categorizing us as queer, gay, lesbian. Well, it's so rude and disrespectful to the kids at our school who do fight every day with those issues. I'm sick of it. A *big* part of me, like really, just doesn't give a damn about what people at school think anymore," Hayden said, ending with a sigh.

Sucking in a deep breath, he closed his eyes. I guess he gathered his composure before he could continue. Hayden motioned over to me. "Tell you what, if I get the urge to walk up to you at school, and I wanna hold your hand—because I bet I will— can I? I want to know I can count on you to go to events with me. Maybe, like, a game? Or dance? Or something in the future?"

I threw Hayden a hint of a smile and nodded my head with a tentative "yes," since I didn't know if Hayden's questions were rhetorical or not. With my eyes locked in on him, I observed his every move. He looked over at me, threw his hands in the air, saying, "Sorry, Gretchen. I'm done ranting. Like my favorite movie character, Forrest Gump, that's all I gotta say about that."

He swiveled around until he positioned himself in front of me, pulling me into him. Hayden burrowed into my shoulder before he whispered in my ear, "Uh, duh. I guess I'm trying to tell you I wanna be your boyfriend. Is that doable?" He asked.

I giggled, nodded my head, and of course, I celebrated with a kiss from my *boyfriend*! We took a few selfies: Hayden giving me a piggyback ride, a group shot with Gene and Dad, photos of the veterinary animals in the adoption area. One cat, in particular, loved Hayden. She perched on his shoulder, purred, and meowed sweet nothings to him the whole time we walked around with her. Hayden eventually cradled her in his arms, and she fell asleep. He spent so much time playing and petting her he wore her out. Once he placed her back in the cage, she woke up and cried for him. Standing up on her hind legs, she peered through the metal of the cage, stretching her tiny paw through the wires, and she swatted for Hayden to return.

Hayden looked at me, "What do I do? Her face looks so freaking sad." I didn't know who to feel more sorrow for—Hayden, the cat, or myself as I watched man versus animal in a sulking match.

Chapter Eleven

As soon as I opened the cage, Hayden's eyes grew wide and softened. The right side of his mouth perked up from his frown, and the left side soon followed. A toothy grin filled his face as he said, "Come here, little girl." *Is this boy for real? How can I fall any more in love?* She pranced back into his arms. Though I swear, she glared at me. "Can I show my Dad?"

"Like a picture?"

"Oh, okay. I didn't know if you could take animals out into your backyard?"

"Let's do the picture and invite our dads in here for safety?" I suggested.

"Dad and Gene come over and see our new friend. She's smitten with Hayden." I texted, attaching three pictures of the two of them: The cat nose to nose with Hayden. The cat curled on his shoulder, purring in his ear. And the cat, asleep in his arms.

Since the clinic is basically in the backyard, it only took Dad and Gene a few minutes to arrive after getting my photos. Dad showed Gene around and discussed the minimum spots we can keep open for adoptions.

Dad finally told Hayden and me the whole story: "This cat was abandoned on the side of the road recently. The mother cat got hit by a car, but the driver didn't bother to stop to save her kittens. Another passerby, near a Gene Tucker Construction work zone, spotted the furry critters and brought them into me, including this one, just the other day."

Dad peeked over at me, shot both eyebrows up in the air, grinning at me with the corniest smile, which caused his eyes to squint and placed his crow's-feet on display. This gave the dads away. Plus, it granted Dad an appearance exclaiming, *Gene and I already masterminded this whole shebang.*

"So, you two have been in cahoots?" I asked. They glanced at each other, grinned, looking back at me before shrugging. "You talked about Hayden's birthday, the barbeque, and the cats, for days?"

"Busted," Gene said.

Turning his glance to Gene, Hayden's smirk showed a bit of embarrassment, but his eyes looked surprised at his dad's efforts.

I walked over to Gene, planting a high five. "Aww, Gene. You softy. You save kittens' lives!" I added, "If we had any Godivas left, I'd reward you." Everyone laughed.

Gene pointed to the kitten, asking, "Hayden, you seem to like her. Is that the one you wanna adopt?"

"What?" Hayden's mouth fell open wide. "Dad, you're not kidding?"

Gene shook his head. "No joke."

"Yes." Hayden saddled up next to his dad, giving Gene a quick arm-around-the-waist side-hug. The cat purred for affection. She enjoyed how Gene scratched her under the chin.

"When your mom and I first got married, we owned a cat. Actually, the cat owned us." Gene stayed close with Hayden, continuing to share a moment with the kitten.

"Really? Dad, do you have pictures? I want to see."

"Sure. I'll find some old photos. Happy birthday, buddy." Gene tousled Hayden's hair and the cat's fur. "You'll have fun being a pet owner. They're lots of work, bud." Gene kept the smile on his face but pointed at Hayden and then to the cat in a serious manner. As he looked Hayden directly in the eye, he added, "I expect you to clean up after her and take great care of h—"

Hayden cut Gene off as he cuddled his new best friend. "I will, Dad." Already, just one day in, I slipped in status to girlfriend number two. As the kitten slept, Dad and Gene left us to contemplate name ideas. We made a list of possible names using an A to Z style, but we deviated terribly from keeping in any alphabetical order due to our disbelief and excitement.

"Let's consider her personality—playful, talkative, loves to purr," I said.

Hayden said, "She's cute with her pink nose, and I like her white paws like boots."

"Her fur has patches of orange, grays, and creams."

We kept an ongoing list, laughing at each other's ideas. Our system consisted of using random checkmarks, circles, and stars by the names in the running, and we drew lines through names we tossed out.

Hayden's Cat:
1.) Autumn for October
2.) ~~Callie for calico~~
3.) ~~Patches for fur~~
4.) Pumpkin Spice-Hayden loves the spice
5.) Boots for white paws
6.) Pinkie for nose
7.) Trixie for trick-or-treat Gretchen's fav.

Patches and Callie seemed cute, but cliché and ordinary to Hayden.

"Miss Spicy Boots Tucker!" Hayden announced, celebrating with an extra-tight hug.

Letting out a little snort, I said, "That's super sweet. The name's a little 'up next to the stage,' but I like the fun and perfect concept. It incorporates her fur, personality, and charm." I pushed back from the table, getting up to circulate, needing to check the adoption room one final time before we went back to join Dad and Gene.

I turned to walk toward the doorway to secure the adoption area, but Hayden touched my shoulder and spun me around. He met my gaze, his forehead resting on mine. His arms locked behind my neck. Hayden started with the lightest brush of his lips against mine. Then he did it once again. His feather kisses on the top lip and on to the bottom lip. He encompassed the scents of barbecue sauce, woodsmoke, October wind, and splashes of cypress cologne. My hands reached for his hair, as his fingertips cupped my face. I squeezed my hands down his arms and reached to caress the contours of his biceps.

"Ouch." He moaned, looking down. "Miss Spicy Boots." She had climbed his leg like a scratching post. I envied that cat for living my dreams and fulfilling my fantasies. Hayden made a desirable scratching post, indeed, Spicy Boots. I had an inside joke run through my head: Cat, don't get too greedy because you've gotta share him.

We discussed a way to post and tag our dads with our photos on Facebook and Instagram. Our caption: Family, Food, Fun, and New Furry Friends. The photo collage we designed included the picture with our dads at the BBQ, Hayden's #41 football birthday cookie, the selfie of us cracking up while Hayden's giving me a piggyback ride. The photo makes us both look deliriously happy— super toothy, with cheesy grins—even showing off the dimple on Hayden's cheek—it showed up if his smile happened to be wide enough. One of Miss Spicy Boots perched on Hayden's shoulder completed our collage. Four snapshots of pure bliss. Four opportunities where I'm part of a new normal. Four times spent in the company of people who treat me like I'm family: I mattered, I'm listened to, I'm understood.

Mom, would it be it okay if I had less guilt and tears since you weren't there? Or if I didn't question myself about all things? Like, what would Mom think, say, do, and feel? For example, "Would Mom like these napkins? What would Mom say about Dad grilling so much food? How would Mom react to her daughter kissing Hayden under the weeping willow tree, in the house, in the vet clinic, and in every stolen location possible?" Well, dang. Now, I'm crying a bit. Only, maybe these tears fit into the labels of joy, hope, and possibility?

Hayden and I flirted through texts late into the night. He thanked me again for my A-Z card. He already hung it up on his wall near his bed. I sent him a funny comment, something like, "Duh, I'm so glad I'm your g/f. That's all I've got to say about that." Our last texts of the night—sheer perfection. It belongs on a calendar featuring athletes and their kittens. Rugged sweetness is my title for it.

Hayden: Spicy Boots & I wanted to say goodnight. ☺ =^..^=

Hayden attached a photo. Dang! First, he's shirtless. Secondly, there's a little cat snuggled up against his bare chest. Too cute. Too hot.

Me: What an ab-tastic pic, dude. Remind me again, which one of you is Spicy Boots? Lol. ☺

Chapter Twelve

Early October 2019

Hey, Ma,

I don't have all the right words to better explain to you how my situation went down, but I wish I did. I also can't put a label on all the emotions behind my stupid actions. A lot about the story I can't piece together. My brain keeps wanting to forget, or my mind likes glossing the details out? Either way, I don't know.

"Momma's Boy Hayden, Queer as Fuck," started again in the locker room with Thomas Sharp's mouth. Sharp scrolled through Facebook, showing me Gretchen's page, "Have you hit that sweet ass yet, you fag?" I ignored him, but my heart thrashed, reaching near explosion— like a boom, it traveled into my ears, and the world started slipping and pivoting into mush. My legs wobbled out of my control, jumping up and down because my brain wanted to shut down. Tears and anger, I reserved, forced them back, with my lips twitching and jaws clenched.

Thomas Sharp continued scrolling, enlarging Gretchen's photos, gawking at her, as he pretended to perform sexual acts on her with exaggerated body movements and then added in his tongue. Sharp's comments and gyrations escalated, and I noticed background laughter. "You're still a freaking virgin, who's queer as fuck." The locker room roared. Some booed; some cheered. The noise blinded me.

"Fuck off, Sharp," I blurted, without much thought. Still, I sat on the locker bench, half-dressed in my football practice gear, staring at the floor, my legs jumpy.

"Yep. I always knew it, Tucker. You wanna fuck me rather than Gretchen." Commentary flew through the locker room. My hearing failed. The world blurred. Coach Ryan says he came running and screamed at both Sharp and me, "Sit down! Stop cursing!"

I remember my hands wound into fists, drawn, and ready at my side. At some point, I bounced off the bench. My mouth spewed words toward Sharp, I didn't care if I controlled them, and I'm not even sure of the exact stuff I yelled. I recalled my feet floating and sinking inside a quicksand-like substance, which turned into concrete. I fell backward but pushed forward, my back slamming into the edge of a locker.

With the taste of blood in my mouth, my senses regained. A throb surged through my hand, I guess from slugging Sharp? The corner of my lip burned, and when my finger touched the painful area, I discovered the cracked puffiness.

Overall, my soul hurt the most, surrendering numb. *What have I done? I'm a total ass-jerk. Dad will flip out. Gretchen will dump me. John will hate me. Coach will kick me off the team. The school's gonna throw me out. My grades may plummet. Seeking revenge, Sharp's plotting his next attack, digging up friends to help him.*

Human barriers: Coach Ryan, Principal Marshall, and Mr. Porter stepped in between Thomas Sharp and me. After sitting me back down, Coach Ryan preached. "You will be benched for the next game!" Coach stomped his foot like he still stood out on the football sidelines. He looked up at the ceiling, cupped his hands over his face, sighed, and walked in a complete circle. "I'm calling your Dad."

At the end of Coach's statement, I swallowed hard and choked down my heart. "Violence is not an option, Tucker." Coach clapped his hands into a murderous red, which matched his face through the "violence is not an option" speech. Three times he repeated himself, using his words as a mantra I better memorize. "Do you understand me, Tucker?"

"Yes, sir. I'm sorry. Please, give me a chance to talk to you in private and try to explain a few things. Please."

"Right now, I'm done dealing with you. Gather your stuff and get out of my locker room. Go wait in my office for your dad. We can talk when he gets here." Coach pointed me out the door. Thomas Sharp received the same foot-stomping, hand-clapping nonviolent speech from Coach.

Separation equaled an excellent thing for Sharp and me. The coach instructed me to his office. Ordering Sharp, he would soon go across campus to Mr. Marshall's office, where his parents would pick him up. Through the glass window of Coach Ryan's office, I viewed and listened to the whole scene. From the way Sharp favored his left eye and cheek areas—he patted at them—so I assumed I popped him good.

God, I'm so stupid. All I could do is sit and stew in Coach's office. I sent Gretchen a text, so she didn't gather exaggerated Ding Dong Darcy rumors and panic.

Me: Gretch, Sharp bullied me into fighting today. I feel stupid. I'm ok. I'm sorry. Bet I'm in lots of trouble. If Dad takes my phone, I'll find a way to talk ASAP.

Before Dad's arrival, I hoped texting him would soothe him, as well as smooth things over before our face-to-face encounter.

Me: Dad, please try to understand. I'm very sorry. This kid, Sharp, bullies me so bad. I'll explain everything. Please just listen when you get here. Please.

Crickets. Effing crickets. More effing crickets. My guts churned sitting in the silence, staring at my phone with no replies, just me, with my negative energies, and my stomach, which I thought might flip inside out.

The second Dad barged through the door, *dang,* I wondered, *why's his face so flushed? Why did Dad have Frankenstein veins popping out of his forehead?* Dad's ball cap, the one he wears on the job, sat on his head backward, meaning he meant business— I can see you, eye to eye, kid. I knew Dad must be way beyond angry. Dad plopped in the chair, inches from me. Next, he grabbed my face, examined my fat lip, sighed, and rolled his eyes, letting out some kind of hissing sound before he crossed his arms. Then he started speaking.

"Coach, I'd love to find out from my nonviolent son, a kid also selected for a sportsmanship award, why he's sitting here banged up."

In a less-than-friendly tone of voice, Dad asked, "Hayden?" He moved his arms, turning his palm up to motion to me. This signal or maneuver meant, "you have the floor, son—so, go—but—you—had— better—go—now, and watch what you say. Because it had better impress the hell out of me."

I wanted to barf. Tears created a murkiness for me, but I struggled through the burning urge not to cry.

Dad had to know. The coach needed to hear. I didn't have to hide this any longer. I didn't do anything wrong!

A cadence of constant pulsating pain with both my heart and lip occurred when I introduced my story. "Last year, during the end-of-the-year sports banquet, which the school hosted near Mother's Day, I became too emotional for the guys, I guess." I sighed, sucking in air, so I could continue. "All the guys planned to buy their mom's flowers to give out during the ceremony, but of course, since my mother's gone, I couldn't participa—"

I held up one finger, pausing for a breather before I could finish this part of the story. Dad touched my shoulder. My hands covered my face, and as hard as I tried stopping them, the falling tears won. Coach handed me a Kleenex, allowing me time until I considered myself ready to share the rest of the information.

"Okay. The time came from the end-of-the-year banquet, so I attended. Dad, your important projects were going on at work, on overtime, so I told you not to worry. I choose not to buy any flowers, so when they did the Mother's Day portion of the ceremony, I sat at the table alone, looking ignorant and unloved. A few guys caught me wiping away some tears. And after the banquet, the whole nickname, 'Momma's Boy Hayden, Queer as Fuck' began. I should've insisted you come to the banquet or bought flowers for y—"

"Stop. Hayden," Dad said. "You did *nothing* wrong. I should've been there: my son, my responsibility, my fault." Dad pointed to his chest. "You're *not* ignorant or unloved. I'm sorry." Dad rubbed my back. "Nobody *ever* has the right to call my son names, and *never* does anyone on this earth have the right to belittle my son's grief." Dad turned his attention to Coach. "Isn't that correct, Coach?"

"Yes. Sorry about your experience, Hayden. Had I known, I wouldn't have allowed such behavior. You're a solid team player. I care about you," Coach said. Dad blinked his eyes, looked toward the ceiling, and with a fist, he wiped at the corners of his eyes before pulled me into a full-on hug.

Dad placed his index finger at the edge of Coach's desk, providing a tapping mantra for Coach: "I want to be assured my child's going to be protected, while in your care at this school."

"I understand, Mr. Tucker." The Coach diverted the attention back on me. "Hayden, help us understand what sparked the issue at practice tonight."

"Something kinda similar, as always. This time, though, Sharp had Gretchen's Facebook page up, asking me why I wanted to still be a virgin. The verbal insults went on with Sharp saying I wouldn't have sex with girls because I wanted to fuck him and the whole 'queer as fuck' name-calling. Then he pretended to jerk off on Gretchen's face.

Plus, he talked about Gretchen. You know, stuff like giving him a blowjob. With his tongue hanging out, he pretended to lick photos of Gretchen on Facebook, acting like he was going down on her. Sharp said, 'I'm going to teach the queer-as-fuck virgin how it's all done.' The world got fuzzy because I had had enough. After all his antics, I grew sick of all the bullying. Sharp made me and continues to make me so furious. I hate people who want to be mean for no reason. I'm done putting up with it. I've had enough, I guess. I don't know. I don't deserve it. That's all I can tell you."

"Hayden, I would be agitated and angry too. Violence at school can never be condoned, however."

"I'm sorry, Coach. I don't recall who threw the first punch." I shrugged.

Coach shrugged back at me. "Hayden, I don't either. Half the team says you; the other half says Sharp. By the time I got right next to both of you, and with all the noise and nonsense, it was hard to determine who said what and what truly happened."

"Who cares?" Dad said. "My concern is for Hayden's safety and education. What type of punishment is he looking at here?"

"Well, I expect him to dress out, but he's going to sit the bench for the next game. The school's policy on fighting is out-of-school suspension for three days on a first offense."

"Can he still do schoolwork?"

"Most teachers favor helping students out. No guarantee all credit will be given."

Dad pushed his chair back, reached for the Coach's hand, and provided him a firm handshake. "Well, then, thanks for the info, Coach. Now that the school has a record of Hayden being bullied, I'm sure it won't happen again."

Dad knocked his knuckles on the Coach's desk. "I don't like the idea of having to think about taking legal action, you understand what I mean, Coach?"

"All things appear under control, Mr. Tucker."

"Oh, I hope so." A little whistle leaked from Dad. "Dr. John Gardener may not appreciate the fact his daughter, Gretchen, has been brought into this sexual harassment/ bullying scenario either. Thought I better provide you and the school with a little piece of advice, Coach."

Dad helped me gather my belongings—my two backpacks—one with my school-related books and the other crammed with bulky sports equipment. Once again, Dad turned back in Coach's direction. "Hayden shouldn't fight at school, and he will fulfill his punishment. Tomorrow, I'll run by the main office and collect all his work from Mr. Marshall. Please let him know."

"Will do, Mr. Tucker."

We cleared the door, where I dropped my backpack on the ground. I begged Dad for forgiveness. "I'm so sorry."

"Let's just go home. Right now, I'm at a loss for words, bud. I might've knocked the crap out of the guy, too, but it still doesn't make it right. Go. Get in the truck."

"Dad, do you plan on telling John? I don't want him to hate me. What if he doesn't let me date Gretchen anymore? What do you plan to do to me?" Loose pebbles in the parking lot provided temporary relief as I kicked at a few. Otherwise, I *felt* dragged alongside Dad as he marched across the lot toward the truck. *What comes next?*

"I'll call John and explain. He's an understanding person, and I think he will appreciate the fact my son defended his daughter." Dad said, situating things into the truck.

In the cab of the truck, Dad glared at me. "And as far as I go, my first thought in dealing with you, I wanted to brain you and confiscate your phone and all your electronics while grounding you. Not allowing you to see Gretchen for a while crossed my mind."

"Fine." I pulled my phone out of my pocket, tossing it to Dad. My eyes glazed over as I stared straight, looking through the windshield.

"Options changed, Hayden. After I considered everything—read your text, and then I listened to the whole story. Pick up your phone. All is well in our world, kid. Start telling me about issues, Hayden. I am *not* putting up with *any* of this bullying *sh*—crap—bud. How in the hell does someone crying at a public event due to the stress of grief turn into some kind of sexual sports hazing?" Dad slapped the steering wheel, asking with sadness in his voice, "Hayden, why didn't you tell me?" After my shrug, we drove the short distance home in silence.

After Dad pulled inside the driveway, I balled my hands into fists but kept my head down. "I never understood why they chose the whole 'queer as fuck' name!"

Dad's seatbelt unclicked. Reaching over, he pulled me to him, so I melted into him.

"Do you really wanna know why I didn't tell you?"

"Yes, I do, Hayden."

"Maybe it's because I didn't think you'd care. You seemed too busy with work to listen. Or I just didn't think you'd wanna hear it since it sounded so freaking stupid." Sobbing against Dad, my lip broke open, so my tears, snot, and blood mixed.

Dad used the bottom hem of his work shirt, wiping everything as he spoke.

"Stupid? Not one thing about my son Hayden is stupid. I hate that you feel this way. I care. I love you. You got that?" Dad pulled me into a hug.

Against Dad's shoulder, I nodded.

"I know I need to be a better dad." Dad squeezed me. "Let's *both* learn from this mistake. Hayden, treat this incident as one minor glitch. This fight doesn't define you. Let's go cuddle with Miss Spicy Boots, catch a movie on TV, and put the day behind us, my little troublemaker." Smirking, Dad said, "Hey, buddy, look up at me again."

"What?"

Dad asked, "Do you realize peach fuzz is growing on your precious *bloody* face?" He used a horrible British accent, making sure he emphasized the word *bloody*, of course.

"Dad! God, you're so weird sometimes. Yes. I shave now. I *borrowed* your stuff—sorry, I should've asked." Reaching for the door handle, Dad interrupted my plan to jump and bail. Dad sprinted around to my side of the truck to help me carry everything. First, he tossed my stuff to the ground because he went in for one of his bro hugs.

Together, we made it inside, dropping everything, including ourselves, at the bottom rung of the staircase. "I love you, Hayden. I'm gonna step it up as a father—be there for you, and all."

I nodded my head.

Playfully, Dad nudged me, "But not if you're gonna be stealing my stuff, though, dude. I'll buy you your own shaving gear, bud."

"Fine, Dad," I said, dragging out the words.

Dad grabbed my football helmet out of my bag. After he propped it on his head, cockeyed, he looked at me and yelled, "Wanna piece of me, Tucker?"

Laughter filled the stairwell.

My body fell against the banister. "Dad. Stop. You're so weird. I guess that's why I love you. Oh, I'm keeping your extra Cremo shave cream, your Quattro razor, and the cypress aftershave I already snagged."

"Deal." Dad smiled at me. "I realize it may not always be easy to talk about some things, but you gotta tell me about events, issues you're having, items you need, so I can help you. I care about my son, but I'm not a freakin' mind reader."

"I'm trying. Okay, Dad? But, to be really honest, I'm just now gettin' used to you actually being around more. Like, you're actually all about showing up? All about wanting to be involved in my life?"

A deep sigh escaped Dad. The sound hit my heart like an apology. "Hayden, I get the look you're giving me. And I hear your concern, bud. I'm working on things, like showing up, I promise."

"Well, okay, then, Dad. Does this mean I can talk to you about *anything*?" Dad nodded his head. "Even if it's to ask questions?" I paused. "About Mom?"

Clearing his throat, Dad answered, "Of course."

My nerves rambled for me, I heard my voice asking, "How would Mom feel about all of this? What do you think she would've said? Or done? Can you please tell me about her reactions? You know: my fight, lip, bullying crap with Sharp, sticking up for Gretchen?"

"Well, those are good questions. I've never told you, but I also think about Mom every time I face tough situations. I wonder what she might say. Or I consider what advice she'd tell me." For a moment, we sat in silence. Breathing a few seconds before talking helps form thoughts and quiets the pain.

"Let's see. First, Mom's primary concern would be her baby Hayden's injuries. Oh, I bet you'd experience Mom's angry side jump out a bit." With a sad half-grin, Dad stuck his index finger on my chest, doing his best at mocking Mom's voice, he said, "Hayden Oliver Tucker! You hit somebody?" My lips attempted to curve into a smile but acted confused and twitchy instead. I was thankful for Dad's acting efforts but depressed because I'm reminded again I'll never hear Mom's voice say my name like this.

"Parents go crazy when their kids go crazy—it's ironic, buddy. Aren't you glad your Dad's *always* easygoing and cool?" Dad paused. Smirking at him, I gave him a well-deserved eye roll.

"See, Mom might've thrown a little flippty-doodle-da (is that what Gretchen calls it?) fit of her own. She'd be protective but on your case."

"It's WTFDD—what the flippity-doda, Dad."

He smirked with a shrug. I just shook my head.

"The circumstances of the bullying would bother Mom the most. I imagine she'd search every way possible, ensuring it didn't happen again." Dad's eyes became a bit glassy. "Your mother would be so proud of you. Like I am for sharing your story with Coach and me. Also, for protecting and defending Gretchen's honor."

"Of course, your mom would baby you, too—like, by goin' and makin' you a platter of her buttery cinnamon toast." Dad patted my back, "Like me, your Mom would've had your back. Because we both love you, Hayden. Remember, death doesn't have to end a mother's love."

Long-awaited words I so badly needed to hear about my mom, I didn't anticipate my father's ability to deliver. Next to Dad, processing all these emotions and pieces of information, realizing he came through for me, caused my chin to tremble. My best-of-intentions eyelashes, which often acted as temporary levees failed, opening my flood gates.

"Dad, I miss Mom—all the time—my birthday, at all my games, rough days, like today."

Dad hugged me. "I know you miss her. I sure do too. I'm here for you, Hayden. I *really* am. If you want, how 'bout we camp out in my room tonight? Watch TV? We've not done that in a while. I'll even allow Miss Spicy Boots to join us."

I nodded.

"Hey kiddo, I gotta an idea I'm gonna run by you. You're gonna work for me while you're suspended. More on my idea later."

Dad spent some time on the phone discussing the situation with John, who rallied in my corner, as far as the whole anti-bullying and protecting Gretchen's honor goes. Yet no one claimed they approved of my punch to Thomas Sharp's eye socket. Well, the feisty feline, Miss Spicy Boots, *maybe*?

Thank God, John allowed Gretchen to remain in contact with me during my suspension. Gretchen sent me a sad face emoji when she got a look at the photo of my swollen lip for the first time. She told me she was going to miss me at school. Thoughts and daydreams about English stirred me into a frenzy. A whiff of Love Spell passing by my desk, I longed to inhale and exhale.

My heart traveled to school, where her feet and legs wiggled and twisted inside my wire basket without me. A peppermint mouth attached to those lips. Her copper hair would be swept up and tucked behind her ears. She's probably reading.

I loved subtle Gretchen with her affectionate discoveries during class. Now, she's starting to drape herself way over her own desk. Leaning up so close to my chair, reading materials in hand, her hands often brush my neck with her fingertips as they turn the pages. In English, my posture's much more, shall I say, laidback. I'm missing every bit of her.

Turned out, Dad's project for me involved aqua paint, along with the letters WTFDD. He and I drafted and sketched out a work order for Gretchen, a marquee-style lamp. This is a birth-day surprise from Dad. We used a light kit acces-sory but still gave it a retro vibe. Dad plans to also gift Gretchen a bowl of Godiva dark chocolate. He blames her for his new addiction to them. I'm glad Dad likes Gretchen. Sometimes I wonder if he wishes he could've had a daughter. Dad's around more, and he's involved in my life. With the new friendships with Gretchen and John, and beyond Dad's working hours, he's actually present now. I'm thankful for all of it.

John agreed to allow Gretchen her "drawers" storage she asked for, and Dad said, "Get busy, kid; figure out how to make it happen. Paint, unfinished cabinet bases, it's already set up in the garage. I ordered aqua knobs and pulls too. You've got plenty to do, kid. Go to work."

* * *

"Ugh, ass-jerk Sharp, made it, so I can't kiss you," I said to Gretchen.

"Doesn't stop me from kissing you," Gretchen said. Out-of-school suspension served me well, minus the bloody lip and the back bruise from slamming into the locker. My back injury "bruise" afforded me a chance to remove my shirt and show

Gretchen my bodily damages. She's so kind and offered to rub lotion on my back. In the evenings, Gretchen's "studying" helped me so much: she collected my assignments, delivered her Love Spell and kisses, and talked and visited. She's the best girlfriend, tutor, and nurse, all in one beautiful person.

I hated admitting to anyone how nervous returning to school made me. My goal on Friday: wear my football uniform, act neutral, pretend nothing happened, and sit the bench without going near Thomas Sharp. I want a life with less anxiety. Some people unnerve me, and Sharp makes my blood pressure explode. I don't like the control others possess over my emotions. They realize, Mom, you are my greatest weakness, and they do not care to torture me.

"Whoa. Woo-hoo! Number Forty-One." Did I catch a round of male and female voices *cheering*? For the first time, I glanced up and into the stands, and I couldn't stop myself—a half-smirk crept across my face. Ironic, I thought, my cheering section chose to attend in support of me on the night I'm benched?

Lined up, from left to right, Mrs. Marks, Dad, John, Gretchen, and some other kids from the grief center (who attend nearby schools)—Kelsey and Miles parked themselves in the stands close by too. Mrs. Marks had sorta ran into Gretchen and the gang and sat down with them. Mrs. Marks chose to be near Dad. She seems to love chatting with him about construction and renovation ideas all the time, I guess. I enjoyed knowing each of them showed up here for *me*. Bundled up in socks and boots, Gretchen's toenails sported gray and blue (depressing Civil War paint—how she describes our school colors). Her Snapchat with her toes in the varying two shades is in honor of me. On each of her big toes, she used white to add the number forty-one in honor of you, Mom.

Gretchen still doesn't understand all the rules of football, but Gretchen gets me. She cracked me up the other night with her analysis of what a tight end does on the field. "They run around, try to catch the ball, hoping not to fumble but praying to reach the end zone, right?" Gretchen asked.

"Yep." I kissed her, turned away, and grinned. "Something just about like that."

"Well, isn't the word *tight end* a euphemism for 'nice booty,' anyway, Hayden?"

Mom, Gretchen can be so sassy. She makes me smile and laugh.

Chapter Thirteen

Gwendolyn Margo Parker-Gardener
November 15, 1970–October 13, 2011
Beloved Wife & Mother

I'M SORRY I'M SO out of breath, Mom. The hills in the residential areas cause a struggle for me, but I huffed and puffed until I got here on my bike. I needed my Mr. Tight End, Hayden Tucker, to work out with me in preparation for this trip, I guess.

Martin's Memorial Shop offered to assist me in making this fall gift. I picked the materials and designed this wreath for you. Dad pays me a small allowance for working in the vet clinic to feed, water, and clean up after the animals. What a blessing it is to know I had enough money today to buy you and Hayden's mom, both something. But why is there no way to repurchase a life, Momma? I want my mom back.

Anyway, I'll dry my eyes and talk about something different. I thought the copper ribbon wrapped around the wreath might be something you'd love. The color reminded me of your hair, how Dad called you a shiny penny—his copper beauty. My hair is somewhat similar. Someday I hope to be as beautiful as you. I wish to be a strong woman, a caring mother, and maybe a wife one of these days. Do I have all that it takes inside of me? I am petrified of what the future might bring. Love and loss confuse me every day. I didn't mean to come here today and break down and cry. My heart just can't help it. I'm so lost and confused and scared.

Maybe I should try to tell more about what I brought you? Since October is here, I hot-glued miniature ceramic pumpkins and acorns around the wreath. I painted some white and aqua for fun. You and I both loved that color combination. For a little whimsy, I paid extra, but I added a small squirrel to the top of the circle. It sits on one of the acorns. It reminds me of my days-of-the-week underwear. I wore that pair today. "Chestnuts Roasting on an Open Fire." I wish I could sing better. Gosh, it won't be long until Christmas is here again. It's hard to imagine all the holidays we missed. I relive our last Christmas every day. I'm sorry I'm sobbing, Momma. Please understand my heart is just so broken.

Let me touch your headstone and feel your name. Do you believe in gifting me signs, Mom? Can you visit me? If so, will you allow me to sense when you're near? Are you the chirping cardinal who appears out of nowhere? Or the yellow butterfly that landed on my windowsill the day I won the poetry award? When I rode through the gates of the cemetery, and the seeds of dandelions caressed my cheeks, were those your kisses? When I'm asleep and dream of you, is it ever for real? Are you the dancing crystals across my bedroom walls?

If there are ways for you to be my guardian angel, please continue to assist Hayden and me. We miss our mothers. As I wrote and told you, he just celebrated a birthday. I'm here today on his behalf. I'm going to his mother's grave. I don't know what to say. I'm in love with her son. I'm nearly fifteen (two weeks), but Hayden's friendship, his very presence, is the most reliable comfort I experience.

Dad takes excellent care of me too. Although I've told you all about his horrible TV news programs and his idea of "fun" games, he does try. He misses you. I hope I accomplish what you want from a daughter. I want to make you both proud. I love you. I'll come back to visit you a lot, in fact, in the months ahead. My birthday, your birthday, Thanksgiving, Christmas—all will arrive soon. A big part of me is excited about the holidays. Hayden and his family might offer me new traditions, new chances, new hope, and a place to be with a family. They will include Dad, also.

On the other hand, I dread the holidays, every single one of them because a nagging element of loss will be around every corner. No one will bake a pie that tastes like your pecan pie. No presents will be "To mom from Gretchen." Your chair at the dining room table will remain empty. This room continues to haunt me. One day, I hope I can learn to decorate it and celebrate in it yet still honor the memory of you.

In the meantime, once I'm at home, I'll continue to write to you in my journal. I'll pour out my soul, spill all (most) my secrets, confess my sins, which is the best way I'm aware of to share all the aspects of my life with you.

Bye-bye, Mom.

Rose Elizabeth-Anne Tucker
December 8, 1969–November 21, 2011
An Angel on Earth "Our Rosie"
*Beloved Wife & Moth*er

Hello, Mrs. Tucker. My name's Gretchen. I promised your son Hayden I'd come here today, with flowers for you on his behalf. Your son misses you so much. But his soul is too crushed to visit you. Sorry for all my tears, Mrs. Tucker. I hope it's okay that I'm sitting down, leaning against your headstone. In some ways, your son is my existing headstone—he's my strongest supporter, my rock.

I'm here today because, on Hayden's birthday, he wished for you. And he longed for the courage to pass through the gates of Summerfort Cemetery, deliver flowers to his mother, and celebrate the women who gave him life.

My gift today is this wreath. I designed it for you. I rode my bike to Martin's Memorial Shop and crafted this, especially for you. I need and want to learn so much about you. For now, I tread lightly. I tiptoe around in my discussions of you. I'm careful not to ask too many questions. I want to protect your son's heart. In a recent conversation, he said someone at school called him a name, and it's eating away at me: "Momma's Boy," and they attached nasty comments with cursing. I'm unhappy about it. When Hayden's ready to share all the information with me, I plan to listen to the whole story. After he does, I'll return to talk to you and explain the story and how it resolved.

But, today, I came to honor the birth of your son. Also, to say thank you, Mrs. Tucker, for giving birth to the kindest, sweetest person I know. Like your headstone says, "Angel on Earth," Mr. Hayden Tucker, your son, is that person for me. Perhaps someday he will consider me an angel on earth? I would love that. You see, I think I'm in love with your son.

I doubt people believe in my knowledge of love. However, after all the massive heartache life tossed out at Hayden and me so young, we see the world in a different light than others our age. I understand I still have so much in life to learn. How unfair, unjust, unnatural for Hayden and me for both of

218

us to have our mothers buried underground. We both understand loss to the very core of our aching souls, Mrs. Tucker.

As I told my mom, if you can look out for Hayden and me, like in a guardian angel way, please do. And, if you can send us signs to let us know you're near, you're watching, or you still love us, will you please? We miss our moms.

My tears just never end some days.

Anyway, let me explain some of the features of the wreath I brought you. I chose the first initial of each of your boys: H: Hayden, D: Drew, C: Cole, and G: Gene. At your house, I loved the spa-like color scheme of the master bedroom in white and gray, so I hope my colors make you smile. I picked a purple ribbon and wrapped it around the circle. When your son Hayden tricked me into our first "study" date/ birthday party, I noticed some throw pillows on the couch with purple and wondered if maybe those might have been something you chose.

Since Hayden just turned fifteen, I added his age on the wreath, along with the number forty-one, which is Hayden's football number. Forty-one equals a bittersweet number for Hayden—he lost you when you were that age.

I placed a tiny cat with white boots on the top of the "H" to introduce you to Miss Spicy Boots, Hayden's new kitten, which Gene rescued and then adopted for Hayden on his birthday. When Hayden and I enjoyed birthday cookies, I witnessed an apron hanging in the kitchen. At Martin's, I found a miniature oven mitt, which reminded me of someone who may have worn an apron with the catchy phrase "Kiss the Cook" and once loved baking. That sure appeared to fit you, Mrs. Tucker. I hope I'm correct.

Lastly, I selected a single mini rose, a symbol for your name. The green wire loops around the letter G for Gene. After all, he must've been the one to call you "Rosie."

I plan to come and revisit my mother's grave, so I'll stop by and say hello to you. My mind captured a photo of your headstone today and the lovely angel that rests against your granite stone, holding a rose. Our visit inspired me. I'll strive to be an angel on earth for Hayden, Mrs. Tucker.

One final thing: I want to thank you and God for your little angel, Hayden.

* * *

Mom,

I'm home from the cemetery and writing in my journal. I didn't have the slightest idea how to tell Hayden I followed through with my promise to visit his mother's grave. Or how I made the trip on my bike to Martin's (I wanted to explain what I created) and tell him about the cemetery. But then he got in his scuffle at school. That just breaks my heart.

No one's blaming me. Why do I feel like I should blame myself for Hayden's fight with Thomas? A part of me keeps thinking it's partially my fault. Not one bit of it is, though. Why should I accept Thomas Sharp degrading behavior? I never wanted my body, sexuality, or gender scorned. Permission and consent were never granted to Thomas Sharp. Who gave him the right to view my body as his sexual outlet, inside the school's locker room? The bodies of women are not jokes. I will not allow myself or others to be labeled a joke. I am not a joke.

Thomas Sharp chose to go all out "Trump" in the locker room. His words weren't exactly, "Grab her by the pussy," but he picked on me. He decided to *use me*. To display my photos and say my name in front of other guys. Did he touch me? No, not in a physical way. But, virtually, he did. As Thomas Sharp paraded around, mouthing Hayden, he did his best to cheapen my image by devaluing the name "Gretchen." Purposely he twirled and spit out each letter of my name, saying each syllable like some kind of gross tongue twister. With his body, he objectified me with jerking and grinding. Cruel and intentional are some of the ways I describe his actions.

Sexual harassment and bullying behaviors, when if left ignored, might resurface. That's one of my fears, anyway. A three-day suspension? I don't know how I feel about that. But I don't recall too many people asking me about it, either? The focus of his punishment became all about football and fighting. Nothing about sexual harassment and bullying occurred. Even after Hayden's called Momma's Boy Queer AF, it isn't addressed because nothing's found in writing about Hayden or me. So, for now, it's only hearsay or gossip. "Boys will be boys" you know, all that locker-room crap—

Dad thanked Hayden for sticking up for me in the locker room. Dad, Gene, Hayden, and I had an odd catch-22 chat. We hate violence, but under the circumstances, we understood why Hayden resorted to fighting. We were proud he spoke out and stood up to defend me but wished the face-punching could've been avoided. We hated hearing that Hayden had lived for years with Sharp's bullying and now his locker-room BS "jokes."

"My tolerance for Thomas Sharp is sitting at zero. I want what happened in writing. Start my file and paper trail on him. I'm not accepting anything inappropriate against my daughter, Gretchen," Dad said to the school.

I think Thomas Sharp's issues are going to be a bit of a battle. The "Momma's Boy Hayden, Queer AF?" It hurts me just as much, if not more than the whole locker-room scene.

At the game, because of the fight, Hayden's punishment was to sit the bench. But that didn't stop us from going and cheering. We had fun in the stands. Mrs. Marks even stopped by, plopping down by Gene again. The corners of Gene's mouth curved slightly upward. As he turned toward her, I witnessed his grin turn into a full-on smile, traveling all the way up to crinkle the corners of his eyes. Mrs. Marks enjoyed the greeting and returned something similar. Miles and Kelsey from our group also sat nearby. So, maybe Marks saw us and picked a convenient place?

Here's what I did concerning Hayden's wreath story. Dad allowed me to go to Hayden's and study while he served his out-of-school suspension. Before I went over to Hayden's one of those school nights, I sent a text prior.

Me: Hayden, I didn't get a chance to tell u much about my recent bike ride when I made a stop at Martin's Memorial Shop. If u want to hear about it, let me know. We can chat—in person or txt if u prefer. In case u wanted to see what I designed, I took pics. No pressure, Hayden.

Hayden: Gretchen, I'm beyond thankful. Idk how I'll ever repay u. It will be hard to talk about Mom, but I want to. I know u won't judge me. Of course, I want to see what u made (in person). HURRY! PS My lip is almost healed. xoxo

Chapter Fourteen

October 2019

Happy Birthday, Gretchen! On my birthday, your creativity astounded me with your A-Z card. Since I built your items with my hands, I hope I earned some crafty points. And you will accept some heartfelt ramblings in the form of a *handwritten* letter because you appreciate old-school chivalry.

I'm so excited to have you in my life. Do we owe George Orwell and his *Animal Farm* book a shout-out for bringing us together? Or your witchy Love Spell potions? Or did the stars align, our worlds collide, and the full moon all shine down on us at the right time? Perhaps divine interventions—God, guardian angels, or our mothers—worked together and guided us and provided ways for us? Sometimes I wonder about all of this.

You asked me once if I believed in heaven. Once you shared the photos and description of the wreath you designed for my mother, I noticed a peacefulness around me. I believe in something even more because of you. Somehow, I accepted the fact my mom understands the pain still in my heart. My guilt and shame about not taking flowers to her grave lifted. The kindness you gifted me stretches beyond the scope of this world.

In all honesty, when I think about it, you have been an essential part of my life from the time we were six years old. And I've cared about you since the beginning of our time together in our group. On day one, we clicked and bonded—you "got" me even though I barely spoke. We understand one another's sorrow (all too well), joys, strengths, and weaknesses. However, we help each other through the hardest things in life. Gretchen, you are my best friend and the greatest girlfriend. Thanks again for everything, from the bottom of my heart up to the top of it too.

Plus, I'm grateful you placed your trust in me, allowing me to play with your "drawers." What a pleasure to build my aqua princess some storage. Cock-a-doodle-do, and shittle-sticks, you make me smile, laugh, do Eagles cheers, and overeat junk food. Enjoy your abundance of Godiva chocolates. I worked hard, keeping Dad out of them. He blames you for his addiction, you know?

WTFDD: Every time you flip your lamp on, I hope it lights up your life and warms your soul with thousands of good thoughts. Now, if you ask me to play One to Twenty-Seven at your party, I think I'll plead the Fifth. However, I expect an invitation to be blindsided for a game of Truth or Dare.

Love,

Hayden

PS Meowzer

=^••^= from Miss Spicy Boots

* * *

Hey, Ma,

My October calendar implied/implies a busy month. Dad celebrated my birthday, carrying it over into an extra day—BBQ/Miss Spicy Boots' adoption. Gretchen delivered a wreath to you (I hope you're pleased—I felt a peace surrounding me about it). My fight and suspension occurred (sorry again, Mom). Football season will come to an end, but basketball practice will begin. Plus, Gretchen's birthday and our Summerfort Grief Center Halloween Party all happen soon.

After my incident with Thomas Sharp, Dad *demanded* I start speaking and sharing more of my life with him—events, programs, games, all the school stuff going on in my life. Instead of relying only on technology, Dad printed out this blank calendar and put it on the kitchen bar. Leave it to Dad, who said, "Since we enjoy eating so much, I realized I'd find you here the most. Write down what's happening. Let's plug things into our phones too.

We can 'sync' up together. Make it happen, bud."
I love how Dad's transformed into the new and
improved "Soccer Mom/Dad" for me.

Once in a while, he runs late or isn't available,
but he's no longer absent from my life. How ironic,
a fight brought Dad and me closer together. Dad's
downloaded a bunch of apps, too, so he's tracking
me. One of them, some family calendar thing, is
called Cozi. I asked him, "Dad, did you rip off this
idea from some soccer mom blog?"

Using air quotes again around his "B-T-W," Dad
asked, "So what if I did, Hayden? 'BTW'—look, you
show up as a yellow dot on dates meaning 'yield/
important thing ahead' and see how I'm red to
indicate, 'time to stop and go.'"

Mom, now I receive text alerts all the time:
"Dad's on the way to pick you up; Dad's leaving for
your game; Dad's checked in at Summerfort High
School." Mother, I'm not sure about all of this. It
might be a bit too Cozi/cozy.

Since I started shaving, should I fear Dad's going
to sign me up for another site, too, and app me to
death? "Dad shipped new razors to the house; a
new can of Cremo is on the way; don't forget to
shave for your upcoming event, Hayden; Hey, it's
four o'clock now, so you're about to sprout a five-
o'clock shadow, bud—on your precious bloody
face!" I gotta love, Dad, though.

Love overwhelms and intrigues. We long for it,
but when we acquire the desires of our hearts, we

get aggravated and tired of it too. This is a human flaw, I'm afraid. We want what we can't have. When we get it, we don't want it; we take it for granted or get rid of it; we miss it; we fight for it all back—around and around in a circle, our lives, like a catch-22? I love Dad with all my heart, but dude, back off—let me breathe.

However, I prefer crazy Cozi Dad over absent Dad; because even in my short life, I already realize the importance of choosing people and love. My mother's love vanished, and I lost my choice. My heart wants what it can never have—*your* love, Mother. Through many trial-and-error moments, my communication skills with Dad keep improving. I will even talk to Dad about my needs, going as far as to ask him questions about you.

Earlier, I wrote on the topic of events, such as birthdays. I added a copy of the letter I plan to gift Gretchen, wishing I could sit down with my mother, listen to her voice as I ask for her advice. However, I'll suck it up, Ma, like I always do; keep on taking my chances. At least, I'm stronger and willing now to try and go out on my own; put myself out there.

When Dad said, "It's a done deal," I thought, Dad's weird and crazy, but once I talked to Gretchen and sealed the deal by officially asking her to date me, our relationship fell into place. I love Gretchen a lot (I show her but do not tell her—*yet*). Spoken words might be too hefty for now, but I'm feeling them. She's dishing out good vibes also.

I still find it difficult (I feel awkward/clueless) trying to do the right things in the romance department with this girl. I don't want to suffocate Gretchen with too much love and affection—yes, I do, but I know it's inappropriate. Sometimes she revs me up. Like I mentioned above, I do not want to go all "soccer mom" love app nutty with her, but I want her to always realize how much I care. I wish I understood how to reach a balance—I try.

On a serious note, Mom, I am sorry I'm still unable to come to your grave. For some reason, going to the cemetery traumatizes me. Most people in the grief group claim to go, talk to their dead parent, and share warm and fuzzy stories. On and on, they ramble about all the relief they felt, but I'm just not there yet. I'm stuck inside the pages of this grief diary: My Big Black GD Grief Diary. But even on these pages, I share more than I ever used to. Although sometimes I'm still your little six-year-old boy in the pantry, playing cars with his mom's spices. Some days, I crave a piece of my mother's cinnamon toast so much I weep. Today, I'm a fifteen-year-old guy, with a big, broken heart, who's in the process of learning how to grow and mend.

My gratitude for Gretchen reaches to the heavens. She offered to bring you some *flowers* on my birthday. I never dreamed Gretchen planned to ride her bike across town, where her day consisted of designing and creating a whole memorial wreath from scratch. And then, Gretchen pedaled across Summerfort again, delivering a gift to my mother, a woman she never even met. What a trifecta: an act of bravery, kindness, and love.

When Gretchen showed me the photos, of course, I got misty-eyed, even sobbed at some points. While Gretchen's only been in our home in such a short amount of time, she somehow captured your essence with her observant behavior. Gretchen understood you—your personality—she envisioned you here. In the pillows, Gretchen found the purple; in the kitchen, your apron; in the bedroom, the colors. Her gift included Dad, Cole, and Drew too. Since the wreath honored my birthday and your memory, she picked out the numbers fifteen and forty-one. For your name, the single rose. Oh, the little whimsical touch for the introduction to Miss Spicy Boots.

Mom, Gretchen, also asked, "Hayden, do you want to see the photo where I displayed the wreath at your mom's headstone?"

I said, "I don't even recall what Mom's headstone looks like, Gretchen. I forgot. I think I chose to block it out—all of it—so I didn't have the visuals haunting me." Gretchen hugged me.

"Give me a minute." With my eyes closed, my heart slammed against hers. She squeezed me extra tight but then rubbed her hands through my hair and pulled away. I sucked in a deep breath, sighed, and said, "Ready."

Rose Elizabeth-Anne Tucker
December 8, 1969–November 21, 2011
An Angel on Earth "Our Rosie"
Beloved Wife & Mother

While I stared at your headstone, the words "an angel on earth" jumped out at me. Although I fought through the tears to say the right things, I pointed to the inscription and whispered, "That's you, Gretchen—'an angel,' thank you, for doing this." I reached over to kiss Gretchen's cheek. She reached around my waist to hug me, her body pressed into me, her head against my shoulder. We shared silent tears.

Gretchen sat beside me on the couch, our arms stayed wrapped around each other, so close. As she held me, she understood my need to gaze at my mother's tombstone while my fingertips brushed each element of the wreath in the photograph. My need to trace out each letter and spell out R-O-S-I-E for Rosie. Then, I could touch my mother, even if it was only through her name. Because my God, I miss you, Ma.

Because of Gretchen's act of service, love, and kindness, she brought my mother right to me. She returned my mother's spirit back 'home' for me.

Gretchen understood my mixed bag of emotions—silent tears mixed with sobs, switching into laughter as I thought of the ugly purple pillows (we were leaning against). I asked Gretchen, "How does such a gaudy inspirational item turn into such a beautiful masterpiece?" We giggled. I marveled at the ribbon color, the silly ceramic cat, and the poignant meaning behind the numbers fifteen and forty-one.

Again, Gretchen, my "little angel," supported me, sitting beside me. Mom, one day, I will give Gretchen her angel poem I wrote about her long ago as the message continues to remain true today.

When our tears dried, my lips longed to relish hers, but Thomas Sharp reigns as a giant ass-jerk. However, Mr. Hayden worked some magic, catching on to a couple ways to operate his swollen lip.

* * *

"Gretchen, you dislocated and rearranged my heartstrings," Dad told her when she showed him the photos of the wreath. I studied Dad's slumped posture, his hand tucked in the front pocket of his jeans as he rested his head against the doorjamb. He stared as I did at all that's left of my mother.

"Dad, Gretchen offered and did a favor for me on my birthday since I don't like going to the cemetery."

Dad shifted, pulling away from the doorjamb. He stood ramrod straight. "That's a big thing to ask of someone, Hayden." Cocking his head to the side, he glared at me.

"No— Gene—it's really not like what you're thinking. Hayden didn't *ask* me to do it. We talked about heavy stuff. The topic came up." Gretchen made a fist then used her thumb to point back at herself, stressing her point, "*I* suggested going because *I* planned on going for my mom."

"How much do we owe you, Gretchen?" Dad asked, pulling his wallet out. Dad crowded in to sit beside Gretchen, ramming me into the arm of the love seat—created for *two*.

"Nothing, Gene. To be honest—it's just a gift. Hayden didn't ask this of me." Gretchen frowned, appeared on the verge of screaming, wailing, or running, either to the bathroom as a hostage or, worse, on out the door.

I tried shifting, but with my hip in a corkscrew, my ass sat frozen in time. I tried plotting an intervention. From my wedged position, I reached for Gretchen's hand, but I sank further into the abyss, with little hope. With Dad's addition to the sofa, the corner cushions devoured me. Gretchen and Dad focused on Gretchen and Dad.

"Da—"

"Thank you, Gretchen. That's a tremendous gift. You're a talented wreath maker. I appreciate it too. The way you included me, Drew, and Cole is thoughtful. Gretchen, does your Dad know you did all this?"

Gretchen shook her head no. She narrowed her glance to the ground, with glassy-eyed introspection. I almost heard her heart. *"Why bother loving anyone?"*

"I didn't mean to upset you," Dad said.

Gretchen sniffled and swiped at the corners of her eyes before any evidence fell. She was using one of her coping techniques, I bet. Either she's biting her bottom lip or the inside of her cheek. Maybe clenching her jaw, making a fist while digging fingernails into her palm, or curling her toes inside her shoes. Over the years, I have observed Gretchen, listening to her speak secrets and painful words, while I fell in love with her. Regardless of her oddball WTFDD quirks. When she hurting or hiding something, I can usually tell. Her eyes and mannerisms give her away. Most of the time, I'm good at guessing what she's thinking.

As Gretchen's teeth attacked her bottom lip, she claimed, "No worries, Gene."

Dad doled out one of his bro pats to her back. "Bring it in for a group hug, you two."

"Dad, move!" I begged. "And get your hands off my girlfriend." I cracked up laughing as Dad picked me up, threw me over his shoulder, and tossed me onto the chair.

"Now, everybody can breathe in their own space," Dad said. Keeping his hand propped on my shoulder, Dad asked, "Gretchen Grace Gardener?"

"Yeah?"

"I believe my little boy plunged into a vat of Love Spell lotion; you aware of this happening?" Dad asked, sniffing the air loudly.

"Nope." Gretchen grabbed a pillow from the love seat and covered her face, but it failed to shield her laughter.

Dad picked up a throw pillow, swatting me once lightheartedly before tossing it toward Gretchen, with a chuckle. Dad suggested, "Call John; make some future plans. We can go out to dinner, your choice of place, Gretchen. My treat. A way for me to say thank you. Celebrate your birthday too."

Gretchen's Birthday Dinner, October 16, 2019. Our evening turned into an indulgent and delicious night at the Golden Dragon Restaurant, which required we travel about twenty miles outside of Summerfort but well worth the drive. As Gretchen described it: a quirky, out-of-the-way location. Gretchen thought the idea of a quick little adventure out of state seemed exciting. We called this border-hopping since we crossed from Missouri into the state of Arkansas.

Dad rolled his eyes at Gretchen and me because I ate the crunchy outsides of her Crab Rangoon because she ripped her food into little pieces and only savored the middle portions, eating just the cream cheese. "Jack Sprat could eat no fat," Dad rattled in a mocking tone.

The hot and sour soup packed too much zippy-do-da for everyone but Birthday Girl Gretchen, who exclaimed, "Best ever." With each sip, she wiggled in her seat, managing to swallow until she'd eaten the whole bowl.

As I bit into my egg roll, my imagination played tricks on me. I thought I caught John's eagle eyes, watching my every move. John's gaze seemed to ask, "So, Hayden, you more than like my daughter, eh?" With a mouthful of Chinese, I grinned "yes" with my eyes, but I almost laughed out loud, spewing cabbage onto the table. John stabbed at a piece of chicken on his plate with a forced smile.

Private Investigators Gardener and Tucker hovered across from Gretchen and me inside the booth. I toyed with the thoughts in my mind of John and Dad appearing like two off-duty police officers in some old TV show, like *Starsky and Hutch*, perched at the edge of their seats. My secret theory put me at ease, and I wanted to nudge Gretchen, so I could share my joke with her. Instead, I turned my attention to the placemats and wondered about Chinese zodiac signs. Twelve animals represented the personality traits of a person, based on the year rather than the month of someone's birth. Perhaps asking, "John, what's your sign?" or "What's the year of your birth?" would sound too forward and creepy.

John, why are you making me edgy tonight? It's not like you can read my mind. "Looks like Roosters for us," I said, motioning to Gretchen and myself. "The signs go by the year of your birth. How about you, Dad?" Dad played along. He scooted his plate to the side and searched for the year 1970.

Dad read aloud: "The Dog is the symbol of honesty, frankness, and loyalty in all groups. People having the Chinese zodiac Dog sign always have industrious, genuine, and righteous characteristics. Also, most of them have a good sense of humor. Their smooth-talking and resourceful personality traits win high popularity among the surrounding people."

Dad reached across the table to fist bump Gretchen and me. "I accept all these good parts."

"Read the rest," I said.

"But those don't fit me," Dad said, covering up his placement, laughing. John started searching for his sign while Dad covered up his "weaknesses."

Dad groaned, stuck his tongue out, and crossed his eyes, but he still picked up his placemat. "Now, before I start reading this incorrect listing of traits, I need to preface with a short statement. I do not concur with negativity; just sayin'." Dad waved one hand in the air, holding his placemat. He gave the placemat a twirl above his head, lowering it back to the table for his reading. We all giggled. "At times, dogs may exhibit some of these following traits: Weaknesses include being emotionally cold—*no*, distant at times—*not*, and irrational when mad—*never*.

Not lifting his eyes from his placement John uses his finger as a reading guide tool. In an excited tone of voice, he reads, "Arrogant and impatient for me." He lets out a snort. Wiggling his index finger like the number one, he looks around the table, making eye contact with each of us. For emphasis, he points back to the placement. "*However*, I problem-solve like a practical monkey." John's simplified summary of his Chinese zodiac characteristics cracked us up.

My first theory of Starsky and Hutch's combined abilities for spying, intruding, and untangling upon any and all issues surrounding Gretchen and me had been debunked. Our dads transpired into real human beings, and they settled down enough to stop throwing their judgmental-parental, fire-breathing Golden Dragon daggers at me. Or maybe my imagination chilled. John even rested his elbows on the table by the time the fortune cookies arrived.

"Stop searching for happiness; look next to you." Gretchen blushed as she announced to the table what her cookie said.

"Aww," I sing-song, forgetting for a moment about the dads as I lunged for Gretchen's mouth. But she kicked me under the table, turning her head in time to embrace me in a hug that allowed my misplaced kiss to land on her forehead.

Another jolt from under the table hit me. I realized Dad provided a little warning. For a second, I *almost* asked, *you ready, John, because everyone at this booth thinks I fear you? Guess what? I don't! I respect you. Wanna kick me now? I hope not. Oh, duh, that wasn't you.* I chilled, leaned back, and opened my cookie. "You just ate a great meal with friends."

"How lame." Gretchen giggled after the grand production of her cookie. It made my cookie appear like a total wimp in comparison. Did Gretchen know the consequences of her cookie on me? On the back of my dessert, my Chinese word for the day was bowling. Gretchen's word: tomorrow. "Hey, everyone read the word desserts backward," I said. "What does it spell?"

"Stressed," Dad answered. "What a fun game— a palindrome? No—wait, does that mean the same forward and backward, like civic?" Oh no. I witnessed John's face glow with American pride. Dad using social studies vocabulary, stirred up ideas, concepts, and adjustments to John's game, One to Twenty-Seven. A new game to incorporate with Gretchen already underway, a mental checklist in preparation. *Thanks a lot, Dad.* "Well, what's it called?" Dad asked.

Gretchen researched her phone, "Gene, 'semordnilap' comes up as the answer, a play on the whole palindrome word." Gretchen looked happy, unaware a new game awaited her at home. But I sure noticed.

Of all the people at the table, Practical Monkey piped up with, "Hey, Hayden, go back to your fortune, and read the word on the back."

"*Bowling*?"

"Yes," John said. "I challenge all of you at this table to a game at Alley Kat Lanes down the road!" John slapped his hand on the table with a grin. "'Follow restless urges and find yourself.' See, my fortune cookie prompted me to encourage all of you to go with me and toss gutters and strikes tonight."

"Let's do this, but I'll share one final thought— soon, you will discover your hidden talent," Dad said, reading his fortune.

The waitress overheard us laughing and talking about Gretchen's birthday. She handed Gretchen two extra cookies, with a smile. "Every person is the architect of his or her own fortune," and "Attention is the mother of memory." After Gretchen read them, the last three words of her cookie entangled us, regardless of the intended meaning. "*Mother of Memory.*"

Chapter Fifteen

Saturday, October 26, 2019

Halloween Party Night

Dear Mother,

Your husband, John, sure can be a bit of a prude. When Mrs. Marks announced the *Back to the Future*-themed Halloween Party, I researched costume ideas online. I found the cutest 1980s outfit—A "Lucky Star" Madonna ensemble. Ensuring a good fit without snugness, I selected a size medium. I especially worried about the size because of my boobs and hips. With John's approval and credit card in hand, I clicked the order now button.

I rocked my Madonna costume. From my iPhone, I cranked "Like a Virgin" because I thought John would get a kick out of the whole thing. Dancing down the stairs, lip-syncing, allowed me to showcase myself in the complete package. This happened before he went all freak fest on me.

Now, John says I can't go to a grief center, "showing my ass off to everyone." Nor can he believe "Walmart.com sells lingerie disguised as Halloween costumes to children." Plus, I had to "take off those fishnet stockings or *whatever* they are and put on something else, anything else—seriously, Gretchen. Wear solid tights or leggings. God, anything else—please!"

Under his breath, he mumbled around, accusing poor Hayden of helping me pick out the outfit. I jumped right up, correcting him of his error. "You sat beside me on the couch, giving me your credit card and final okay. Every single piece of this costume for this party I selected." Doing a little spin, I had no problem owning up to it.

I'm appalled John cussed at me. Mr. Khaki-Pants-Button-Collars-News-Watcher-Constitutional-Dude-Animal-Doc also enjoyed spouting off tacky words? How friggin' rude. Like, #RUDE.

God, I hated him tonight. If you were here, Mother, where you belonged and like I wished you'd been, you'd have been able to talk some sense into his narrow-minded brain. I got so pissed I wanted to climb out of my second-story bedroom window and find a way to shimmy or jump down to the first floor, so I could run off and still go dressed full-on '80s. Or I just thought about ripping the whole thing off and going to bed. However, I had to see Hayden's costume. Otherwise, Halloween and Dr. John Gardener could kiss it.

Here's what happened: Trailing up the stairs, right behind me, taking leaps, and skipping steps was none other than your Man of Steel, Mr. Superman. Not the usual upstanding Clark Kent that I remember. Because I ran back to my room after John's "rude ass comment," slamming my bedroom door right before he could reach me. He rapped rather loudly on my door in quick successions with another offensive remark: "Tone down your attitude, Gretchen Grace, and the costume, or you're not going at all."

Like, your Man of Steel practically banged down my door. Plus, his shouting reached a new decibel level. As he stood outside my door, like the big bad wolf, I worried he might huff and puff and blow the house down. I almost considered opening the door and telling him, "Go away and practice our purple octopus technique."

Well, I didn't dare because since when did John become so energized and athletic? And why did your husband have to be so mean, rude, hateful, and cussy tonight? He hurt my feelings.

For a while, I refused to change. I just sat in my desk chair, staring at my "Lucky Star" reflection. Madonna's "Papa Don't Preach" and "Express Yourself" played on as I dabbed at the corners of my eyes to stop as much of the makeup as I could from streaking down my face. All the blurred images in the mirror still appeared as just Gretchen, but with some extra blush, mascara, eyeshadow, puffier hair, and a lot of black lace. The new accessories empowered me—more fun than my usual me, with the gloves, blingy cross necklace, big black bow for my hair, and two chain belts, one gold, and one silver, to clip around the miniskirt. Maybe a Gretchen 2.0 version, an upgrade to understand what fun is all about. Amusement beyond the twenty-seven amendments of the United States Constitution called to me.

Fine. You win, Doctor Gardener. So, Mother, I reapplied my makeup because of Dad's "rude ass comments." Deep down, I misheard Dad's concerns. I assumed he called me a whore, a slut, or a bitch, but I know he had done none of those things. However, Dr. John Gardener's actions and tones felt much harsher, louder, and ruder than usual. He played his toughest game with me tonight, throwing down his dad card.

I found boring-*ass* black leggings from the 2000s equaling nothing Madonna, but I wiggled into them anyway. All in all, I guess I might've still been a passable Madonna. Secretly called myself the "The Unlucky Virgin" whose star would not shine so bright.

In all the commotion fighting with Dad and with the music going, I missed a call from Hayden, which went to voicemail. Thank God for Hayden. This message brightened my day:

Gretchen, I hope you listen to this voicemail soon. Where are you? Please, save me. Dad brought me here early to consult with Marks about remodeling her house or something. Listen, I'm pulling a Gretchen. I'm calling you from the bathroom, where I'm hiding. Marks had me playing Emotions Bingo with those nutty young twins, Timmy and Jimmy, and that other boy, oh, um, you know, that kid who jumps and he crawls on the furniture. Anyway, he calls himself 'Toad.' Well, a *happy* flashcard hit me in the face. Can you guess my emotions now? Six-year-olds are supposed to be cute and quiet, like us—we—were. Oh my God, their party is over, but their living parent won't come and claim them. Wonder why? Hey, if this is a Halloween prank that you and our dads are pulling on me, please make it stop. Sorry, this is the longest voicemail rant, ever. Happy Halloween. Just get here soon. Please. Please. Please.

As I listened to Hayden's voicemail, I laughed out loud, forgetting for a moment my aggravation at Dad. To smooth things over, I found Dad in the living room. I pointed to my new look. "Black leggings? Better?"

"Much." Dad surprised me. He'd cooked a platter of junk to eat—nachos and wings. Said he planned to stay in tonight and watch a movie. Or he and Gene may get together for *a drink*. Dad made sure he enunciated "a drink" like I needed to know he'd be going back to do-gooder Clark Kent.

"Hey, GG, I want to show you something I found. It will only take a second." Dad handed over a photo. It was from the '80s—Mother, you were dressed for Halloween as a hippie wearing a shining smiling, waving the peace sign with your fingers, while another peace sign symbol dangled from your necklace. "Do you see yourself in her?" I nodded my head, staring in stunned silence at my twin.

"Thanks, Dad." We hugged.

"I made a copy of the photo for you." I tucked it inside my bag, so I could show the others at the center. "You ready to go, Madonna?"

I smiled. "Yep. Hayden left a message. He's already there. Gene dropped him off early." From the car, I texted Hayden: **On my way. Costume/ dad issue resolved. Got your v-mail. Sorry, not a trick or treat prank.**

Dad asked me, "What's making you grin over there?"

"Oh, Hayden's message cracked me up. He said kids tossed Emotions Bingo cards at him or something?"

"Hmm—you'll have to explain the rules of the game to me sometime." I thought about it, weighing the idea of which game I might prefer. Sharing my personal woes with my father versus our continued game night of constitutional fun, playing One to Twenty-Seven?

As we pulled into the parking lot, Dad started in on his general comments of acceptable behavior: Please act respectful, yadda yadda. "Okay. Yes.

I know." I jumped out, started to wave him off with "good-bye," but instead, I decided to try something different. I said, "I love you, and thanks again for the picture of Mom." Dad stayed until I cleared the front entryway before he drove away with a smile.

Oh, my dear God in heaven. Hayden stood inside the foyer, appearing as if somebody plucked him fresh off the TV set *21 Jump Street*. My eyeballs drank in every 1980s inch of him, from head to toe and then from toe to head. I admired the whole style. His faded and torn-at-the-seams denim vest, along with the form-fitting long-sleeved black T-shirt, looked good. His leather belt was black with silver chains. The necklace, Swatch watch, and leather bangle accessories in black and silver were pure perfection.

I noted Hayden's jeans matched his vest, as the fabric wound around his legs, fitting so snug. As my eyes crawled down him, I stopped to marvel at the holes in the knees. Black combat boots, similar to mine, covered his feet. His, however, offered an air of half-laced bad-boy quality to them that I found quite appealing. Hayden transformed himself into a man of the '80s. What a decade worthy of admiring. Hayden Tucker, otherwise known as Johnny Depp from *21 Jump Street,* showed up at the Summerfort Grief Center to attend the Halloween party as my date.

"Wow!" Hayden mouthed as he walked toward me with wide eyes, his hands shoved into the front pockets of his acid-washed jeans. As I slipped through the door, he did an about-face to bring himself to me, front and center. He pulled his hands free, grabbing me by the hand to wheel me around. Repeating himself, but this time aloud, he said, "Wow."

With a toothy grin, one which showcased the tiny dimple on his cheek, he led me to the side hallway. Near the offices, away from where everyone else milled about, Hayden propped me against the wall. He offered a quick kiss and hug. When he released me, he placed his hands on my hips, smiled, and said, "Dang, you're hot." His cheeks ignited into a rosy glow.

"Likewise."

"Likewise?" Hayden asked, giggling at me with a poke to my side, tickling me. We both laughed and enjoyed making fun of my juxtaposition of Madonna attire with my virgin-like vocabulary.

When I gave Hayden the rundown of my fight with Dad, he provided me a lopsided grin. "Well, if I had a daughter as sweet, smart, and as pretty as you, my protectiveness would pop out too. Like, I'd be, oh my God, flippin'-out-crazy-protective, I bet." He gazed at me, the corners of his healed mouth turned up into a heartfelt grin. The slightest gap in his two front teeth glowed white.

While we leaned into each other, forehead to forehead, he did one of those Hayden kisses where he caressed each of my lips, one at a time.

Those types of kisses leave me wanting more of him because he starts with only a graze to each of my lips. My heart and my stomach fluttered. And I just wanted to hang out on *21 Jump Street* all night without anyone to interrupt us. As we heard footsteps approaching, Hayden pulled away, but anchored against the wall side by side, our fingertips and hips remained touching.

Mrs. Marks caught us in the dimmed hallway. "Hey, there you two are. Hayden and Gretchen, your group is going to be set up in the Blue Room tonight." She pointed to the end of the hall. I thought about saying, "He's only playing Emotions Bingo with me, Mrs. Marks." But instead, we sniggered, tiptoeing to the group wing of the building. The center represented a second home to me, a refuge to hang out with kids who understood the pressures of the world of loss.

As we walked the halls of the Summerfort Grief Center: A Place to Heal, A Place to Hope, A Place to Belong, I thought about coming here for years, on and off. Dad and I attended events and group sessions here. So did Hayden, Gene, and his brothers. Because of our age, Hayden and I remained in the same cohort, and I never minded. The Blue Room is the best location in the center, in my opinion. In fact, it's the best of all the rooms, not only because the color soothes me but also because the décor speaks to me most. Mrs. Marks is somewhat of a photographer/historian and several large prints of kids, just candid shots of them, some with smiles, as they complete activities hang on the walls. My favorite photo in this whole place resides in there.

A picture of my little group sitting around a tree hangs in there. Mrs. Marks photographed it. The center hadn't been opened long. The photograph of the tree decorated in a variety of colorful hearts tells a compelling story. Each heart represented a different soul-crushing grief story. As Mrs. Marks told of her mother's stroke, I bonded to her. Because she understood my pain since my mother died from complications of a stroke as well.

Mrs. Marks explained her mother wore a *purple* church dress. One boy's dad took him to the circus, where they ate *pink* cotton candy. I remember I picked a *brown* heart to share how my mom loved to garden, and I placed it on the tree. Hayden, who barely spoke, said his mom died from cancer, but she was a nurse, so he chose a *white* heart.

After Hayden sat back down, he squeezed my hand tight with tears in his eyes. Hand in hand, we gazed up at our grief activity. A small wood-and-paper tree filled with the stories of our sorrows. Sharing painful memories made the tree bloom with colorful hearts. The photograph captures a significant moment. I understood the word "hope" for the first time since your death.

Hayden appeared as a little angel to me since that day. He's always been there for me at the center, along with others. So, we do not have to choose to be alone. I am not alone in this journey with grief. There are other children like Hayden and me, such as Miles, Mia, and Kelsey. And people, such as Mrs. Marks, who rise above the pain of grief to help others. The photo reminds me every time I step through the Blue Room doors: Do *not* lose hope; continue believing in love, and keep coming back, even when it's not always fun or easy.

For almost eight years, I've stood as firm as possible. And I know I'm a survivor of grief. Mother, because of your death, I attend a program with more than twelve steps because, lady, this grief crap is never-ending. However, with time, learning new techniques, journaling, and the connections to others, they all do help me.

Since I wrote and told you all about the Blue Room and our photo, I wrote this poem for Hayden. One day, I hope to have the courage to share it with him. Life takes an awful lot of fearlessness, Mother.

To The Little Boy with My Heart:
Colorful hearts sprinkled the ground
One little boy barely made a sound
In his silence, he squeezed my hand
Our grief we could not understand
Beyond colorful stories of pain and sorrow
His heart painted in mine a new tomorrow
With hearts and minds, we learned to cope
Through togetherness we planted hope
We sat, cried, watched love grow and bloom

As a white painted heart brightened the room
Oh, precious little boy, if you only knew
On that day, I shared my heart with you

Since I spend a lot of time at the Summerfort Grief Center, I want to describe the place to you. A large taupe semi-circle couch invites people into the Blue Room. It can seat about six to eight teens comfortably and opens up the conversations while we're all sitting together. Our prints from over the years hang above it, and on the opposite wall, two oversized chairs with a funky abstract pattern rock, and glide but they do not recline. They somewhat match our taupe couch. We bring in bean bag chairs as needed to stretch out on the floor, if we want to watch a movie, or write in our journals. The TVs travel from room to room on a cart, tied down with black straps. It works but in a bit old-school style, so it makes me smile.

I like it when we turn down the overhead lights, using only the floor lamps instead. We keep them in two of the corners. Sometimes I think people spill more of their guts in the perceived darkness than when they believe they are under a sad interrogation. Only one mini-blind-covered narrow office window, which runs from almost the ceiling to the floor in the room, brings light into the room. But it gives the room a cozy effect. They (maybe Gene's crew?) replaced our shaggy carpet with dark laminated wood, which runs throughout the whole center. For the main areas, the shininess makes the entire place look uniform, but in the Blue Room, we need a rug so we can sit on the floor again. The carpet offered ugly warmth. I miss it, but I don't tell anyone.

The center has a foyer, which offers a couple of chairs and a desk for the secretary who welcomes guests. A small hallway then branches off into the offices if you turn left, where Mrs. Marks and a couple of full-time counselors work (*21 Jump Street Hallway*). But if you go right, you run into the commons area location. A play area for the kids, the bathrooms, even an apartment-style kitchen setup in an "L" shape, are nestled in the back corner. A library of book resources, a craft center, and a storage bin area all are hidden by large bookcases that create a wall or a cove. This design adds privacy for the groups while they work. It reminds me of the hub of what a small office might be like. Off this open area, the Blue Room, Yellow Room, and Green Room line up next to one another.

The banner on the door to the Blue Room read ***"Back to the Future: Happy Halloween."***

When we were all accounted for, Mrs. Marks asked, "When we consider the American way of celebrating Halloween, we often associate it with spooky stories, sights, sounds, all related to death. For some, grief gets heightened or triggered. Who might relate or can share a thought?"

"I guess all holidays stir me up to an extent," I said, "I find myself going back. To revisit my childhood memories—Mom allowed me to pick a costume, or sometimes she made them. One year, she took old bedsheets in the pattern of red, white, and blue stripes. Somehow she sewed together the sweetest clown costume for me. It's in my A-Z memories scrapbook I made with your help Mrs. Marks, under 'C' for Clown. I find it incredible just how many memories I still manage to have or rec-reate even though I lost her so young. I thank my dad and the grief center for keeping her alive for me in positive ways. Holidays are still rough, every one of them. Today I argued with my dad over my costume choice, but before I came here today, he shared a photo of mom with me." I pulled the pic-ture out of my bag and passed it around.

"Wow, Gretchen, you could be twins," Mia, the girl who lost both parents to a drug overdose, announced. When I listen to her speak, it brings me so much perspective. She lives with her grand-mother now. A new home, life, and school to nav-igate after losing two people. I'm so thankful for Dad and our Mr. Rogers/Clark Kent-nerdy life-style. As the other teens open up about their lives, the same feeling holds true—I'm thankful for Dad. Some, like Miles, had parents die due to suicide, and they harbor guilt, even when they could have done nothing to stop the death from happening. My heart aches for every one of them. Each of us suffered a significant loss, but we travel through our grief journeys differently. What we share in common? The various pains of grief.

"Gretchen mentioned a fight with her Dad. That brings up an important topic associated with grief. *Regrets*? Anyone want to share a story that relates to that topic or still stay with the holiday theme?" Mrs. Marks asked.

Hayden cleared his throat. "I'll try," he said. "I had a birthday recently, which is weird for me because my mom, who gave birth to me, is gone." He paused, and the other kids nodded their heads in understanding. Hayden reached for my hand, so I latched on. "Gretchen knows I bottle up my feelings, and she saw in me that I was hiding something. And, she waited for me . . . pushing me in her Gretchen way to talk. . . ." Hayden took a deep breath.

"I confessed to Gretchen how much I hated going to the cemetery to take flowers to my mom's grave, and I thought I appeared weak because I still can't." Hayden's eyes began to water. He held up his finger to ask for a second. "Gretchen not only rode her bike to the cemetery, but she stopped at Martin's to design a thoughtful wreath for my mom. I regret that I can't go to see my mom's headstone, but I don't want to regret not saying thanks and sharing this story. May I show everyone the photo—it's on my phone, though?"

"Of course, Hayden!" Mrs. Marks clutched her hand over her heart. Whenever Mrs. Marks finds herself on the brink of tears, we witness this signature move. "Hayden, I'm so proud of you. You've come a long, long way with opening up. And, Gretchen, what a beautiful gift to give to someone. Let's add this to the list of topics we need to discuss. What is the best kindness someone shared (or greatest gift you've received) to help you with grief? Or what could you give someone who's hurting? Please think of those things. Look around for opportunities. It seems when we help others, we heal in the process somehow too."

Marks paused for a moment to lighten the mood. "Remember, tonight, we need to eat all these snacks and have fun too. Let's view *Back to the Future*. I set up crafts and journal prompts in the lamp corner, if you want to do those, while you view the delicious, young Mr. Michael J. Fox as he portrays Marty McFly."

"Mrs. Marks, did you really just say that?" asked Kelsey, who choked on her drink and nearly snorted it out through her nose.

"Hmmm. I don't recall my exact words." Marks laughed. We all giggled as she scooped up buttered popcorn in a black Solo cup with googly eyes and exaggerated eyelashes glued on to the side. Ace bandage wrappings ripped into strips had been wrapped around it to design a silly-looking mini mummy. Picking from the pile of orange Solo cups, Mrs. Marks poured herself a glass of tea. A couple of those cups offered eyes shaped like candy corns and jagged teeth from those Ace bandage strips. Fun and cute homemade party décor. "Oh, markers over here to design your cups and put names on them." Marks lifted the pens to show us, before strolling to the couch.

Under our photo collage, Marks found a place to lounge. With all the lights out, except the faint corner glow, she stated, "Imagine, *if* time travel were possible, like in this movie. You're given the ability to go back in time to visit your loved one. What conversations would be essential/vital for your grief journey?" She paused while her words soaked in before adding, "Okay. Roll it!"

Hayden slid his arm around me, rubbing my gooseflesh arms. PDA at school and the center get handled with care. The Center allows hand-holding or looped arms, but Mark's isn't the fan I am of the *21 Jump Street* intermission hallway locked lips. As we walked into the Blue Room for the Halloween Party, holding hands, Mia, Kelsey, and Miles had said, "Duh, about time!" and laughed. *Everyone* said they knew we liked each other. They were glad *we* finally figured it out.

But Mrs. Mark's words about time travel conversations with a parent *if* we could go back in time rattled my heart.

I reclined into Hayden's shoulder and said in a whisper, "WTFDD, *everything's* vital to me." Hayden stretched his arm around me, taking in all of me, squeezing tighter, brushing his lips against my temple with a quick kiss, apparently his signal of agreement.

Earlier, I had picked up some of the journals prompts Mrs. Marks placed around. Since I write to you all the time, Mother, I wonder how many questions I've already answered. I enjoy thinking of you, sharing my days-of-the-week secrets with you, and writing in my journals.

Chapter Sixteen

Dear _____:

If I could travel back in time, I would pick
the time we (event/place/memory):

It meant this to me/or made me aware of:

_____

_____

_____

_____

_____

_____

_____

_____

_____

Draw the scene of your memory if you prefer

No Rules. Fill in. The storyline's yours to tell as needed.

Dear _____,

If time travel were a possibility, I would love to have you come back to the year _____.

You could see me: _____

_____

_____

_____

_____

Maybe you could meet: _____

_____

We could do the following activities: _____

_____

_____

_____

_____

_____

_____.

I'd finally have the chance to say to you: _____

_____

_____

_____

_____

(Good for suicide/overdose grief)~

Dear _____:

Sometimes I still wish I could travel back in time and help you. I realize I can't fix a broken past. Your death isn't my fault. But I still wish you could've seen yourself through _____ (my, child's, mom's, dad's, etc.) eyes.

There are so many good things _____ saw in you. Such as: _____

_____

_____

_____

Plus, there are so many happy memories of you, such as: _____

_____

_____

_____

_____

_____

These are some of the things _____ want/wants you to know. They are: _____

_____

_____

_____

_____

_____

These are some things you might be very proud of _____ for accomplishing:

_____

_____

_____

_____

These are some questions _____ still has/have about you: _____

_____

____

Using "My Powers of Three— Grief Won't Outsmart Me" Game:

Dear Grief,

I can name **three** people I can count on in spite of grief/to face grief:

I can name **three** places I can go for help when down:

I can name **three** things/techniques—books, movies, TV shows, hobbies, etc.—

I use to work through pain—answer more than one—build a list

I can name **three** people I've helped through their pain:

I can name **three** suggestions/resources IF someone asks for them:

I can name **three** things about myself I'm currently proud of:

I can name **three** positive goals I'll set for myself

The Ghost of Christmas Past	The Ghost of Christmas Present	The Ghost of Christmas Future
If time travel were possible and you traveled back to your childhood, who would you want to meet and what would you want to see, feel, hear, taste, and touch? Explain or draw grief-related emotions:	What do you expect to see, feel, hear, taste, touch in this year at Christmas? Explain or draw grief-related emotions of the upcoming (present) Christmas	If time travel were possible and you could travel to your future, who would you expect/hope to meet and what would you expect to see, feel, hear, taste, and touch? Explain or draw grief-related emotions:
Who I was before the death: My Past~	Who I am now, dealing with the death: My Present~	Who I will become/what I am going to be, despite the death: My Future~
My List From A–Z About All The Things I Remember About You:	My List From A–Z About All The Places We Traveled or The Places I Wish We Could've Seen Together:	My List From A–Z About All The Goals and Things I Want to Tell You About Me:

Chapter Seventeen

Dear Mom,

Sometimes on ordinary days in November, the world crashes down.

"GG, I need the truth!" Dad said, wearing his new shades of blue polo. I designed it, talking Dad into purchasing them. John Gardener, DVM, embroidered in navy blue on the background of sky blue. I focused on the colors, but my mind shifted. A fire ignited in my brain. Acids burning inside my chest, I held my breath, pressing my hands over my heart.

"Well, Gretchen?" We sat at our Shaker farmhouse kitchen table, the one you picked, Mom, because of the craftsmanship. In the nearby utility room, the dryer buzzed. The washer whirled in a spin cycle nearing complete. Downy fabric softener filled the air with an April Fresh scent.

Lightheaded, I rose to my feet. "Laundry?"

"No!" Dad slapped the edge of the table. He snapped his fingers, pointing to the bow-backed Windsor chair. "Sit down! Now, Gretchen." I longed to escape. Flopping down, I thought, "my mother chose this seat," as the bones in my body melted. "We're dealing with this situation." As Dad spoke, his face contorted between anger and sadness, his eyebrows twitched and cocked every which way. A load of towels, half of them folded, littered the table-top. Dad's elbow propped up on some of my favorite days of the week: the monkey, turtle, and turkey.

"I'm sorry, Dad. I know it makes me look weird, but I just wanted Mom around me in some way." I scooped them up and squeezed them all in one hand. "I'm not hurting anyone. God, stay out of my stuff. Why did you get into my laundry today? I usually do my own."

Dad reached for me. To hug me? Or to steal from me? I didn't know, so I flinched. He frowned and reared back against the spindles of his chair, scratching the whiskers on his chin. His fingertips tapping at the edge of the table as he stared at me with droopy-dog eyes. I think he puffed a round of purple octopus breaths.

"Gretchen, I'm really trying to understand and consider this as some kind of grief solution." Dad shook his head, his eyes glazed. He spoke in stutters. "But it's way, way too un-unacceptable . . . even . . . unhealthy." Dad hung his head for a moment, his fingertips raking through his hair before he raised up to look at me. Dad motioned to me, opening his arms.

Clutching my panties, bawling, I agreed to collapse into him.

"Gretchen, I love you, but you may require hospitalization if you can't make yourself give up harmful items. You're obsessing over odd things. You're hoarding. This might actually be some form of obsessive-compulsive disorder, I'm afraid."

"No. I'm okay."

"Gretchen Grace, no, honey, you're far from okay right now." Dad kissed the top of my head. His legs jolted up and down. Dad grasped my face with his hands and put his head on top of mine. His jaw shifted—I believe I felt it clenching before he again started to speak.

"I need a decision from you—leave the underwear with me and go into one-on-one counseling services with a psychiatrist for OCD or else you can get inpatient treatment for OCD. Or do I need to call an ambulance for my daughter because she's hoarding any other secrets? Or because of any desires to hurt herself? What can I do to help my daughter?" His hands cupped my cheeks as he pulled me closer toward his face, making me look him in the eye.

"Dad—"

"Dad what? Gretchen, please answer my questions. Plus, if we go upstairs to your bedroom—what else?"

"Nothing."

"And?"

"I'll turn the underwear over to you. And not wear them. *If* you promise not to toss them out." Dad released my face, reached down, prying my palm open, finger by finger. Tears dripping, I latched back on to the underwear before finally surrendering the three pairs on the table.

"Let's go to your room for the remaining four," Dad said. Recovering from sobbing, my body hiccupped, so I sucked in air and swallow back the lumps in my throat. "Gretchen, lead the way."

Once in the room, I recovered the others. "Three? Gretchen, I'm not playing games with your life. That's not all of them."

"One pair on, Dad."

"I'll expect you to change later. I'll wash and store everything."

"Alright, alright." I scoffed, with my arms crossed, staring at the floor.

"Do you need more money or help to buy bras and panties, Gretchen?"

"No, you gave me enough when I went shopping with Darcy and her mom, remember?"

"So, you do know what size you wear? Understand the appropriate styles for your age group? You realize I'll always take care of your n—"

Using a harsh, robotic tone, I answered. "Yes, I know all these things, Dad,"

"Gretchen, if you put yourself in my shoes, like, as a parent, would you search this room right now?"

"No. Stop it."

Dad pointed an accusing index finger at me. "No, Gretchen. You stop it. Stop worrying me." Dad hovered over my shoulder, his vulture eyeballs swooping, scanning everything inside my dresser, uncovering death evidence. I prepared for another attack.

"Sorry, I disappointed you. I never meant to be such a freaking joke." My stomach plummeted. The impact of handing Dad the last items was so intense. *Did every strand of hair on my head fall out? Did my heart resign?*

"GG, you're neither of those things. I'm disappointed in myself as a doctor but even more so as a father. My kid scurried around our house, tidying up with her laundry—performing secret service acts—because of this." He lifted and shook the scraps. "Your mom wouldn't want this for you."

"Dad, remember, you promised you wouldn't throw them away."

"Let's let professionals guide us on the best decisions. I'll set them aside for now."

"I wish I could be more like you, Dr. Perfect."

"Perfect?" Dad asked. Letting out a little sigh or snort, he patted the bed, motioning me to come and sit down. "Right after Mom died, I struggled, late at night—lonely with a little girl to raise alone—so I self-medicated with alcohol. I realized quickly,

I better pull it together for you. Ever notice how I pace and limit myself around booze? Now you know—a must for our successful survival." Dad rubbed his temples like someone with a migraine.

"Really?" I squinted up at Dad in shock.

Dad nodded.

"After the alcohol, I thought if I dated, the companionship might ease the pain of missing your mom. I was very lonely."

"What? When? Booze and women? Who are you?"

"Oh, I had friendships. Things like lunch dates. Or while you played at Darcy's or Meghan's. Sometimes after I dropped you off at the grief center for events. Just whenever."

"Who?"

"Not important."

"Dad, tell me. I hate the cop-out attitude."

"Well, I feel a bit strange sharing info like this with my daughter. You sure?"

I grinned and nodded. My face started drying out, so I stopped wiping away my salty remnants. For a change, it seemed freaky but exciting, almost even funny, having Dad in the hot seat.

"Hmmm, some ladies were from out of town. I met some when they brought in pets. Others I call *happenstance* situations—see somebody at the post office and learn about a recent divorce and plan a lunch together and such."

"So, my uptight dad ran around as a man-whore?"

Dad laughed, putting his hands over his face. When he first spoke, he mumbled his words, creating awkwardness in Dad, so I longed to listen to even more of his side of these stories. He glanced over at me with a smirk, scratching his stubble.

"Gretchen, I doubt words like 'uptight' and 'whore' describe me."

"Oh. No. Those words do fit you in this situation." I put my arm around Dad. "My dad, Mr. Uptight Doctor Man-whore."

"Hey. This day started out all about you, GG. Don't get sidetracked and forget."

"I know, but at least give me some deets—names?"

"Well, I don't look at this as a solution to anything? And I'm conflicted about telling my daughter too much private information—what do you say, 'Yuck, Dad, TMI, Dad!'"

"So. Today, I struggled a lot. Maybe I deserve to know. Spill."

Dad paused. He glanced at the floor, over to me, scratched his wooly face *again*, cleared his throat, and—against his better judgment—shared TMI!

"The lady who used to cut my hair, a pet food supplier I met—first online and then in person, a vet in a nearby town, customers, post office chance encounters, grief moms, and one of your classmate's moms."

Yuck, Dad. TMI. What was I thinking? Shut up, Dad. Gross. Who are you?

"Jesus, Dad. Too cryptic. You still mentioned no names."

"Hon, I'm not with these people. The best way to deal with the problem—not go around like a kiss-and-tell type. Remain discreet and anonymous."

"Obviously, I see where I formed my fabulous skills. I guess I got my OCD secretive methods from *you*, Dad?"

"Jesus, Gretchen, that's a bit harsh and uncalled for."

"It's too bad if saying how I really feel hurts your feelings. I guess I'm sorry." Using air quotes, I asked, "On any of your discreet '*dates*,' did you find any hope of a '*real*' relationship?"

"A great question. Not really, which led me to reflect on the road I was on. I knew I needed to get back on track in life. I had self-destructed a little too much."

Really, Dad? I shrugged. "Not one person in all these years?"

"I guess I enjoyed the company of one lady over anyone else. She and I talked a lot. We used to slip away for lunch. Sometimes, we caught movies in the afternoon. Laughter and conversation flowed easily. She understood the unique demands of parenting a daughter."

A gleam popped into Dad's eyes, talking about "Single Mom." The edges of his mouth curved upwards, creeping into the area of a hint of a smile until it burst wide open. So much so even his crow's-feet became pronounced. That's how I knew he more than liked her. Odd to consider my dad giggling, flirting, and digging into buttery popcorn in the daylight hours with some woman other than my mother. Then claiming her as only a "friend."

Dude, get real. Also, get a grip. It's called friends with benefits, hit it and quit it, no strings attached, hooking up, or Netflix and chill. Gross. My dad's a man-whore.

"What's the daughter's name?"

"Lilly."

"Effing Lilly? Like, Lilly P.?" I fell back onto my bed, covering my face. "I hate Lilly. You slept with Debbie? De-*BORE*-ah, her mother? Oh. My. God. Dad!"

"Enough, Gretchen. My se—personal life—off-limits."

"Fine. By not saying no, you said a big, fat, juicy-ass yes. Dad, you slept with the enemy? Wait, what did you call it? Oh, I remember. *Happenstance?* Right? Of all the people in Summerfort, Dad?"

"Hey, Debbie moved on. No worries. Forget about Debbie and Lilly. We need to get the best treatment for us and not focus on other people right now."

"Fine, sure, alright, okay."

Dad stood, his arms crossed in front of him. "Switching gears, Gretchen. I placed a call earlier today. I set up an appointment with a therapist. Tomorrow, you go first thing."

"Can I still go to my group stuff at the center?" I sat up, my eyes brimming with tears, my mouth slipped into a frown. Dad plopped back down next to me. He wrapped his arm around me.

"Yes, of course, you can, but also, you will receive one-on-one care for a while too. The center offers a psychiatrist on staff who will counsel and monitor a treatment plan. Deal?"

"Okay, Dad." I closed my eyes while silent doubts flowed down my cheeks. Dad leaned my face against his collar bone until my world stopped spinning.

After Dad left my room, I felt like a complete failure. Dad confused the hell out of me with his own grief revelations. Hayden deserved a better girlfriend than I could be. I'd give anything to tell him, "I love you" instead. When you love someone so much, you want what's best for them. Three bombs of ugly truths he needed to know about me. So, I texted.

Me: Hey Hayden, Dad and I worked through a lot of crap today.

First bomb: Dr. Man-Whore, who I call DAD, slept with Lilly's mom, Debbie, or DeBOREah. BOOM!

Second bomb: As an OCD hoarder, I require treatment for wearing and stashing underwear Mom bought me for X-mas so long ago. BOOM!

Third bomb: I understand u probably no longer wish to be w/ an effing weird g/f. Sorry. I'll miss u so much. Bye. ☹ XO. BOOM!

Chapter Eighteen

Hey, Mom,

I love you. And miss you a lot. At the Summerfort Grief Center, the question presented to us for November: Who or what makes you thankful? Who helps you or has helped you with your grief?

Gretchen's hurting right now, and I respect her wishes to break up with me but backing down without any kind of fight? Not happening—Boom. Her text destroyed me and annoyed me, but in the end, I ignored it with no reply, allowing both of us time to think about things first.

Even though I picked up the phone, staring at her contact photo, ready to hit call, I never did. And I typed message after message but deleted every single one of them. Some of my thoughts, when putting them in black and white, looked pretty rude on the screen. I'm glad I didn't act on impulse, adding more regrets and hurts. But really? "BOOM—you don't want me as your girlfriend"—shouldn't I get a say in the matter?

Instead, I decided to busy my mind, along with my heart, by writing a story from Gretchen's point of view, expressing how her support always helped me. In the garage, I used Dad's tools to carve a tree figurine, leaving small spaces for hearts. I designed them as the leaves. I painted each heart, planning to hotglue them, matching up with our story and photo. My tree accompanies my words and poem, wishing her a Happy Thanksgiving.

Mrs. Marks printed a copy of the picture for me. Gretchen adores aqua, so I painted and designed a frame. At the photo kiosk, I requested an 11" x 14" of the shot. Gretchen stares at this photo at the center with a hauntingly beautiful expression on her face. My wish—my gifts will grant hope to Gretchen's life every day, whether I get to play a role or not. God, I hope that I do, though.

To one of my greatest blessings:

Happy early Thanksgiving. The photo, tree, story, poem, all came from the inspiration of a little angel I call Gretchen. Thanks for all the ways you've helped me over the years. I hope you'll be surprised to see the names of some of our old group members from this childhood story. Gretchen, I guess you and I are the last two standing together through grief. I pray that never changes, and we stay united to help each other. Sometimes I remained silent through activities, but I want you to know, I still listened, heard, and noticed you in everything.

Chapter Eighteen

Gretchen's Grief: Sharing Her Heart
Written by Hayden Tucker
Dedicated to Gretchen ~ with all my heart

Welcome to the Summerfort Grief Center: A Place to Heal, A Place to Hope, A Place to Belong. I enjoy coming here, where I can talk with other kids like me, who understand grief. My name's Gretchen Gardener. My Dad and I live alone since Mom died. I'm almost seven and about to attend second grade.

First, I made a lot of new friends in my group. Mrs. Marks, the leader, is called a facilitator. I like her because she teaches us how to listen to one another. We learn so much about others this way. Plus, we encourage each other not to be afraid to talk about the death of the person or people we miss.

At times, we read helpful books, like the one about an octopus who demonstrates deep breathing techniques to help us relax. You try: take a deep breath in—hold it—hold it—now, slowly, let it out. Imagine this purple, silly sea creature! Does it make you want to giggle?

On other occasions, we watch videos. We also complete memorial art projects. For example, I wrote a note in the shape of an angel, which turned into a Christmas ornament. So many exciting things happen here. Let me describe my all-time favorite activity:

Imagine a rainbow of hearts, the pieces a little bigger than the size of my hand, scattered across the floor. Colors galore—red, orange, yellow, green, blue, purple, pink, brown, black, gray, and white—piled in a mess. I counted about three of every color or thirty-three total.

In the corner of the room, a handmade structure stood, a bit taller than me, or four feet tall. The bare branches extended out. Fuzzy strips of material stuck to the tree and to parts of the hearts, too, I noted.

"Gather 'round while I tell you the directions," Mrs. Marks said. Pointing, she asked, "How do you believe the tree feels inside this room?"

"Sad, different, cold, angry, mad, lonely"—words erupted from everyone at once.

"Hayden, you said, 'sad'—why might the tree be sad?"

"Cut off from others."

"Alright." Mrs. Marks nodded.

"Finn, you used the word, 'mad' —why might the tree be mad?"

"No leaves—so empty."

Again, she smiled with a nod. "Maria, you said, 'scared.' Explain."

"I think different, like scared of love, maybe it feels unlovable."

"How interesting. The emotions, mad, sad, and scared, which can come from fear, can be so alike sometimes." She repeated the words: MAD, SAD,

FEAR, ANGER, and HAPPY, helping us and checking for understanding. We looked over a chart of emotions with faces to guide us. "Does grief sound and look like this some days?"

"Yes!" we shouted in agreement. Mrs. Marks asked all the right questions. She's smart about grief.

Mrs. Marks bent down, selecting a heart from the floor, "My mother wore a purple dress when she sang in the church choir. In her memory, I want to add this to our tree. Now, each of you will choose a color and tell your story. We can go around the room."

"I miss my dad. He got killed racing. I picked gray like the chrome on his cars." Adrian slapped his heart topsy-turvy near Mrs. Mark's purple.

Emma scooped up green. "All my life, I grew up with my grandpa, so he acted like my dad, and he drove a John Deere." She put a finger up to her lips, saying, "Shhh, don't tell Mom, but she thinks she can operate his mower well, but she can't." We giggled. Emma layered her heart sideways, near Adrian's.

We almost needed a microphone to catch Kasey's thoughts for choosing orange. "My mom got hit by a drunk driver. Dad wears orange jumpsuits when I visit him. Granny's who I stay with now."

Henry's reason for pink surprised me. "Dad and I shared the same name. Carnivals, circus, rides, fairs, and lots of fluffy cotton candy were the fun side of him before his brain tumor. Most people just thought he was a serious lawyer."

"I lost both parents in a car wreck during an ice storm. I live with my grandparents now. Shiny black paint covered our car. We once traveled a lot. I miss them." I knew Finn's black heart overflowed with pain. But next to Henry's candy pink, the colors blended and looked pretty.

Finn plopped down by Emma. She reached for his hand. Emma's kindness started sweeping around the room. Hayden leaned over to hold my hand. He's shy, like me. He barely speaks in full sentences. Thoughtfulness gave us all more courage. With a smile, I leaned over, offering my hand to Maria.

"My heart is white. My mom. Cancer. She was a nurse." After he spoke, Hayden squeezed my hand again.

"I need two hearts," Maria said. "Before my mommy hurt herself, my family vacationed in Florida. This blue heart is for the sky, and the yellow one is for the sun. Happy sunny days—that's how I like to remember her."

Tyson collected one red and two blues. For him, they represent love but a different kind, not the romantic stuff. "My mom and baby brothers died in a house fire late one night, while my dad was working. I pushed my little sister out the window. We climbed out to the firemen."

Chapter Eighteen

I chose last. "Brown makes me remember gardening. Mom enjoyed plants and flowers before her stroke."

Hand in hand, we sat, smiled, and stared. Holding on tight, each branch stretched to the limit. The heartbreaking stories we shared turned into a colorful creation.

Mrs. Marks clutched her hand over her heart, gazing at our tree. "How lovely," she said. "By working together, we allowed hope and beauty to enter our lives."

Have you ever witnessed happy tears? Because many of us had them sneak into our eyes.

* * *

Mom, remember my poem, the one I started a while back? It's done. The timing seemed perfect for the hand delivery of my gifts to Gretchen's house.

Oh Little Angel

Grief filled my childhood
then an angel sat beside me
our timid hearts connected
our little hands interlocked

Her hair glowed like
a summertime sunset—
layerings of amber,
copper, flecks of gold—

Her small-town smile,
brightened my broken world—
she quieted my inner storms
shed her silent tears with mine

Our moments—grief-filled
our little hands now growing up
will timid hearts stay connected
her kind eyes—a vision of hope

When should I confess to her
since she doesn't appear to know
oh little angel who sat beside me
long ago, you captured my heart

With everything in my hands, I took my gifts to Gretchen's house. At her front door, I stood knocking with a confused, broken heart, knowing I had nothing else to lose. This was it. I had to offer her what I could. I needed to show Gretchen how she helped changed my life.

"Hi, John, will you do me a favor and deliver these as a surprise to Gretchen?"

"Come in. Gretchen's upstairs. You want me to get her?"

"No. Wish I could stay, but I gotta run. Please tell Gretchen to update me if she likes everything. Thanks, John."

"Wow, I can already tell you, Hayden, she will flip over all this. You carved every detail of each item?—amazing."

"Thanks, John. I hope she loves everything, and I hope I can visit again soon."

BOOM, Gretchen—now, it's all up to you, I thought.

After delivery, I walked away. The cold wind mixed with hot salty tears stinging my eyes. Courage to love someone hurts like a mother-effing ton truck plowing you down but not enough to kill you, though. Life support hooked up to you, but the inhaling and exhaling become a chore, not a priority for survival. Hope. Mom, sometimes that's all a person possesses. I guess that's me: hope for the hopeless?

Well, today, I walked to read you my story and poem. Plus, to share all the current issues going on in my life. Mom, I realize I still may not be able to stand right next to your grave, but I stretched as far inside the cemetery as my heart would allow. I came closer than I ever dared before. Maybe someday? I'm here, even close enough when I peek—I recognize your angel.

Chapter Nineteen

November 2019

Dear Mom,

In nasty haste, I overreacted, screwing up. Hayden became my punching bag. My anger toward my OCD and the Dad fiasco turned into a mess of my own creation with Hayden. Boom? Break up with someone via text message? That's pure tackiness. What's wrong with me? Why do I keep making these dumb personal mistakes? I owed Hayden an explanation—face-to-face of my problem or at least a kinder note asking for a couple days to sort out some things with Dad.

Oh, and speaking of *him*, Dad—what a joke. He's a big faker hypocrite—I think I'll call him "Dr. Love." Or maybe Sneaky Clark Kent with his secret sexcapades! Dad gives new meaning to the word "action figure" when I think of Clark Kent/Superman. Especially when I'm stuck living with him, witnessing him sitting around acting all casual. Dad's on my radar now. I've noticed things. Such as his excessive cologne scents. And like how, after taking his contacts out at night, he plops down to watch TV or read, sporting those dang black-rimmed glasses of his. Does he think he's some hipster? He sits there, pretending—all quiet-like.

~~Mom, is this why *you* called him Clark Kent and Superman? Switcheroo, dude! If so, that's understandable and sweet. Otherwise, I HATE it. Changing subjects. With you gone, it's too hard. You're not able to chat with me about this stuff. Ugh! Grr! Men! I don't know if I'm ready for Dad to *just date around*? I don't want Dad to be slutty. Honestly, I don't want him lonely either.~~

My biggest problem. . . . I don't know what I want? No, what I want is you, Mom. And for some resolution with Dad and Hayden.

Mother, do I even deserve a guy like Hayden, who seems to love me so much? Hayden writes stories about our childhood, remembering tiny details of who said what. He takes his time, crafting thoughtful gifts by hand. My favorite photo from the Summerfort Grief Center now hangs in the dining room (of all places), next to the engraved colorful tree of hearts. In my bedroom, I framed each page of the story and poem. About "Oh Little Angel"—no words yet—what can I possibly say? I tried texting.

Me: Hayden, Thanks for every gift. I wish I could tell u which item ranks as my favorite, but each one means so much to me. No. I put YOU at #1. Please come to the house so we can talk. I'm sorry about the "boom" thing. Let me explain. Plus, I want YOU in my life.

Moments later, dots danced across my phone screen as Hayden constructed a reply but then disappeared. I waited. Three polka dots jiggled again, but again, he decided to send me nothing. Over an hour, drifted. I waited, picking up the phone, staring at a blank screen. Nothing—boom—Hayden dumped me for good.

Me: Hayden, Txt 2: Sorry to bug u again. I'll leave u alone, but I feel u should know one more thing. I'd love to talk in person, but if I'm never given a chance, u need to be aware of how much your poem, "Oh, Little Angel," means to me. The title alone holds power for me. At our mother's graves, I asked for a sign. I expressed to ur mother, "I wanted to be an angel on earth for your son, Hayden." The idea her son already thought of me this way—I'm forever grateful. Thank u. Sorry, I never meant to ruin our relationship.

Another hour drifted. I waited, picking up the phone, staring at a blank screen. Nothing—boom—Hayden's gone.

Dots again danced on my screen as a reply from Hayden lit up my screen. As they appeared, my body felt enlightened. Then they vanished. What was he going to say? Why did he keep changing his mind? I wanted to text again. Beg him to please finish his messages. Please speak to me, Hayden. Nothing for hours. Silent tears exhausted me to sleep.

* * *

A touch tickled down my forearm, in feather-like strokes. "Wake up," says the voice in my dream.

"Shhh, I need my sleep," I said, muffled by my pillow. Some giggle, so familiar to me, filled the air. *Stop laughing at me.* A kiss brushed my forehead then my cheek. My body, or soul, must have traveled overseas. A young British man spoke to me in some odd dialect—he sounded more Southern American than British, but I liked his style—the hot breathy tone near my ear, "Four legs goo—"

"Hayden?" I raised out of bed, throwing my aqua comforter off like Princess Ariel arising from the waves. "What time is it? Why is it so dark outside?"

"Think it's 4:30, or maybe 5 o'clock." He lifted my hand to his face, stroking his chin with my fingertip. "Any shadows lurking?" We giggled. He patted my hand. "You need sleep? Want me to leave? Come back tomorrow?"

"No, stay." I pulled him to me, tightening my grip. "I'm so sorry, Hayden. Are we okay?" He nestled his head against my shoulder, nodding. "Um, does my dad know you're here? Did he let you in the house?"

"Of course. I wouldn't walk inside your house, uninvited." Hayden reached across me and flipped on my WTFDD lamp. "Gretchen, you alright?"

"Better. I think with my hoarding problem, yeah." My eyes shifted to the floor. I pulled my knees up, buried my face into the comforter, "I'm so stupid. It's embarrassing to admit. For days I slept, cried, wrote until I reached a layer of numbness." Hayden's arms encircled me.

"Gretchen, don't be ashamed to reveal *anything* to me. I think you just missed your mom so much, and on some level, I understand all that. Listen, I rubbed cinnamon on my arms to smell like my mother's breakfast toast—I needed to feel her around me in some way. Okay. I get it. You're not alone." His grasp grew tighter. "So glad you texted me and told me you agreed to go to therapy."

"Thank you." I reached for his hands, lacing our fingers, loving the warmth, the calm. I closed my eyes and rested against his chest. Hayden leaned his head down on top of mine. "So comfortable, I might fall asleep."

"Mhmm. I could easily sleep with you." Our foreheads collided after Hayden's unusual choice of words slipped out, but we laughed, untangling. "Well, true," he said, mumbling and stuttering, his face shifted into a rosy glow traveling all the way to his ears. "Hey, the way the words fell out of my mouth—all wrong." Hayden hid his eyes behind fingers in a game of peekaboo, until he lowered his hands to cover his lips.

"I wanna kiss your dirty mouth."

Hayden transformed. His bunched hands fell away, unveiling the corners of his lips, tugging up from my invitation. The smile grew wider until it reached his eyes. I had a front-row seat as our smiles merged. Hayden held me close, threaded his fingers through my hair, wrapping curls around one finger.

Cross-legged in silence, we enjoyed each other's company, huddled together.

"Hayden, can I talk to you about the other stuff, which sent me raging?"

"Of course." He offered a quick peck. Hayden straightened up, cleared his throat, and glared at me sideways. "*If* you don't drop your BS boom bombs on me anymore, Gretchen."

"Oh, shittle-sticks, stop staring at me with your daddy-like eyeballs. I can't kiss you if you keep acting ridiculous. Boom."

"Gretchen!"

Hayden tackled me, peppering me in tickles and kisses. The last kiss ended as a lingering reminder of how much he missed me. We decided to bundle up and take a brisk walk. Summerfort closed school for the entire week of Thanksgiving (next week). My undies episode had occurred Thursday night, and I had missed school on Friday. No one called the "Boom Squad" on me. Yes, mother, I realize "not funny," but sometimes humor defuses a situation—again, poor choice of words. Or perhaps maybe the best? I hated the four days Hayden and I broke up. Time to enjoy Sunday night. Forecast for the week ahead: sunny with less boom.

Small towns, like Summerfort, provide hidden elements of charm. "Everything's Sweeter in Summerfort"—swing open the doors to the holidays because, according to the Chamber of Commerce calendar, Christmas began November first. Downtown flickers and glows, every sparse twig in the park, found a wrapping this year in red-and-white lights. So, the walking trail makes me think I will locate the North Pole if I follow Candy Cane Lane. The gazebo represents a Christmas tree with lights woven in, appearing as pieces of candy.

Hayden draped his coat around both of us. We rested on the bench, between the gazebo and the entrance for the candy canes. Hot chocolate rests in my hands since Hayden disappeared into the store across the street to surprise me with extra marshmallows.

"Want to chat about the nuttiness with my dad?"

"So, you said, John slept with Debbie? The lady who receives Botox like a religious rite and who lives vicariously through Lilly?"

"Yes, De-*bore*-ah? Plus, half the women in the neighboring counties. He switched his barbershop since he got too snippity-clippity with what's-her-face, even."

"Dr. John? Your dad?" Hayden bit his lip, holding in his laughter. I nudged him, and he busted. "Sorry, Gretch, but I just can't envision it."

"Well, don't, weirdo! Your turn. Tell me something funny or embarrassing about you and your dad."

"Dad calls you Strawberry Shortcake and me Huckleberry Pie—"

"What?" I furrowed my brow in confusion.

"You know, the cute doll. Red hair?" Hayden raised an eyebrow waiting for my nod. "That's my dad for ya." Hayden smiled.

"Your Dad's funny. We need to make sure we prank him soon." We laughed. I offered a fist bump and said, "Boom."

Hayden threw a scowl my way, adding a playful growl, before he said, "Ugh, Gretchen, stop it with the booms."

I snorted. "I'll try to behave. Hey, speaking of your dad, I saw him Friday, hanging with Marks at the center." *Hayden, do you not see what I see with them?* But I never speak the words out loud. "Your dad waved to me with paperwork in his hands, so I bet stuff for her house project—what else you got, story-wise?"

"Yeah, Dad must be working on her house. Oh, I know—my birthday party story. Dad commented on you coming over after the game. I panicked about being sweaty. Dad said, 'I would allow you to take a shower, Hayden'—see what happened there—twisted wording, just like with me earlier today? It got very humorous."

I grinned at Hayden. "Hmmm—you never followed through with the offer yet."

Oops. Too bold? Hayden licked his lips, his Adam's apple bobbed as he swallowed hard. He smiled. "I think. No. I hope, one day, I will. Keep talking about it, and I'll need a cold shower *now*." He almost tossed me into his lap, capturing my bottom lip inside his mouth.

Prove it. Words I left unsaid. Did I dare torture the boy, shower him with more commentary? My body yearned for him. Ratty Christmas underwear once created a bit of a barrier concerning Hayden Oliver Tucker.

Hayden removed his coat, fanning himself. He looped the leather sleeves around my waist, lasso-style, using them as a way of luring me into him. I loved the way he grabbed both sides of my face, putting everything into the power of a single kiss.

"Boom," I said, joking. In a fit of laughter, I sprang off, skipping down Candy Cane Lane. Over my shoulder, I asked, "Think you can catch me?" His arms located me moments later. Hayden hoisted me over his left shoulder. "Mr. Tucker, do not drop me."

Hayden showed off by performing mini-lunges for me while I remained anchored to him. He jogged in place and said, "Oh, I know, a cheer." He maneuvered, working his moves toward the ground, shaking his hips, mocking me, "Crotch shot, crotch shot, wiggle, wiggle, down.'" By the time he finished, we both cracked up. He hurled me into the air again, my arms dangling down his back. Down the trail, he ran, but the spinning began.

"Ha-Hay-Hayden." I squirmed, my arms reaching far enough to slap his butt. I hoped my message would make him stop. My first attempt failed, so I tried a second and third time. Words of protest no longer formed, and I tasted acids mixing with hot chocolate, which I pushed back. Out of control, my head swirled, my brain no longer functioning.

"Wow, feisty. You want more?" He misunderstood. Hayden only twirled faster. Hot chocolate flung through the air, splattering, coating candy canes. My body twitched, convulsed, continued to spew. "Oh, fuc—Gretchen, I'm so sorry." Hayden carried me to the gazebo to lie down.

He tucked my hair behind my ears, rubbed my back. Dry heaves racked my stomach. I wrapped my arms around my waist, falling forward, hacking, and choking. Puke clung to the ends of my hair, gagged me. "I'll run across the street and get you some water," Hayden said. "I'm sorry, Gretch—I didn't realize you were getting sick."

"I'll be okay, but I get motion sickness." My eyes fixated on the ground, limbs unmovable. Hayden's shirt lands on the ground beside me.

"What—why—your shirt off?" *The day I touch his butt surround me tossing chunks?*

"I got a bit covered, so I'm going to just use my coat. I'll hurry, Gretch." Flares of red, white, and green lights glowed all around me. I'm stiff, sprawling on the cold concrete floor of the gazebo. Hayden squatted down on the bottom step peering up at me, gripping my hand, offering another apology. "Gretch—please forgive me. I'm such an ass-jerk. I promise I'll be quick." He released a puff of air before dashing off.

I squeezed my eyes shut, begging the world to stop the whirling. All the wrong parts of my body revolved tonight. Caught in a Christmas vortex of hell—in November. Upon an imaginary merry-go-round, my head still spun 'round and 'round and 'round. *Christmas candy—Christmas candy— peppermint sticks—and curling ribbon—candy canes— chocolate Santas—lollipops.* My brain operated in a looped fashion, demanding lyrics. The weirdness, no matter what I tried, nothing shut down the madness or nausea. I dropped off the edge of the ride, with my head aimed toward the ground.

Red crawled across my body, signaling a warning, the color of danger came for me intensely: to reach inside the recesses of my stomach, to yank on the contents within, to force them up through my esophagus, and to fight for an explosive exit. The green light giving the whole action a "go."

Against the white flashes, I became too powerless, my body drained of every ounce of food or liquid inside me. Empty. Tired. Weak. A cheap milk chocolate Santa, now hollow—likely to melt, easily forgotten, crushed, left for dead—*Happy Holidays, Gretchen.*

Chapter Twenty

Hey Mom,

Of course, life serves up piles of roadblocks when someone requires speed. Summerfort Foods parking lot hosted a plethora of vehicles. Even from a short distance, I could tell I needed to prepare for the head-down-dart-dodge-grab-and-go method. Well, what else remained opened in a town our size? And this close to Thanksgiving *and* Christmas? *This town?* At least my coat zipped and buttoned high enough, hiding the fact I strolled in shirtless with bodily fluids attached to me—but not the kind I longed for (sorry, Mother). Thank God we left my jacket on the bench while I had the bright idea to spin my girlfriend like a circus act, not realizing she'd act possessed and projectile vomit.

When Gretchen went all *Fifty Shades* on me, hoping to get me to stop, I thought she liked it, wanted to go faster, so I spun her harder. Kind of charged me up with all of her reachings, wiggling, touching, and slapping. I had fun through the process—if you know what I mean. Hmmm—I think I'll mention it to Gretchen, offer my words with a smile or laugh. At the correct timing—tell her she's allowed to do it again as a way get me back for the spinning? Prepare more cookies to put frosting on that evening as well. . . . ☺

God, I really felt terrible. Gretchen's face looked drained of life before I left. Like, she appeared super sick. I win her back for less than a couple hours, and already, she's dealing with more crap because of me. Why does love create so many complications?

Only a few carts remained in the store, but I found the one with the wheel that was sure to *clunk, clunk, clunk,* so I ditched the idea like how I felt I ditched pitiful Gretchen waiting on me. Gatorade. I went with what Gretchen calls the "*pretty aqua blue one*"—Glacier Freeze (she had taste tested mine via a kiss—said she liked), bottled water, and some kind of sensitive skin baby wipes because I ain't taking any more risky chances.

An exciting new development in small-town gossip transforms before me. Thomas and Lilly might be on a date at the grocery store with Debbie or De-*bore*-ah, as Gretchen likes to call her. "Hey," I stammered, bypassing them. My arms juggle everything as I make my way toward the checkout lines. Thomas offers me another strange look, taking inventory, scanning me from head to toe. Plus, he gives the skank eye to the stuff I carried. Sharp cared too much about a dude with twenty items or less in his hands.

I'm on the fence as to whether Thomas's gazes toward me lately mean he would like to filet me open, turning me into a dead animal he loathes? Or instead, if Thomas desires to treat me like taxidermy—stuff me full, mount me in secret, so he can keep me like a prized trophy? I sense eyes *fixated* on me, so I glance around, finding Thomas's face the only one zeroed in on mine. My whole body pivots away.

Creepy overload. Thomas Sharp's one dude I totally dislike because I don't understand him. I'll never relate to people who choose cruelty toward others for sport.

When Gretchen's 1000% better, I will relay this tidbit of information with her, but I'm not sure she's ready to talk about the trio I dealt with seeing at the store—Lilly (no), Debbie (no), Thomas (no).

Run, Hayden, is all I can muster my mind and body to think and do, except for the nagging *I'm starving.* First, I need to help rehydrate Gretchen and then make a plan to get us both fed, as long as she could function through. "I'm back, Gretchen." No answer.

Her arms dangle over the edge of the gazebo. Evidence of sickness plastered to the walls and lights on the side of the gazebo below her. The scene illuminated with Christmas lights. She looked pale, even more so than usual. "Gretchen—effing answer me. Please." I stumble and stomp up the three wide stairs as loudly as I could. "Hey." She lies there, motionless, a sleeping angel, my Aqua Princess. My feet fail to move forward. The grocery bag lands hard. "Gretchen!" I scream her name again, but I hear nothing in response.

Silence screams. Only my heart pounds so hard my eardrums feel like they might explode. *I can't—why God? Why? Why would you put me through this? I only spun her. This can't be happening.*

Dizzy and through watery eyes, I search and find her by dropping down, sliding across the concrete. My knee throbs. Blood pools to the outside of my jeans. "Gretchen?" I place my hand on her back, shaking her, ensuring she remains among the living. "Jesus Christ, why? Why didn't you answer me?"

"I did. You just didn't hear me." Gretchen says in a mumble, her voice faint.

I try nudging her. "Can't you sit up?" Stretching out my legs, I pull gently to collect Gretchen until her body leans against my chest. "Gretch, your forehead feels super hot. Will you drink something?"

She swats me away. "No. In a minute. Maybe?" I take this as a good sign.

"Gretch, I can't accept no as an answer to everything. I can't let you lay there all night and not help you. I'll put you back down, so I can get our drinks. I think I gotta take my pants off and check my knee. Okay? I'm bleeding, I think." I wonder if saying something crazy might stir her up.

"Okay? What?"

I did pull my pant leg *up*, noticing the scrape on my knee. Not as bad as the blood and pain are making it out to be. Cut but not deep enough for a stitch-worthy hospital visit. Like playing baseball and experiencing a horrible slide into home plate while slicing yourself open on a small pebble.

I prop her against me again. "Gretchen, I bought Gatorade—it's the pretty blue one you like." She sips at the drink. Fumbling, I open the sticky part of the baby wipes and show them to Gretchen. "While you rinse your mouth out and drink, can I wipe your hair and stuff to help you?" Gretchen gives me a thumbs-up. She leans forward like she might blow again, so I hold her hair back and rub her back until she softens.

"Thank you, Hayden." Gretchen falls back into me for a minute, looping her arms around my forearm. She's a beautiful mess, but I love her. The words "I love you" almost tumble out of my mouth right then.

"I'm glad you're speaking in full sentences. Plus, with your eyes open again." I bend down, kissing the top of Gretchen's head (one safe, sick-free location). "You still feel warm, though?" My palm rests against her forehead and cheeks.

"I think I'll be okay. Gatorade fixed my puke face. Starting to see straight again. My world's not flying in circles. Even though my head's hot, I'm actually kind of cold."

"Let me share my coat." I unzip the coat, encircling it around both of us, pulling her against me. "You had me sweating with nerves a bit ago. I've got lots of body heat to offer."

"Oh, yeah. You took your shirt off. I remember now."

"Mhmm." Gretchen escapes from me as she turns halfway around, using her right hand to touch my skin. I loved allowing her time to explore my chest, neck, and stomach, which tickled. My reaction was to flinch and giggle. "You might corrupt me with your magic fingers, little girl." Gretchen's mouth starts moving over me. She peeks up at me, her tongue slightly exposed. I don't anticipate her next bold move.

Gretchen leans down, kissing my chest, following up with tiny nibbles of her teeth—"Whoa." I grabbed Gretchen and lay beside her, kissing her full force, with my whole body on high alert, tingling. My eyes cover over in a needy fog—like a hot, breathy, loopy glaze.

More than anything, I want to give in completely, with an eagerness to explore. "You create issues for me, Gretchen, but I'm glad you feel better—in fact, you know how to feel *real* good. Hella good!" A moan, growl, roar, or whatever the heck

301

one might call this animalistic sound of ridiculousness escapes from me. We chuckle.

Gretchen slugs down more Gatorade, which runs through her veins like an aphrodisiac/energy drink combination. To buy stock in the product someday enters my mind, if this little preview showed me only the beginning of what could happen for us. Too nervous and unprepared for the whole shebang of *sex*, but *some* things seem debatable after tonight?

Mangled in innuendo, this girl carried evil skills on twisting words around. And she never disappointed me in that area. I plan my question with anticipation. "Are you getting hungry, Gretchen?"

She bites my ear. Words follow in whispers. "Starving for hunks of Hayden."

"You make it almost impossible for me to behave, Gretchen," I flop over on my side before I lose all sense. All I could think of is myself performing like one of the neighbor's dogs. He's a whiny canine who spends each night humping stuffed animals because the neighbors insist on placing them in his doghouse.

Snagging Gretchen's hand, I lace our fingers tight, so she doesn't roam. My body has survived all the *near-loving* I could handle. I kiss the back of Gretchen's hands. "I want you *really* bad, Gretchen, but can I talk and ask you some questions first? About, you know, some *sexy stuff*?" My heart surges, banging against my breastbone because I worry Gretchen's expression means, "Hayden, I brand you as a complete and total fool."

"Yep. But did I do something wrong?" Gretchen asks, her mouth forming a straight line before it falls into a slight frown.

"No. No. No—nothing you did seems wrong, Angel. In fact, I love everything a whole bunch. *A lot*." My exaggerated "a lot" caused a react at the corners of Gretchen's mouth, her lips tugged up into a smile, lighting up her face again.

"I only mean things like—where do you rate us on the comfort scale? Like, what are *we* ready for? Or not ready for? Do you know what we should do about protection? Ugh. I don't want to take all the fun out of it. But I want to do things right, you know?"

Gretchen nods in silence.

"What do you think you like? Do you know what's special or important to you? Or what you don't like? What's off-limits? For example, you pulled some fun *Fifty Shades* action on me earlier tonight."

Gretchen spins her body until she's on her back, cackling at me. "Hayden! I tried alerting you to stop spinning me."

"Well, your plan didn't work because it excited me to go faster instead." I smile, kissing her, careful not to linger too long, dragging myself right back into a territory I teeter on the verge of anyway. "So, I guess we know an item we can add to 'Hayden's pro-list column' when the time comes." I squeezed Gretchen's knee.

Gretchen, holding a finger to her chin, tapped it with thought, before pointing at me with a little smirk. "Wonder if I'm pro too?" She shrugs. "In the future, I'm willing to find out if you go easy on me—no twirling involved, though." She laughs.

I hug her. "I look forward to learning all your pros. And even your cons. Gretchen, I'm a total virgin. I figured you guessed that." She nods. "You excite me, but I'm nervous as heck too."

"I understand everything. Me, too, you know, with the whole virgin thing." We glance at each other and smile. Grimacing, I sit up, pulling my knee up to examine the area. "You okay, Hayden?"

"Sure. I just scrapped it when I tripped with the grocery sack. You worried me *a lot*. God, you know, Gretchen, you didn't bother to answer me tonight—that kind of behavior is so naughty—" I wink and start cracking up.

"Oh. My. God. Hayden." Gretchen gives me a playful shove and rolls her eyes. "You want me to pour water on your knee and clean the area for you?"

"You tryin' to get me out of my pants again?" She pretends to choke me before rewarding me with a kiss. I fold my pant leg up until reaching my knee area. "Baby wipes or water—what do you think?"

"Water, first?" I watch as she pours it on the wound.

I hiss, "It's so cold," I stomp my other foot. Gretchen stands with her hand on her hip, head cocked to the side. She finishes with a baby wipe (perfect for me). "A Band-Aid and antibacterial cream for the area, later, sir." Gretchen offers her hand, guiding me to a standing position. "We should eat and take care of your knee."

"Text John for permission. Wanna head to my house for the rest of the night—eat, watch a movie, hang with the cat, or play a game?" Gretchen nods and texts.

"Hayden, I put your shirt down in the grocery bag. I'm so sorry. I'll wash it at my house, tomor—"

"Hey, I don't expect you to. A few squirts of Spray 'n Wash, and I'll soak the crap out of it before I wash it. I appreciate your offer, though. Besides, it's all my fault. Well, wait just a minute, your little escapades created quite the stirring in me." I bump Gretchen with my hip, teasing her.

We start walking in the direction of the house, assuming John will go along with our plan. Gretchen's phone lights up. "Dad doesn't care. Oh, you mentioned some game?"

"Hmm. Yep, I heard about a new one that came out tonight called 'Show Me a Pro from the Sexy List.'"

"Sounds intriguing. Tell me all about the rules and how to keep score, Hayden." Gretchen slowed her pace until we stop, facing toe to toe.

"God, your comebacks amaze me—you win. But I feel like I win because I'm with you. We make up our own rules as we go along, I guess." Gretchen's stomach growls. "Please tell me you're not about to be sick again."

"Hayden, with you around a hunger resides deep within me," she says, then giggles.

"Gretchen, thank you for performing every word tonight with poetic sex appeal." Then her show begins. She talks in her feathery voice, using her hands to guide me down the sidewalk, luring and talking:

"Imagine, Hayden, one night will arrive as the final curtain falls down on the stage. Only you will possess a backstage pass to the after-party—*Our Party*." Gretchen comes up to walk by my side, our legs so close, the materials of our clothing rub and swish, as we hold hands.

"Effing hot damn, I got the Golden Ticket." I clutch my heart with my free hand, and we share a grin. Gretchen reaches around my waist, hugging me, but her hand slips down, lands in my back pocket, stealing a squeeze—a first.

At the post office, I pick Gretchen up, wrap her legs around me. Giving her feathery kisses, gentle pecks, and even near misses, while walking her backward. Until I twist my body, slamming against the bricks at the back of the building. I pressed her into me, knowing, even realizing, she feels my body responding. My mouth smashes into Gretchen's hard. With both hands, I shimmy my way through Gretchen's hair, snaking my fingers beneath her shirt, skimming and cupping new territory over lace. Her skin, satin beneath my touch. Fingernails bite into my lower back. Remembering how much I loved her recent move, I return the pocket favor.

"*Signed, sealed, delivered, I'm yours,*" Gretchen sang, catching her breath. Her eyes snapped wide open.

"You okay, Gretch—I didn't scare you, did I?" I ask, my hands now behaving, resting on her hips. My head goes into hiding on her shoulder.

Oh my god, I'm the neighbor's whiny dog, after all. My girlfriend's against a brick building in public. Happenstance—and at the dang post office? Isn't this what she said her dad called it? Isn't this even where John said he had it occur? Do not utter a word of this to Gretchen out loud, Hayden.

"No, I liked it. I mean, no, wait, yes—I'm okay. Ugh, Anyway, I understand what you mean about things—the questions, safety stuff. I'm a little overwhelmed."

"Cool deal. I'm with you on the overwhelmed stuff. I just told my body to be more chill *AF*. Sorry, Gretchen, poor choice of words." A tiny chuckle came from us.

"Let's go eat," I say, I hold Gretchen's hand until we reach the house, but most of our steps seem awkward, unsure of each other's needs. The trip grows quiet with a cloud of uncertainty as to what we should do or say.

When we reach the house, Dad gives Gretchen and me the once-over, zoning in on my knee, her strangely wet hair, my shirtless situation as I unzip my jacket. "What in the flippity-doodle happened to you two?" Miss Spicy Boots prances figure eights through Dad's feet, so he scoops her up, saying to her, "Lookee what the cat dragged in here tonight for me to deal with." Dad props himself against the banister, staring down at Gretchen and me as we sat on the bottom step, removing shoes.

Our blank stares and silence failed to impress Dad. *Stay calm, Dad.*

"I'm past WTFDD. I'm just at WTF now, Hayden." Dad lets out a sigh and shrugs before saying, "If I had to guess, I'd say you two got in a drunken brawl?"

"No, Dad. Not the case. A little incident at the park. That's all."

"Hayden, did you fight again? Why's your knee banged up—Gretchen's all roughed up too?"

"No! Nobody got in a fight. It's hard to explain." *A little help here, Gretchen. Open your eyes and quit leaning against the damn wall.*

"Well, somebody better start explaining something to me." Dad's voice grew louder.

"Gene, I got sick at the park. I drank some hot chocolate and threw up."

She's alive. Thank you, Gretchen.

I watch Dad throw up one of his hands in the air as he holds Spicy Boot with the other. So far, considering Dad's pulling off his best behavior for Gretchen, thank God. Still, how humiliating sitting with Gretchen while enduring a heated lecture from Dad. *What am I supposed to say to him about how all this occurred?*

"Hayden—Oliver—Tucker—I accept Gretchen's *part* of the story. Was this hot chocolate spiked? Start talking *now*."

"Okay, I bought Gretchen a hot chocolate, and no, it wasn't spiked. No one's drunk or was drinking. We went walking, and I, like, picked Gretchen up, you know, tossed her over my shoulder. I spun her around. Before I know it, she's goin' all freakin' *Fifty Shades* on me, slappin' my butt, so I thought she liked it. Guess what? I went faster. But, no— Gretchen's only trying to warn me she's gonna blow chunks. I didn't understand her signal. Happy now, Dad?"

A growl hurled in my direction, "Hayd—*Huckleberry*, I can't believe you said all that in front of your Dad!" Gretchen rams her back against the wall of the staircase. Using her hands, she does her best to cover her entire face.

Dad's throat creates a noise, almost like a croaking frog, stifling laughter. "Oh my goodness, did you hear them Spicy Boots? The cats out of the bag about Huckleberry and Strawberry Shortcake—"

Dad lets out a small snort, adding, "There's even more to your convoluted story. So, the knee, no shirt—what gives, Huckleberry?"

"Let me try to summarize, Dad. Thankfully, I didn't wear my coat when spinning Gretchen, so only my shirt got puked on. I used my coat to cover up. Here's my shirt." Picking it up, I offered to open the bag for show-and-tell with Dad. He stepped back, holding his palm up to stop me.

"Gene, I get motion sickness. Like the whole world twirls off its axis. Hayden carried me to the park's gazebo, so I could lie down until I stopped vomiting. It took me a while to come around."

"I ran to the store to pick up Gatorade, water, and baby wipes."

Dad closes his eyes for a second before the next phase of his inquisition began. "That's all you bought?" Dad asked smirking. "That sounds like the start of a terrible, horrible, dirty joke, Huckleberry. A young, single guy walks into a store alone, buys water and baby wipes."

I slap my forehead, "Uh, duh, no wonder people threw creepy and shady looks my way."

"Like who?" Gretchen asks as her nose crinkled.

"Nobody important—nobody we like. Nothing to worry about. I planned to tell you when you felt better. I promise." I make prayer hands toward Gretchen.

"So, Lilly and ... who?" Gretchen asks. Of course, she guesses the negative factor of the equation.

"Her mom Debbie, and of all people, I think Lilly's maybe dating Thomas?"

A collective "Ugh."

"Weirdest day and night," Gretchen says.

"Huckleberry, please loan Shortcake some clothes. You two need to clean up. I don't even care if you take 'separate' (Dad uses air quotes) quick showers."

Our eyes take turns darting around at Dad and then each other, knowing we'd told secrets. We crack up.

"Get that stinky stuff you're both wearing in the washer ASAP. Eat and relax a little bit. Here's my last question. How did you get hurt? Give me the knee details." Dad signals using Spicy Boot's paw to look at my scuffed, almost-torn jeans. A small stain of blood had seeped through.

"When I got back from the store, Gretchen acted dead. I got scared, so I bolted over to her, slid, falling on my knee. Seriously, end of the story."

"Wow, Huckleberry and Shortcake, you incorporated a lot into one night: *West Side Story, Romeo and Juliet,* and *Fifty Shades—*"

"Gene, "Everything's Sweeter in Summerfort." The whole town has gone Christmas crazy. Add a Christmas title to our outing—know any nutty small-town Christmas movies with a character who throws up all over the décor in the city park?"

"I don't know about you two," Dad says, strolling away. "A new work proposal came in that I've got to finish sketching. It's a holiday rush order. Please behave. And Gretchen?"

"Yeah, Gene?"

"No more hot chocolate," Dad said, chuckling.

GRETCHEN

Chapter Twenty-One

Dear Mom,

It's almost Thanksgiving. Here's a little story about what happened when I went to watch Hayden play basketball.

The rattle of shaking glittery pom-poms nears the bathroom. Some perfumes show up way before their owners arrive. Since I'm hiding in a stall, I'm forced to taste test a suffocating blend. A sensual bouquet: thorny rose, skunky musk, luscious lavender, and vivacious vanilla extracts. I switch off, holding my breath and pinching my nose. *Sniff it or choke it down?*—my internal dialogue stays running. The voices belonging to the fragrances bother me also, too much plastic fakery.

My conscience tugs at me: right versus wrong. I hit record on my phone because something, somewhere, deep inside of me urges me to do so. Was I wrong when I hit the button? Perhaps I broke the law or school rules by recording, eavesdropping, invading the privacy of others in the bathroom of all places?

"Thomas looks hot out there tonight. I love dating him," said Lilly. "He's so funny and flirty."

Suppressing thoughts to barge out of the stall and barf, I squeeze my eyes shut, hoping not to visualize Thomas, taunting, harassing, bullying or he and Hayden punching each other. "Queer AF" and his past dumb FB messages and IMs: "Hotty, send me a screenshot of the assignment; wanna party with me, Little Red Riding Hood?" Gathering in front of other boys in a locker room, gesturing at my photos like a jerk-off freak (yes, pun intended).

I withstand their makeup reapplications and practice cheering. "Shoot two; shoot two; shoot for two *and score with him* (someone changes the actual cheer)." I couldn't always tell who rambled, except for Lilly. I know some of the crowd, like Jun Wong. A super funny, artsy—if at times a bit eccentric—character. Of all the cheerleaders, I like and even respect Jun. In some ways, she's like Hayden, in the fact she's an athlete but not a stereotype. Being subjected to Mean Girl antics is something I don't fear around Jun. She's in some of my honors classes. Cheerleaders from the upper classes round out the other girls, and my knowledge of them equals acquaintances at best.

"Hayden can also dribble the ball. Know what I mean?" *Not Lilly's voice.*

"Hayden's hot but too quiet and weird. Plus, he's got *Constitution Girl*. He fought with Thomas, remember? Too many negatives," Lilly said.

Hey girls? Wanna play Face Ball? Shoot two; shoot two; two basketballs to the face for each of you! Crotch shot; crotch shot; wiggle, wiggle, down—Gretchen wants to knock you on your ass and break your crowns!

"Oh, yeah, right? Lilly, you had a moment with Hayden once, right?" A Perfume asks.

"Oh, sort of," Lilly replied with a fake-sounding laugh, adding, "you know what they say about quiet types—he can talk with those thick puffy lips of his, girls," Lilly smacked her lips together applying another layer of lipstick. "It only happened once at a party, but I think he liked it as much as I did."

My blood surged through my body, my heart hammering against my chest bone. I'm surprised, I stay quiet. With the click of the keyboard, I text Hayden: **Imagine my surprise when I stood in agreement with Lilly, who claimed you could really talk with those thick puffy lips of yours. Sure seems impressive, though, for "just a little peck" to be so dang memorable? Eh, Hayden?** Then, I never hit send after I consider the source.

Plus, I realize Hayden's contending with Coach Ryan's cliché clipboard session of hollering and stomping in the locker room during this halftime crap. Or he's tangled up with Principal Marshall in photo ops and banners. A blue-and-gray Civil War "Go, Summerfort Eagles" freak flag must be flying down one of these school hallways tonight. God, this high school cracks me the eff up—a mini insane asylum—people rushing around being noticed while others hide, and people like me, the stowaways, wishing way down deep they belonged.

Lilly starts speaking again after all the giggles died down. "Hayden and Constitution Girl, they're both kinda cute though. The whole dead parent thing makes me think of something else—"

"Where's this going, Lilly?" Jun asks.

"Well, consider how much social media attention we can get for our school if we nominated a basketball player for court warming and his smart, pretty girlfriend who both attend the Summerfort Grief Center," Lilly said. "Oh. My. God. Can you just imagine the thousands of people who would like—no, wait—they would *love* our post!"

"I don't know about that idea," Jun said. "Sounds like you're taking advantage of people or something?"

Lilly announces to the crew, "Why? We'd go viral, and they'd get noticed too."

Oh, the dang jumping and squealing. And then more squealing and jumping. Pom-poms fly up, and I worry for a second that one wayward one might land in the toilet with me.

Thank God I pushed play on my cellphone for this piece of information.

"Wait," Jun says. "Lilly, did you ever stop to consider what it would be like to lose if you try to pull a stunt like this? You're taking away your chance of winning against Gretchen—she's got a real chance for votes with *a lot* of kids—band, drama, foreign language, basically all the smart clubs around here. Plus, she'd have all the secret Hayden sports followers versus those claiming they're for Thomas. Really, it's something for you to think about."

"Um, I think Thomas and I will win no matter who or what goes down," Lilly said, her tone so matter-of-fact and less rah-rah.

"Oh, you know, what-the-flippity-do-da, do you think Gretchen would let me rub fake bake on her before our court warming dance? Especially before they put the winning crown on her head! That girl's a serious indoor girl with a hot bod. I just wanna give her a little glow. You know?"

"Jun, you didn't just say those words?" Lilly asked, gasping for air.

"Hey, I like to keep you people guessing about what I'll say next," Jun said. "Besides, boys or girls, I appreciate all the fine works of art." After a few laughs, she adds, "Hayden can jump his sexy self in the mix too. When the time comes, I'll make sure I bring enough tanning gel."

Their voices trail off as they exit the bathroom to perform their halftime showstopper. A cockeyed grin of disbelief spreads across my face—stunned, appalled, but a teeny-tiny piece of me flattered if I tell the whole truth. Sure, those girls think of me as the quiet and weird Constitution Girl. On the other hand, they'd labeled me cute, smart, pretty, worthy, a work of art even—but, for all the wrong reasons, I understand.

But in Jun's odd way, she stood up for Hayden and me. I appreciate and admire her for that. At least I don't think this is my imagination. Jun's secret message to Lilly seemed to be that a lot of kids at SHS mirror the same beliefs about Thomas that Hayden and I do. Jun said, *"Those claiming to be for Thomas."* Even if I still think I'm stuck out on the fringes of everything, maybe I'm still going to be okay.

"Ladies and gentlemen, I'm Principal Marshall, your halftime host tonight. Please, put your hands together. Help me welcome to the center of our very own Summerfort High School stage, the Chheerriinngg Eeaagglleess." This greeting slapped me head-on as I walked back into the gym.

In the bleachers, I spot Gene, so I plop down, asking, "Gene, this halftime business or show, whatever—is a game-show host required? I mean, is this normal?"

Gene pats me on the shoulder with a grin. "No, Strawberry Shortcake, definitely not typical of high school basketball."

Hayden glances up at us with a little wave. He holds up his aqua Gatorade bottle, giving it a little shake, winking at me. It makes me giggle.

"Shortcake, I don't even wanna know what kind of weirdo flirting that is, or what that's all about. You and Huckleberry better not throw up blue all over my house later." Gene tosses a piece of his popcorn at me before offering me some. Gene opens his wallet, pulling out a twenty. "I can buy you anything under twenty dollars, *except hot chocolate*."

"Hilarious, Gene. No, thanks, I'm good." From my purse, I retrieve a water bottle along with a box of Junior Mints. Shaking my candies, I sprinkle a few pieces into Gene's awaiting hand.

As Hayden dribbles the basketball, I eye his biceps in motion. Out on the court, number forty-one in the blue-and-dark-gray jersey stands out. To shift from outdoor football season to the short sleeves, shorts, and the inside court warms my heart. When Hayden controls the ball, I tune out the constant squeaky shoe noises, the grunting, and the odor of sweaty feet permeating the gym.

I admire sporting events, like watching Hayden as he passes the ball, running back and forth, from basket to basket, dodging opponents, slapping the ball, sometimes jumping or shooting. And Hayden also scores a few hoops. Coach Ryan's clipboard obsession annoys me, as does his constant, "Get your head in the game rants," while he paces. He favors standing next to the orange Gatorade watercooler.

Sometimes I space out so much I feel like Coach Ryan's "Get your head in the game" temper tantrums are meant for me. Doesn't Coach Ryan know

I put my whole body in the act of spectating for number forty-one? My mouth, mind, soul, and heart follow the curve of Hayden's fingers as he grips the rounded edges. As the ball drifts, leaving his hands, my eyes travel through the arc and contours of each muscle in action from a single jump—arms, torso, back, and legs.

A replay occurs afterward, verifying whether or not Hayden even lands the points. Gene's clapping alerts me back to reality. Other times, Principal Marshall—who insists on volunteering as a sports announcer—interjects, "Hayden Tucker, number forty-one, what an excellent three-point shot. Swoosh, that's another free throw point for Thomas Sharp. So-and-so got two points on the rebound. Go, Eagles, Go! Wow. This week is Thanksgiving, and don't we have much to be thankful for, Summerfort?"

"So, when do Drew and Cole plan on getting here?" I ask Gene.

"Both preoccupied with serious relationships, so they're Skyping with me. It looks like it's just Hayden and me—I'd like to still invite you and your dad. You want to learn how to cook a turkey and some sides?"

"Sure. That sounds fun. Do you really mean it? You trust me in your kitchen?"

"Well, I'm willing to try," Gene says. "Besides, I see a lot of Hayden's mom in you, personality-wise—caring, smart, and funny." Gene covers his mouth with one hand before mumbling in a super-fast voice, "Plus, bossy, hardheaded, and sarcastic, but each used only when necessary." Then he laughs at his own joke.

"Gene, thank you for your warmhearted and kind compliment. But me, *sarcastic*?" I shake my head at him, smiling.

I think about asking Gene if he thought about dating again, falling in love, remarrying. Stalling, I think of the best way to approach the situation, with this inkling or vibe I get about him and Mrs. Marks. I'm surprised Hayden hasn't noticed or brought it up to me.

"You know, Hayden's mom, Rosie, loved her boys, but she would've enjoyed having a girl around. Shortcake, she would've liked you. Rosie would be happy Huckleberry has someone so kind. I don't think you're so bad either."

My eyes fill with happiness, but I withhold the tears.

"No, no tears, Shortcake." Gene pinches at the bridge of his nose. Without looking at me, he says, "You know, you help me be a better dad, I think. I miss my wife a lot. So, I used work as a crutch to forget, but Hayden's the one who suffered in the process. It killed me to come to these games alone. I threw mean fits and even got too aggressive with Hayden once. I don't know, but I assume he's talked about it with you."

"I knew you'd missed games in the past because of the fight with Thomas. But, no, I didn't know about the other stuff. Hayden never talked about that aspect. I'm glad things are better."

"Well, I'm happy you're around, Shortcake. Continue being kind to each other. Both of you have been through enough already."

Hayden approached us, sweaty but willing to fist bump or hug. I picked both. Plus, I pull a handful of jersey into me for a surprise kiss. Not often do I like full-on PDA, but tonight's mood calls for a little extra attention for Hayden.

In the hallway, my back rested against the school's blue lockers while I waited for Hayden. Gene excuses himself to warm up the truck. The Perfumes cluster together for their hallway parade, strutting in a manner I call the "tricky-trot." Making sure my voice sounds extra chipper, I say, "Hey, Lilly, I learned we could've been sisters. Did you know our parents dated?"

"No way. How funny. Wouldn't that have been cool? A little sister." *No! We're the same age?* Lilly pats me on the dang arm, strutting on past like I'm an afterthought. Not cool. Not funny. I know, though, Lilly's never cared about me at all.

But Lilly wiggled her fingers, motioning the others to go ahead. After the Perfumes got out of hearing distance, her words floor me. "Gretchen, your dad probably blabbed all my family's dirty little secrets to you."

I shook my head.

Chapter Twenty-One

"Oh, sure," Lilly said, snorting. *Go ahead, call me a liar, Lilly!*

"Anyway, if our parents had stayed together, I'd have dealt with it. Okay? I know that you know about my dad's gay affair, and that's why he chose to move away. Things are better. Calls and visits happen sometimes. My dad's happy. My mom's happy. I'm more than okay. Thanks, I guess, for protecting my privacy and not spreading rumors."

Lilly peers at me for the first time with an expression of someone worth liking. Maybe I liked the humanity I saw reflected in her eyes? Too fleeting, though. Seconds later, her eyes narrowed into slits. Her glares turned into something on the verge of threatening.

WTFDD, Lilly! You just dropped a big bomb! Why the daggers? Why not a truce? "You'd do the same for me, *right*? I get it. No problem with keeping the secret, Lilly."

"Thanks, Gretchen."

"I'm sorry about your dad. I know how hard it is to lose a parent in *any* capacity. I suppose even like moving away. In the end, you didn't have to share a dad. Or you didn't have to feel like you had to *steal* mine away from me. So, I guess we're all good." I said.

Lilly's face crumples, but she offers no comeback. My passive-aggressive words leaked out before I could stop them. After living in the shadow of hurt and anger over Lilly's "dead mom stealing," this seemed mildly mean in comparison.

She spins and waves good-bye with her balled up hand, her cheer skirt swishing as she picks up the pace. She reaches jogging status, catching up with her "friends" as they point, laughing at her but not with her, and scream, "Hurry up!" Living inside her land of golden hair, resort wear, pompoms, and glittery cheer, Lilly's bubble—all of it—reeks of make-believe. She doesn't even have a real supporter with Thomas Sharp as a boyfriend. I feel sorry, or maybe it's sadness for her. She said: "Dad's happy; Mom's happy; I'm more than *okay*."

The distaste of Lilly lingers but lessens after finding out about her dad's infidelity and abandonment. Could this explain *some* behaviors? No free passes or excuses. On my phone, I debate deleting the audio I recorded earlier in the bathroom. Delete. For now, I'll focus on a well-deserved and decent upcoming holiday season. What ifs are bugging me, though. That whole grief boy/grief girl nomination BS—what if it does get brought up? What if Lilly and Thomas gang up as a duo to bully people?

The day before Thanksgiving, Gene tells Hayden and me he needs us to open a gift. He wants us to begin preparing as many of the dishes as possible ahead of time. On Thanksgiving Day, we won't be scrambling, rushing, and stressing, which causes people not to enjoy the holidays.

Each of us picks out a side dish and dessert we want to devour, and then we plan to narrow down the options. Turkey remains the main dish. Gene votes for green bean casserole and pumpkin pie. Hayden chooses mashed potatoes and pecan pie. Dad selects macaroni and cheese and pumpkin pie. I pick macaroni and cheese and pecan pie. So, everyone wins. I also thought a bagged salad, cranberry sauce, rolls, and some corn will make the table look complete. Gene assures me I can have a tablecloth, candles, and a centerpiece.

Mom, inside the Tucker's dining room, I don't suffer the weight of haunting visuals, like seeing my mother's empty chair. The echoes of my mother's voice planning a birthday party she never attended are silenced. At the Tuckers' home, I enjoy being a teenage girl in love. Because at home, I identify with a trapped little girl in our dining room. Nothing will change the fact that I will miss you on Thanksgiving, no matter what table I'm sitting at or where I'm located in the world. The new traditions this year give me hope. Finding a place with welcoming people makes their home appealing. This feels like the intended meaning of Thanksgiving.

The camera on Gene's iPhone sits open on the kitchen counter next to the two matching white gift boxes. A red bow adorns the top of one, while a blue one is on the other. Written on the outside in black Sharpie: **To Gretchen, Love Gene, Happy Thanksgiving.** The other package follows in the same pattern: **To Hayden, Love Dad, Happy Thanksgiving.**

"Dad, do you want us to open at the same time?"

With his camera aimed and ready, Gene instructs us, "Tear open the presents."

"Gretchen, a.k.a. Strawberry Shortcake," I said, reading the inscription on my new apron. Gene designed a caricature of me as Strawberry Shortcake drinking hot chocolate, reading the Constitution, and wearing a WTFDD necklace.

I run to hug Gene, laughing. But knowing how much effort he put into the project created a lump in my throat. "What a perfect gift, thanks, Gene."

"I'm glad you like it," Gene says.

"Dad—" Hayden stares at his. He traces the threads, inspecting everything.

"Read the inscription," I say.

"Hayden, a.k.a. Huckleberry Pie," he states, placing the garment back down on the bar. We chuckle at Hayden's caricature. Gene went with an athletic Huckleberry Pie Hayden, with his letterman jacket opened minus a shirt on but inked with the number forty-one on his chest, along with exaggerated six-pack abdominal muscles. He's juggling a football, basketball, and Miss Spicy Boots. I'm tossed and kinda peeking over his shoulder, holding a baseball bat.

"I hope they make you two happy. When Hayden first mentioned inviting you here, I remember how looney but excited he acted. This makes everything all worthwhile for me," Gene says.

Hayden reaches out to Gene, "Thanks, Dad."

"Can I be in the group hug?" I ask. Gene and Hayden yank me in.

Chapter Twenty-Two

November

Dear Mom,

Gretchen and I cooked up quite a mess, along with a lot of fun while preparing and setting up for our first Thanksgiving meal together. When I took her into the pantry for the spices, she paused, saying, "What's up with this little room? I like it. It feels so *homey in* here."

The moment enveloped me like a spiritual sign or message. My heart rattled out of tune. Goosebumps ran down my arms. Gretchen saw my eyes overflowing, so I would have to explain.

"Remember when I said I used to put cinnamon on my arms to smell my mother?"

Gretchen nodded.

I stepped on my tiptoes, pulling down the storage container hiding the old spices, toy trucks, and some of the cookbooks. I shared my story of playing day and night inside the pantry, searching for "*Home*." How Dad found me here with your apron, cookbooks, and spices. My arms dusted, spices piled up, creating roads, the aroma of my mother all around, longing, and always searching. This pantry became a place I could find a little piece of heaven, a bit of "*Home*."

"So, your mom's apron holds extreme value to you. Wait. I suppose, the aprons Gene made us? Gene filled them with so much humor but not as a gag gift—they contain a ton of sentimental worth?"—Gretchen narrows her eyes—"more than I even realized when I opened it?"

I nodded my head as I embraced Gretchen. Like on my birthday, God granted me another moment of thankfulness. Sometimes in life, people wish to be anywhere else or to be anyone else. But I'm Hayden. I'm the proud son of Rosie and Gene Tucker. I'm happy. And I'm "*Home*."

After touching old memories, the aroma of spices lingered in the air—the spirit of my mother. Vanilla, cinnamon, baked goods, all of these scents trigger emotion. For so long, loss strangled me with the secrets tucked away on the top shelf inside the pantry. Homesick and alone, a lost little boy, afraid to talk, open up, share his heart about *his* "*Home*."

As the youngest boy of Rosie and Gene Tucker, my heart tends to backtrack, knowing my mother told me not to worry, not to hurry to grow up too fast. Today, however, I sensed a *little* push, an urging. With my face buried in the warmth of curly hair, which shined in color as a cross between paprika and nutmeg, I smelled courage.

Noticing a small card table we used for the holidays and the extra stack of chairs, I pulled out two chairs. I unfolded them, placing them in the center of the pantry for Gretchen and me, so we could sit and chat. Gretchen slid into place, facing me, our knees and fingertips touching.

"Mornings often consisted of toasted bread, with Mom's signature formula of gooey butter, ensuring the cinnamon pooled on top. If extra time allowed, she drew a heart outline with the knife before serving me. Other times, Mom cut out shapes with the cookie cutters matching the seasons or celebrating the holidays. The cinnamon toast was our big thing."

Gretchen swiveled sideways in her chair to motion up near the ceiling, "So, the tall canisters filled with cookie cutters all mean a lot to you, huh?"

I nodded. "Before hospice arrived, Mom realized she was sick, but I didn't yet know. She'd only told Dad. Mom adorned me in her apron and this little chef's hat. Dad took a few pictures, I now recall." I smiled at Gretchen as I retold the story. "For the first time, I understand how much trouble my parents went to in making these memories for me." Gretchen angled toward me, placing her hands on my thighs before embracing me.

"Aww, I need to see these pictures." Giddy anticipation sprang from Gretchen's voice.

"I haven't wanted to look at photos for so long. Now, I think I'm prepared. Oh, that apron hung on me like a dress, but I'll show you so we can die laughing together." I scoffed. "Still, I loved wearing 'Kiss the Cook' across my chest."

"'I'd Kiss the Cook,' for sure." One chair became enough as I pulled Gretchen onto my lap until she collided with my mouth. "Tell me more about your childhood."

"Mom propped me up on the counter with the bread, butter, toaster, and all the cooking utensils. We worked together on perfecting a platter of treats. After hospice set up, I would sneak toast to my mom. In the beginning phases, she nibbled on the bread with praise for my cooking and decorating skills."

"You've always been so sweet." Gretchen rested her head against my shoulder. My arms wrapped around her while she sat in my lap. I grew fidgety, clamping down on Gretchen tighter. My breathing deepened.

"Hayden?"

"This part of my story is hard to share, but I want and need to get it out. I've never told my story in front of our whole group. Just Mrs. Marks knows." My eyes, half-filled with tears, closed for a moment.

"Hayden, you can tell me anything. I'm here for you."

"I remember saying something like, 'Mommy, I brought you our treat. Wake up.' I shook her arm. 'Mommy?' Her head rested on the pillow, motionless. My words—'Mommy, wake up'—repeated, growing louder and louder. Through blurry eyes, I begged her, until I literally screamed, 'Mommy, please, please, open your eyes!'"

Gretchen swallowed hard. She listened without interrupting me, but the corners of her eyes grew wet, and using her knuckles, she tried disguising the pain, swiping at it before it ran down. "Gretchen, do you need me to stop? Is this too much for you?"

"No. Tell me." Gretchen rooted closer to me.

"Hospice had helped Dad set up Mom's hospital bed in a portion of our den. We had created a whole makeshift bedroom downstairs. A baby monitor allowed him to keep tabs on her when hospice nurses took breaks. When no one else was up or around, and no scary medical treatments were underway, I enjoyed putting on Mom's apron, so I could give her an early breakfast surprise visit. Because for a few moments, I had her all to myself. Dad heard the plate of toast shatter as I screamed, 'Mommy, please, please open your eyes and wake up,' coming through the monitor on his nightstand."

"Hayden, I had no idea you were the one who found your mother." Cradled inside Gretchen's arms, I found peace for a moment.

"'Where are they taking my Mommy? What did I do wrong? Why won't my Mommy wake up?' I remember asking all these questions to all these adults milling around this house, Gretchen." I puffed out my cheeks, releasing a heavy sigh through my gritted teeth.

"You had the right to ask those questions, Hayden."

I positioned my right hand onto Gretchen's right shoulder, and the left side followed the same pattern. "I asked, but the biggest issue became that nobody cared to listen to me. Or nobody had any answers or even responded to my voice. Maybe they just didn't know how to tell a six-year-old his mother died? Or they wanted to spare my feelings? Or they didn't want me to think it was my fault? Damn it. I needed someone to say something and listen sooner."

Situated on top of Gretchen's shoulders, my fists bunched, I swear they almost took on a persona, staring me down. Even through burning, watery eyes, I could see them. Gretchen reached up, hauling my hands into her lap. "You have the right to be angry about this situation, but I want to hold your hands. Keep sharing, Hayden."

"Do you realize the effing nickname, 'Hardly Speaks Hayden,' comes on the scene because of all this? After I witness a blanket draped over the head of my dead mother as she's wheeled out of my home? If I didn't deserve words, people around me didn't deserve words, so why should I share effing words? I labeled myself unimportant at six years old, silencing my voice, but really my heart, too, I guess."

"I'm sorry this happened, Hayden. You know you're important to me, right? I hear you and understand." Gretchen sniffled, blinking back a flood, but I mopped the unruly mess skating down her face with my fingers.

"Gretchen, remember—you're the little angelic girl with the copper hair who stole my heart and held my hand. Never once did you join other kids in laughing at my emotional silence by chanting or calling me, 'Hardly Speaks Hayden.' You never saw me like others did as a 'Momma's Boy' or 'Queer AF.' Somehow, Gretchen, you got me all along, even when you didn't know the whole story. I think I've always been just Hayden to you." We shared a quiet embrace for a few moments.

"Well, I have a secret pet name I call you," Gretchen said before she slapped a hand covering up her I-should've-kept-my-mouth-shut smirk. Her eyes widened in this uh-oh flare at me.

"What?"

"Hot Boy for Hayden Oliver Tucker. Get it?" She let out an embarrassed giggle.

"Gretchen! Hot Boy?" We cracked up so much. Her body tilted, almost falling off my lap and onto the floor of the pantry. One glance at each other led us right back into another fit, unable to speak, our bodies wobbling. Once the tears of laughter stopped, I shook my head. "Hot Boy—seriously, Gretchen?"

Gretchen licked the tip of her finger, caressing my arm as she made a hissing sound. "*Sizzzzling hot,*" she said, adding a closed-mouth snigger. Snuggled close for a hug, whispered lyrics started pouring out, "I'm hot-blooded, check it and see. . ." She continued her notes and movements. Pauses occurred for only split seconds, enough time for nips at my ears. In a hot breathy method, Gretchen whisper-sang Foreigner's tune, squirming on my lap—she longed to dance.

Visuals in my mind had me smuggling dollar bills in unmentionable places. Hardly Speaks Hayden may have been silent, but his thoughts spoke volumes. Gretchen's skills could make it rain money. Green cascaded, flooding my brain. . . .

"I love this *too much.* Ugh. You're killing me, Gretchen." I said each word in an achy tone because that's exactly how I meant it. Every part of my body throbbed. My lips latched on to her mouth to quiet her, my hands grabbing hold of her hips to stop the sway. I wanted this girl I so loved. "I'm about to go postal again if you know what I mean."

Gretchen playfully pouted. "Okay. I'll settle down. Mailman Hayden, as I recall, well, he was hella Hot Boy, though." She said each word with her fingertips like they were dipped in paint, tracing imaginary zigzag patterns down my chest. A tiny chuckle escaped us. All her moving around rustled up her signature scent, Love Spell, and I further drifted. Some abracadabra stuff is being done on me, I swear. One look-see inside those blue-green pools of Gretchen's, and I'm under the influence. I'm about to dive in and drown.

No, don't stop dancing, Gretchen. Keep on entertaining me. I love you. Ass-jerk, say it. Do it. Be brave. Stop the one-sided conversations inside your head. Put the words out there.

"Gretchen, I'm so thankful for you. I appreciate how you get me, how you listen to me, all you do to help me. I hope through my actions, you know all this already." Gretchen nods with a smile. "With my whole heart, I also believe you deserve to hear some more *words* from 'Hardly Speaks Hayden' today." I intertwined my fingers, then stretched them out, cracking my knuckles.

Gretchen stared at me wide-eyed, her lips in a straight line. Maybe unsure of me? Fearing what I might say or do next? I've never been much of a knuckle cracker as a way to stall before. She crossed her arms and asked, "What's up?"

"Everything's fine. I hope so, anyway. Is it okay to let you know that I love you, Gretchen?"

Her arms swung open, uncrossing with speed as they flung around me. "I love you, too, Hayden."

Chapter Twenty-Three

Dear Mom,

Mom—I wanted to write the dog story before I explained what occurred at (under) the Thanksgiving table. I really hate revisiting the actual incident. I'll write as much of it as I can remember. A few details may be missing or forgotten as to what everyone said to me that day, but you'll get the gist.

* * *

Early December.

"The Fall Out After Thanksgiving."

"Please, help me! I need you to save my dog!" an unknown male voice said, crying out as he barged through the doors of Dr. John Gardener's veterinary clinic. Dad's closed on Sunday afternoons, but after receiving a warning call on his emergency line, Dad picked up, saying, "Sheriff Lowell?"

At first, I found it odd Sheriff Lowell accompanied the young man. Dad and I had assumed the injured animal belonged to Lowell. The wailing boy's large breed of dog, which appeared to be an older Boxer, came wrapped inside his arms, presented in a blanket. All of which obstructed my view of the boy's face. As he stood there, he was just Crying Guy with Dog to me. Not an unusual scene at a vet clinic.

Dad jotted down information from Sheriff Lowell. I overheard him say, "John, I accidentally hit the boy's dog out on Country Club Road. Dang it, you know, the spot where the hill curves and everybody wrecks. The boy and dog jog, but Cliff got too close to the edge of the road—"

My focus turned to the eyes of the dog as they fought to open as he looked at me. As I continue to assess the dog, Cliff's tongue hung out of the side of his mouth. Blood began pooling at the location where the collar attached to the leash. A slight gash, along with a patch of missing fur I noted mentally, so I could show Dad later.

In a calm tone, I said, "Dad, he's losing blood, so the dog needs help here." I knew Dad would recognize my comment as "hurry."

The boy wailed louder before he said, "Help us, Gretchen."

No! I froze. I detested the sound of his voice. Even his sobbing annoyed me. Summerfort's "class-clown" jock, Thomas Sharp. No matter what,

I desired to help any dog survive. Regardless of the owner's status as the biggest ass-jerk in town.

Dad's voice boomed. "Sheriff, escort him out of here, *now*!" An accusing finger pointed in the direction of Thomas Sharp. "Sheriff, I will *not* allow a sick bastard kid who bullies my daughter and other kids inside my place of business. He's not welcome here. Look, he's over there boohooing about his Boxer Clifford, but if the tables got turned, he'd be the first to call someone else in this same situation a fucking dog fucker." Dad's face flushed bright red the more he rattled on.

"John, I understand, but let's calm down," Sheriff Lowell said.

Please, God, don't let my dad die of a stroke over this. Dad just breathe like the purple octopus we once read about. Please, Daddy. Please!

My eardrums exploded with hammering. Every heartbeat detonated bursts to my brain. I stood swaying. But I realized I couldn't move. Fear kept me stuck in a position near Cliff and Thomas, who continued sobbing behind his blanket. Sheriff shuffled, nearing closer to Dad, going toward him in such a slow motion I worried he was preparing to use force. Dad saying or doing something else to escalate this situation seemed and felt like a real possibility. I wanted to run closer to Dad to calm him down. I tried helping Cliff, but I wanted to shove Thomas as far away from me as possible. Shove, run, help—how could I do it all?

The earth swayed. Hives or goosebumps dotted my skin. My gut dipped and fluttered. Puking or passing out, maybe even both, became very likely.

Dad's voice spewed like a volcanic eruption. "Thomas Sharp pretended to dig up my dead wife and Gretchen's mother. He sent photos of shovels and boots, lurking at the gravesite with a private online message: **'Hope you're buried under six-feet of treats for Thanksgiving'**—calling the incident just a prank, a silly joke."

"I'm sor—" Sheriff Lowell tried breaking into the conversation, but Dad wasn't going to stop talking.

"Thomas may never understand how Gretchen, Hayden, Gene, and I were haunted and set back by his words and images forever. Like a hot iron branded on my brain, there's my wife's gravesite and those—those horrible thoughts—" Dad coughed, choking down pain. His hand curled into fists that went to the edge of each eye, as he wiped at the corners. "John?" The sheriff stepped toward Dad, offering comfort, but Dad swatted Sheriff Lowell's hand away before continuing his speech.

Sheriff acted like a referee—his eyes glued on Dad as he stayed within grabbing or helping distance for each of us. What was I supposed to do?

Through clenched jaws, Dad said, "Thomas, thanks for ruining the first *perfect* Thanksgiving meal we sat down to in years. We hadn't even made it to dessert, but Gretchen seemed determined in her happiness to take photos of the food, the table settings, all of us smiling. Then *you* happened. Gretchen experienced a panic attack over the trauma. One minute my daughter's thrilled. Next thing I know, she's hiding under the table, shaking, wailing, pleading from someone to go check on her mommy's grave. She could've ended up in the hospital, you little fuc—"

Dad glared at Thomas, stopping himself. Instead, Dad slammed both fists down, pounding the top of the counter. I jumped. My eyes popped open as wide as possible. A noise from beneath the front desk made me wonder if Dad had kicked the door where we store the flea and tick medicines.

Cliff whined. Sharp begged and pleaded, saying, "Please forgive me. Help my dog. I've offered to volunteer at the grief center as part of the community service my parents are making me do to make up for my mistake. I'm sorry. I understand what I did was horrible, Gretchen and Doctor Gardener."

Dad started rambling again and flailing his hands, saying, "I'll tell your parents, police, courts, or whoever the hell finally listens how I disagree with you being at the grief center. Unless you've got an armed guard with you. And then only if you're assigned trash duty. You need to stay away from kids, especially my daughter." Sharp's still blubbering, sucking his snot.

"You not only go to the gravesite as only a sick fuck would, but you also verbally assaulted

Gretchen in the locker room. I know all about your jack-off antics and oral sex rants. Oh, while we're face-to-face wanna tell me how you'd like to fuck my daughter?"

Sharp sounds like he may asphyxiate tears, snot, and words as he says, "No, sir. I'm sorry. The guys in the locker room were just egging me on. It was only a joke on Hayden. I was only kidding and trying to tease Hayden."

"A jokester? There's having fun and teasing people, and then there's just being a dumbass. And guess what? You're *not* funny. Stop including my daughter in all your dumb bullshit."

Dad's voice rises once again as his hands twisted back into angry cannons, ready to punch. "I don't understand a reason for your brand of cruelty. You're a popular athlete from a stable home."

"John—" Sheriff Lowell offered a calming but stern voice, approaching Dad with his arm outstretched.

Right on his heels, Sheriff Lowell stepped in line with Dad. Lowell's hand went immediately to his nightstick as Dad stomped toward Sharp. My eyes squeezed shut. Wobbling back and forth, praying to wake up from this nightmare. A pulsing rush from my heart surged into a ringing inside my eardrums. Sweat beads trickled down my back. I longed to switch off the sniveling sounds of Thomas Sharp, Dad's thundering footsteps, Sheriff's clanging cuffs, and Clifford's weakening yelps.

Imagining the worst, I didn't want to watch as my father was beaten or arrested should he attack Thomas Sharp, who's just a teenager. I might not always like Dad, sometimes even calling him Dr. Love and Mr. Happenstance, but he's also the very kind Clark Kent who enjoys playing One to Twenty-Seven. But he slept with Lilly's mom. Today, I detected a grief-filled rage expel from him. Doctor Gardener, my father, isn't a violent man. He's human. And being human means having pluses and minuses and reaching limits, *including Dad*. I once thought his Halloween behavior over fishnet stockings seemed over-the-top. What a harsh way to learn this lesson about how much passion and ache still resides inside Dad's human heart. I didn't comprehend how much Dad loved the people in our life.

Dad's roaring announcement jolted me to open my eyes.

"Imagine, you're six years old, but instead of worrying your dog might die, you have a mother's death to deal with. Cliff will survive. But not Gretchen and Hayden's mothers. Or other kids hurting. Think about that and consider it for the rest of your life." Dad said, as his final words for Sharp before turning his attention to the dog.

Soon, I witnessed Dad gently rubbing fawn-colored fur. "I will fix you up," Dad said, whispering in Clifford's ear.

"John, sorry you guys have this FUBAR situation with Thomas. Man, thanks for treating the dog

343

since my car caused the injuries. I'll take care of things: Take the kid home, tell the family about the dog, even arrange all pickup and delivery, Doc." As the sheriff prepared to leave, he gave Dad one of those hardy "on your side" pats to the shoulder.

Dad continued attending to Clifford's basic needs as he nodded at Sheriff Lowell, who walked sobbing Thomas out the door.

Once Dad finished caring for Cliff, he said, "Gretchen, I'm sorry I spoke like that. My language was asinine—my tone and my choice of words. I threw the F word around more today than I have in years."

"Que sera sera," I sang. "Things happen."

We both laughed.

"It freaked Thomas out. Got your point across. Sheriff Lowell got the hint. I didn't want you pushing things until you got arrested. And, Dad, if you talked to me like you did to Thomas. . . . Um, holy heck, I think I'd crap myself."

Dad chuckled. "Gretchen, sometimes, I don't know how to respond to you." He pulled me into a hug. "Just know I will defend and protect you. I love you, kid."

"I know, Dad. I love you too."

* * *

Chapter Twenty-Three

Thanksgiving

Mom, again, a few details may be missing or forgotten as to what everyone said to me that day, but you'll get the gist. As Dad mentioned, I decided to take photos of our meal with Gene and Hayden when I noticed a message. What would a quick check hurt?

BIG MISTAKE!

Your headstone and a pair of boots came into view. A shovel gave the impression of grave digging. Someone's feet had stomped down the grass nearby. Words appeared: **Hope you're buried under six-feet of treats for Thanksgiving!**

From what I recall, I screamed, "Why?" shoving my phone over to Hayden, who had been posing near me for the photos.

"Oh my God, that low-life freaking idiot. Thomas Sharp, again!" Hayden said. I slid out of my seat onto the floor until I reached a place under the table in hiding. Following after me, Hayden said, "Gretchen, come here. I'm so sorry."

By now, I was under the table in the fetal position, mumbling. Images of my mother's grave freshly dug, stomped on, and destroyed ran through my mind. Hayden's trying to hold me and console me, while Gene and Dad begged for answers. Everyone's words sounded like gibberish. Hayden realized he's clutching the photo proof and handed off the phone to Dad, saying, "John, I'm so sorry." It's probably best I didn't see Dad's reaction or remember every detail.

Dad reached me in seconds. "Please! Please! Go! Go check my Mommy's grave," I begged over and over, rocking back and forth. My body trembled so out of control.

"Shh, baby, I'm here. I need you to breathe for me, Gretchen. Come on—can you focus on me?" Dad kept saying things like that.

"Please—my mommy's grave," I cried over and over, gasping, kicking, protesting until nearly collapsing.

Hayden asked, "John, her heartbeat?" Holding my wrist, Hayden offered Dad a thumbs-up, suggesting the beats were too fast? Through the blasting, woozy palpitations, I remember Hayden whispering things to Dad, "John, I'm worried. What can we do?" Struggling to listen, my mind battled against my body.

"Gretchen," Gene said, "I'm headed to your mom's grave for you. Your dad and Hayden will stay here. Shortcake, I promise to hurry. Sit up and do me a favor, okay?" Holding a half-full glass of water, Gene asks, "Will you sit up and drink this? And, hey, will you watch Hayden and your dad for me while I'm gone?"

Pulling myself up with Hayden and Dad still near, Gene offered me the water. With shaking hands, I accepted.

Hayden rubbed my back. "Want me to help hold the glass until you're ready?" I nodded.

Gene's requests were so odd they required me to stop and think. *What? Why? Do I want water? Do I need to be in charge of grown men? Gene, you're so weird! But you're also kind, loving, and competent. I love your welcoming home. I love your son. I love your friendship. I guess I simply love you too.* I nodded my head. My sobbing turned into silent tears as my body began to slowly calm down. The first words I spoke after Hayden helped me, so I could swallow a sip of water were for Gene. "Thank you." A silent hug, his only reply, as I heard truck keys jingling in his hand.

As promised, Gene worked fast, returning with his news. "Thomas Sharp didn't harm the grave; he's just a freaking jackass."

"Dad, let me go to his house and pulverize that ass-jerk. We own a shovel and some boots. I'll gladly give him a few treats," Hayden said, punching his right fist into his left palm.

Gene said, "I hear you, bud. I understand, but you've got to stay away from him because if you respond to him online or in person, it makes you just as much a bully as he is."

Hayden scoffed.

A gruffer version of Gene's voice filled the room as he pointed his finger at Hayden. "I mean it, Hayden!" Quickly, though, Gene squeezed Hayden's shoulders, relaxing the mood.

My heart played a ballad, beating out the narrative of this day. Some moments so dramatic, I almost refused to write one word of it. Broken down, my gaze climbed from the ground to Dad, who spent time on the phone, sorting out details with the police.

He looked as if he were pretending. Like his late wife's grave hadn't been violated. But the mother of his daughter's had been. Dad couldn't fully disguise the droopy-dog eyelids. I noticed. He stood on that day as a pillar of strength because he loves me.

In a glass of water and through the sound of Gene's odd questions and even his truck keys, I witnessed love. On my behalf, Gene went to the grave. Past experience tells me that's deep friendship or love.

From the whispers of fear underneath the dining room table, through the noise of anger, I realized every word Hayden spoke expressed love, protection, and respect. No one had the right to disrespect and hurt me. Hayden would be there, sitting beside me. Even if it's to wrap his arms around me beneath a table through tough times.

In fact, all three of these crazy men have nothing else to prove. My heart beats to a tune: I am loved.

The chief of police invited Dad and me to come in person, so we could file a report on Thomas about the online cruelty and photo harassment.

He said, "This paper trail is your best bet, but honestly, Missouri's law is such a gray area on juvenile cyberbullying. In 2017, Missouri was one of seven states in the US with anti-bullying laws, but they didn't back it up with any real policies. This came in the wake of the poor little girl Megan Meier who committed suicide after being harassed by an adult pretending to be a boy."

Chief Kyle placed several articles on the round table for Dad and me. Shuffling through each one, he pointed out headlines. In a monotone voice, he rambled. "Look. Here you can see far too many elected officials don't want to criminalize teens. Not in the arena of cyberspace, anyway. History shows me they'd say something like Thomas didn't actually dig the grave. He didn't threaten bodily harm. Gretchen appears physically fine. He made a poor judgment call, which is a mistake, but it isn't a crime."

Dad sighed.

"I know, John. If I were Gretchen's father, I'd be unsettled too." He went on, "It seems the elected officials want to debate PSA on parenting, online safety, and then turn the issue over to the schools to teach. John, I'll reach out to Thomas Sharp's parents. I know them, and they'll be devastated. As a person of law, I can recommend to the parents they might consider getting him some juvenile services. Sometimes I work behind the scenes of Summerfort to make things happen. Do you want any kind of meeting set up with the parents?"

"If they request anything, I'd want it done here," Dad said. "Otherwise, not at this time." Dad turned his attention to me. "Gretchen, do you want to speak to them? Do you have any questions for Chief Kyle?"

I shook my head.

Dad pushed his chair out and shook hands with the chief before he said, "Sometimes laws don't seem to protect younger victims very well. I'll file anything that kid does against us from here on out. Please be sure to tell every member of the Sharp family that for me." Dad led me out of the police station.

In the car, I glanced at my phone. Dad and I were included in a group text that had come in from Gene and Hayden while we were inside the station:

Gene and Hayden Tucker request the honor of your presence at their Thanksgiving table to finish dessert. Plus, we have leftovers to share. Martha Stewart, eat your heart out because Gretchen Gardener gave us the greatest Thanksgiving blessing by decorating our home with so much love and care. Because of Gretchen, we are in awe of our dining room today. Look at the evidence—in the food and décor she created. What a Happy Thanksgiving she offered us.

Three photos followed the invitation. One focused on a portion of the centerpiece with the baby pumpkins in the colors of white, turquoise, and orange. Another snapshot captured the table with all the food set up, each place setting ready to go, as the battery-operated candles flickered. The last image included Hayden and me. In the photo, my smile reflected a 'dang, girl, you look so happy,' quality. There was no denying it.

Dad sat in the driver's seat, fiddling with his seat belt while reading his phone. A few happy tears slipped after reading Hayden and Gene's words and viewing those pictures. I stared down at the photos, smiling. Three dots appeared, letting me know about another text coming in from someone in the group.

Dad: Screw Thomas Sharp

In disbelief, I looked up, meeting Dad's eyes and smirk. What an unexpected moment. It's Thanksgiving Day. Stuck parked at the police station, sitting inside Dad's Rogue, I decided to say, "Dad, you definitely know how to 'go Rogue' when it's fitting!"

Sadness melted away. At the same time, we died laughing. "*Screw Thomas Sharp*?" I attempted repeating Dad's words, stuttering and stammering, cracking up until no sounds at all would come. Slapping my knee and stomping my feet, trying to regain my composure. I sucked in some much-needed air. Seemed Gene and Hayden mirrored Dad's sentiment.

Gene: I concur, John

Hayden: YES! I agree, too, John. LoL ☺

Dad and I continued to chuckle, wiping wetness off our cheeks. Through watery eyes and giggles, Dad added another line of text before putting the car in drive and moving us forward.

Dad: Got a lot worth celebrating. On our way.

Me: Happy Thanksgiving! ☺

Chapter Twenty-Four

December

Dear Mom,

It's the most wonderful time of the year. . . . There'll be scary ghost stories and tales of the glories. . . . This journal entry addresses these issues.

It's the holiday season. A *flurry* of activities are happening—you like that? Another pun and play with words, Ma. Gretchen said to me, "Intelligence is sexy, Hayden." With her loving me, I'm marching on Smart Street and traveling daily down Studyville Lane because I want to see her smile.

Barring any of Sharp's BS, I'm hopeful we will have an enjoyable Christmas. When I think about Sharp's ass-jerk message and the photo he sent to Gretchen on Thanksgiving and what it did to Gretchen, it pisses me off. To realize what a sicko he is and how much crap he seems to get away with, all in the name of juvenile "jokes, mistakes, and misdemeanors."

I've got an idea for community service. Take Sharp to the cemetery at night when they've freshly dug a six-foot hole. Plop his creepy ass down into the earth. With a shovel full of dirt, toss one load on top of him, listening as it bounces across his body. Throw in a gift—a thorny rose, in honor of Hayden Queer AF without uttering a word because Hardly Speaks Hayden would accompany me. Over my shoulder, I'd say, "Stop crying, phony grave digger. It's only a joke. Besides, I'm playing your game, Jokester Dumb AF." Mom, I realize this is way too scary mean. It's better to vent than to act out.

The best reaction to Sharp came from John on Thanksgiving. John texted: **Screw Thomas Sharp.** It shocked Dad and me to the point of laughter. Most of the time, John's upstanding "Doctor" Gardener. We loved and understood John's message. He didn't want us to let Sharp ruin the day or get inside our heads, taking over our lives. In the future, we won't accept mistreatment, but for now, we won't react. John reminded us of an old saying to consider: "Living a good life is the best revenge."

On the day Sharp came in with his dog, Cliff, I must admit I wish I could've seen John in action. As Gretchen recounted the event, she gripped my arm and said, "Dad screamed the actual F word multiple times, like telling Sharp something about being an effing dog-effer!" Can you believe it, Hayden?" It must've been a scary scene for her.

She seemed proud of her dad for the way he poured his heart out in standing up for both of us. I'm glad Gretchen and John got back to a better place in their relationship. A bit of distance and testiness with each other happened after Gretchen learned about his fling with Debbie, Lilly's mom. Debbie's daughter Lilly's the one who hurt Gretchen so bad with her comment like, "just because her mom's dead doesn't give her the right to go stealing someone else's mom." It's Darcy and/or Meghan's mothers involved in the situation. Speaking of these girls, Gretchen doesn't talk much to them because of how they handled the underwear situation (doing nothing) or with Gretchen's grief in general, even from an early age. Gretchen doesn't feel those friendships are healthy. Gretchen's cordial to them, but she's doesn't seek them out anymore.

We're building friendships outside of the center with Miles and Kelsey. Gretchen and I think Miles and Kelsey date on the DL. They, for sure, really like each other. Gretchen said she overheard Mrs. Marks giggle and ask Dad, "Am I working at a grief center or running a dating service?" I *assume* Mrs. Marks is talking about Gretchen and me, plus Miles and Kelsey. At some point, we plan to try to do something fun together—go to the movies, ice skate, hit the amusement parks in Branson. Mia, who also attends the center, lives farther away and is still not ready for much. Once in a while, her grandma brings her to a game.

Basketball's been fun. Much less drama than football. I'm less Hayden Queer AF these days. Sharp's mouth stays pretty silent. He mumbles out of my range. I think John got his point across to Sheriff Lowell about not taking any of Sharp's nonsense, and it got passed on to him. Gretchen enjoys coming to the games. She's reading magazines less while she's there. She avoids hiding out in the bathroom too. Gretchen sits with Kelsey, Mia, and Miles during the times they can come. Or she's next to Dad—he misses only on rare occasions. Mrs. Marks even pops by, seeking out Dad and Gretchen in the stands.

Sometimes I'll hear John cheering me on. On those nights, Coach often pulls Sharp out of the game since he can't "get his head in the game," even though Coach goes on his mission of turning beet red, his clipboard in hand while he's stomping down the sidelines near the bench. Maybe Sharp can only think *I'm a fucking dog fucker* when John's there. ☺

Sorry, Mom. . . . I used the actual F word, but John did it first. LoL. Gosh, that sounds so much like a "Dennis the Menace Drew" thing to say. I've been missing him. He told Dad and me he'd see us at Christmas. This *newest* girlfriend, Ava, appears to be sticking around. Either Drew's met his match, she's crazy, or he's ready to grow up enough for just one girl? Ariana and Cole are coming for Christmas too. Do you like how I acknowledge her before your son, Cole? Probably not. Well, I hope he cracks a freaking smile when we open the door. I'm feeling bold. I might shock Dad by asking, can I say, "Merry Christmas, Cole. Please at least effing grin, effer." Enough ranting about Christmas and my brothers. Back-to-school stuff with Gretchen.

Gretchen cringed when the school's first-semester highlights newsletter came out with one of the headlines reading, *Dr. John Gardener Saved Poco.* Below the article, other columns included news of upcoming school events for the second semester, photos from the games and clubs, names of those on the A and B semester honor rolls (woo-hoo—Gretchen Gardener and Hayden Tucker), and a display called Miss Gabby Garcia's "Coun-selor's Corner." Miss Gabby shares her thoughts on the latest school news, scholarships, or even such things as college safety, pointers, and ideas for students.

Miss Garcia felt inclined to include a photo of Poco lavishing John with "Thankful Kisses," which is how Miss Gabby explained the situation. Another "Happenstance" relationship for John, the Love Doctor? Gretchen and I wondered, assuming and remembering some history of events—Gretchen's time in Gabby's office when she described John as "A hoot and an American Gentleman," John's

357

questions about Gabby to Gretchen, John's ER call with Poco the night of my birthday/study session. We guessed some "Happenstance" moments may have been occurring for a while. They're still not official, but they aren't hiding their interest so much, such as sitting by each other at the games. Gretchen says they chat some on the phone. John's taken Gabby out to dinner. He told Gretchen, "I'll take it slow, but I like her and *only* her right now. If at any time it's uncomfortable for you that I'm dating Gabby, please talk to me about it. I promise, no other craziness with women is going on with me."

Gretchen's reaction to accept this pairing surprised me at first. "Well, Hayden, it could be worse. Garcia's not a total nitwit, and she's nice, don't you think, *sweetie*?" My mind raced with worry, thinking: *For now, John and Gabby don't flaunt their dating in front of Gretchen. They go out of town to eat. When they spend private time together, they spend it at Gabby's. In public, like my games, they show no PDA other than maybe him putting his hand on her back to lead her through doors and such. The way they sit close together, their attraction is undeniable. Even to strangers, they would appear as a couple. What happens when Gretchen catches them kissing? Will going to school be awkward if Gretchen deals with John having a sexual relationship with Gabby? Then at school, what if Gretchen needs her to step it up and be a counselor too? Is she fine as long as it's not Lilly and Debbie?*

Gretchen said this, falling over with her giggles, snorting even. "Oh, my dad kills me with his secret, flirty ways. My dad's more popular than us at Summerfort High School. That's freaking hilarious." We cracked up about the incident. "Oh, well, let's see what happens, sweetie." Gretchen patted me on the arm, trying to get out other words, but she laughed so hard no words or sounds came out. Then I heard random words begin tumbling out of Gretchen's mouth: "Happenstance, post office loving, sweet doggie." Gretchen rolled on the floor until she was in the fetal position, wiping her eyes.

"Do what? Say what? Gretch, is this a bunch of your nonsense innuendo?" I asked. She tried answering yes, but she managed to form only a half-nod of agreement. After that, I took in the scene, and I joined her in rolling on the floor.

No one seemed to care or even found it peculiar when Miss Garcia, Poco, John, Mrs. Marks, and Dad showed to my games as a group of friends. Principal Marshall sometimes stirred through the crowd, sitting with them. Somehow, they've all formed a little cheering section, along with Kelsey and Miles, all in support of me. I especially didn't care. In fact, I love it. Every game, I still long for my mother to be there, but I'm learning to open up and share these thoughts.

Speaking of grief counseling, Gretchen and I chatted about one of Mrs. Mark's holiday-themed journal prompts, which she introduced to us during our Halloween party. We brought it back up because it seemed more fitting during the Christmas season.

While Dad lounged upstairs watching TV, Gretchen and I took over the downstairs den. Miss Spicy Boots roamed from Dad to us, prancing around, deciding which location offered the most playtime and cat treats, before she curled up and crashed on the sofa. Gretchen hemmed and hawed, agonizing about telling me her backstory of the days-of-the-week underwear and how her mother's death led to her hoarding behavior. "I'm too embarrassed, saying the details out loud will make me sound crazy. . . ." Gretchen said, stalling. We've scratched the surface of the details.

After I led Gretchen into the kitchen for a break and taught her how to butter toast like you showed me—sprinkling just the right amounts of cinnamon and sugar to make a platter of treats we could devour—she looked ready to tell me just about everything. What is it about food? Its magic can draw trust and love out of others.

"Come with me," I said, leading Gretchen into the pantry. After placing our plates on the floor, I stood reaching up for the cinnamon. I sat back down, facing Gretchen, flipping open the spice lid. Gretchen watched as I lightly sprinkled cinnamon on my arms. With my eyes wet and my voice choked, I said, "I will always miss my mom and her buttery cinnamon toast." Gretchen grabbed me into a hug. "You can tell me your whole story too, Gretchen."

Gretchen and I reread the questions again, pondering our past, present, and future issues with Christmas. What a difficult journal prompt. The topic of grief and the Christmas holiday digs roots so deep for each of us. Of course, more so for Gretchen, I believe. Together, we tackled the questions.

Gretchen yielded the most painful memories to me, traveling back to her childhood, reaching into her Christmas stocking, pulling out the gag gift of underwear, which became an issue she outgrew yet couldn't let go: Her Ghost of Christmas Past. Through tears and moments where she paused, saying, "I'm too ashamed, Hayden. I can't—it's embarrassing," I gave Gretchen the time she needed until I heard the whole detailed story.

Starting with Monday, I learned about the monkey. We went on into Tuesday and the turtles. The wolf made up Wednesday's pair. Gretchen's attention to detail about Thursday's turkey dressed as Santa made us chuckle. Frog Fridays and squirrel Saturdays, with those squirrels being Gretchen's all-time favorites. She talked about wearing the squirrels for special occasions. And how she almost spilled her guts about having the squirrel underwear on during my birthday. It was when

The Ghost of Christmas Past	The Ghost of Christmas Present	The Ghost of Christmas Future
If time travel were possible and you traveled back to your childhood, who would you want to meet and what would you want to see, feel, hear, taste, and touch? Explain or draw grief-related emotions:	What do you expect to see, feel, hear, taste, touch in this year at Christmas? Explain or draw grief-related emotions of the upcoming (present) Christmas	If time travel were possible and you could travel to your future, who would you expect/hope to meet and what would you expect to see, feel, hear, taste, and touch? Explain or draw grief-related emotions:

we had the moment in my room about being upset about the little car set you got me, Mom. As we got to Sunday, Gretchen's face fell, and she said, "Can we not go there—it's really awkward."

"Gretchen, it's just me. I can handle it."

Gretchen closed her eyes and sighed. "Fine," she said. She threw her hands in the air. "I'm going to be super blunt then. This isn't something I want to tell you, though." In a gravelly voice, Gretchen

362

went on to say, "You have no idea how incredibly uncomfortable this is right now for me, Hayden." She paused.

"I'm sorry, Gretchen." I hugged her. "No judgment. I'll hold you, so you can whisper to me if that's easier."

She nodded.

"While wearing the starfish pair at school"— she swallowed hard—"um, I started my first period and destroyed them." Gretchen cleared her throat. "Okay, I threw the words out in the open for you to hear. Now, I'm mortified." Gretchen's tone verged on edgy, which meant maybe I'd pushed her too far. Especially as her last remark came rolling off her tongue, word by word: "There. You. Have. It."

Yep. Duh, I asked for that. Making sure Gretchen didn't feel bad for exposing such a personal moment, I stuttered around. God, I felt weird for knowing. Like I'd violated the hidden crossroad she'd been denied with her mom.

"Uh, don't be mortified. I'm okay. I bet—bet it was . . . traumatic, Gretch. I'm sorry." I squeezed her tightly. *Think and say something decent.* Gretchen latched onto my arm with a death grip, putting her head on my shoulder.

"Imagine being a girl. It happened at school! It started in May before school got out. Couldn't wait for the summer break? I hated it. I needed my mom. I never felt comfortable asking for help from friends or their moms. I'm not dumb, but I didn't entirely know what to do. My dad's kind, but how awkward to confront him about my period. That summer, I went to the Branson Landing shopping. Later, I effing hated all the new underwear I bought because I attached Lilly's words to them. Her hateful words were always running through my mind. Even that night, before we first kissed, I heard her mocking me. After I rediscovered the Christmas underwear, I started wearing them daily to feel closer to my mom."

"Can you remember when and how you felt when you started wearing them?"

"Over the years, I knew I had them in my dresser, like a keepsake. Last year, in October, on the anniversary of her death, I took them out, forcing them to fit. And on my birthday, I wanted to feel *any* kind of connection with her. Wearing something she bought me made me feel like I could celebrate my birthday with her. Thanksgiving came, and the underwear with the turkey seemed perfect. Of course, the Christmas season gave me a chance to sample all of them, repeatedly. I didn't think I had a problem. Maybe my underwear was too tight, and they hurt? My reasoning for wearing them seemed legit. I loved and missed my mother."

Noticing Gretchen's eyes welling with tears, I asked, "Gretchen, do you need to take a break?"

She shook her head. "I'm okay. I don't think my problems really started until I ruined that one pair because of my period. After the shopping trip and Lilly's words, I refused to wear new underwear. The morning rituals began around this timeframe. Like obsessing about every detail of the underwear. A form I called an inventory sheet kept up with every pain. Basically, I wrote a diary about underwear."

"Can you explain more or how you felt?"

Gretchen shrugged. "In my twisted OCD way, I attached my mom's words and memories to each pair. If I didn't hang on to every pair, every secret, I'd lose everything. Like my mother, Sunday died. Monday, Tuesday, Wednesday, Thursday, Friday, Saturday, every day of the week I spent in fear I'd lose every one of them. Just as I lost her. Sometimes I felt like they were all I had left of her. I know. I know. I'm so—" Gretchen's voice cracked, ending mid-sentence.

Hot tears soaked my shirt. I offered all the support I could, keeping Gretchen wrapped inside my arms until she wore herself down sobbing. "It's okay, Gretchen. Let it all out. Say anything you want or need to."

I waited for Gretchen to pull away from me. She brushed her lips against mine.

"Thank you for listening, Hayden."

"You're welcome, but thank you for having the courage to tell me your story. I know that wasn't easy for you."

"Yeah." Gretchen shrugged, offering a hint of a smile.

"Hey, does it help knowing I plan to love you all seven days of the week?" I asked, planting a kiss on the top of her head. She gave me a closed-mouth giggle. My kisses moved down, brushing her forehead, nose, leading to her mouth with intensity.

We fought the ghosts together.

My Ghost of Christmas Past: My mother, wearing a smile and her "Kiss the Cook" apron as she prepared my toast, with a full family—Dad, brothers, and mother, all at home.

"The Ghost of Christmas Present is my favorite choice," Gretchen said, leaning over, offering me a buttery-lipped kiss. "I will miss my mom, but I have no secrets to hide this year, and I'll be surrounded by people I love. My dad and I have plans. I feel included. I have new traditions now, new hopes, and less anxiety. I'm actually giddy with anticipation about time off from school. I've not been this happy in a long time about Christmas. I know there's maybe more therapy to go, but I'm not resisting that either."

"Gretchen, I'm stealing some of your answers— they're too good. I love you so much. I'm proud of you, and how you've worked through things you're dealing with this year and still willing to keep on working. You've faced a lot this year. I'm looking so forward to all the corny holiday movies, decorating the Christmas tree, wearing our Strawberry Shortcake and Huckleberry aprons while baking cookies, aggravating our dads, kissing you, over and over," I pulled Gretchen to me. "Here's a bit of a sample." I pressed my top lip onto hers and moved to the bottom one, so tempted to roam on. "I'm happy doing anything with you—"

"You don't have to get heavy or deep with your thoughts or answers. It's okay. But, what about the Ghost of Christmas Future, Hayden? Is that too much to talk about at our age?"

"I'm willing to dole out some particulars. You don't scare me, little girl—" Glancing at Gretchen, I wiggled my eyebrows.

She cocked her head before smirking.

"Well, not too much anymore." My face flushed—I think even my ears turned red. "Anyway, I'd be thrilled to take on the past, present, and/or the future, Gretchen."

"What if I confessed and told you my mother was born a twin, but her sister died at birth?" Gretchen asked. "And did you know my dad has a special needs sister—she lives in an assisted living facility. She's awesome. Jolene was born prematurely, causing a lot of issues for her. I love her so much. For the most part, she's considered developmentally delayed but advanced too. Dad said she functions on about an eight-year-old mental level—needs help with the bigger issues in life. She can walk, speak, cook some minor meals, and live somewhat alone, but she can't make the best decisions. For example, no driver's license. Dad offered to let her live here, but she likes living as independently as possible in Columbia, Missouri. You need to come with us when we visit her. Jolene's a couple years younger than Dad."

"Wow, you never divulged those tidbits of info. I'd be honored to meet Jolene, Gretchen."

"No, not a lot of people know all my stories. I'm a secret keeper. Anyway, I'm genetically predisposed to give birth to multiples—*if,* in the Ghost of Christmas Future, you pictured a life with me? And with tiny Haydens or Gretchens? Did you happen to see more than one of them? Or think about it this way—little Genes or Johns. . . . Oh, my God. . . . Can you imagine that, Hayden?" I watched as Gretchen's hands clasped her stomach, holding in her belly laugh.

As I stretched out on my back beside Gretchen, I stared up at the den ceiling, smiling. I glanced over at Gretchen, who at fifteen already resembled a perfect wife and mother for my children— Ghost of Christmas Future (of course, very *distant* future), but I kept those secrets to myself. I rolled over, wrapped myself around Gretchen, reaching for her hand, lacing my fingers into hers.

At fifteen, I knew I carried the heart of an old soul. My body may be young, but my thoughts drift, and I often feel like I'm at least thirty years old. Does the death of a mother do that to a child when they lose her so young? Constant conflict— afraid to love, but once you do, you fall so hard you aren't scared to reveal your whole heart, to genuinely love. Understanding how fleeting and precious life is, you decide on love.

The minute I touched Gretchen, it was Hayden's future *heart* envisioning copper-headed babies framed in photographs hanging on the wall. My heart smelled cinnamon toast piled on a kitchen table, tasted Gretchen's peppermint kisses, and heard children laughing. And while I held Gretchen inside my arms, against my chest, my heart time traveled to my future home.

"I can imagine lots of good things about the Ghost of Christmas Future, Gretchen," I said in quiet tones. "I bet you will be a loving mother to every kid lucky enough to call you Mom. Twins sound like a houseful of chaotic fun."

"Really?" Gretchen turned to meet my gaze.

With a nod, I answered, "Yes." Gretchen curled up as close to me as humanly possible, resting her face inside my shoulder. My arms stayed wrapped around her.

Tears flowed down her face as she said, "Thank you, Hayden, because I've been terrified to think about those things, much less dream about them. Since I didn't have my mom for very long, I didn't even think I'd know how to love anyone the right way."

Gretchen's comment hit me at the core. My chin quivered. "I understand, Gretch." My voice sounded so shaky. "But, angel, you're the most loving person I know." I clung to Gretchen, confronting Christmas ghosts. Healing our Past, relishing in the Present. With hope, we dreamed of belonging to a family with a Future.

The Summerfort Grief Center sign flashed in my mind: A Place to Heal, A Place to Hope, A Place to Belong. Making the parallel connections between the journal entry on Christmas past, present, future, and the sign left Gretchen and me in awe but ready to face a Merry Christmas.

Chapter Twenty-Five

December 2019

The heart thumps out beats. I believe it thrives, functions, and continues to grow and heal. Candles, once stored away, now decorate the dining room table. The glowing creates flickering and dancing. Light illuminates every wall, bouncing off surfaces as a showcase. Before this big reveal took place, a long journey occurred with a lot of heartaches and effort. Here's the story:

One night, I couldn't fall asleep, so I went downstairs for a snack. Dad keeps a low wattage bulb in the lamp in the hallway on the console table as a nightlight, so I didn't bother flipping on lights. In the faint glow, I spotted a figure flopped over in your chair at the dining room table. A head rested on the tabletop while his other hand stretched out, gripping a bottle of alcohol. Sounds of light sniffling and soft music drifted. "Dad?" I asked.

Springing to posture perfect, he asked, "Hey, GG, what're you doing awake?"

"Can't sleep." Worried he'd slipped into old patterns, I asked, "You okay? Are you drunk?"

Dad actually rolled his eyes at me. "No, I'm not drunk. This is the only drink I'll have. I'm just having a mini pity party." Dad took a swig from his bottle. "No, honestly, I'm allowing myself some Gwen time. So, I'm sitting in the moonlight, reminiscing, missing your mom. Think I've come up with something that might help us, though."

"Oh. What?" Dad's weird mood concerned me. I worried he may say or do just about anything.

"GG, just like you, I struggle with grief. Your mother accounts for years of my history. She was supposed to love me as I grew old. How do I fix that? I can't. But your mom granted me the gift of a healthy, intelligent daughter who's still here. I thank God and her every day for that. I can't bring Mom back. I know we will always miss her. I know we will have bad days. But can we try to be happy? I've come up with a mantra to say." Dad paused, smiling up at me. It goes: "Aren't we lucky she's worth missing?"

As I listened to Dad's profound words, my eyes filled and spilled over. Nodding, I wiped at the tears. I couldn't help but smile. My heart understood what he meant.

"Aren't we? Think about it. Aren't we lucky she's worth missing? Let's honor her life. Weave

Mom's memory into new traditions. Starting in this godforsaken dining room. Let's decorate it for Christmas. Take some of Mom's things from the attic and add new items. Gwen would love us smiling, GG."

Absorbing Dad's profound mantra and ideas, I stood, stunned, staring at him. Still, I cried while smiling, experiencing that bittersweet ache of pain surging with hope. All I could think of doing was hugging Dad. Late into the night, we sat at the dining room table, sorting through photo albums, sharing stories, laughing, and remembering why we were so lucky.

* * *

In the attic, Dad and I located the snowman centerpiece. I tossed out the traditional red-and-green color scheme, opting for blue and silver. My personal theme: "Frosty" meets "Silver Bells." In the corner of the room, I displayed the white tree, adding only silver snowflakes, tinsel, and blue garland. White lights accent the whole thing. A new tradition, Mother, and it's a beautiful vision.

A tree of hearts highlighted on the wall ensures me your heart remains in hope every day in the dining room. I once sat beneath your brown heart at six years old, but I granted authority to the little girl in that photo, allowing her permission to release her pain.

"Chestnuts Roasting on an Open Fire" pours out in the background, reminding me of my days-of-the-week illness—my inability to move on, to let go of you—much like a squirrel, I hoarded underwear, afraid to watch the last items my mother purchased for me, slip away, so deadly afraid my childhood would vanish.

Therapy:

"What caused me to develop OCD?" I asked Dr. Han, my therapist.

"Unresolved, or complicated, grief—the fear (anxiety) of letting go of your mother. In your case, you tied love to her last gift of the days-of-the-week underwear—having reoccurring thoughts—like hearing Lilly's hurtful comment created fears, which began the keeping of the detailed inventory log, which became the obsessions. The repeated behaviors of wearing underwear and morning routines are the compulsions. And the long-term secrecy too, Gretchen.

"Yep, I'm good at keeping secrets." My lips made a popping sound. "Last time, you encouraged me to photograph the underwear and say good-bye to them. I did." I sucked in a hefty breath. "Not easy, but here I am, I survived."

Doctor Han adjusted in her chair. She crossed her legs and propped her elbows onto her desk. She tilted closer toward me in a more casual stance. "Some secrets need to be released, Gretchen. I'm proud of your work so far. You're making good progress. OCD is an unhealthy illness, but with therapy and time, I see a lot of real possibility for you."

"Even though I no longer do my morning routines, keep the detailed inventory, or wear the underwear, you don't think I'm okay to stop therapy?"

"Be patient with yourself, Gretchen. Things may take time. I want you to think about your own question from earlier. Remember asking me, 'what caused my OCD to develop?'" I nod. "I'd like you to explore those issues."

Three photos on the wall above Doctor Han's head were hanging cockeyed, but if I said anything, would she announce it as another sign of my nit-picky personality or a symptom of the OCD poking me in the ribs? A set of gray hands painted the corners of the first frame. By the second frame, the one which required adjusting, a flock of birds were about to be released to take flight. *Look away, Gretchen.* By the third frame, the birds flew away until they went off the edge of the canvas. *Did she cock up the picture on purpose—are you testing me, Doctor Han?*

"I think you're well on your way to healing, but several more months of therapy will benefit you. Why don't we take it one session at a time? Slow down and monitor everything, Gretchen."

I nod again.

"A lot of turmoil going on, Gretchen—you and Dad arguing, girls at school annoy you, Thomas

Sharp's recent Thanksgiving behavior—say, I noticed you've been admiring my paintings."

"Wow, you created those? So pretty." *You do realize it's crooked, though, right? Fine, sue me. . . . I'll come back with my nutty self for more sessions.*

"Hobbies help the mind, Gretchen. Tell me about some of your hobbies."

"I like writing my mom letters in my grief journals, reading, writing poetry, scrapbooking—small crafts, coming to my group helps me a lot—hanging with my boyfriend, Hayden."

"Oh, explain what small crafts mean." She pushed her reading glasses up, snug on her nose, magnifying her dark brown eyes. Sitting across from her, if I glanced at certain angles, her eyes appeared unusually large and distracting. She offered another tight grin. I'd like to hear her laugh and see her teeth one day.

"I made memorial wreaths for my mom and Hayden's mom. I have photos on my phone. Do you wanna see?"

She nodded. "Of course." Doctor Han glanced at the photos with a sincere interest. "Beautiful, I bet you could take special orders and sell those at craft fairs."

"Thank you," I stuffed my phone back down in my purse but not before I realized a message awaited me from Hayden when this hour ended: **Thinking of you.** xo

I smiled. No wondered Doctor Han asked me to silence my phone before talking—so distracting. My mind, perhaps my heart, or specific body parts?—anyway, I drifted to images of a bare-chested boy in the park—

Dr. Han interrupted my fantasy. "Well, let's focus on marching through the holidays with success. I know they can trigger a lot of harsh memories, but last time you said you and your Dad decided to address Christmas with a new tradition this year. Remind me of your plan."

"Dad agreed to sort through Mom's old Christmas décor in the attic and allow me to use what I liked to decorate the house this year. Dad suggested we host a small dinner party—well, just Hayden and his dad—if you call placing an order for pizza delivery, a dinner party." I laughed.

Doctor Han grinned, her eyes crinkling in the corners, magnified by her glasses, which kept slipping down her narrow nose. "But I plan to go overboard, making the dining room fancy—candles, tablecloth, centerpiece, you know, all those sorts of things."

"What significance or sense of closure might this event bring you concerning your mom?"

Snatching the box of Kleenex off the desk, I dabbed at the edges of my eyes. My voice trembled. "On my seventh birthday, I stood inside our dining room under balloons, streamers, and just literally felt crushed. My mother prepared things way ahead of time, so I saw her in the Little Mermaid candles flickering on the table and in the "Under the Sea" décor but felt haunted by her memory since she didn't attend a party that she'd planned. I want to learn to embrace her there and get happier again in the space. Guess I wish I could get a sense of normal."

"Gretchen, your willingness to share this with me benefits you and starts your process to wellness. This memory seems to take you right to the core, the very center of your pain. Grief takes everyone on a journey."

"There's a line I once heard or read I like. Something about how grief hurts so bad because it's pent-up love with nowhere to go or something near those words. About like that, anyway. Grief slowly dies but never love. Right?"

"Absolutely, Gretchen. Love and memories last, but pain and grief subside. Please use the saying as a mantra for the holidays. Come back with positives to share with me. Do you have anything else on your mind today?"

"No, I'm good."

"I agree." Doctor Han waved good-bye.

Mrs. Mark's office door sits diagonally to Doctor Han's at the Summerfort Grief Center. As I slipped into the hallway, Mrs. Mark's craned her neck, seeking eye contact with me. "Gretchen, do you have a moment?" I tiptoed near.

"Sure. What's up?" Adults who call impromptu meetings with me cause the corners of my mouth or eyes to twitch. As my lips and eyelashes twerk, I pussyfoot toward her desk, where I'm being summoned to sit in one of her chairs.

What? Why am I here? What do you want? Wondering when I found out about your little secret? You will not cause my stomach to gurgle, and I will not crap myself over this, right?

"You don't have to answer since you've got rights to your privacy with Doctor Han, but I hope all is going well for you." Mrs. Mark's brushed her hair behind her ear and smiled. I realized in all my years at the center I've never been to this particular room, and I knew little about Mrs. Marks. Photos of herself as a child with her parents hung on her wall, along with her framed diplomas, but no images of children or a husband. Books on photography, counseling, grief, and love after divorce lined a small bookshelf behind her desk. Stacks of papers, magazines, and camera equipment littered the tops of file cabinets and other areas.

"I'm good. I like Doctor Han. She believes I'm making progress."

"Gretchen, I'm so proud of you. Glad to hear such good news." Mrs. Marks sighed. She then gave me a nervous grin. "I want to show you something, okay?" Instead of glancing at me as a counselor, she looked at me with the eyes of a worried friend. My heart surged with uncertainty, but I nodded.

From her desk drawer, she pulled out a frame, handing it to me, "Merry Christmas, Gretchen." My eyes blurred as I attempted to stare at the black-and-white photo collage she had titled *Love at the Center of Grief*. In the middle, of course, the prominent photo of Hayden and me, grief-filled, holding hands. Mrs. Marks captured pictures over the years of events I'd forgotten about until now as I viewed them. In nearly everyone, Hayden's by my side, holding my hand for an activity as I'm looking up at the picture of us under the tree. In the most recent one, she caught us stealing a kiss at the Halloween party.

"We didn't even know we'd been caught," I said, giggling. "Wow. This is so nice. Thank you so much. I appreciate it. I can't believe you took all these."

"Photography's a big passion of mine. Gene redesigned a portion of my utility room, transforming it into a dark room, so I can pursue my hobby more."

"Gene's a great contractor and guy. He's good to my dad and me. I spend a lot of time with Hayden at their house. Gene's sense of humor is off the charts." Mrs. Mark's face met mine with a tell-tale grin of agreement.

"Gene and his crew did an amazing job here and at my home. I'm glad I took a chance on hiring them." Mrs. Marks squirmed in her chair.

"Gene checked in with you at the center *a lot*, I guess, making sure he performed every job to your satisfaction 100 percent?" I asked rather than stated this because the time had come for Mrs. Marks to reveal more.

"That's Gene, Gretchen. Mr. Perfection-*ist*. He starts out all serious, sometimes even a bit grumpy, but finds solutions by the end, which create laughter for everyone."

Nice, Marks. Adding the "ist" rather quickly to your Mr. Perfection—what a beautiful way to save face.

Glancing around the office, I cleared my throat, giving myself time to formulate the right words but stuttered out, "Can you talk about your personal life? Or does that go against any policy rules?"

"What would you like to know, Gretchen?" Mrs. Marks gazed at me in amazement. "At this point, with your age and in our relationship, I'm an open book, hon." I perched on the edge of my seat. Mrs. Marks pointed to the center of her chest before she rambled. "Let's start with some basic stats: Hi, I'm Lisa, divorced, pushing into my late 40s, with no children." She shrugged like she had nothing to hide. The gleam in her eyes said, "Bring it on. I'm ready for the next line of questioning."

"Did you ever want kids?"

"Yes, very much," Lisa's mouth sagged downward at the corners. She gathered in a deep breath.

"Never happened because of a medical issue. My ex-husband used my infertility as an excuse to end our marriage. Later, he apologized to me for having an affair. And he was sorry for not coming out sooner and living an authentic life. I'm glad he's with his new husband."

"Wow." *No way—could it have been Lilly's Dad?* I sat, listening with the thought festering. People in small towns, like Summerfort, think we know everything about someone. We find out lives intertwine with a history of secrets no one ever discusses.

She nodded. "Infertility, divorce, along with the grief of losing my parents, did a number on me."

"I'm sorry. That's a lot to go through. Did you think of remarrying? Or adopting? You'd be a great mom. In fact, Hayden and I call you 'Grief Mom' sometimes."

Lisa's hand flew up, covering over her heart. "Gretchen, knowing you and Hayden think of me in that way makes my day." She glanced up to the ceiling and waved her hands over her face as a way to hold in tears. "I didn't want to cry today." She giggled, tapping at the corners of her glassy eyes. "Over the years, working with lots of children at the center fulfilled my parenting wish. I liked taking part in watching you and Hayden grow up." Lisa tapped her fingers on her desktop. "What did I forget to answer?"

"Will you ever remar—" Lisa Marks cut me off, her words started falling from her mouth in a nervous tone, softer than her usual speaking voice, almost like speaking about the emotions of love rendered her helpless.

"Oh, yes. Right. *If* life brings me the right man, I will remarry, but I'm happy alone too." Lisa grinned, but her lips sat in a closed fashion. I'm more accustomed to her toothy grin.

Dear Lisa, you're not a good liar. In fact, you're terrible at it. Perhaps you might already be in love? What a straight-faced phony grin. An actress or poker player, you are not.

I asked, "Love feels risky sometimes, doesn't it? It's scary to open your heart to someone when you consider yourself as damaged goods or something, even if it's because of grief. Why are there so many complications in life?" After, I blew out a heavy sigh of relief.

Mrs. Marks, or rather, *Lisa*, titled her head, hanging on my every word. "Gretchen, your use of the word 'complications' seems accurate. Love acts as both a burden and a blessing throughout our lives. At times, love breaks us down, but then the power of love builds us right back up stronger than we ever thought possible. Sometimes even at our darkest, weakest moments." She sucked in a deep breath before continuing.

"But I will still always tell you to work through the pain. '*When in doubt, choose love.*' I know I've heard others say words similar to these before, yet the concept now seems different as I tell them to you, Gretchen." Lisa patted at the edge of her desk when she said, "When in doubt, choose love" with as much passion as a preacher delivering a Sunday morning sermon.

Are you saying this for my benefit? Or for yours, Lisa?

"That's profound. You sound like a Hallmark card. I love it. Do you really believe in all of it? Even for yourself?" I asked Lisa, peering into her troubled face.

Lisa's feet shuffled beneath her desk. Her gaze bounced around her office, searching for answers she didn't seem to find before she said, "I want to, Gretchen. Adult life adds extra layers of problems, though." Lisa held up her hand. Starting with her index finger, she announced: "First, there's the *guilt*." Lisa's emphasis on the word "guilt" made me empathize with her.

"Next, or the second thing, among many, Gretchen, is the shady blurred *ethical* lines you fear may be crossing, and it could hurt others." As Lisa spoke, she wiggled the second finger to emphasize her issue.

"Can't ethical lines ever be worked out? You know, talked out by people? I don't know, like a compromise?" My face fell, my mouth edged into a pout. "Sometimes, what others think or feel is wrong might be the best solution for a lot of people? Don't you agree?"

Chapter Twenty-Five

Unblinking, Lisa stared past me, like a zombie. A deadpan expression blazed across her face before hunching her shoulders into a mighty shrug. In all my encounters with Lisa, I've never witnessed her in such a blah state. "I don't know. Nice thought, Gretchen."

Internally, I screamed a lecture at Lisa. I almost had to sit on my hands to silence them as well.

WTFDD? You're deeper in love with Gene than I first thought. Hayden loves you too. He will adjust with you around. In fact, a mother figure—that's what Hayden already sees when he looks at you, Lisa. I realize you once served as his counselor, but that was years ago. Now you're a teen volunteer. You're the children's one-on-one. That's not unethical! You're not a bad person. We all adore you. Don't you get it?

"Gretchen, can I flip the subject and share why I snagged you to chat today?"

No, Lisa, you may not. I'm angry at you right now.

"What's up?" I asked.

Lisa presented me with a half-smile. "I called your dad first. John's given his approval, and he's on board if you want to do a project with me." Lisa pulled a stack of papers and photos from her desk. "My work at Summerfort Grief Center tells stories of tragedies and triumphs." As Lisa spoke, she spread pictures of Hayden and me across her desk. "Watching this particular journey unfold has been among my favorite. I titled it *Love at the Center of Grief*."

"I love the pictures, but I don't understand what you're asking of me," I said.

"Throughout the years, I encouraged you and Hayden to write in grief journals, do self-discovery fill-ins, and share your hopes, fears, and dreams. I saved all of our group projects. I hope you might be willing to offer your *most personal* thoughts with me for a book?"

"Seriously?" I asked. "I jotted down some odd-ball stuff over the years that I don't think certain people want to read or know about. Sometimes the thoughts in my head come out way too honest. Even on the verge of rude? One minute I'm child-ish. Then in the next sentence, I'm a horny teen." I scoffed. "Hashtag, awkward."

Lisa stifled her laugh and instead reassured me with a smile. She stretched her arm across the desk and patted my hand. "Gretchen, that's perfect. People need to hear what's real. Names and locations can be changed to protect you. You and Hayden endured years without mothers, and your grief stories could touch the lives of other teens all over. What do you say? Are you in?"

I let out a squeal. "This is so exciting but scary. I guess I'm in if Hayden's in."

"Gene and Hayden said the same thing you did—'If Gretchen's in—we're in.'" Lisa clapped with an added "Yay!"

"So, *Miss Lisa Marks*, this *Love at the Center of Grief* book opportunity, means you'll be required or *urged* to spend some time at Gene and Hayden's house researching and gathering information for this book?" My eyebrows arched up then wiggled as I asked.

Lisa giggled. "Oh, Gretchen, indeed." Light shone back in Lisa's eyes. I rejoiced in possibilities with her. Lisa claimed her signature gesture: placing her hands over her heart.

As I was leaving, I spun around. Inside Miss Lisa Mark's office doorway, I said, "Wait. You know, good vibes are surging through me about *Love at the Center of Grief* and for all of us involved in the project. The promise of a new year lies ahead. And also: 'Tis the season of miracles, merriment, and mistletoe."

Inside my purse, my phone buzzed and buzzed. A quick glance revealed a text from Hayden. A photo displayed across my screen. The cell lit up a cheery number of two faces: Hayden and Gene, dressed as twins. The guys were wearing identical Rudolph pajamas along with Santa hats topped off with red noses. Another ping came moments later. Dad shared his Rudolph pajama attire, but Dad's message stated, "Don't worry, Hayden, Gene, and I all decided you should also have a matching set to go with ours for our pizza party." Gawking at the red-nosed faces on my screen, I leaned against the wall in the hallway, doubled over with laughter, deciding this situation seemed too funny to keep to myself.

I ran back inside, where Lisa reached out to embrace me with one of her famous side-hugs, as she enjoyed pointing and cracking up at my photos with me. "Maybe by next year, you'll have a matching pair?" I nudged Lisa.

"Oh, Gretchen." She giggled. Joy leaked from the corners of our eyes and streamed down our cheeks. After we composed ourselves, we sent Gene and Hayden a snapshot of the two of us with the photo collage, *Love at the Center of Grief*, from Lisa's doorway.

I texted, "Marks said she'd like a matching PJ set too."

Gene texted back in all caps: DONE. Lisa's eyes flew wide open when I showed her Gene's reply. I gave her a told-you-so smirk and then showed her Gene's next text message that soon followed. "Huckleberry says I should ask Lisa to be my plus one for some of our holiday events? Any thoughts, Shortcake?"

My free arm clutched even more proof the heart *can* indeed survive a loss. Years of living without a mother's love will leave gaping holes, but allowing others in and giving others a chance to fill the pain makes all the difference. Sometimes grief will not be smooth—days and moments, so debilitating, hit out of nowhere, and sorrow never completely disappears. When the pain subsides, the memories and love remain.

Evidence of that stayed tucked next to my heart in the form of a photo collage displaying a history of love I built at the Summerfort Grief Center. But, now, I even dare to love and dream beyond these walls. Lisa's impact on my life is monumental: center activities, photographs, and prompts for journal entries. She's creating an honest and real way to distribute the story of Hayden and me in hopes of helping others. In so many ways, this is really Lisa's story too.

When I consider my life, I always imagine Lisa playing a significant role. First, she served as Mrs. Marks, my childhood group facilitator. She never corrected other kids or me when we assumed she was a "Mrs." all those years, claiming it became a term of endearment. Through our awkward tween years, Mrs. Marks morphed into what we nicknamed our nagging "Grief Mother." Hayden and I wavered from distaste to admiration of her, like most kids do with their mothers, I assume. Mrs. Marks then became Miss Marks, one of the kindest souls I know who learned to overcome the troubles of her past. When I stop to consider her as my friend Lisa, I recognize her capacity to share her heart with others as immeasurable.

Life presents many challenges, but I also believe all the people I love deserve happiness, and the future hinted at so many promising adventures. New routines, new normals, new traditions (like dining room décor, friends, matching Christmas PJs), might come into all our lives.

It was the holiday season and closing time at the Summerfort Grief Center: A Place to Heal; A Place to Hope; A Place to Belong. Lisa's phone vibrated among the papers stacked on top of her desk. Biting her bottom lip, she studied the screen, her eyes narrowing, debating whether or not to answer. She reached out, touched it, but her finger withdrew from pushing accept. She slid the phone on her desk, tiptoeing away until the call stopped.

Lisa frowned at the iPhone in question. Changing her mind, she retrieved the cell from on top of her pink Post-It Notes, where she'd written her to-do list. She studied the screen. In seconds, noise reverberated inside her hand. A deep breath flew into Lisa's lungs, and I heard her exhale.

Lisa paced in circles, contemplating—holding out the phone, double-checking the phone number calling. But then I watched as the corners of her mouth inched upward, her finger crawling dangerously close. Almost ready on this round to push accept.

If only fear didn't toy with our hearts so much. *Oh, Lisa, at least try to accept love.*

Imagining the hearts of the people I cherish—Dad, Hayden, Gene, Lisa, and soon *maybe even by "sweet" Happenstance, Miss Gabby*, I realize we offer a link to each other. We help one another heal through life's battles. When seeking hope, we become a team when one of us needs to be cheered on by the others. At the end of the day, we discover multiple locations in which to land, all welcoming us, like home. It is with the right people that a heart accepts its place to thump out the beats of belonging.

I cupped the outline of my mouth as I backed out of Lisa's office, and using my free hand, I whisper-shouted, "Miss Lisa, just one more thing, I promise. *Someone* once told me to borrow these words: 'When in doubt, choose love.'"

At last, Lisa's hand went into her best signature move, plastered over her heart. She pushed accept, choosing to answer. "Hello."

At the corner of Cinderella and Golden Streets in Summerfort, Missouri, oh, my heart jolted in an overflow of love. As I exited the very center of grief, I thought, *now this memory and these emotions are worth hoarding.*

Chapter Twenty-Six/ Chapter One

Love at the Center of Grief
How it all Began
by Lisa Marks

GRIEF LIVES IN OUR hearts as a puzzling notion. No one's sorrow measures the same. Each of us acts as a jagged piece of the puzzle, hoarding a unique story. Unable to tell these stories because too often we choose to hide behind the pain in silence. What if we share our hurts? One by one, we each make an offering, adding a piece until the rough edges smooth, slipping into place. Might we visualize a full photo of togetherness, worthy of displaying?

Will Summerfort, Missouri, grant me, Lisa Marks, a place to belong? Can I turn my Summer of Despair 2012 into a perfect summer project?

To entice visitors off Highway 65, billboards paint scenes of the quaint downtown. Concocted with seasonal changes, the ads on the signs jazz up small-town charm—antique shops, hand-dipped ice cream, and a gazebo decorated in the park. All elements serving up a family-friendly yesteryear appeal. Visitors must act fast because there's only one exit to the town of Summerfort, with its population remaining steady at just under five thousand.

With my parents gone, their home sold, graduate school behind me, and a failed marriage too, I became a permanent resident of Summerfort once again. It happened because I opened my mouth, found myself uttering the words "sold" while standing in the kitchen of a ranch house in need of new carpet, paint, fixtures, cabinets, and appliances. But crazy ideas come to us at odd times in life. Even in small locations, grand dreams present themselves.

After grappling with a wrench in my hands, I adjusted the fittings, *again*, on my overflowing toilet. I ran out of my fixer-upper, jumped into my car, took off speeding. I'm quick to slow down, but with full force, I never stop arguing with myself. *You had no business buying a house with three bedrooms and one-and-a-half baths for a single person—what were you thinking?* Looking back, what had I told the realtor? My new job as a school counselor will afford me the time to remodel. I'd called *this* the perfect Summer Project of 2012.

What a joke. I'm overwhelmed, needing to hire some help, but I hate admitting defeat. Picking pineapple delight paint for the hallway to brighten the house had started out as a good idea. Wearing globs of the color in my dark blonde ponytail, with the humidity pulling out frizzy wisps of hair, isn't my best look. Every which way I pivot, glancing into the rearview mirror, produces an unappealing sight. With the AC cranked on high, I suck in the frosty air and puff out the angry steam deep in my lungs. Taking a break from my house "project" to roam my old stomping grounds seemed needed.

Visions of Mom singing in the choir of a Methodist church on the edge of town triggered my search. I recall attending church with my parents as a child. The congregation grew, so the little one-story country church merged with a mega-sized church in the city of Branson. What had become of the old place? I'd never heard. Traveling Summerfort's backroads to where the church stood offered corkscrew curves, roller-coaster hills, and trees lining both sides of the road. All of it created a beautiful adventure. Questions racked my heart as I navigate each twist and turn.

What am I supposed to do with all my grief? What am I doing with my life that makes a bit of difference to anyone? Who can I turn to and not lose hope? Where do I belong? When will I trust and love again?

Black mascara flows like rivers down my cheeks. Yellow center lines blur as I battle to keep my eyes clear, watching for the changing curves in the pavement. With the back of my hand, I try wiping away the gloom.

Cinderella and Golden Streets—how very misleading! My first impression when I turn into the parking lot to view the vacant property: unholy. Like a combined effort of episodes of *Trading Spaces* and *Swapping Spouses,* it seemed God had relocated to Branson, so the Devil had swapped, moving right on into this single-story redbrick building and wreaked havoc.

This old building and me—kindred spirits, I think, grasping at some of the particular conditions of the building—run-down, abandoned, in need of a smile, longing for love, a purpose, a breath of life.

Where to begin? Missing and rippled shingles on the roof require replacing. Upgrades to the cracked front window and door would be mandatory for modern safety standards. An overgrown yard and cracks in the sidewalk now allow weeds to peek through the parking lot. Who knows what's lurking beneath? A "for sale" sign pokes through the grass, but due to the elements of time, weather, and nature, the phone number of the selling agent remains a mystery.

I close my eyes, allowing my mind to drift back in time. My hands pull open the glass double doors, and I walk through. I see my mother standing upfront. She's wearing her favorite purple dress with the white lace collar. The lyrics to the hymn "Take My Life, Lead Me, Lord" ring out in my mother's voice. My father sat next to me, dressed in his Sunday best, his hand latching onto mine. The lyrics continue. Dad smiles at me and glances toward my mother with admiration. As a child, love enveloped me in this location.

When my eyes open, the reality of life stings: I'm alone. Footprints of my past lie in ruins. Piece by piece, the little church and I are crumbling. But with a name like Marks, I should have a plan, a place, a goal. Dad always used his joking line, "Lisa, go and leave your 'Marks' on the world with your big heart."

Inside my purse, I fumble, searching for his letter. Unfolding it once again, I reread my father's final words, hoping to find inspiration.

Dear Lisa,

Please use the trust fund your mother and I set aside to help others. We always believed assisting others helps open up the world to love. When we do for others, we become better versions of ourselves. It's time to put that fancy psychology degree I helped you pay for to good use but do it creatively. Leave your 'Marks' in the world!

Take care of yourself, too. Complete updates on your fixer-upper by placing a checkmark next to each of the wishes you keep plastered to the side of the refrigerator door. When the repairs are complete, celebrate by replacing the refrigerator.

Do not let the deaths of your mom and me make you bitter. We worried sick about bringing a child into the world at our age, but having you was the biggest blessing of our lives. Over the years, when asked, 'What's your greatest accomplishment in life?' I never hesitated to answer: Lisa, my daughter.

I know you didn't bargain for a husband to walk away, but in time, a resolution will come. Life throws out topsy turvy things. People we believe in don't always turn out the way they should. Our plans don't always fall into place. Then, somehow, life designs some fancy schemes, serving up miracles, by guiding us with faith. It teaches us to believe in something unrealized as our culminating dream.

Don't be afraid to try adventures—travel, photograph the world, find new love. Show people your heart through kindness. It will be easier for them to forgive mistakes. Remember, mistakes can be made, so stop being so hard on yourself. If you're surrounded by the right people, they aren't looking for you to fail. Embrace this kind of love.

Above all, I <u>hope</u> you find a place to <u>heal</u> your heart. Or maybe a place or a person will find you? And you will know that's precisely where you <u>belong</u>.

I love you,
Dad

Mom, I'm singing your tune, "Make my life useful. . . ." Dad, I think you'd rejoice at my creative idea.

My treasured note finds its way back into my purse for safekeeping. Not sure if service would reach through this wooded area, I researched my phone for a person mentioned to me by my realtor. Punching in the numbers on my cell, I fumble because my fingers tremble. I'm amazed when my second attempt at dialing works.

"Hi. Gene Tucker Construction?"

"Yes, this is Gene."

"My name's Lisa. I got your number from a local realtor. I'm out at the old Methodist church on Cinderella and Golden that's for sale. I'm looking for a ballpark estimate on outside repairs before I make an offer."

"Lisa, I'm not far away. I can swing by in a few minutes and give a quick look-see."

"Great. Thank you, Gene."

When the Gene Tucker Construction truck pulls in the lot, parking near me, I expect an older guy to climb out. Not someone within my age range, late thirties or early forties. He was standing inches above me, with his six-foot frame. As he wraps his tool belt around his waist, the song "YMCA" jumps into my head. Does he think he's been summoned for some weird bachelorette party? Those dark denim jeans lack Velcro, appearing securely in place. Tan work boots, showing a bit of scuff at the toes, look legit. I wait, but gyrating his hips doesn't seem to be part of his plan.

For a slight second more, I worry. Have I called a unique business offering singing or dancing telegrams? Because Mr. YMCA Construction Man rakes his aviator sunglasses through his dark wavy hair, depositing them on the top of his head as he steps toward me. I wave, offering a smile. Up close, he reminds me so much of actor Paul Rudd that I perform a gawking double take.

With a firm handshake, he says, "Hey, Lisa, I'm Gene. I'm so glad to meet you. Have we met before? Did you go to school in Summerfort?"

"I did go to school here. I'm a '93 graduate. Right after graduation, I went off to college in a different state. Now, I've decided to move back to the area. Are you a native of Summerfort?"

"Pretty much lived here my whole life. I also moved away for college, but I came back with my architecture degree and started my company. I graduated before you in '88. Welcome back to Summerfort."

"Thanks, Gene. Come to think of it, I guess you're the Tucker football star that Summerfort High School displays in their photo and trophy case?" *Oh, I remember you now, Gene. I recall girls calling you Tucker the Total Ten.*

"Maybe they've taken those down and put up some new athletes by now," Gene says with a smile.

I grin back.

Motioning with his hands to the whole church grounds, Gene asks, "So, what's going on 'round here, Lisa?"

"The Fundamentals of Caring" is a great film, Paul. I loved you in it, I think, and chuckle. "Well, Gene. Good question. I'm considering restoring this old church into a grief center."

"Hmm, okay." Pointing at the building, biting his lower lip, Gene hunches his shoulders but remains silent. He turns to me as if he's about to ask me something but fumbles around with his tool belt instead. His nonverbal communication skills speak volumes. My problem: I don't understand this "strong-silent-type" language. *What are you thinking?*

As Gene pulls out an invoice sheet attached to a small clipboard tucked into one of the pockets of his tool belt, he shakes his head. Gene yanks a pen from his bag of tricks, pushing down so hard on the clicker and releasing it with a loud pop. Writing each item brought on his added, "hmms" and "ughs."

"Lisa, if you want to walk the perimeter with me, I'll try to explain things or answer some questions."

Black ink from Gene's pen digs into the to-do list:

Crude Estimate Only for Lisa at Methodist church on Cinderella and Golden

Overhaul roof with repairs and shingles, $8 K, outside lighting/electrical updates $1K, Research vestibule door deals/exterior doors/all windows $10K, stamped patterned concrete porch/sidewalk repair (approximate 20 x 20—$3K), HVAC

unit replacement $6K, parking lot/lawn fee— clean up before estimate—any asphalt salvage- able? Many hidden costs.

Pausing from his scribbling and his moaning and groaning, Gene glances down at me with his piercing blue eyes. Gene's finger taps at the list he's written.

"So, Lisa, does a grief center set age limits? Does a grief center use classrooms? Would you be able to use the preset Sunday school rooms inside, maybe?"

"I'm thinking kids that are at least in kinder- garten. Or if an individual case comes in, I could consider younger. No age limit for adults. I'd like to have all age groups—kids, teens, and adults. Yes, I'm hoping to keep the business offices and class- rooms pretty much intact, if possible. Change the entry area to a greeting center, the sanctuary into a commons area for a play area, craft center, and library. Currently, the small church doesn't have a kitchen, so I'd like to install a simple kitchenette to serve treats."

"Oh, so you know the layout of this church inside?"

"As a kid, I came here with my parents. I remem- ber a lot."

"What's your last name, Lisa—who are your parents?"

"Marks. You might remember my dad, maybe even mom?"

"Yes. Your dad was my school counselor. Your mom taught music. A super nice and patient lady. I took her class, but I can't sing."

We chuckled.

Are you good at dancing? "I didn't inherit my mother's singing abilities either."

"Oh, I think your dad became the assistant principal around the year I graduated."

"That's my dad." We shared a smile.

"He was a great guy. I'm sorry for your loss, Lisa."

"Thank you, Gene. I miss him and my mom a lot. They're the reason I'm moving forward with this project. It's written as part of their will for me to do something important."

"Wow. It's admirable, but this is a big undertaking. Do you have a written business plan in place on how it will all go down? How many kids per class would you take? Is it like a Sunday school? Is this faith-based?

"Yikes, Gene. That's a lot of questions at once. No, I don't have a specific business plan drawn up, but I've been a school counselor for a while. I've visited grief centers, youth groups, and sat in on therapies, so I have a clear vision. I want the center to be nondenominational and not necessarily church-focused. Often times, faith does seem to come up with people as part of healing, so I'm open to that as needed. More on a focus of spirituality, mindfulness, and less on a specific organized religion if that makes sense."

Using the toe of his boot, Gene kicks at a stray limb. "I bet a lot of people give up on faith when dealing with grief anyway. Won't it be hard to get people to come, open up, and talk about all their sadness?"

"Yes. For some people, it's tough to accept all that happens after death. Our society doesn't like to discuss the 'taboo' topic. They hide away in their anger and depression for a long time. Others find great relief doing activities and talking about their hurts with others."

"Sounds expensive. How much will you charge for these services?"

"My dad taught me how to apply for grants. I've done some for educational purposes. Plus, I plan to gain support from area businesses with donations and shared resources, so I won't have to charge anyone a cent unless they want or need one-on-one counseling."

Gene lifts his gaze off the costs, shifting his glare to me, before pointing a finger at the church, spouting off, "So, you're telling me, you're gonna spend maybe tens of thousands of dollars on this place, so kids and people can come and make macaroni necklaces and sing 'Kumbaya' for the dead and not charge for it?"

My eyes well up at his harshness. "I'm so sorry you feel that way, Mr. Tucker. That's not exactly my plan. I hope the center helps people. Thanks for coming and for the estimate." I sigh.

"Wait, Lisa. I'm sorry. Sometimes I come across gruff about things I don't completely understand. Then I go off saying idiotic stuff." Leaning forward, Gene offers to hand me a business card but instead straightens up, going motionless. His lip snarls up like Elvis. Of course, not with a sexy vibe, it seems more like—"what the heck?"—when he asks, "Have you been painting inside here already?" He points to my hair with his mouth now gaped open.

"Nope," I answer, snatching the card from his hand. "But, thanks for your time and estimate." I attempt to stomp away, but flip-flops don't gracefully skid across leaves, gravel, and unseen blacktop. Gene springs into action, grabbing my arm as I tumble.

After a quick squeeze of his muscled forearm, I push him away, proving I'm capable of getting to my feet. Up close, his skin smells like leather, earth, Irish Spring, and fresh-shaven face. *Stop envisioning Mr. YMCA in a towel with a razor. You're at church, Lisa.*

I pretend to laugh, dust off my legs, smooth my hair, and wipe any further remnants of mascara off my face. Dressed in wonky black flip-flops, homemade cutoff shorts, and a lime green tank top speckled with bleach stains, my ability at making a good first impression with this man—doomed already. Before turning to face him, I plaster on a phony grin. "I'm painting *my* house," I say.

"Busy lady," Gene says, leaning against the door of his big ole diesel truck, finishing the never-ending invoice. "I can research costs further if you decide to look inside. Other than just peeking in the windows, Lisa. Good luck with this place. Your house too." Nodding to the weed-covered sign, he adds, "I work some with this listing company—tell the realtor and banks I'm willing to work with you. Here's a copy of my 'guesstimate.'

If I work here, I'll put photos on the Gene Tucker Construction website to promote your grief center—a win-win, Lisa. I'll help you look for vendors who might donate in exchange for advertising. Extra supplies leftover from other jobs might come in handy too. I'd give you those materials if they help. I'd work fast with my small crew, and we'd do a good job."

"Thank you," I say. This time, I saunter away, staying upright, paperwork in hands, and my back to Mr. YMCA Construction Man/Paul Rudd Look-A-Like Tucker.

Sounds of twigs and leaves crunch and stir as footsteps approach behind me on my way to my car. I turn around, and the noise stops. He clears his throat like he's preparing to say something but follows through with nada.

I shrug.

Locking his icy blues on me, Mr. Construction Man stares at me a moment. It dawns on me how his eyes imply a hint of glassiness. He slips his sunglasses on, hiding anything from further viewing.

Typical, I think. So, I spin to bail.

Fine. Good-bye. I dive into my car, turning the engine on, locking my doors, cranking the AC. *Why's he lurking? Maybe he really is going to dance the YMCA?* He stoops down and, using one knuckle, knocks gently on my window.

His voice carries a heavy, serious tone. "Lisa?" I can't read his eyes anymore since he's covered then over with sunglasses. Dear God, he's got the best poker face. To show him I'll consider listening, I roll my window halfway down but only halfway since I'm also questioning every motive.

"Yes. What can I do for you, Mr. Tucker?"

"My wife died. She had cancer. I suppose I'm just one of those angry people we talked about earlier who hate discussing death. But I've also got three sons. My youngest boy, Hayden, is only six years old. So, I think Hayden needs a place to make macaroni necklaces and sing 'Kumbaya' for his mom. What you're willing to build for others— I can't imagine. And, Lisa, you've already made me realize something. Maybe there's even hope for someone like me to get beyond my grief."

Acknowledgments

WRITING A BOOK TAKES a lot of courage. It would not be possible without the love and support of so many wonderful people. I'm thankful to be backed by many family members and friends. For all—McIntyre, Sluder, Tucker, and Lawrence clans.

Mom & Dad: For giving me a lifetime of memories worth remembering. I love and miss you.

Lost & Found: For providing an outlet that gives people a chance to breathe inside new memories of loved ones. And for allowing me a chance to experience it. Thursday night groups/volunteers, you rock!

Shirley Rash: For taking a chance on a new novel writer. As an editor, you taught me so much. Your guidance and experience elevated my story to a new level. For that, I'll forever be grateful.

Dr. Phillip Howerton: For using your writing connections to suggest Shirley. Our friendship/

co-working status over the years has been a rewarding one. From the foundation of Drury on to educational issues with rocks, candles, sticks, and stuff—

Hillcrest Staff: For being a mini-family, support system. Some of you read portions of the story and provided feedback along the way—Donna, Janet, Lesli, Kati, Regina, Toni—it's a blessing to work with you gals. Happy retirement, Donna. I will miss you. HRDC guys, Brandon and Austin, you're special too.

HEC students: For overcoming, surviving, and opening up to me about grief-related topics recently. Some served as beta readers. A special shout out to Rose Wilson, "Rosie" and Breanna Lowell, "Sheriff" who took a particular interest in the story.

Siblings: For Theresa, John Jay, and Sandi—thank you for your support. Theresa, an extra thanks for being the "keeper" of the rough drafts. Often, you were my first line of defense. You took over, like Mom, stashing away the stories.

McIntyre cousins: For Benita, Richard, Kathy, Tim, Chuck, Dee Dee, Billie—I couldn't ask for a more loving group of cousins/support from "afar": Kentucky/Illinois.

Acknowledgments

Nieces/Nephews: For standing in line because I always supply Tic Tacs! Thanks for letting me be your cool aunt and for all your love and support. Who's the best at rubbing my shoulders?! Kelsey, Lauren, Bria—you remember this game the most.

Concord Christian Church: For Lee Todd, and all church family, thanks for your continued support and prayer.

Ryleigh Tucker: For bonding with me, even deeper through our grief. Thanks for reading portions of my rough draft.

Lisa Jones: For the lemon cakes, thrift shops with tiny bags, and outing for Italian, Chinese, and Mexican—our friendship is full of adventure and fun! I'm thankful for your encouragement as you read early versions of the manuscript.

Jim Tucker: For sticking to the "plan." You're the best fish in the sea! You supported me when I spent a lot of nights camped out in Summerfort. I promise, there are no "Happenstance" issues going on with the fictitious Gene or John. I love and appreciate you.

About the Author

CINDY MCINTYRE, AUTHOR OF *Eulogies Unspoken: Stories of Worth* and *Caring for Dad: With Love and Tomatoes,* has served as a secondary at-risk teacher in Missouri for twenty years. She holds degrees in psychology and human services, with an emphasis in education. After the loss of her parents, Miss McIntyre, set out assisting others, volunteering as a group facilitator at the Lost & Found Grief Center. She is originally from Earlville, Illinois, but now calls Missouri home.

www.ingramcontent.com/pod-product-compliance
Lightning Source LLC
Chambersburg PA
CBHW071140100726
47908CB00002B/194